Praise for *Canyons*

"Cacek delivers with this gruesome Denver-based werewolf thriller. *Canyons* is adeptly written. The plot moves and builds steadily straight through to the end. Cacek's dialog is fresh and entertaining, and her characters are well developed, unique, and engaging. Frequent pop-culture references are good fun amid the mayhem."
—Jennifer A. Hall in *Locus*

"Werewolves tear up Denver in what looks like the first of a series by Bram Stoker-Award winner Cacek. Brisk, and the constant flow of bizarre headlines lends a light heart to a dark fable."　　　　　　　—*Kirkus Reviews*

"Cacek doesn't pull any punches. The funny parts are very funny and the violent parts are very violent. What starts as a light-hearted romance unfolds into a deeper and darker story."　　　　　　　　　　　—*The Denver Post*

"Like any good heroine worth her salt—or wolfbane—Cat's got a feeling she would get into big trouble with her rescuer once she finds him. Things get considerably more complicated when Cat discovers that the city is something of a continuing battleground [between werewolf clans]. A hardnosed romance *for* lycanthropes."
—Ed Bryant in *Locus*

"The most original werewolf tale to come along in a while."
—*Boulder Camera*

Canyons

P. D. Cacek

TOR®

A TOM DOHERTY ASSOCIATES BOOK
NEW YORK

This is a work of fiction. All the characters and events portrayed in this book are either products of the author's imagination or are used fictitiously.

CANYONS

Copyright © 2000 by P. D. Cacek

All rights reserved, including the right to reproduce this book, or portions thereof, in any form.

A Tor Book
Published by Tom Doherty Associates, LLC
175 Fifth Avenue
New York, NY 10010

www.tor.com

Tor® is a registered trademark of Tom Doherty Associates, LLC.

ISBN: 0-812-54534-6

First edition: December 2000
First mass market edition: October 2001

Printed in the United States of America

0   9   8   7   6   5   4   3   2   1

To the Cacek pack:

Joe, Mike, and Peter—
Alpha Males, all

Acknowledgments

The book you are now holding would never have come to be without the help, guidance, and support of a number of remarkable people. To that end I'd like to thank—

Melissa Ann Singer—editor par excellence
William Smith—fastest editorial assistant on the block
Rebecca Springer, Jeff Dreyfus, and all who tightened down the nuts-and-bolts
S. P. Somtow—who taught me what a werewolf novel should be
Edward Bryant—whose editorial voice and comments I continually hear inside my head (Now get out! You're driving me nuts!)
Ellen Datlow—who gave me real insight into the wonderful world of publishing (over cheese blintzes)
... and to all the rest of you (you know who you are) who kept me on track and occasionally had to talk me down from the edge.
Thank you!

—P. D. Cacek
Arvada, CO

June 1, 2000

1

The wind had come down from the high mountains
with the taste of snow clutched in its teeth. An offering. From
the natural canyons of ancient rock and hidden springs to the
unnatural ones of steel and concrete.

To *them.*

As an equal, the wind brushed against ice-flecked muzzles
and ruffled winter-thick coats; joining them briefly as claws
tapped soft sounds against the rutted blacktop and bellies
grumbled in anticipation.

They ran. Slow. Steady. Ears forward, bodies tensed. This
place was new, unfamiliar except for the smell and feel of
the wind, so they stopped only for a moment or two to scent
the cold newness of the place with familiar musk. To mark
this new place, this territory as their own.

They ran. Silent. And kept to the deeper shadows between
the towering buildings. Avoided the places and yellow-tinted
avenues where MAN walked.

In the real world, the world of predator and prey, the prey
animals would already have found safe hidey-holes for the
night.

But not here.

The moon had almost set, but still MAN—the prey—walked his artificial canyons. Or drove through them. Or huddled against the wind's snapping bite in the hollows and tunnels and alleys that dotted the cityscape.

MAN didn't understand his true place on the food chain. Never had. And with luck, never would.

And so *they* ran—bellies tight, tongues lolled, noses high and glazed with ice as each sorted through the known and unknown, familiar and unfamiliar scents that washed over them. Garbage and human waste, exhaust and gasoline. The smell of hunter and prey.

At the mouth of a narrow brick gully, *they* stopped and lifted their heads. Snuffled at the wind's breath and felt drool begin to fill the hollow places beneath their tongues.

food

Heads lowered and lips curled back, they entered the alley. One by one. Each according to its rank.

The boy shifted his weight in the nest he'd made for himself from the half-filled garbage bags and cardboard boxes he'd found behind the brew-pub and groaned. He just couldn't get comfortable, and that was pissing him off. Shoulda been able to get comfortable with all the shit he had in him, unless . . . unless . . .

The thought took a moment to rise through the haze behind his eyeballs, but once it did it flared up like a fuckin' bottle rocket.

Pockets had screwed him. Screwed him like he was virgin pussy on a first date and after swearin' on his fuckin' Mama's life that the stuff was prime. Ninety-nine and nine-fuckin'-tenths pure muthafuckin' Primo that would take away all the cold and pain and hard and hurt.

"Shit," the boy mumbled as he looked down at the needle sticking out of his arm and felt the rocket fizzle out in his brain. Fuckin' stuff wasn't any more Primo than any of the other junk he'd gotten off Pockets in the last fifteen months. "Gotta get me a new supplier. Shit ain't workin'."

'Cause he could still feel. *Dammit.* Could still feel fuckin' everything that he fuckin' felt before.

Dammit dammit dammit.

It wasn't fair. It wasn't fuckin' fair. Not that he expected fair . . . even from Pockets. Like his mama told him when she kicked him: Ain't nothin' in life fair so don't make believe it is.

Yeah. Right, nothin' fair. But who woulda thought Pockets woulda screwed him over like that?

"Shit."

The boy stopped looking at the needle since it didn't seem to be doing any good and squirmed deeper into the bags and 'board, and groaned again when something hard goosed him through the seat of his jeans. God, he hated winter. At least in summer the garbage got all warm and squishy and felt just like a nice, soft bed . . . if you ignored the smell. And he could. Shit, he was used to it. His whole world, for as long as he could remember, smelled like garbage, inside and out.

But in winter. Shit, in winter everything got as hard and stiff as old bones. Even the smell.

He hated winter.

And he hated Pockets *(fuckin' little piece of shit)* for selling him stuff he claimed was Primo but wouldn't even make his kid sister high. If his kid sister was still around and not in some foster home somewhere probably getting it up the butt from her legally appointed guardian.

For some reason the idea made him laugh until the snot was loose in his nose. The thought of his little sister taking it up the butt was just too damn funny. *Little Miss fuckin' Prissy . . . all the time walking around with her fuckin' nose in the air like she was too good for them . . . like someone made a mistake somewhere and given her to the wrong family.*

"Too friggin' damned funny," the boy said, and wiped off the slime from under his nose. The needle in his arm danced a little two-step with the bulging vein. And flopping ends of the rubber tubing. Which he'd forgotten to untie once he got the needle in. It took him a minute to recognize what he'd done. Then another minute to remember how to fix it. And when he did all the laughter went away.

"Well, shit." The encrusted needle jumped and kept getting in the way when he tried to find the release end of the tubing. "Hold still, asshole. Gotta start the fuckin' engine 'fore I can fly."

The tubing started playing the same game as the needle, playing hard to get, but finally he managed to snag a loose end and yank. The tubing stretched out fine and thin, just like a rubber band aimed at some fuckin' substitute teacher's fat ass, but nothing else.

Tonight was definitely not his night.

His throat made a growling whine sound when he ducked his head and grabbed the tubing's other end between his teeth. And pulled. Jaw clamped and head reared back like he was some kind of friggin' wild stallion trying to fight a lasso. Stretching that motherfucker until his neck felt like it was going to snap before the rubber did.

But it didn't.

The tubing let go of his arm in a rush of fire that cooked away all the cold and hard and hurt and pain and smell.

The boy sighed and let the warmth ooze through him as he settled back against the cardboard and garbage bags. Life wasn't so bad after all, he decided just as the shadows started moving in on him. Big fuckin' shadows that slip-slided along the alley like black water.

"Cool," he said, and smiled when the shadows condensed and stepped up to say howdy.

Dogs. Big fuckin' dogs. Dogs and a half. Biggest damned dogs he'd ever seen in all his fourteen years of life. And not city dogs either . . . that he could tell just by looking at them, although they looked skinny enough to be. These looked like the kind of dogs that should be pulling a fuckin' sled across the North Pole. Or bringin' down a moose. Or . . . or . . .

The boy blinked eyes that suddenly (finally) felt too heavy to stay open, as the biggest of the big dogs moved closer and sniffed the air. Shit it was big! Bigger-n big. The fuckin' Hercules of dogs.

But it didn't seem mean. Just big. Fuckin' big.

"Nice puppy," the boy said, and stuck out his hand, friendly-like, the way the PBS Afterschool Specials said you were supposed to when you meet a strange animal. The needle in his arm waved its own howdy-do.

"Got yourself a gang, huh, puppy?" he asked, as the other shadows surged forward and jelled into animal shapes. "Good. 'Cause you need a gang in this fuckin' world, right? Yeah. I got me a gang, too. Real *fresh* . . . don't take shit off nobody. Right. Never take no shit but dish plenty of it out. Yeah."

The big dog lowered its head and whined, soft and low in the back of its throat.

"Yeah, good ol' puppy. C'mer, puppy. It's okay. I won't hurt you."

The dog glanced back at its gang, and the boy could have sworn it nodded its head before it turned and trotted straight up to him; tongue hanging out and prancing, happy-like.

He'd never had a dog—pets weren't allowed in any of the busted-down roach motels he'd lived in with his mother and sister . . . before his sister got outted by the Feds and his mother kicked his ass into the streets—but he'd always wanted one.

Always.

Still wanted one—"Good puppy. Nice puppy. C'mer, puppy."—right up until the fuckin' big puppy snapped off two fingers on his outstretched hand and gobbled them down like they were candy.

"Fuck."

The stumps were running red, spurting like fire hoses, but for the moment the pain hadn't reached his brain, and that was good. Damn good.

Proof positive that Pockets hadn't been lying about the shit. It *was* Primo. He'd have to thank the dude next time he saw—

A wet growl made him look up. Eyes the color of piss glared at him above a muzzle stained with blood. Pain and reality hit him like a double-barreled shotgun blast to the belly.

He wasn't going to be able to thank Pockets for nothin'.

Or complain about the cold and hard and pain. Or worry about the garbage smell of his life or if his kid sister was getting it up the ass or if he'd live to see his fifteenth birthday.

Or even if he'd live to see the morning.

Because he probably wasn't going to live to see the next hour.

The boy's mouth stretched almost as far as he'd stretched the rubber tubing when the big fuckin' dog tore away what was left of his hand.

"Noooooo—

—oooooooooooooo

The scream rolled down the sides of the narrow alley like thunder. It was a familiar sound—one that wet the mouth and pricked the hackles into spikes, and one that had been sorely missed in the months and miles that stretched between their old hunting ground and this new one.

Lifting his head, the Alpha Male added an undulating counterbeat to the scream and tasted the boy's blood on the back of his tongue. That was familiar, too. The blood. And the taste of carrion it held. Even without their help, their blessing, the boy would be dead before the hunger moon rose.

When the voices of hunter and hunted faded, swallowed by the night, the big Silverback lowered his head back toward the prey and felt the crush of the pack behind him. They were growing bold in their eagerness. A growl quieted them.

The HUNT would begin when *he* decided and not a moment before.

The boy had clutched the mutilated hand to his chest, blood soaking the front of his faded *Rockies* jacket, the forgotten needle quivering in the crook of one arm. A waste. Drugs and alcohol soured the meat.

But the pack had gotten used to it over the years.

The Leader took a step forward, stiff-legged, and snapped at the air just in front of the boy's fear-rimmed eyes.

"Go away! Leave me alone! Bad dog. Get!"

Commands. Demands. If he'd still had the mobility of flesh, the Alpha Male would have smiled at such nonsense. But since he didn't, he tensed his haunches and lunged.

The HUNT had begun.

The boy didn't want to believe what was happening. Couldn't believe because if he did, that would have made it real . . . and it *couldn't* be real. 'Cause dogs didn't do this kinda shit. They didn't attack people. Dogs were cool and nice and even the nasty-lookin' ones you saw noisin' around the junkyards could be scared off with a rock and shout.

Dogs just weren't *supposed* to eat people like this.

Unless they weren't. Unless the shit he got off Pockets really *was* Primo, and he was just stuck inside the baddest bad-ass drug nightmare he'd ever had.

Yeah. That *coulda* been what was happenin' . . . if his god-damned hand didn't hurt so much and there hadn't been so much blood spurtin' out of him and that big ol' dog wasn't still chompin' up his arm like it was a fuckin' breadstick and his head was a fuckin' plate of spaghetti.

When the dog crushed the bones in his elbow the boy knew it wasn't any kind of nightmare. It was real. And he was going to die.

"No! Go *away!*"

He swung with his good arm (the only one he had left) and caught the dog upside the head. It wasn't much . . . shit it wasn't practically anything . . . but the dog let go just enough for him to pull the shreds of meat and bone that'd been his arm for fourteen years out of the animal's jaws. The boy stared at the broken head of the needle, still stuck in the tattered remains of his flesh, when the dog lunged forward and ripped out his throat.

The boy felt his face slip to join the stinking hot puke that barreled up from his belly to spill out of the gaping hole just below his chin.

The attack had pushed him back into the hard, sharp pile of frozen garbage, but he still tried to fight; punched and kicked and felt his K-Mart specials caught and held and then felt the cheap canvas go all hot and gushy inside.

After that his arms and legs didn't work right and all he could do was lie there and continue the fight inside his head.

For as long as he could.

While the dogs chowed down. *crunch chunck snap crackle pop* Like they were eating fuckin' breakfast cereal.

It wasn't supposed to happen this way . . . Pockets 'n' him 'n' maybe T-Job were supposed to go down fighting with some other gangbangers or maybe get caught by mistake by a stray bullet while waitin' for the bus or take one hit too many from a dirty needle and waste away or . . . or . . .

The boy only got to another dozen "better" ways to die before he remembered that better still meant dead.

And dead was what he was.

Not like this not like this notlikethisnotlikethis The boy clutched at a stiff plastic bag with his remaining hand and screamed—loud and long and frightened. But only inside his head. The real sound that came out the ragged hole in his throat was as soft and puny as a baby's fart.

The blood was hot and succulent despite the taint of drugs.

Animal flesh, the Silverback had discovered years before, was tolerable. Mediocre at best. Unpredictable at worst. A constant diet of beef, dog, and cat made the pack irritable . . . constantly challenging one another—or him—for power.

In the last six months, he'd had to kill three promising members. All because they had tried to break the cycle that had driven their kind over countless generations. *He'd* tried. And failed.

And the pack had suffered for it.

That wouldn't happen again.

Lips curled back in a grimace and hackles raised, he placed a forepaw over the boy's chest and turned back toward the remaining members. Despite their hunger and bloodlust, none, not even the Beta Male challenged his right to the kill.

He snorted through his nose, acknowledging their submission, before returning his attention to the night's meal.

Red foam bubbled up from the torn throat as the MAN-child's lungs still struggled for breath. MAN always took so long to die . . . and always seemed so surprised when the actual moment arrived.

Regardless of the situation that had brought him there.

Murder, accident, or suicide—the Silverback had seen them all, and every time the look was the same, the *"But this can't be happening to me! Not to ME!"* wide-eyed wonder. It was almost as if, until that very moment, MAN believed he was immortal.

If his mouth hadn't been full, the Silverback would have laughed out loud, but instead he nosed the boy's cheeks and watched the MAN-child's eyes finally begin their last slow roll upward. At least the boy'd had a reason to look surprised.

Behind him, the Beta Male whimpered and snapped his jaw impatiently. Any other time that sort of behavior would have gotten the big blond male a new set of muzzle scars, but the Silverback decided to let it pass in the light of this, their first kill.

Huffing air through his cheeks, the Silverback lowered his head and gently nudged the limp arms away from the front of the blood-soaked jacket. The downy material ripped apart with only the slightest tug from his canines. As did the stained sweatshirt.

And the flesh beneath it all.

Steam and the stench of emptying bowels and bladder rose in the air from the opening as the Silverback sank his teeth into a succulent coil of intestine and pulled.

The rest of the pack moved in, tails and heads lowered in deference, when he trotted off down the alley, tethered to the kill by its umbilical of uncoiled gut. When he found a suitably protected position between the back wall of a storage company and its oversize metal trash bin, the Silverback dropped his length of prize and glanced back at the killing place.

The Beta had eaten his fill and retreated a small way off

to gnaw contentedly on a lower leg bone; leaving the three other mature males and twin Juveniles to challenge one another for the rights of the remaining limbs.

But not one so much as toed the quivering, blue-gray entrails that spilled from the denuded corpse. The Silverback growled and snapped the air the way his second-in-command had done earlier—a warning, but also a promise that he *might* leave some of the delicacy—before lowering his head and slicing open a section of intestinal wall with an incisor.

The partially digested pizza was still warm, and the Silverback slurped it into his mouth with greedy delight.

Pepperoni and black olives.

His favorite.

As he ate he listened to the pack sounds echoing through the alley. There were grumbles and growls, the occasional yelp from the adolescent, and once or twice a duet of snarls that lifted the hair along his spine. He would stop then and listen, his meal momentarily forgotten, trapped between tongue and palate.

Once, he'd encouraged combat between the lesser males as sport and diversion, and to cull the weak, but now he shuddered each time a "discussion" escalated to the point of physical attack. It was never any more than a glancing snap to the muzzle or flank, just enough to draw blood, but still his belly would grow cold and his muscle tense.

They had lost too many to the months and miles that stretched from their beginning to this new hunting ground of concrete and glass. The females had gone first, and finding suitable mates in the MAN canyons was not as simple a task as it once had been.

Not simple at all.

The pack sounds changed from growls and threats to a series of yipping whines as the Juveniles begged scraps from their betters.

Satisfied that all was well, at least for the moment, the Silverback swallowed the mushy lump at the back of his throat and smacked his lips.

McDonald's apple pie.

Dessert. He'd always been a sucker for sweets.

He was about to search out another bite when a siren's lamenting howl raced through the alley and one of the Juveniles forgot himself, his place, and *theirs*, and lifted his head to give answer.

Less then a heartbeat later, that voice was stilled between the Beta Male's fangs.

"stop." One step forward, ears flat, lips curled back, fangs bared, the Silverback tensed his body and made ready to lunge if the Beta's fangs parted more than just the coarse off-white fur at the youngster's throat. *"i think he got the message."*

The Beta didn't seem convinced. He growled and shook his head, taking the hapless Juvenile along for the ride.

"you're too soft. they have to learn the ways."

The Silverback took another step forward, the apple pie forgotten. He didn't want to fight the Beta Male . . . they were almost equal in strength, and the big blond was five years younger; but he couldn't let this challenge go unanswered.

"yes, they do." The Silverback deepened his growl to Alpha strength and lifted the hackles at the back of his neck. *"but how much will he learn if he's dead? let him go. now."*

The Beta's lips trembled, but he released the Juvenile, who instantly scurried away to a position of safety—belly fur scraping the blood-splattered asphalt, head low, haunches pressed tightly together. If their kind had tails, the Silverback had no doubt that the Juvenile's would, at that moment, be tucked firmly into the crack of his ass.

The Beta Male was still glaring at him.

"cool it, bro," he huffed, *"the kid's learned enough for one night."*

Then just to add a little insult to the Beta's already injured pride, the Silverback Alpha Male lifted his head and looked up into the blue-black sky beyond the alley. The moon was almost set. He could feel it even if he couldn't see it. The night was almost over.

But it had been a good night. A good start.

His own howl was soft and melodious, a lullaby from a forgotten past to a promising future.

life was getting better.

He was half out of bed before he remembered to wake up.

But even then, the nightmare still sang in his ears. A song that refused to fade even when he knew he was fully conscious and standing in the shadows of a recognizable but unfamiliar room.

He turned back toward the bed and saw the outline of the woman—recognizable but unfamiliar as well—her bare skin tinted blue from the moonlight seeping in through the open windows at the far end of the room.

The woman was beautiful in her way, long-boned and slender . . . perhaps a little too narrow in the hips and small of breast, but appetizing enough in looks and more than enthusiastic in their lovemaking.

He knew her from the pub. A regular—every Tuesday and Thursday after an aerobics class at one of the trendier loft/gyms off Larimer. Always alone. Always finding reason to sit at the bar directly in front of his station. Always ordering the same thing—tonic laced with bitters and a twist.

He'd grimaced the first time she'd ordered it, imagining the taste on his own tongue, and then laughing when she quipped a variation on *Cold hands, Warm heart*.

"Nasty drink, sweet disposition," she'd said, and the microbrewery's hops-and-grain-scented air was suddenly overpowered by the aroma of her musk.

He'd doubted if anyone else at the long mahogany-and-brass bar had even noticed the change, but he had . . . and some part of him knew that *she* knew it, as well.

That was a little over three months ago—two months, three weeks and five days exactly before they became lovers up in her tenth-floor, security-patrolled, roof tennis court, one-and-one plus view condo apartment on Tremont.

After which he'd struggled down a tonic and bitters. With a twist. And then treated her to an inch-thick blood-rare steak at the Buffalo Company.

He thought it was only fair that they sample each other's tastes as early in the relationship as possible.

Even though he knew from the very beginning they would never get to the ". . . And They Lived Happily Ever After."

Too bad.

He touched her shoulder to see if she'd be receptive and watched her roll over, pale hair whispering across the pillow as her semiconscious fumbling found the sheets and wrapped them around herself. Childlike. Innocent. She didn't want sex. She was cold.

He tiptoed to the foot of the bed and picked the quilt up from the floor. She'd kicked it off them, complaining—as he thrust up inside her—of the heat. Now she was cold.

But Christ, she was beautiful. Too bad.

The quilt settled over her without a sound, covering the yellow sheets and winter white flesh with a new layer of midnight blue shadow. He watched, standing naked in the cold, while the warmth trickled down and she stretched out, muttering something soft and incomprehensible into the pillow. A song.

For the first time since leaving her bed, he felt the cold and trembled. Another kind of song had woken him up. An ancient lullaby that terrified him.

"Only a dream," he whispered to the dark, then quickly inhaled as if he could suck the words back into himself when the woman stirred. The last thing he wanted to do was wake her up to tell her it was over between them.

Three months and a couple of days and it was over. A repeat performance of the dozens of other "relationships" he'd had since reaching maturity. A given number of days—more or less, depending on the situation—but always ending the same way: standing in the dark of the familiar room, ready to sneak out in the middle of the night instead of waiting until morning to tell her, whichever *her* it was. It was over.

He'd known from the very beginning how it would end, but only felt the tug to escape for a week, maybe two. Not that he'd let it stop him from going to bed with her. One last time. Or from sneaking out afterward, while she slept, child-like, without so much as a note.

The coward's way out. No note. No regrets . . . once he took care of things.

Smiling, he touched the heavy squash-blossom necklace that encircled his throat. Three months and change . . . almost a record. For him.

A shadow within a shadow, he crossed the room, sorting through the scattered piles of discarded clothing. Somehow, in their haste to consummate, her panties had gotten tucked into his jeans. They were damp at the crotch and rich with her scent. Honey and musk.

He let them fall from his fingers as he slipped into his jeans.

No matter how many times he'd succumbed to the urge, leaving them was always hard.

He almost to the door when the woman, his soon-to-be ex-lover, moaned deep in her throat. It was a sound he'd heard a great deal over the last three months, especially in this room, but tonight it caused the hairs at the back of his neck to lift.

Tonight, it carried the memory of the sound . . . the ululating *song* that woke him. In the nightmare.

He touched the necklace again, drew the heavy silver blossom into the hollow of his palm and changed directions in mid-step until he came to the window. Despite the night chill and shadows that had gathered in the room while he slept, the necklace radiated a heat that made his hand tremble and glowed in the reflected city lights.

The night was dark, the moon set or about to beyond the high-rise offices and condo/apartment complexes, and quiet. Few sounds made it up into the rarified air of upward mobility.

He pressed his forehead against the cold glass and looked down at the "view" that had probably cost her an extra $400 a month—building and the street; a few cars crawling along, a few clutches of tourists and clubbers traveling in tight packs for protection, the occasional lone figure pushing a shopping cart . . . the glare from the U.S. Mint a half block away.

Not much else.

Actually rather empty for just past midnight on a Wednesday. No, he corrected himself, Saturday—the day she, who would wake to find him gone, had planned a picnic lunch for them in Morrison Canyon.

Maybe he'd leave a note, try to explain the unexplainable.

The woman—for he'd already begun to think of her as just that, as just a woman he once knew—turned over and muttered again. He'd never heard her say anything in her sleep before. It was almost as if she'd also been frightened of the sound from his nightmare.

He stood up, back and shoulders going rigid. He hadn't been frightened of the sound. Had he? If anything it had made him want to . . . Want to . . .

What?

He took a deep breath and tightened the grip on the necklace. Felt his heart pound against the back of his fingers. What had he heard? Even though part of him could still hear it, *feel* it, the actual memory of *what* he'd heard and felt was fading. An old song. A lullaby some grand or great-grand family member had sung to him over the edge of his cradle.

Or maybe he'd been less asleep than he thought and a siren had simply triggered some half-assed illusion. Like hearing a plane overhead and instantly picturing yourself becoming the pilot.

Except that he was afraid to fly. And, living deep within the urban sprawl, he barely noticed sirens anymore.

Then, from ten stories down, another siren suddenly wailed through the narrow valleys below and made him a liar. He started, and small flashes of light—red/green, yellow/lavender—burst behind his eyelids as his forehead smacked the window.

He grunted, softly. She, the woman, was—amazingly— silent.

He turned and looked at her, all cuddled up and warm, peaceful and happy and blissfully unaware of the direction her life was about to take. Until morning.

And by morning, he'd be gone. But not forgotten. And she'd suffer. Even when she finally convinced herself, over bagels and espresso with a covey of tsk-tsking gal-pals, that she really was better off without him. They all did. But until then, she would hurt and wonder if it'd been something she'd done that made him leave.

In the middle of the night.

Like a thief.

He'd promised himself the *last* time he left a woman (five weeks, three days) that the *next* time would be different, straightforward, without tricks. The next time . . . *this* time.

The best-laid plans of mice and men. And *others*.

Letting go of the necklace, he walked back across the room and carefully sat down on the edge of the bed closest to her. She was so beautiful. *Dammit.*

And she'd been so trusting. *Just like all the others.*

And just like all the others, she deserved to be spared this one humiliation.

He pushed back the covers until her hand, fisted like a child's, appeared. He lifted it into his and kissed the curved knuckles softly. Though still asleep, she smiled as he lowered her hand to brush fingertips against her throat, her cheek, and finally her forehead. He stopped there and spread his fingers wide—middle finger lost in the tangle of her hair, thumb and small finger closing the circuit at each temple.

Her smile faltered as he squeezed, tiny worry lines furrowing beneath his hand.

"Shhh," he whispered, "it's all right. You're still asleep." The lines of worry deepened. Her breath quickened, tickled the hairs on the underside of his arm. "No, don't be afraid, you're only dreaming . . . and the dream is about why you decided to break up with me because—"

He frowned, creating and rejecting a hundred different reasons that a woman might pick before deciding on the smallest, but most plausible.

"—because I thought the idea of having a picnic in Morrison Canyon was stupid."

She sighed, her breath quivering.

"Shh, it's all right. I'm not the romantic you thought I was. I'm not even close to what you want in a man."

Her breathing steadied, softened.

"If you see me again, you'll remember letting me down

easy . . . with no regrets or harsh words. But you can tell all your friends how you broke my heart."

Her forehead was smooth when he lifted his hand away. She slept. She'd remember it as he'd told it. A wonderful fairy tale.

If only *he* could be so lucky.

Her scent on his skin and the fading hum of nightmare sound kept him company while he dressed and, after making sure the apartment door locked behind him, trotted down the ten flights of stairs to the street.

The elevator would have been easier, quicker, but he needed the hard hammer of steel against shoe to keep himself focused.

He was so focused by the time he reached the cold night beyond the building's security door, that he'd forgotten he left his car in the parking lot behind the microbrewery.

"Shit."

He turned north and squinted as if he could actually see the distance between himself and his car. All seventeen blocks and God only knew how many panhandlers and/or muggers and/or gang-bangers and/or . . .

"Screw it."

He wasn't afraid of the night or anything that might lurk within it, but he wasn't in the mood for any more "social confrontations." His skin itched as if it'd suddenly grown too small for his body and he could still hear/feel the song that had jerked him awake. That, on top of the way he'd just left . . .

. . . just left . . .

What was her name?

The wind ruffled the few strands of hair that had come loose from the leather tie at the back of his neck and snapped at the hem of his coat as he walked to the edge of the curb and looked up at the tower of glass and wrought-iron balconies. Despite the late hour, there were still a few windows, curtains drawn against the night, flickering blue. Insomnia. Or the Playboy Channel. But the window on the tenth floor, west corner, was dark.

She was still asleep. The woman he'd just left. His most

current ex-lover. And he could no more remember her name at that moment than he could remember the final score of his first Little League game.

But he did remember that he'd felt better about how the game had ended.

No. He was definitely *not* in the mood to face anyone— good, bad, or indifferent.

The wind caught him again and whipped the coat out behind him as he hunched his shoulders and headed down Tremont toward Thirteenth. One short block and he'd catch the bus on Colfax and then ride it until the itch went away.

Or until morning.

Whichever came first.

At the corner of Thirteenth, he kicked an empty Coors bottle someone had stood up next to the signal post and watched it explode across the intersection in a shower of piss yellow glass.

He crossed against the red and offered the verbally irritated driver he'd stepped in front of a single-digit wish for all his future endeavors.

Life sucked.

2

Life was good.

Good? It was *great*!

And not even the overheated, rocking sway of the bus or the four extra hours tacked on to her two-to-ten split shift was going to change her opinion. Or darken her mood.

Especially not since the extra hours had been devoted solely to the agonizing labor and birth of her firstborn. It'd been a long, hard fight, but she'd done it. *Goddammit, she'd done it! Finally.*

Cat took a deep breath and wrinkled her nose at the too-many-people-not-enough-deodorant-scented air as the bus jerked to a stop to let another passenger on.

Journalistic curiosity made her look up, just as it had since she'd got on at Blake and Speer. The man looked like a cross between an Elvis impersonator, complete with rhinestone-studded denim jacket and jeans, and a gorilla.

Hmmmmm.

ELVIS: ALIVE AND WELL IN DENVER ZOO

It might work.

Cat decided to tuck the idea away for next week's staff meeting and watched The King (Kong) stumble up the center aisle as the bus pulled back into traffic. She crossed her fingers and held her breath—no small feat all things considered—until the man-beast finally selected one of the few remaining empty double seats, four rows in front of her.

She exhaled and uncrossed and thanked whatever God of Transportation had been watching out for her. Not that she'd probably had any cause to worry. None of the other late-night/early-morning travelers seemed any more interested in striking up a conversation than she did. Most slept, and those who didn't were busy talking to the voices in their heads.

Her usual bus was generally filled with overachievers and clubbers, so she didn't know if it was standard RTD practice or if she'd happened upon a driver who wanted to add saint to his résumé, but she had the distinct impression that she— give or take a few graveyard shifters—was one of the few paying customers.

Not that it bothered her.

Really.

Cat had commandeered her own double-wide one row back of the rear exit, her briefcase and umbrella next to the window, herself perched on the outside. Her baby in her lap.

Her baby.

I WAS BIGFOOT'S LOVE-SLAVE
—by C. K. Moselle

Okay, so it wasn't Pulitzer Prize material. Hell, she wasn't so self-deluded as to think that. And maybe it wasn't exactly what she had in mind back when she was ten and watched *60 Minutes* while all her friends reenacted the antics of *Laverne and Shirley*. Real life had always fascinated her more than fiction. Always. At least up until twenty-nine months ago when, B.A. degree in journalism clenched in one hand and newest batch of rejections to her textbook-perfect inquiry letter in the other hand, Cat received a long-distance phone call from the managing editor of *QUEST News Publication (The Fastest Growing Promulgate Journal in America)* offering her a position of associate editor.

She hadn't even bothered to check her dictionary before

packing it and all her worldly goods into her fourth-hand Toyota and headed west, bidding a fond farewell to her family, friends . . . and anything even slightly related to real-life journalistic integrity.

Or reality.

Cat looked down at the grainy retouched cover photo that showed a very pregnant teenager (Bigfoot's Love-Slave) standing in front of her parent's single-wide trailer as an oversized, cartoonish Bigfoot grinned at her from around the side of the trailer. A child could spot the cut-and-paste job. So it was fortunate that few children bought *QUEST*. More fortunate still that the typical *QUEST* reader—aged thirty-eight to fifty-six with a jump again between ages sixty-nine and seventy-five, lower-to-middle-middle-class, blue-collar, 3.5 children and two cars, only one of which worked at a time—would have thought it odd if Bigfoot *hadn't* been on the cover.

Cat smiled and pulled off one of the woolen mittens her mother had sent and turned to the page indicated just below her byline, page 38. The intoxicating scent of ink and paper overpowered the bus's other scent. There it was, *her baby*. Page 38. Second column. Right-hand side. Directly below an ad for herbal hemorrhoid relief.

It was beautiful, truth and justice be damned.

A giddy "Christmas morning thrill" surged up from her belly as Cat stamped her boots softly against the floorboards and looked up, ready to meet whatever spontaneous adoration of her talent might be coming her way.

None came.

Those passengers who'd been asleep when she'd gotten on remained asleep, and those who weren't stared indifferently out windows or talked quietly to themselves. *Elvislopithecus* was slumped across both seats and humming.

It could have been "Hunk-a, Hunk-a Burnin' Love" or it could have been "Ode to Joy." It didn't matter. All she had to do was tell her loyal readers, 11,053 in Denver alone, that she'd seen Elvis-Ape on a bus headed for the capitol and there'd be a bigger riot downtown than when the Broncos finally took the Super Bowl. The *first* time.

Cat smiled. She'd definitely have to bring the idea up at the staff meeting.

The printer's ink was still fresh enough to leave a gray smudge on her naked fingertips, and the pungent aroma of chemicals made her eyes water, but Cat couldn't stop re-reading the article she'd already memorized.

Her first. In what she hoped would be a long line of similar *enfants terribles.*

Cat closed her eyes and felt the bus shimmy under her rump as it headed for the curb. At this rate it would probably take another hour to get back to her studio apartment, but it was okay. In fact, if she got home just as the sun was coming up, it would mean that she, and her issue of *QUEST* would be hitting the streets at the same time.

The back door *whoosh*ed open and cold, exhaust-scented air ruffled through her hair. A moment later the doors *whoosh*ed closed and Cat opened her eyes.

The newest passenger boarded the bus, a woman wearing nurses' whites and a plum-colored quilted coat. The woman was late forties, early fifties. Glasses, graying hair cut short. Twenty, twenty-five pounds overweight. And a copy of *QUEST* tucked under one arm.

Cat sat straighter in her seat and watched the woman (the wonderful, wonderful woman) take the seat directly behind the driver's "safety grill" and snap the paper open.

To page 1. The winners of last month's chicken parts recipe contest.

Page 38, Cat thought at her. *Turn to page 38!*

The woman ignored her and studied the page with the single-minded intensity of a brain surgeon about to remove a tumor.

Bitch, Cat thought and immediately replaced the woman in her mind with things she wanted to do when she got home.

Because she knew she wasn't going to be able to sleep.

Celebrate. Definitely number one, although difficult with not so much as a Starbucks open this late/early in the morning. Number two—cut out article and plan trip to Pier 1 for a glitzy frame. Number three. Write up proposal for Elvis-Ape article.

Four . . . Call Mother.

Cat felt herself shrink beneath her skin. Cancel celebration and call Mother. She had to. It was one of those obligatory things like asking for your first box of Kotex even though you were so embarrassed you would have rather bled to death. Call Mother.

Her baby rustled when the bus went over a pothole. Cat pushed back the cuff of her ski jacket and frowned at Mickey Mouse's ever-smiling face. Add two hours, Philadelphia time and . . .

If she didn't call, her mother would be furious. If she did, her mother would suspect the worst.

"What's the matter? Were you in an accident? Are you hurt? Did you get raped? Mugged? Shot? Didn't I tell you Denver was dangerous?"

As if living in Philadelphia was any safer.

Thirty-two years, twenty-nine months, seveenteen hundred miles, two time zones, and a good job and Cat knew exactly what her mother would say once she knew "her precious baby" was safe and sound:

"How nice *for you, Catherine."*

Always Catherine or Catherine Kelly. Never Cathy. Especially not Cat.

"But I thought you wanted to be a real journalist. Dear."

Right, Cat thought. "And fuck you, too, Mom—"

The words came so quickly, so *effortlessly,* that if it hadn't been for the sound of them in her ears, she wouldn't have realized she'd said them out loud. But say them she did. Loud and clear.

Fortunately, her outburst got about as much attention as her smiling invitation for acknowledgment had. Not even the recipe-studying nurse looked up.

They didn't understand. Her mother didn't understand.

And it didn't matter. Not really, because somewhere on the road between Philadelphian hope and Denver reality, Cat had finally come to understand that it didn't matter *what* was written as much as *how* it was written.

While the bus took the curve from Speer onto Colfax, Cat brushed her hair out of her eyes and studied the article again.

The *what* behind Bigfoot's Love-Slave had been a simple case of pubescent hormones gone wild. The "innocent victim of the creature's monstrous desire" was actually a fifteen-year-old in love with a forty-five-year-old married trucker who saw an opportunity to escape her parents' trailer-trash existence and took it.

And who was returned one rainy night, barefoot, bedraggled . . . and five months pregnant. The girl had told Cat, in a private interview over the phone, that when she found out her middle-aged boyfriend had been two-timing her with the thirteen-year-old daughter of a truck-stop waitress, she hitched home and told her parents she'd been kidnapped and raped by Bigfoot.

Her parents, true believers in all things UFO and Unexplained, not only bought the story but offered it to *QUEST* for the tidy sum of $275.00.

And a free six-month subscription.

Cat had gotten the story due to the simple fact that she'd been the one sitting closest to the phone when it rang. Before that, her job at *QUEST* had been picking out the winners of the monthly recipe contests.

The *how* of the story was pure C. K. Moselle.

"Absofuckinglutely," Cat whispered, and kissed the tip of her bare index finger before pressing it to her printed name.

For luck.

And gasped when the *C*-period and *K*-period smeared into one another. Period.

My baby!

Cat snatched the mitten up off the seat next to her and brought it to her lips. The greased wool tasted awful, but it didn't stop her from tonguing spit into it and gently trying to coax the smear clean. Her mother had done it to her often enough, usually right before recitals, dates, and graduations, so Cat didn't have any doubt she could manage.

But after two dabs and a wipe, it became apparent that there were subtleties of cleansing that she had yet to learn.

The smear had worsened and tiny pulp balls all but obscured the *C*. The period following no longer existed. And the *K* . . .

Her baby, her first byline now looked like it had been written my someone named *OX Moselle*.

From Cat to Ox in one fell swoop. Her mother would love it.

Cat sat back against the seat and dropped the mitten over her poor mutilated baby. It wasn't the end of the world, she could always pick up another copy first thing in the morning, it wasn't like it was the *only* one in the city . . . but it *had* been the very first copy, hot off the presses as they say.

And she'd ruined it.

The bus made two more stops before Cat shook her head and decided staring out the window was slightly more constructive than staring at the ink stain on the mitten.

Her reflection glowered back at her from the glass.

Genetic Russian Roulette had taken bigger scoops from her father's Black Irish gene pool than her mother's Nordic Jacuzzi, resulting in thick black hair that frizzled in the slightest hint of moisture, gray-green eyes, and cinnamon-colored freckles that refused to be hidden regardless of the amount of makeup applied.

Since the seventh grade, Cat had offered a nightly prayer of transformation—to take away the thin, dark-haired, freckle-faced five-foot-six-inch duckling with skin the color of a fish's underbelly and leave in its place a beautiful and tall, blond swan with skin the color of honey.

Cat gave up praying in the ninth grade, and C. K. Moselle (not OX) would undoubtedly be too busy in the months to come—what with the Elvis story and an exclusive on Bigfoot's Love-Child once it was whelped—to worry about her looks.

Much.

The bus squealed up to another stop when Cat noticed the smug, "Oh, do you really believe that crap" sneer on her reflection's face and did what any mature, self-assured, professional journalist would do in a similar situation—she stuck out her tongue.

And instantly heard the low bark of laughter that spilled into the bus when the doors opened.

The laughter belonged to the man on the sidewalk, directly

in front of Cat's window. She couldn't see much of him from
where she sat—dark, almond-shaped eyes, long strands of
muddy-russet hair blowing in the cold wind, the hint of a
smile bunched along the rims of his cheeks—but it was apparent he'd seen more than enough of her.

Cat sucked in her tongue and turned away from the window so quickly she heard the vertebrae in the back of her
neck crackle.

The bus idled, rumbling while the early-morning dark settled down around it and steam rose like the ghosts of dead
sewer workers from the manhole covers. And the man at the
curb kept looking at her.

Cat knew that without having to look. She could feel him,
almost see him from the corner of her eye . . . and knew he
was probably still grinning.

At her.

"Hey, pard," the bus driver shouted, so sudden and unexpected that Cat jumped and added a few new wrinkles to
her smudged baby. "You getting on or what?"

The man didn't budge a muscle for another moment or
two, and Cat could feel her own muscles tighten under the
unwanted scrutiny. *Pervert,* she thought, and was about to
offer her lookie-loo more than just a stupid look when he
moved quickly out of Cat's periphery.

Thank God.

Cat felt the tension begin to leave her muscles when he,
her curbside admirer, swung onto the bus, black duster bil-
lowing behind him like wings.

He was apologizing to the driver. Cat could just make out
the words and cultured clip to his voice above the pounding
of blood in her ears. It might have helped if she'd looked
away, pretended to read her article again or just stared out
into the now-deserted street . . . but she didn't.

Cat found herself openly staring while the man fished a
handful of change out of his pocket and fed three coins into
the depository next to the driver.

The sodium streetlight at the curb hadn't done justice to
his hair. It was the color of autumn sweet-gum leaves, fox-
bright, and tied into a loose ponytail that hung just below

the shoulder yoke of the black-canvas duster he wore.

Had he been younger, paler, Cat would have suspected him of being a Goth . . . one of the late-teen/twentysomethings who wandered the streets and clubs decked out in tattered black outfits and carefully applied kohl shadows to heighten the effect of otherworldliness.

The man, however, had a good decade or more on the oldest Goth she'd ever seen, nor did his red hair appear to be from a bottle. He just happened to be wearing all black. Expensive, nontattered black. Duster, tab-collar shirt open to the black-leather vest, designer jeans, and spit-polished Wellingtons.

Black and red, a great contrast, and there was no doubt in Cat's mind that he knew it.

He stayed next to the driver when the bus rumbled back into the traffic lane, and then started slowly up the aisle. When he saw her still staring he winked, and Cat felt her neck, cheeks, and forehead burn.

WOMAN DIES OF TERMINAL EMBARRASSMENT ON BUS

"Head just exploded," says one witness

She should be so lucky.

The man was five rows in front of her when Cat finally managed to crank her neck muscles down toward the paper and found herself staring at her mitten. She could still feel him, however, moving closer with each step.

Christ, she thought, *why do I have to attract every pervert and psycho and . . .*

"Do I know you?"

Cat looked up into a face that was only a shade or two lighter than his hair. Burnished copper skin and raven black eyes. Red and black. The ol' gene pool had played a harder trick on him than it had on her—high cheeks, hooked nose, red skin . . . and Irish setter hair.

PROOF OF VIKING LINK TO NATIVE AMERICANS

He was, without a doubt, the most striking man Cat had ever met. On a late-night, crosstown bus.

And she might have said so, or at least broached the subject of the article as a prelude to conversation, had she been able to get her mouth to form actual words. Instead, she felt her mouth do the goldfish-out-of-water bit while she stared and he smiled.

And stared back.

"Sorry," he said, "didn't mean to bother you."

Something flashed at his throat—a concho or necklace—when he nodded to her and continued up the aisle to the back of the bus.

Do I know you? Sorry didn't mean to bother you.

Ten words and the lingering scent of a musky aftershave and it was all Cat could do to keep herself facing the front of the bus. And to keep the sudden moistness in her palms from doing any more damage to her byline.

Her baby. Her firstborn. And ten words from a complete stranger of indeterminate breeding had made all that, her greatest achievement to date, seem . . . adequate.

Cat folded her bare hand over the mitten-covered one and turned back toward the window. But this time, instead of making faces or watching the streetlights and shadows of the city, she lowered her eyes and ran down the list of names (and dates) on her mental "Date Scoreboard."

And cringed.

Her last "real" date—those which included sex along with dinner and a movie—had been four months ago . . . four long, lonely months.

He'd been an associate editor at *QUEST* for almost a full year when Cat was hired. After introductions were made, he offered to show her the ropes of "jaundice journalism," as he called it.

She liked his irreverent sense of humor immediately, and they started dating three weeks later. A week after that they went from casual to real dating on the foldout bed in her apartment. And two weeks after that she made the mistake of saying the *L*-word in the midst of passion.

She knew it was a mistake the moment it slipped out. He slipped out soon after complaining of a sudden headache. But Cat knew better—she'd said the *L*-word when he was definitely only an *F*-word kind of guy.

She wasn't really all that surprised when he called in sick the next day. And the next. And the next. Although it did come as somewhat of a shock when she found out a week later at the staff meeting, that he'd quit and was now working for a New Age nudist magazine somewhere in the redwood forests of California.

Four months. Four long, lonely, *frustrating* months of forced celibacy . . . maybe that was why every nerve ending in her body had been sent into overdrive by the Indian-Viking. Geronimo of the north.

Cat closed her eyes and leaned back against the seat as the bus squealed to yet another stop. And saw his face—copper skin and black eyes framed by flaming hair. It was not a good sign and one that pointed down the garden path of carnal misconduct. She'd never, *ever* walked up to a strange man . . . especially a strange man on a bus, for God's sake . . . for the raw purpose of having sex with him.

It just wasn't *her*. And yet . . .

Cat unclasped her hands and folded her arms, put palms to elbows and squeezed. No, dammit, it wasn't like her, but there was something about the man that tugged at her, something that lingered in the air above her far longer than his dark, musky cologne.

She tried to figure out exactly what the *something* might be while the bus idled next to the curb. And idled. And idled.

Cat opened one eye. And then the other. And then her mouth.

"Ohmygod!"

"Shut up, bitch," the too-young, too-nervous boy yelled at her, and punctuated the command with the chrome Saturday night special he held in his hand.

The boy could have been anywhere from fourteen to twenty-four. Cat couldn't decide if the gun and backwards Rockies baseball cap made him look older or younger, not that it mattered. Life on the street acted like salt brine to the young, it aged and toughened them.

The bus continued to idle while the Kid and His Gun glared at Cat.

"Wha'choo lookin' at, bitch?"

Anything cute and glib would probably have not been ap-

preciated at the moment. Cat bit furrows into her lower lip
to keep from answering and shook her head.

Neither the Kid nor his Gun seemed to notice. For the
moment.

"Wha'choo *all* lookin' at, fuckin' motherfuckers?" The
Kid's scream echoed up one side of the bus and down the
other before fleeing for its life through the open rear door.
One of the passengers, who'd been happily talking to himself
when Cat got on, suddenly looked very sane and followed
the echo out the door. He didn't stop running until he was
only another shadow among shadows.

The Gun backhanded into the side of the driver's head and
somebody—maybe a lot of somebodies, maybe only Cat—
screamed.

"Shut the fuck up," the Kid screamed. "And shut that
fuckin' door. Ain't nobody gonna book it until I say! Close
the fuckin' door!"

Only Elvis-Ape slept on while the doors closed and the
driver, bleeding high on the cheek, tried to reason with the
Kid. And his Gun.

"Hey, look, calm down, okay?" The driver's hands
gripped the steering wheel as if he was afraid to let go. "Like
the sign says, I can't open the collection box, and there
wouldn't be anything in there but chump change anyway. So
why don't you just leave and—"

"Shut up!"

The Kid jabbed the Gun at the driver's nose before turning
it toward the passenger compartment. The Gun's single black
eye gave the sleeping King only a fleeting glance—

"You just shut the fuck up and get this fuckin' thing
movin', man. We gonna take us a little ride."

—and lingered only an eternity on the spot between Cat's
eyes—

"Cops come snooping if a bus sits too long. So get this
piece of shit moving!"

—before coming back to the side of the driver's head. The
bus pulled away from the curb as gently as a mother pushing
a stroller over velvet.

"The rest of you start diggin' out whatever goodies you

got. Cash, plastic, or drugs." The Kid suddenly giggled and the Gun dipped into the hollow of the driver's ear. The bus jerked forward, but the Kid didn't notice. He was enjoying himself too much. "I'm an equal-opportunity man. You gimme something, and I don't give you shit, got it?"

The Kid peeled off his cap and held it out in front of him like a street performer accepting offerings. Hair the color of old grease spilled down over the angry red pimples on his forehead and half covered his eyes. Colorless eyes, Cat thought as a few coins and fewer crumpled bills began to add weight to the cap. Dead eyes.

ZOMBIE HOLDS UP BUS

No. Bad idea. Dumb.

The Gun and the Kid noticed her staring. Very, *very* dumb idea.

"Wha'choo staring at *now*, bitch?"

He came at her like a tornado, all bluster and destruction, smelling of dog shit and gasoline and sulfur. The smell made her eyes water as the Gun found the hollow beneath the point of her chin and tipped her head back. The Kid was younger than she'd originally thought. And a hell of a lot harder.

"I asked wha'choo was staring at."

She didn't have time to answer or blink. The sight at the tip of the muzzle cut a bloody groove in her flesh as it pulled away. A new, unwanted headline flashed sickly green across Cat's forebrain.

QUEST REPORTER KILLED

"I asked you wha'choo was staring at, bitch!"

REPORTER KILLED

"N-nothing."

The Gun's eye lifted toward hers, and the Kid's dead eyes were suddenly very much alive. Cat could see herself mirrored in them.

"You sayin' I'm *nothing*?"

"God, no, I—"

The Gun rose up and stopped all explanations. Cat sat back slowly, her nails leaving furrows down pages 37 and 38.

"I have about twenty dollars in my purse," she said, nodding toward the large canvas tote bag at her feet. "And a couple of credit cards. I'll get them for you."

Cat started to lean forward, her mittened hand reaching for the tote when the Kid backhanded his cap across her face. The few coins and bills he'd collected hit the window like hail.

REPORTER KILLED

"You tryin' to pull something stupid, bitch?" the Kid asked while the Gun listened for her answer. "You got a little ladylike gun in there? You thinkin' 'bout playin' fuckin' *Superwoman*, you stupid cunt?"

The empty cap fluttered in the overheated, dank air of the bus as the Kid cocked the Gun and pressed the barrel against Cat's forehead. Part of her remembered reading or hearing or seeing something about how a gun will explode if the barrel is capped or blocked. A good thing to remember, unless you were what was blocking the barrel.

Like she was.

WOMAN KILLED IN BUS HOLDUP. STORY AT 10.

Cat closed her eyes and held her breath, not minding the smell so much now and hoping that the end of her life would be as hazy as her memory of its beginning was.

"Fuckin' bitch!" The Kid's voice sounded farther away with her eyes shut, the pressure of the Gun less somehow. "You ain't gonna be nothin' but victim number uh—"

The Boy's voice broke and shattered into a scream that rained across Cat's face. More screams followed, competing with the sudden screech of brakes, and then her stomach clenched and shifted to one side as the bus started to fishtail.

Cat opened her eyes just in time to catch herself from slamming facefirst into the seat in front of her. The seat, her hand, and the Gun were covered in blood.

At first, even though she couldn't feel any pain and was perfectly aware that the bus had come to a sudden stop against a streetlight, Cat knew she was dead. Knew that the Kid had pulled the trigger and blown off the top of her head.

She had to be dead . . . although Cat couldn't remember ever having done anything in her life—creative libel notwithstanding—that would have consigned her to the same Hell as the Kid.

And the Kid most certainly was dead, even though his mouth still tried to form words against the bloody tide that washed over his lips and chin to the ragged hollow that had been his throat.

He was dead, but he stared into Cat's eyes as if he didn't know he was dead. Didn't know he was in Hell and put there by the demon that was still feeding on him.

Cat could feel the scream build inside her. Growing. Growing. Waiting . . . waiting until the thing, the demon, had finished with the Kid and looked up.

Then she screamed, and the demon flattened its pointed ears back against the shaggy silver-red fur that covered its head. A look of pain came to its coal black eyes as it tossed the dead Kid to the flooring.

Bloodstained, it lowered its face toward Cat's and curled black lips away from yellow fangs.

"Shhhhhh," it whispered around one upraised, bloodied talon.

Cat stopped screaming, probably stopped breathing for a moment or two while the demon

. . . no, not a demon . . . a dog . . . like a dog . . .

knelt and lowered its hand

. . . paw . . . it has a paw . . . like a dog, but bigger . . . much bigger . . . like a dog . . . a

to her lap. Squeezed gently. Cat heard the sound of paper rustling.

"are you all right?"

The words were slurred and thick, but she could understand them. It was talking to her, this dog-thing that wasn't a dog, but like a dog, this

wolf

More screams filled the night, but from the outside. Sirens. Police and fire it sounded like. Ambulance, too, Cat thought, although the Kid wouldn't need it. Was already dead and the thing . . . the wolf that talked and killed the Kid stood up and touched her cheek. Gently. Before it hurled itself against the sealed back doors and burst them apart.

The hot, musky scent lingered in the stifling air of the bus as Cat watched it . . . *it*, the demon . . . the wolf-thing flee into the night, its black duster swirling around it like bat-wings *(no . . . wrong monster . . . it was a . . . a . . .)* while the dead Kid finished bleeding out, and the witnesses . . . the survivors retched or gasped or prayed. But the words were jumbled, the phrases incomplete.

"What was that? What was that? Oh, my God, my God, my—"

"God damn gangbangers . . . when's the city gonna do something about this—"

"—Evil, for thine art the power and the glory and the—"

"Freakin' crack addicts! Don't have the decency to kill each other in private like—"

"God! OhmyGod. OhmyGod. OhmyGod."

It was a—

And suddenly, there were other words, louder, stronger, coming from inside her head: *Do something! Take notes, for Christ's sake! This is news . . . this is—*

Cat nodded to the *QUEST* reporter in her head, but couldn't stop watching it, watching *him*, until the shadows had swallowed him.

It was—

And then she looked down at the paper—*her baby*—in her lap and saw that the bloodied print of a giant paw had obliterated her smudged byline, the hemorrhoid ad, and half of Bigfoot's smiling face.

Not a demon. Not a dog. Not a wolf.

Cat lifted her hand over the print and stretched her fingers as far as she could within the mitten's knitted confines. The paw print was bigger. Much bigger.

QUEST EXCLUSIVE

WEREWOLF SAVES REPORTER'S LIFE

Oh God. *It was real.*

Cat was only slightly more hysterical and less coherent than the rest of the passengers when the police and *real* reporters arrived.

———

He ran the seven blocks without stopping, without no-ticing where he was or if there were any witnesses to his flight. Instinct kept him to the shadows and hunched low, but intellect fought his every step.

He'd killed. Murdered. And that had gone against the greatest law of Man that he'd been taught. And that he had strived to teach others. Thou shalt not kill.

But he'd saved her. The woman on the bus . . . the one who'd made a face at the night and blushed when she saw him instead.

He stopped running when he got to the northwest corner of Cheesman Park. Still in a half crouch, he leaned against a tree trunk and sniffed the air. There was always the scent of the long-forgotten dead in the winds that drifted over the well-manicured lawns, a delicate and faded perfume from the past when the park had been one of the city's first cemeteries.

He turned and flared his nostrils against the breeze, sorting the dead from the few homeless encampments beneath the spruce and cedar groves farther to the east.

There were fewer homeless living in the park now that it was cold, but the heavy sick-sweet smell of them clung to the shadows and made his mouth water.

No!

His claws, sticky with the adolescent's blood, tore deep grooves in the cottonwood's papery trunk. It was just the circumstances he'd found himself in. Just the bad emotional taste left on his soul from his most recent break-up with . . . with . . .

He couldn't remember her name and her face, the face of his most recent ex-lover kept blurring into the face of the woman on the bus. He let his claws sink deeper into the wood to keep from licking them clean.

He'd saved the woman's life by taking another's and had absolutely no idea why he'd done it. Men and women died in the city every day from random, mindless acts of violence, no less horrible or horrifying than the one that would have claimed her . . . that *should* have claimed her if he hadn't interfered.

Thou *shalt not kill.*

Extracting his claws from the mutilated tree, he turned and loped slowly down the ice-frosted slope, ears pricked backwards to listen for the sounds of pursuit. Angry villagers with torches, the stuff of childhood terrors. More likely police in riot gear and semiautomatics, secure within the steel-reinforced wombs of their cruisers, looking for the man who'd murdered the boy on the bus.

Looking for a *man*. Not him.

He ducked into a thick bramble of bushes near the western edge at the back of the botanic gardens and vaulted effortlessly over the eight-foot-high fence.

There was a strong scent of urine, both human and dog, along the shadows that lined the park side of the fence. He fought the urge to add his own to the layers of territorial markings.

It would have been a useless waste. The Family never came to the gardens.

Silence gave him passage as he picked his way carefully across the water smooth pebbles that surrounded the koi pond. He was almost home. He looked up at the high-rise condo just behind the northern most fence of the Japanese garden section and easily spotted the swatch of darkness that was his. The Family hated that he had chosen to make his way, singularly, in the world of men, but they couldn't really say much about it.

Except for Mother. Her displeasure was well-known. And constant.

He followed the paving stones around the edge of the pond and paused beneath the leafless fingers of the weeping willow and sat down. Beneath the black water, kept fluid by the hidden recycling pumps, he watched a large silver-and-orange fish nudge a smaller red out of the way. On land or water it was the same, the aggressor makes the rules.

Sitting on the man-made "natural" rock bench, he reached into the pocket of his duster and felt the tingle radiate upward from his fingers as they closed around the silver-and-turquoise choker. It glowed, moon bright, against the bloody, now-hairless palm of his hand.

He was a mess. The blood had already begun to dry on

the coat sleeves and the front of his vest. Damn.

Setting the necklace down on the rock next to him, he took a deep breath and began to lick himself clean. It would probably take the rest of the night, but it was better than walking into the lobby and trying to explain his appearance to the semivigilant night security guard.

"No, I'm fine, Brian . . . just ran into a monster on the bus. Hah. Hah."

"Hah," he whispered, and watched a large silver-and-black koi start at the sound. "Sorry."

He had no choice.

Closing his eyes, he used his right canine to scrape the congealed blood off his claws. It was the consistency of raspberry jam. It made him sick . . . just a little, if he thought about it. If he didn't think about it . . . just a little . . . he almost enjoyed the coppery sweet taste against his tongue.

Shit.

Life really did suck.

3

Cat watched the rippled circles dance across the surface of her coffee as she brought the mug to her lips. Her
hand was shaking more than any wino's or druggie's coming
off a fix. And the worse part was that she couldn't stop it
from shaking any more than she could stop herself from
thinking about *why* it was still shaking.

And remembering every little detail.

So she could tell it again to *QUEST*'s managing editor just
like she'd told it to the police (and *two* police psychologists).

In case he didn't believe it.

The same way the police hadn't believed her or any of the
other hysterical eyewitnesses. There was something to be
said about "blind justice" and, by God, she'd have to remember to use that line in her article.

"And you want the headline to read . . . ?"

Cat looked up too quickly, and the minute she did, a couple of the stronger ripples took the opportunity and splashed
over the edge of the mug. They landed, going lukewarm on
the way down, on the right leg of her corduroy slacks—just
above the knee and just below the smear of blood.

Cat watched the coffee soak in. She'd stared at the blood

smear enough—first at the police station when she'd noticed it and then in the back of the cab as it crawled through the morning rush on Speer to get her back to work only fifty-eight minutes late. It was shaped a bit like Italy. With the toe of the boot missing, cut away in a straight line.

The toe was on Page 38. With *her baby*. And the bloody paw print.

Cat looked back into the mug and watched the ripples dance.

" 'Saved by Werewolf,' for the header," she answered—automatically, professionally—while her hands shook and the coffee danced. "Followed by '*QUEST* Reporter Eyewitness to Bizarre Bus . . . um, Bizarre Bus . . .'"

"Homicide? Murder? Attack? Let me know if I'm getting warm here."

Cat didn't take any chances this time. Scooting her chair forward, she set the mug down on the desk before she looked up. To meet the managing editor's hard stare.

"It wasn't really like that," she said, and suddenly wished she hadn't . . . or at least had stopped before adding "He, *it* saved my life. That kid was going to shoot me. I know it! If he, *it* hadn't killed him . . . the kid . . . I . . . wouldn't be . . . God."

Something hot and not tasting a lot like coffee tickled the back of Cat's throat and made her swallow. Hard. Twice.

"It was real," she said when she could. "I mean it. This thing was *real*."

Tanner Boswell—"Call me Tanner" to all his employees, but called Ol' Tannenbutt, secretly, by those same employees . . . or so Cat had been told—sat back against the padded desk chair that squeaked regardless of how many applications of WD-40 were applied and stared at her over the tops of his gold half-frame glasses. Her copy of *QUEST* lay on his desk, in the center of a stained, fake-leather-trimmed blotter, folded in half and half-hidden beneath her hastily written, unspell-checked, and printed three-page, single-spaced accounting of the *Bizarre Bus . . . whatever*.

"Real," he echoed.

Cat nodded. "Real," she answered, and watched her boss's

bald, milk chocolate–colored forehead accordion pleat into wrinkles.

"A *real* werewolf. Here in Denver. Saved you."

Cat nodded each time. Yes. Yes. Yes.

"You're absolutely certain."

Yes, yes, yes, yes.

"I knew you were going to be special when I hired you." He leaned further back, much to the chair's audible protest, and changed the wrinkles' direction—from frown to smile. "Hell, maybe I should have hired me *real* journalists years ago. Might have been bigger'n the *Enquirer* by now.

"A real werewolf . . . damn, you almost have *me* believin' it!"

Cat's head had stopped nodding like some back-window car novelty halfway through his adoration of her talent.

"But I'm telling you the truth. It really happened."

Tanner smiled and held his hands up in surrender.

"Hey, look, you don't have to convince *me*, okay? I'm gonna run it page One . . . Cover story."

Cat's protests died. "Cover?"

"Damn straight." Tanner leaned forward into the loudest squeal Cat had heard the chair make yet and picked up her *real* account of the incident. "Look, you were smack-dab in the middle of some serious shit last night. Hell, you still looked pretty much up to your eyeballs in it when you walked in, but . . ."

His grin spread across his face, ear to ear and eyeballs to second chin.

"Lord knows if someone, kid *or* adult, stuck a gun in my face and cocked it I'd probably be seeing a whole lot of nothing, but here you are, fresh-faced and right out of college, and *you* come up with this Lycanthropic Knight in Shining Fur. And, by God, don't you stick to that story like it was covered in honey. Hell yeah, I'm going run it front cover!"

Cat felt the hot liquid against the back of her throat again, but this time she ignored it. Regardless of her poor showing the night before, she was, as he had just reminded her only a moment before, a *real* journalist. She cocked her head to one side and nodded. Humbly.

"I'm glad you like it."

Tanner waved the pages at her. "Understatement doesn't become you, kid. And neither does complacency. Now, there are a couple of things I want you to do to this . . . bulk it up to make it *sound* real. Don't touch the werewolf bit, that's choice and our readers will go absolutely wild, especially the ones here in Denver; but we gotta remember we've got a duty to the public, so throw in a paragraph or two on the general ills of society and youth gangs. Yaddah, yaddah, yaddah. You know the kind of stuff I'm talking about . . . social import and all that crap. Got it?"

Cat nodded. There were gold flecks in her boss's brown eyes, the same shade as his glasses, that sparkled whenever he heard a story that he knew would be a grabber. And at the moment those flecks were throwing off more sparks than the mother lode.

She'd struck it rich. Her second child was going to be a protégé. So why did she suddenly feel like throwing up? Cat had to swallow twice before she could answer.

"Got it."

"Great." He picked up his coffee mug, the one showing a snarling Garfield over the words "Have a Nice Day" and leaned back. *squeak squeal* "Now tell me about the other witnesses to last night's bus ride to hell."

So Cat did. Again. Just as she had for the police and their psychologists. And herself.

"They were mostly homeless, sleeping or . . . not paying attention for other reasons."

"Drunk," Tanner said, and nodded while Garfield rode the swell of his belly between bow tie and Broncos' (First) Super Bowl Win commemorative belt buckle. "Good. No reliable witnesses."

"Except the bus driver," Cat added quickly. "And . . . *him.*"

"Him?"

"The . . . you know. Werewolf."

Tanner chuckled. "Right." Then sighed. "I am worried a

bit about the driver, though. Any *real* eyewitness can flush this whole thing right down the crapper. Remember last issue's lead story?"

Cat nodded. How could she forget.

SCIENTISTS DISCOVER KILLER VEGETABLES

It had put her off broccoli for a week.

"Yeah," she said, even though she didn't see the connection between that *(fake)* story and hers.

Tanner didn't seem to notice the question in her voice.

"All we had was one throwaway item from the ten o'clock news about how some of the tomato seeds that went up on the last shuttle mission appeared 'different' "—he used the pinkies of both hands to curl quotation marks in the air— "when viewed under a microscope here on Earth. And that's all we needed.

"We didn't have one *real* witness that could stand up and say, for a fact, that the government *wasn't* breeding man-eating carrots in the Amazon jungles. It was a perfect story. But with yours being set in Denver, on the other hand . . ."

The other hand had *always* been the first thing that got Cat into trouble.

"If a witness does come forward, we can do a retraction and say it was only some lunatic wearing a mask."

Her mouth was the second.

She snapped her jaw shut so quickly she bit her tongue, but saw her boss smile through tear-filled eyes. He didn't notice the tears anymore than he'd noticed the lie—about it *not* being a real werewolf.

"See," Tanner said, saluting her with his mug, "that's what a degree will get you. Logic. Okay, rework the article. Hey, give it a Beauty and the Beast angle if you want; sex always adds to the sales figures. And have it back on my desk by—"

He quarter-turned as the chair complained and looked out through the glass wall/partition that separated his office (an eight-foot-by-ten-foot section of the loft *QUEST* rented in the same building that housed the printing facilities . . . in the basement) from the "newsroom" to the wall-mounted clock above the personnel (freight) elevator. Cat followed his gaze and saw that she'd already been there two hours.

Time certainly did have a way of flying.

"Oh, let's say, noon. How's that?"

The chair's continued squealing told her she'd better say something, quickly and with the right answer.

"Sure," she said. "No problem. I'll have it on your desk before lunch."

"That's m'girl. But just remember, *QUEST* readers want fantasy that's cloaked in plausibility. Give them that and they'll be seeing werewolves on every Metro bleepin' bus."

He took another sip of coffee as Cat stood up and walked to the glass-in-glass door. She could hear him swallow as her fingers, still shaking, closed around the knob. The brass was cold against her skin, and it made her tremble.

"So, you think you could work this into a four, five part series?"

Cat almost fell backwards into the doorframe before she got her legs to cooperate as a unit and turn.

"Whom do I have to kill?"

Tanner looked up at her and chuckled like a jolly black Santa.

"That's exactly the answer I want from my reporters. Instinct tells me that story is gonna hit more nerve endings than a nun with a ruler." He leaned back, the mug resting on the crest of his belly. This time the chair springs were silent. "And do you want to know *why* I think this?"

Cat nodded at the same time she realized that he'd been waiting for *her* to ask that question. She felt as if she'd just missed an easy question on a final exam.

And it was obvious by the look on his face, the smirk working its way into the wrinkles at the corners of his mouth, that Tanner knew it as well.

Cat suddenly understood the endearing, and enduring, nickname. *Dear ol' Tannenbutt.* She returned the smile.

"Because," he said, "I learned this business firsthand . . . not out of books." He paused to let the barbs sink in. "Okay, I want you to start with the bus incident and play up the fear and loathing in Denver bit—people not being safe, yaddah, yaddah. You know, the kind of tweaks that'll make it sound like what our hairy friend did was a public service.

"Keep the first story simple enough to be plausible and end with the standard 'police are withholding information' crap. Toss in a couple lines on the werewolf legend and make it about eight hundred fifty words."

His smile widened. "Can do?"

At 850 words . . . 250 words per page, give or take, that would put it out at—Cat bit the inside of her cheek—*250 times 3 is . . . 750 plus 100 would put the whole thing at just under three and a half pages. Double-spaced.*

She smiled back. "Can do."

"Good." The mug trembled and the springs squealed when he sat back up. "Oh, and make sure you check in with Tomi before you start. She has connections in the sheriff's department and can give you a body or two."

Cat's grip on the doorknob tightened. "Pardon?"

Tannenbutt rolled his eyes toward the ceiling. Her GPA continued to fall.

"Color, kiddo," he said when he finally allowed himself to look at her. "In a city as big as Denver there's got to be at least *one* gruesome unsolved homicide that isn't gang-related. Just ask Tomi if there's been a real juicy one we can pin on Lon Chaney the Third."

Cat blinked.

"Old-time actor," Tannebutt answered without waiting to be asked, although the roll of his eyes told Cat she should have already *known* who this person was. "Christ, don't you watch American Movie Classics? Well, anyway, his dad was the more famous of the two, but he was pretty big in the B-grade monster movies. Used to play the Wolfman. Semilocal boy. Grew up south of here in Colorado Springs. And make sure you go introduce yourself to Ed . . . he's the new guy down in Photo. A wizard with overlay and touch-up. I stole him off one of the bigger Florida tabs . . . if you catch my drift."

He reached up and pulled down one eyelid like it was supposed to mean something. Which it didn't. But Cat nodded anyway.

"Right. Got him for a song because he said he'd always wanted to live in the mountains. Didn't tell him the moun-

tains are about thirty miles away, but . . . hell, the man only
has to face west to see them, right. Right. Tell him to show
you a picture of ol' Lonny in makeup. If it's a good one, we
might even use it for the cover. I think he's probably public
domain now, but check with him anyway. What?"

"Um . . ." She took a deep breath and smelled the stale
tang of cigarette smoke on the man's clothes that no amount
of Brut aftershave could conceal. It'd taken a moment of
mental calisthenics to jump from talk of the new guy down
in Photo to Lonny the Wolfman. "I don't think we'll have
to worry about pictures. I have . . . something we can use as
a cover shot."

Her earlier bungles were forgotten. "Oh? You mean to tell
me you got a picture of Mr. Big Bad himself? Jesus Hum-
perdink Christ, girl, you mean to tell me you withheld evidence from the cops? Now *that's* being a journalist."

God she hated to burst his bubble . . . and the fragile respect it carried with it.

"Not exactly."

-pop- "Then what *do* you have for old Papa Tanner?"

"It's a . . . paw print."

"A paw print?"

Tannenbutt's mug made the long, slow journey back toward the clutter on his desk.

"He . . ." Cat tried to clear the sudden thickness out of her
throat. "The werewolf sort of fell on me after he . . . when
the bus crashed into the streetlight. I had my copy of *QUEST*
open on my lap and he . . . it . . ."

"*His* paw print."

"Yes."

"A *bloody* paw print."

Cat hadn't let herself dwell on that particular aspect until
that moment. And wished to God she still hadn't.

"Uh-" *swallow* "-huh."

"And you're sure you didn't show it to the police."

Cat nodded. Slowly. "Do you think I'll get into trouble?"

"Hell no," her boss said as another smile accordion-pleated
his cheeks, "they'll think it's as fake as the article."

It took a moment for the words—and their meaning—to sink in. "You mean we're going to use it?"

"Hell yes." He gave her another *dumb kid* look while he reached for the multiline phone on his desk. "We not only got an exclusive but an actual werewolf paw print? She-it."

Cat didn't know whether to laugh, clap, or just back slowly out the door, bowing and genuflecting, when he fit the receiver next to his ear and waved her to a stop.

"Hang on a sec," he said to her, and then louder into the receiver, "Yeah, Ed? Yeah, it's your Lord and Massah. One of my Chosen Few is coming down with something special . . . *very* special and I want you to dupe it. What? Yeah. Cover. Center on what she gives you and a teaser . . . upper right. Wolfman."

Tannenbutt winked at her. "Right. Lon Chaney, Jr. Great, she'll be right down. And remember . . . you're still on probation, pal. You haven't worked here long enough to have me thinking you're a genius. Huh? Yeah—I'll believe that when I see it, m'man."

He hung up the phone and leaned back, fingers folded over his belly while the springs sang.

"There you go. Ed'll take care of you. Then check with Tomi before you start on the rewrite."

Cat nodded.

"Oh, and one more thing—"

She straightened like a soldier awaiting inspection . . . or execution. "Yes?"

"Not too much on the Beauty and the Beast angle this time around. You can hit that around the third, forth article. Right now I want people to think there's a *real* monster walking the streets of Denver. Now . . . get that paw print to Ed ASAP."

Cat took a deep breath as she stood up. "Do you want to see it?"

He looked up, the intense interest in her story already beginning to fade. "See what?"

"It . . . the paw print. I left it folded on my desk and—"

Tannenbutt waved her silent. "There are two things you need to commit to memory right now if you want to keep working here. First, never try to pull the wool over these peepers. I publish this shit to make money, period. I don't believe in monsters or aliens using anal probes to control people or that Elvis is still alive and pumping gas for Diamond Shamrock. I believe in bank accounts and the continued gullibility of the buying public." He lifted two fingers. "Second . . . never, and I mean *never* leave anything on your desk that you wouldn't mind being snatched by another reporter. This is a dog-eat-dog field, little girl, and you just left a meat loaf unattended."

Cat wasn't sure if she should say "yes sir," "thank you," or "but there really *is* a monster" or gasp . . . so she mumbled something that sounded like the first two while thinking the third and hissing the fourth as she left the enclosed office.

One or two heads lifted as she raced through the narrow run that separated the rat's maze of cubicles, the displays of articles and bylines that were pinned to the various fabric-covered presswood "walls" flapping in the breeze. Her fear about her coworkers' possibly "sticky fingers" was only part of her rush.

There were too many stories floating around the portable espresso machine in the lunchroom about her employer's love of cancellation. Rumor was that he'd seen too many 1940s movies and lived for the times he could yell "Stop the presses" and replace one story with another.

It'd happened ten times since Cat had started working there, and she didn't want it to happen to her *baby* . . . not after all this. If her *baby* was still there.

QUEST REPORTER BLOWS BIG CHANCE
Exclusive . . . by Someone Else

Cat's heart skipped a beat before she spotted the paper exactly where she'd left it, wrinkled and folded over on itself, the bloody paw print hidden from view . . . and the predatory gaze of scoop-hungry coworkers.

REPORTER SAVES BUTT
Cites Clean Living and All-Banana Diet

"Thank you, thank you, thank—*ooo!*"

Cat jumped when her desk phone rang, the outside-line button flashing amber.

After a quick glance over her shoulder to see which of her coworkers (scoop-stealing predators that they were) might have seen her less-than-mature reaction, Cat exhaled slowly and almost managed to sound professional when she picked up the receiver.

"Moselle, Associate Ed—"

"Catherine, you have to come home immediately."

Cat pressed the phone tighter against her ear. "Mom, what's wrong? Are you okay?"

The concern in her mother's voice disappeared. "I'm fine, Catherine, but I heard about that murder on a Denver bus last night. My God, Catherine, how can you stand living in a city like that? People aren't even safe on public transportation."

Cat pulled her copy of *QUEST* across the desk and picked it up, holding it against her chest while her mother sighed in utter dismay. "I've been up all night worrying."

"Oh?" Cat resisted the urge to check the small desk clock. "Well . . . I'm sorry you felt you had to, Mom."

"Felt I had to? Catherine Kelly, you're my daughter and I love you and I worry about you. Now, why don't you stop all this nonsense and come home? I'm sure we can find you a real job where you won't have to deal with . . . less than sane individuals."

And monsters, Mom. Don't forget about monsters.

"I have to go now, Mom . . . big meeting. I'll send you a copy of my first byline. I'm really proud of it."

"Catherine Kelly, did you even hear one word I was say—"

"I'm fine, Mom. Gotta go. I'll call you later this week. Promise. Bye."

The line went dead before Cat could hang up. There might . . . *would* be some repercussions when she called her mother again, but at the moment that seemed hardly worth the effort to think about. She had to get the print down to Photo and start on the article.

Larry in the cubicle catty-corner from hers shouted something as she ran for the elevator, but Cat ignored it and tightened her grip on the paper.

Her paper. Her baby.

Her firstborn.

Marked forever by the bloodied paw print.

The sign of the wolf.

The *werewolf*. For real.

Cat felt her belly drop down to her shoes long before the elevator doors whooshed open.

Tanner Boswell counted five Mississippis after the girl hightailed it out of the office, pretending to reread some article that linked spontaneous combustion with the misuse of dietary amino acids, in case she glanced back, before sliding a finger into the recessed pull on the bottom right-hand drawer. He counted three more and added one Lou-eeze-E-anna before he looked up to cast an eye into the sea of partitions beyond the glass wall of his office.

Not one of his little fishes swam into view.

All was quiet—beyond the muted ring from phones and fax and burbling grind of printers. All was calm. At least for the moment.

Reason enough to celebrate.

One more Mississippi and he lifted the bottle of Southern Comfort from the drawer and added three fingers to the stain of coffee barely covering the bottom of the mug.

Hell, he knew it was "early," but time was relative in the newspaper game. Mornings became afternoons became late-night-gotta-stay-because-I'm-the-boss too quickly for a man not to take the advantage when and where he could.

The when was *now*.

And the where was currently pouring like liquid honey down his throat.

Better. Tanner closed his eyes as the first warming rays began burning off the late-autumn chill that had followed him into his office and settled in every arthritic joint in his body. Much better.

When he opened his eyes the mug was three-quarters empty even though he couldn't remember taking a second

. . . or third swallow. Oh well, just another reason why getting old was a bitch.

He poured another two fingers from the bottle to bring the level back up and took a *conscious* mouthful.

The cubicle sea was still quiet, so he let himself settle back against the chair and think about the woman/child who'd just left. God, had he *ever* been that young? That enthusiastic? About anything let alone the fanciful crap more people than not eagerly consumed as "fact."

"Shee-it," Tanner said to himself as he closed the bottle back in its drawer. Out of harm's way . . . for the moment. Up until he had to fortify himself against the night chill before making his way home.

To another bottle, a little TV if there was a Jackie Chan movie on cable, and a whole lot of nothing on the side. Gwen had split his first year back from 'Nam and taken the twins with her. Nappy-headed little bitches probably had their Ph.D.s or made him a grandpa a couple of times over by now without him ever knowing.

He didn't even know if they were still in Denver. Shit, you pop a woman once . . . only once and then just hard enough to maybe bruise up the skin a little and she calls you a fucking baby-killing psycho and takes your children away.

His babies—grown women now. Women who could turn on the evening news and *tsk-tsk* about the awful killing on a Metro bus the night before. Women who could pick up a newspaper and *tsk-tsk* about the decline of society.

Women who had to shop for groceries and couldn't keep from sneaking looks at the lurid, "we all know it's all made-up" tabloids while they waited for their frozen vegetables and ground round to be rung up and bagged.

Paper or plastic?

If his girls were anywhere in the reading free world, he'd make sure *they'd* know their daddy was still alive and kicking.

QUEST-The NewsJournal for a New World
presents
THE DENVER WEREWOLF
Tanner H. Boswell, Managing Editor/Publisher

His ex would shit when she saw it.

And his girls would be proud.

And that was more than enough reason to give the nod to the stupidest story he'd heard in a long time. Werewolves in Denver . . . right. He didn't know what that little girl had been drinking, sniffing, and snorting last night, but he sure wouldn't mind taking a little of it home.

Tanner finished off the mug before he leaned back and reveled in the sound the chair springs made.

He might not still be able to feel any of the probable drug-induced enthusiasm anymore, but, dammit, he knew how to exploit it. For fun and profit.

Tanner swiveled the chair around until it faced the window and saluted.

"To the Greater Denver reading public," he said. "You don't know it yet, but your lives are about to get a whole *hell* of a lot more interesting."

He dropped his hand to one leg and scratched the sting it put there. He couldn't really remember when he first realized the power lies concealed as truth had . . . maybe a whole other lifetime before he'd convinced that cracker son-of-a-second-lieutenant that the cooing gook baby was really a cleverly disguised bomb.

Tanner grunted at the memory of what the nineteen-year-old officer had done to the baby, but felt no personal responsibility for it. Not now, or then. He'd just been the catalyst.

Then *and* now.

A fat rat-gray pigeon settled on the top of the glass-front enclosure of the building opposite and bobbed a hello. Tanner bobbed his head in return and took a deep breath. It had taken him twenty-one plus years of scrimping to finally realize his dream: *QUEST-The NewsJournal of the World . . . the Paper That Dares to Ask.*

Answers, optional.

And even if it was only a supermarket tabloid and First Bank owned 45 percent of it, *QUEST* was still his. And still being read. Religiously.

Praise the Lord.

Tanner stopped watching the one pigeon and looked further east, toward the skyscrapers, the roosts of a much bigger flock of two-legged pigeons.

Direct market sales and subscriptions had risen in the last year by 15 percent. *QUEST* had gone nose-to-nose with *The Sun* and *Enquirer* and still managed to make a place for itself. Sure, some of the supposedly well-educated literati might roll their eyes and chuckle over the lurid "grabber lines" like: GREAT-GRANDMOTHER GIVES BIRTH TO DEVIL CHILD, ELVIS SAVES GIRL FROM SUICIDE, or THE ALL BEER-POTATO CHIP DIET — LOSE UP TO TWENTY POUNDS A DAY! but that still didn't stop them from sneaking copies onto their purchases at the check-out lines.

Tanner squealed the chair back toward his desk and reached for the phone. Smiling, he punched the line designated PRINTING and hummed along with the electronic rings.

The connection was completed after the seventh ring.

"Yeah?" a voice shouted over the *clank-clink-hiss-clank* of the press machines.

Tanner felt his smile widened. "Stop the presses," he shouted back.

4

A small flying saucer dive-bombed Cat as she stepped out of the elevator.

"Incoming!" A man's voice echoed from somewhere deep within the labyrinth of clutter-filled steel racks. Footsteps followed the echo, and a moment later Cat was face to face with a long-haired, mustachioed middle-aged man in the loudest, vilest, most revolting puce-over-lime Hawaiian shirt she had ever seen.

The man smiled at her before bending down to retrieve the fallen spaceship. "Cool, not a scratch on it. These things are a lot tougher than they look. And how about you?" He looked up at Cat and tucked a thick strand of gray hair behind one ear. "Didn't take out an eye or anything, did it? I almost killed a guy at my last gig."

Cat stepped back just as the elevator doors whispered closed behind her. Trapped.

MIDDLE-AGED PSYCHO KILLER FOUND
IN NEWS-JOURNAL'S BASEMENT!

—As Told to. . . .

"Oh?"

"Yeah, I was setting up a UFO invasion at an"—he held

up both hands and made the universally accepted sigh for quotation marks with his fingers—" 'unidentified Midwest farm' . . . all in quarter-scale so I could get a cool overshot, and I guessed I used just a little too much flash powder in the laser strike. An entire flock of plastic chickens went airborne. I think the guy who was helping me still has one implanted in a rather delicate portion of his anatomy."

The man dropped one hand and reached forward with the other. His hand was warm and callused against hers.

"I'm Ed, by the way. And you must be the lady with something special." Cat felt a slight increase in pressure in his grip. "Extra special, if you don't mind a dirty old man's opinion. And believe me, I *am* a dirty old man, so you can trust my opinions."

Cat felt a blush race into her cheeks. He was a letch, but apparently an honest letch. "Um, yeah, okay. I'm Cat . . . C. K. Moselle."

Ed's grip tightened almost to the point of pain as he lifted Cat's hand to his lips. The kiss was quick, the lips chapped.

"My lady." He clicked the heels of his ultrahigh-tech running shoes and bowed. Cat caught the faint scent of fabric softener and patchouli as he straightened.

Cat forced an embarrassed chuckle and pulled her hand back to the protection of the paper in her arms. He was, without doubt, the strangest man Cat had ever met.

"So, what do you prefer?" he asked. "Cat? C. K.? Or Ms. Moselle? 'Cause I gotta tell you, you instantly struck me as a Kit-Cat."

The blush worked its way deeper into her skin. "Uh . . . People usually call me Cat."

He smiled and swept a hand toward the steel racks. "But I bet your mother calls you Catherine, right? Yeah, mothers are like that. Mine still calls me 'You Little Bastard.' So, come into my parlor and let's see this something special you have." This time he looked embarrassed. "Sorry, I just seem to have a way with words. I can say 'Good morning' and get arrested for sexual harassment. Sorry."

"That's okay," Cat said as she followed him back through the maze of shelves. Most of the shelving was taken up with expensive photography equipment, but there were a number of other items Cat recognized from various *QUEST* covers. Rubber skeletons and Bigfoot masks competed with model rocket parts and various latex body parts. A jar with two glowing green eyeballs (PRIEST FINDS DEVIL'S EYES IN SISTER'S PANTRY!) stared at her as she followed Ed to a large white "setup" table in the middle of the maze. In the middle of the table, a one-one-hundredth-scale diorama of San Francisco sat baking beneath the glare of two five-hundred-watt bulbs. Two silver spaceships, identical to the one that had almost hit Cat, hung suspended on fishing line over the Golden Gate Bridge. An old-fashioned-looking view camera hunched on its tripod directly over the scene.

"No, it's not," he said, "but you're sweet to say it. And I apologize now for all the verbal missteps to come. Now, let me just get a couple shots of this and then I'll do you . . . I mean—"

"No problem," Cat interrupted. "Go ahead."

Ed rolled his eyes, thanking her, as he walked over to the layout and began reattaching the third spaceship to an almost invisible thread. A mug of coffee sat on one corner of a work-order sheet. Cat moved closer until she could read the subject line: *Aliens Land in CA*/Lawrence Witmore.

Cat smiled and fingered one edge of the wrinkled paper. More aliens, how boring. She could just image Larry's face . . . *all* of their faces when they read her article.

"Damn fishing line . . ." Ed muttered when he finally got the model to hang where he wanted it. "You'd think with all the money the boss man is paying me, he'd opt for decent equipment. I told him I had a source for spider silk, stuff's great, strong and sticky . . . holds without crinkling, like this shit . . . but it's costly. Almost a full dollar more." Ed grinned at her over the top of the tiny spaceship and winked. "Ready for some magic?"

Cat nodded and stepped back as Ed walked around to the back of the camera and picked up the cable shutter release. An adjustment here, a dimming of the lights there and—*snap snap snap*.

"Voilà, the aliens have landed. And now for something

completely different . . ." Stepping away from the camera, Ed lifted the coffee mug out of harm's way and swept the alien diorama to the floor. "Don't worry about it, I have an alien crash I'm supposed to shoot later. Here"—he leaned over and wiped the table with his shirttail—"show Uncle Ed something special."

Cat took a deep breath and put the paper, still folded, down. "Before I show you, I have to tell you that this isn't fake. It's real, I swear."

Ed took another sip from the mug and reached over to turn the lights up. Cat could feel the intense heat against her skin. It might be winter outside, but here in Ed's domain, summer could be instantly achieved with the flick of a switch. The God-awful Hawaiian shirt now made sense.

"Okay," he said, "I'm ready."

"Okay." She decided against using her own rendition of *voilà* and simply opened the paper.

And felt the basement floor suddenly slide out from under her.

Ed caught her, one-handed, before her legs gave way completely. For an old guy, he was a lot stronger than she thought he'd be.

"Whoa! What's the matter? You okay?"

Cat forced herself to look up into his eyes, to stare at the tiny image of herself she saw reflected in them. Forced herself because her eyes kept trying to shift back to the bloody handprint.

A handprint.

"Cat?"

Ed set the mug down and snapped his fingers in her face. Air rushed into her lungs behind the startled gasp, and Cat realized then that she hadn't been breathing.

"Hey, come on . . . you're scaring me now. What's the matter?"

Cat licked her lips and pointed to the paper . . . to the bloody *hand*print.

"It's not the same."

Ed looked at the paper without letting go of her arm. "You think someone pulled the ol' switcheroo?"

Yes, that was it, someone had pulled the old switcheroo. That was the only explanation that made sense. Paw prints don't change into human handprints unless . . .

Shit.

Now she really did feel like she was about to throw up.

Without thinking, Cat grabbed Ed's mug and downed a good mouthful before the flavor, and Ed's shout, stopped her from taking more. It was . . . horrible. The fluid equivalent of the Hawaiian shirt. Beneath a cloying sweetness was the taste of rotting flowers and copper pennies.

Ed grabbed the mug from her hand and set it back down before he began pounding her gently across her back.

"Oh, jeez, are you okay?" She could barely hear him over the wheezing sounds of her own gasping hacks and sobbing coughs. "I'm sorry, I should have finished that. It's not tea."

"N-no kidding. What-what . . ." It took another twenty seconds of pounding before she was able to take enough of a ragged breath to answer. Another dozen before she was able to blink away the tears and actually see his face. Beneath the blue-white lights, his hair and mustache looked almost totally gray. "What *was* that?"

"Vitamin supplement. I can't swallow pills. I'm sorry. Are you sure you're okay?"

Cat's stomach quivered, but held firm. "I'm fine. It's just that . . . Ed, it *is* the same paper, I know it is. See those drops up near the top edge? They're shaped like a question mark, right? I noticed that last night. It's the same paper, Ed, but the print is wrong."

Ed took a deep breath and let her go to take a closer look at the print. Cat saw his nose wrinkle at the smell.

"What's wrong with it?" he asked.

"Last night it was a paw print."

"Paw?" Ed nodded. "Paw like on a dog."

"Like on a werewolf."

She'd expected braying laughter, stunned silence, or a raised shout of alarm. Maybe a combination of all three. Because that's what she would have done . . . a week ago. Hell, a *day* ago.

It was amazing how perceptions change.

"So, what you're telling me is that last night *this* was a paw print."

Cat nodded. "Uh-huh."

"But now, obviously, it's the print of a human hand."

Another nod.

"That means it changed from paw print to handprint . . . like its owner probably changed from wolf to man when the sun came up this morning, right? Just like in the movies."

"Yeah."

Ed took a deep breath and tugged at one side of his mustache.

"That is *way* cool. And it works! God damn it works like a charm!" Cat jerked when he grabbed her shoulders and gave her an enthusiastic shake. "I don't know how long you've been in this business, but you're a natural. You almost had *me* believing it, and I'm one of the world's oldest skeptics."

Cat had to catch herself from pitching backwards when he released her to try and match the size of his hand to the print. And came up short.

Ed whistled softly through his teeth and rubbed his fingers.

"Damn, your boyfriend's a biggun, ain't he? Remind me never to try anything funny with you. Unless you want me to, that is."

He wiggled his eyebrows up and down and smiled to show that he was only partially serious about the whole concept.

"Hah," she said. "Hah."

And he understood. "Gotcha, but you can't condemn a man for trying. Now . . . since we've got the *after* shot I suppose you want the *before*, right?"

She was lost. Utterly and completely. "The before?" she asked.

"Yeah." And without clarifying it more than that, Ed moved her out of the way and jogged slowly to one of the storage closets off the Photo Lab's main room. Hair and shirttail flying. "Stay right where you are, Kit-Cat. Sorry. Mind if I call you that? No? Cool, 'cause you look like a Kit-Cat to me. Okay, ready? You're gonna love this."

Cat didn't have the strength to ask "love what" and part

of her really didn't want to know. He hadn't believed her about the print changing . . . transforming, but it had, god-dammit. She'd seen it with her own eyes. *Right?* And it'd been a goddamned paw print. *Hadn't it?*

She looked down at the paper and the bloody print embossed on it—four outstretched, segmented fingers and a curved line for the thumb. A large hand to be sure, but only a hand. Human.

A sudden crash made her jump.

"Shit . . . sorry. Shoot." Ed's voice echoed off the concrete floor and walls. "Every time I take a new job I promise myself I'm going to throw away half of this . . . stuff and somehow I never do. Probably because I know that if I do, the one thing I'll need for a shot will be the thing I tossed."

He reappeared a moment later carrying a Dinty Moore Beef Stew box, smiling around the cobwebs and dust that clung to his mustache and hair.

"Uncle Ed's Magical Mystery Box," he said, and dropped it next to the bloodstained paper. Dust motes sparkled like snowflakes under the light. "One of about a dozen, actually. No one under eighteen admitted without a parent or legal guardian. May I see some ID, young lady?"

Cat smiled and rubbed the dust-induced tickle out of her nose with the back of her hand. Ed didn't seem to notice, or care, how many particulates he was expelling into the air as he rummaged through the box. He reminded Cat of a little boy going through a long-forgotten treasure chest.

"My, oh my, oh my, just look at all these goodies. Man, some of this stuff I haven't even thought about in years. Lookee here."

Ed held up an ovoid shape that looked to be two paper plates glued together at the rims and spray-painted silver. A string of miniature Christmas lights drooped miserably at the center, overburdened by their layer of dusty cobwebs.

"Man, this is a classic," he said, and blew across the top plate. The dust flakes became a dust blizzard. Cat sneezed without even trying to sound ladylike.

"Sorry. But just picture this under a single high-intensity spot, blue-filtered, and one click off focus for effect"—Ed held it up over his head—"hovering in midair above your typical bucolic backdrop. Fear, terror, despair!

"This baby right here was the cause of most, if not all of the UFO sightings in the late sixties early seventies."

When Cat just stood there, Ed shook his head and tossed the dusty UFO back into the box, where it expelled another small mushroom cloud of dust.

"What? You thought I'd spent all those wonder years going one toke over the line with Janis and Jimi?"

"Oh," she said, "you and your friends did a lot of traveling back then?"

Ed gave her a look similar to the one she'd seen on Tanner when he was talking about Junior Chaney the Wolfman, muttering "God save me from the young," before reaching back into the box and producing a bathroom plunger rimmed with white-plastic shark's teeth.

"Surely you can't have forgotten the Man-Eating Earthworms of Tulsa? Summer of '87? It topped the tabloid charts, man. But I guess you were probably still reading Mother Goose back then instead of—*Yes!*"

The plunger with teeth sailed back over Ed's shoulder as he grabbed something that had been wrapped in yellowed tissue paper.

His eyes glistened as he unwrapped it.

"M'lady," he said, "I give you . . . the Paw."

Cat gasped and backed up until her rump hit another layout table directly behind her. But even then her body from the waist up tipped back away from the dark, dust-matted limb.

"A real beauty isn't it?" Ed asked, turning the leg over. The paw flopped bonelessly to one side, exposing pale gray pads and yellowed claws. "I got this in an estate sale way back in . . ." He flipped the leg up and waved it at her. Bye-bye. "God, let's see, must have been '63 or '64, and then I think it was almost twenty years old. State-of-the-art—back then. Infused latex mold with each hair individually placed while the rubber was still war—"

He sneezed, and dust filled the air.

"You mean"—Cat's nose twitched at the musty, tickling smell—"it's rubber?"

"What'd you think it was? Real?" Laughing, Ed wiped his nose off on the back on his hand, forgetting it still held the paw, and sneezed another cloud of dust into his face. "Shit! I really should take better care of this stuff. Especially him."

"Him?" Cat asked, and pressed a hand to the queasy grumbling coming from behind her belly button.

He stared, openmouthed, at her.

"You mean you don't recognize the famous Wolfboy of White Plains? He was the scourge of Upstate New York for a couple of months back in the 1890's—that was back before TV, y'know. My grandfather told me all about it." Ed dropped the incredulous look in favor of a wide grin and gently brushed a layer of dust from the brown fur. "Grandpa was a newspaperman, like you. Just like you. If there wasn't anything interesting to report he'd sort of . . . put an interesting twist to what he did have.

"Just like you, Kit-Cat."

Cat brushed the hair away from her face and straightened, walked back to the table, and grabbed the dusty *(fake)* limb from his hand. She thought better of her original plan of shaking it in the old hippie's smirking, drooping mustachioed face when the dust she'd already caused made them both sneeze.

"Your grandfather sounds like an interesting man," Cat said, sniffing. The dust was making her eyes water. "But I'm not making this up, Ed. I know what I saw last night, I *know* what left the print and it wasn't a man. I swear."

Ed stopped smiling and ignored the swirling dust as he reached out and took hold of her shoulders. His hands were hot, as if he'd just held them under scalding water. Cat shivered as her body readjusted to the warmth. The poor man was spending way too much time under the lights.

"Hey, okay. I'm sorry." His eyes locked onto hers. "You really believe you saw a werewolf last night?"

Cat opened her mouth. And closed it.

"I mean, you did go through some pretty heavy shit last night if what I heard on the morning news . . . aka the

QUEST grapevine . . . was right. But the bottom line is that you witnessed a murder and that can put some powerful mojo on the brain. Hell, if that had been me on that bus and the murderer was wearing a green suit I'd probably think I was seeing the Creature from the Black Lagoon."

Cat shook her head. "I know what I saw," she said slowly, "and it wasn't a man."

"Not even a man in a Halloween mask and gloves?"

It was a little disconcerting to hear, as a question, the same conclusion that her boss had made—that the killer . . . no, the man who *saved* her from being killed had worn a mask.

"But the paw print . . ." she said and then made the mistake of looking down at the paw in her hand.

Big mistake.

"Uh-huh," Ed said, and dropped one hand to cup hers. "Now, I'm not saying this guy in the mask didn't think *he* was a werewolf . . . I mean, how many normal guys do you know go around carrying little wolfie masks and furry gloves in the hopes that they'll get a chance to use them? Well, if this were California, the numbers would go up, but since it's Denver . . ."

He waited for her to chuckle, but accepted the half smile she finally managed to produce.

"As for the print? You thought you saw a werewolf, so you thought you saw a werewolf print. Your basic optical illusion brought on by trauma." He patted her hand then squeezed it into the fake fur. "Psych 101, San Francisco City College. So, you think grandpa's Wolfboy'll do for your wolfman?"

Cat looked at the bloodied *hand*print covering her article and shook her head.

"It's not big enough," she said and heard Ed grunt.

"Humph. That's what they *all* say, Kit-Cat. But it ain't the size . . . it's what you can *do* with it that counts. Now watch and be amazed."

Cat did what she was told and watched the winterized Flower Child boogie over to a desk near the back wall— twirling the paw like a drum major's baton—where he picked up a small jar and boogied back again.

"Theatrical *blaud*," he said in the worse accent Cat had ever heard. "A tabloid photographer's best friend. Or maybe I should say best *fiend*. Here . . . hold these while I prepare my canvas."

Cat didn't have time to refuse or move out of the way before Ed thrust both the paw and jar into her hands. The paw was heavier than it looked, the jar colder.

The rustle of paper made her blink.

Ed had another copy of *QUEST* opened to page 38 and was smoothing out the creases above and below her story. Her baby. Her firstborn. The first byline of C. K. Moselle, the Kit-Cat Woman of Colorado.

"Now, for a little makeup."

Ed took back the jar and opened it. Smiling, he scooped out two fingers worth of the thick goolike red paste and smeared it across the paw's latex pads. The fake blood smelled rank, rotten. It reminded Cat of the time she and her parents went away for two weeks one summer only to discover that the electricity had gone out and everything in her father's upright freezer had spoiled. She could feel her nose and belly wrinkle in unison.

Ed winked and wiped his fingers off on the seat of his jeans as he took the paw and held it over her article.

"Okay, now just stand back and prepare yourself to be amazed." His head did quick pigeon-jerks, left-right-left, from bloodied handprint to clean paper and back again. "Gotta get it as right on as possible . . . okay, okay . . . little more to the left, shit—sorry, oops—back a little . . . just a little . . . more . . . Yes!"

The latex pads made a soft squishing sound when Ed pressed the paw against the paper.

"And as I used to say back in my dealin' days . . . Presto-chango." He lifted the paw carefully, holding the page down with his free hand until it came away, then smiled at the results and kissed the dusty fur. Sneezed and wiped his lips. "Yuck. Pardon . . ."

Clearing his throat, Ed clutched the paw to his chest as if it was a scepter and bowed.

"Ladies and Germs, I give you the Wolfman of Denver . . . before and after shots."

Cat held her breath against the dust and smell and leaned forward, her shadow casting itself between the two prints. Ed was good. Ed was *damned* good. He'd managed to place the paw print as close to its "mate" as was humanly possible.

"Impressed?" he asked.

Cat watched her shadow bob up and down. "Very. You've got a good eye."

"Among other things. Now, a few little artistic dribbles here and there—" Ed dipped a finger back into the gooey fake blood and splattered it against the paper. The splatter pattern wasn't the same, but Cat didn't think anyone would notice. Except her. And maybe the owner of the real print. If he was into reading supermarket tabloids.

She was shivering again by the time Ed finished. "Whadda ya think? The before and—gasp—after paw and handprint of the Denver Werewolf . . . transformed before the very eyes of the photo tech, yours truly, as he was about it make a print." He paused and shook his head. "Or something more melodramatic that'll have your readers creaming their jeans. Like you need to hear that from me. You're the writer, right?"

Cat met his eyes and folded her arms over her chest.

"Right."

Ed puffed out his chest and smiled down at the two prints. "Right. Man this should really mind-fuck some of the complacency out of the sheep out there, don't you think?"

Cat nodded. *Yes.*

"Look real, too, don't they?"

Too real, she thought.

"So, want to grab lunch?"

Cat heard the bones in the back of her neck crackle as she jerked her head up. "What?"

"Lunch," he repeated. "You know, that meal between breakfast and dinner. Ah'm a stranger in these here parts, ma'am, an' would be much obliged iffen you could see it in yore heart t'show me to the greasiest, messiest burger joint this town has to offer."

Cat felt the skin crawl across the back of her neck as she started inching her way back in the direction of the elevator. He followed her.

"I have—I *have* to write up the article. Besides, it's a little early for lunch, isn't it?"

Ed cocked his head to one side as if he didn't understand the question. "You aren't hungry?" he asked.

"Not right now." Cat checked her watch; it was 10:20 A.M. . . . she had less than two hours to write the article and get it okayed. "Um, maybe later. I really have to get to work. Tannenbutt's . . . Tanner's . . . Mr. Boswell's expecting it ASAP."

Ed shrugged and scratched his chin with the back of the paw as they exited the maze. "Okay, I'll check with you later."

Cat punched the UP button three times while they stood there, side by side. She could hear the rumbling echo of gears from the floor above. The elevator seemed to be taking a lot longer to get to the basement than it usually did.

"Did you hear about a young couple who went out to look at a brand-new apartment complex and then got trapped in the elevator?" Ed asked, rocking back and forth on his heels. "When they finally found them the wife had killed and eaten her husband. I took the pictures. Great gal."

Cat was just turning to look for the staircase, when he tapped the fake paw against her shoulder. "Want to hear something *really* scary?"

The elevator doors opened, and Cat bolted into the car.

"Later, okay? And thanks. For everything, Ed." She reached over and punched the first button she felt. "I mean it."

"Anytime, Kit-Cat. I'll let old Tannenbutt know when the prints are ready." He lifted the paw and waved it at her. "Say *bye-bye*, Grandpa."

Cat laughed and waved back. She stopped both the moment the doors closed and she felt the car begin its jerky ascent. He was the strangest man she'd ever met.

Except for the man on the bus.

With the red hair.
And the *werewolf* mask.

Ed waved the paw until the light above the elevator blinked off and the rattling echoes died, then leaned back against the steel shelving and brushed the dusty fur against his cheek.

She was the most appealing woman he'd seen in a long time, in a *very* long time, and he'd sniffed around enough of the fairer sex to know that for a certainty.

"So, whadda ya think, Grandpa?" he asked as he slid the paw down his cheek to the point of his chin. The fake blood left a cold slime trail against his skin. "Is she the one?"

Chuckling softly at the question—*Of course she was the one*—Ed closed his eyes and squeezed the paw just above the central pad. The paw closed forcibly, the sharp claws tearing into his flesh.

His little Kit-Cat didn't know it yet, but she was about to get a photo spread that was unheard of in the world of tabloid journalism.

5

He held the goblet in his hand without looking at it and ran a thumb slowly over the intricate pattern that had been cut into the glass. He knew the interwoven design of stylized oak leaves and vines by heart. By memory. The goblet was one of a dozen his family had sent—an *apartment*-warming gift—while he was still trying to unpack. The design one of a hundred his family had acquired throughout the centuries.

Still without looking, he lifted the heirloom to his lips and finished the buttermilk it held. Holding the thick liquid a moment in his cheeks to warm it before swallowing, he leaned forward and set the goblet onto the narrow balcony railing in front of him. He could barely make out the design through the opaque liquid.

Good.

He swallowed at the same moment he flicked the goblet off the railing. The sound of his esophagus opening, then closing, was more than loud enough to cover the single note the crystal left hanging in the air before the wind swept it eastward.

A heartbeat, two, later he hear the crystal shatter.

One down, eleven to go.

All of which his family would eagerly replace. If they were ever to find out. Which they wouldn't. Couldn't. In order to discover the "accidents" they'd first have to visit . . . and that, he knew with some small pleasure, they'd never do.

Mother would make sure of that.

Standing, he folded the robe tighter across his bare chest and leaned against the railing. The wind tugged at his hair, whipping it to the side like flame. There was the smell of snow on the wind, the taste of bitter cold. Winter whispering its icy promise of things to come. He closed his eyes and listened.

Tried to.

But wind and winter and promises could not stop what formed in the darkness behind his eyelids. Her face. Hers alone—frozen in time and terror as the blood arched around her head like a profane halo. Her face . . . every time he closed his eyes.

All night.

Both metro-area papers had whitewashed the crack junkie's death, although the *Post* had hinted at something more sensational. He was safe. No one on the bus had actually seen what he'd done.

Except her.

"I'm sorry," he whispered and opened his eyes to watch the squads of volunteer horticulturists move through the botanic gardens like ants swarming an anthill. Ants with hoes and shovels and wheelbarrows filled with either mulch or bulbs wrapped in burlap and headed for the greenhouse to wait out the long winter months in safety. Putting the last of summer away.

Directly below, a male ant and his female counterpart were scooping willow leaves from the koi pond that dominated the Japanese garden section of the arboretum. The pond was the main reason he'd chosen the apartment over the others he'd seen.

There was a peace that he'd never found anywhere else in watching the random flashes and sparks beneath the muddy green water. Had never felt anywhere . . . or *anywhen* else.

Mother had seen to that, as well.

She had never let him forget his place in the Family or in the world, and although he didn't hate or resent her any more than any son did a parent who refused to accept him as an equal, thinking about the old bitch at that moment only added more curds to the buttermilk already fermenting in his belly.

Groaning, he left the balcony to the wind and promise of snow and walked back into the quiet stillness of his apartment.

The mitten lay in the center of the marble coffee table, exactly where he had placed it, palm-side up, the night before.

She had such a tiny hand. Almost the size of a child's.

But she wasn't a child. He caught her ripe scent the moment he'd gotten on the bus . . . deep and rich, the animal hiding beneath the thin layers of her flesh. He'd smelled her and wanted her even before the boy had pointed the gun and . . .

. . . the boy's scent . . . rank with fear and need . . .

He picked up the mitten and pressed it against his cheek. Her scent was still there, trapped in the unbleached wool like a memory. He closed his eyes and breathed her in. Her image came with it—fear making her face pale, but not fear of the crackheaded boy or his gun. She'd been afraid of him . . . for what he really was.

Monster.

He tossed the mitten back to the coffee table just as the phone on the kitchen counter rang. He didn't hurry. There was no doubt in his mind as to who would be calling that early in the morning. With added care, he filled goblet number eleven with buttermilk and took a swallow before picking up the receiver.

"Hello, Mother."

"Mother?" The voice on the line was vaguely familiar; female and soft. It wasn't the Old Bitch. "Luke, it's me."

Luke. Me. He frowned and set the streaked goblet down next to the phone. No one called him Luke except . . .

"Luke?"

. . . his ex-lover. She thought Lucius sounded too fancy for him so she changed it, shortened it to Luke. Lucius had all but forgotten she even existed.

"Oh. Hi." He let his voice soften into the pantomime of pain. And then the truth, "I didn't expect to hear from you again."

"I know, Luke. I was thinking about that. I never meant to hurt you."

He let silence speak for him.

"Okay, I guess this was wrong, too. I just thought—Well, I just wanted to say I'm sorry I hurt you, Luke. You're a nice guy, and I know you'll find someone someday."

Lucius leaned back and watched a raven fly past the window. Her hair had been that dark . . . the woman on the bus. "I'm sure I will. Thanks for calling."

She heard the dismissal in his voice and accepted it. "Okay. Take care of yourself, Luke."

"I will. You, too."

She hung up without another word.

Lucius lowered the phone back to its cradle and stood up. She wouldn't call again, her conscience was clear.

Picking up the goblet, he downed the rest of the buttermilk and snapped the goblet in half between his fingers. Oops.

Another accident.

Only ten of the priceless heirlooms left . . . and counting.

Mother would be so angry with him.

Cat tapped the four pages against the top of the printer, making sure they were even before she stapled them together.

It had only taken two hours and three double-shot cappuccinos for the birth of her second child. And an easier labor it had been.

Once she stopped fighting and accepted the fact that the red-haired man on the bus the night before—the man who'd saved her life—was no more a mythical creature than she was. The police and her boss were right, her hero was only another urban psycho with a fetish for latex masks and monster movies.

But, Cat thought as she carried the papers to her desk and sat down, that was a fact the reading public was never going to find out.

At least not from her.

Or her *newborn*.

Cat leaned back into the thin padding of her desk chair *(no squeaks, thank God)* and gave the article one more quick visual.

Even after all this time it still felt strange to be holding actual paper instead of reviewing it directly on her monitor. But that's what he wanted, Ol' Tannenbutt. Hard copy. The kind he could blue pencil and fold and shred and crush into a ball that *clunked* when it hit the side of the large metal trash can next to his desk. Because, as he'd told her five minutes into her job interview, he hated e-mail and attached files and anything that used electrons instead of paper.

"If the good Lord had wanted us to switch to disks and hard drives and e-fucking-zines then He wouldn't still be making trees to pulp down into paper, now would He?"

It was hard to argue with such logic. Especially when your first real job hung in the balance.

So hard copy it was. Then and now and forever, amen. Or until Tanner Boswell retired and *QUEST* got a new managing editor who could take the information super-highway in the fast lane and never look back.

A managing editor like . . . *her* for instance.

Cat smiled at the thought—vague though it was since she couldn't really see herself remaining a tabloid reporter for more than another year or two—and ran her thumb across the boldface header exactly ten spaces from the top edge

> WEREWOLF SAVED
> MY LIFE
> A *QUEST* EXCLUSIVE
> — BY C. K. MOSELLE

and left behind a pale gray smear.

"Oh . . . crap."

Cat sat up and held the pages under the high-intensity beam of her desk lamp. The ink snail-poop trail was barely visible, the words MY and LIFE blurred into one another but still readable. It was okay. Not perfect, but okay.

But "okay" wasn't good enough.

Cat tapped the pages against the top of her desk and slowly tore them in half, lengthwise. Then quartered them and smashed the remains into a ball.

There was nothing but air when she tossed it overhand into the plastic trash can opposite her chair.

"Two points!"

The sound of applause filled the "doorway," and Cat twisted around to find Ed standing there smiling at her. If it was possible, the room's overhead fluorescent lights seemed to enhance the colors in his Hawaiian shirt.

"From what I've heard the Nuggets could sure use you," he said, stepping into the cubicle space as he bent to retrieve the ruined pages. "Not going well?"

The blush from having being caught doing something stupid deepened at the idea that he'd thought she was having trouble.

"No," she said, too quickly, too loudly. Cat recovered by pretending to cough. She added a few chest pats for good measure. "Sorry. No, I just smeared the ink on that copy."

"Oh." Ed tossed the wadded pages back into the trash without opening them. He was smiling, mustache twitching when he looked up. "So I guess that makes you sort of a perfectionist, huh?"

"Something wrong with that?" Cat asked as she double-clicked the computer's printer icon and okayed it for one more run.

"Nothing at all, Kit-Cat," he said. "I just find it an endearing quality. Especially in one so young."

Ed wiggled his eyebrows, which, Cat suddenly noticed, were as bushy as his mustache. She laughed despite the fact that it only seemed to encourage him.

Without waiting to be asked—either to or *not* to—Ed gathered up the four newly printed pages as each was expelled from the printer and stapled them (sans tapping) before presenting them (with flourish) into her hands.

"A perfect copy for a perfect lady," he said, and retreated back to the cubicle opening. "So, guess this means you're free for lunch."

"Lunch?" *The man was nothing if not persistent.* "Um . . ."

"Almost noon," he said, pointing to her watch. "See, Mickey's big hand is on the eleven and his little hand is on his . . . Oh, Mickey, stop that or you'll go blind! So, Mickey and his primal urges notwithstanding, think I can talk you into a burger or something? My treat, naturally."

Cat slipped the new copy into a protective manila folder, then held up her hands in surrender. The man might be old enough to be her father, but hell, a free meal was a free meal. And he was kind of lovable.

In an annoying sort of way.

"Sure, just let me give this to Mr. Boswell, and then you're on. There's a couple of fast-food places close by."

"Or we could even go to a sit-down with actual tablecloths kind of place." Ed's bushy eyebrows inched up into an arch. "Just as long as it isn't one of those New Age bistros that specialize in free-range tomatoes and picked-without-stress eggplants. I'm a meat eater, plain and simple."

Cat mentally shifted gears—having been about to suggest one of the newest New Age bistros her most recent ex–blind dates had taken her to—when her desk phone rang.

She glanced over at her would-be dining companion, who nodded, understandingly, as she lifted the receiver to her ear.

And cleared her throat. "C. K. Moselle here."

"Your boss here," the voice answered. "How's it going?"

Cat picked up the manila folder and winked at Ed.

"I just printed your copy: eight-hundred-fifty words on the dot."

"Nose."

Cat frowned and Ed followed. "Excuse me?"

"Nose—eight-hundred-fifty words on the *nose*. Old expression used around the time Lon Chaney, Jr. was the only werewolf known to the public."

He paused as if he expected her to say something. Cat coughed.

"Okay, you drop it off here and I'll let you know if I want any rewrites. Ed told me about the paw thing . . . sounds like a killer. This thing should all—" The rest was lost in the sudden squeal of chair springs. "—lunch and I'll let you know about if I want anything redone. Okay?"

"Sure." She'd been a reporter long enough to know you never asked your boss to repeat himself. "I'll be waiting."

He mumbled something else that was lost in another barrage of squeaks and hung up.

Cat thanked the dead air and hung up. Ed cocked his head to one side when she turned.

"What? The old butt-man want you to work through lunch? Can't do it, Kit-Cat, there's laws in this country last time I checked. No employer can make you work through your lunch hour. If he tries, we can stage a walkout . . . have a protest march right out in the middle of the frigging block if he tries to pull any of that fascist-pig crap here I'll—"

He kept getting louder and louder, his voice echoing through the cubicle canyons like thunder until Cat reached out and touched his arm.

"No, Ed, it's okay. Really." He was red-faced and didn't look convinced, but at least he stopped shouting. "Let me just drop this off and then we'll grab lunch, okay?"

"Yeah, okay. But I'm coming with you and if he starts anything . . ."

Cat let go of his arm just long enough to grab the folder off her desk. He'd calmed down to the point of smiling by the time her fingers reestablished contact.

"Ready?" she asked.

Ed bowed and stepped back, giving her the lead but following close behind. They must have made an interesting diversion if the looks she was getting from her coworkers were any indication.

Tanner Boswell didn't seem to notice that she had a pet photographer in tow when she entered his office. Or care. Or say more than "okay" when she said she'd be back in an hour. From lunch.

Cat's heart didn't slow into a more normal rate until they,

she and her self-appointed rabble-rouser, were riding the elevator down to the lobby.

"So, you never did say what sort of more substantial lunch you had in mind," Ed said as he helped her on with her coat. He was coatless, with nothing but the lack of good taste to come between him and the autumn chill.

Cat shivered in sympathy when the elevator opened into the unmanned, and therefore unheated lobby.

"How about steak? About an inch thick and bloody," she said, then quickly added, "Dutch treat, of course."

"No, no, I invited you, remember," he said, holding open the outside door for her to pass. "And besides, I love the way you talk. See, I knew you were a meat eater, too. We make the perfect couple. You lead, and I'll follow at your heels like a well-trained cur."

Cat laughed and took off down the street at a fast walk— with Ed following almost exactly at her heels. He was a nut . . . but in the nicest way, and she was more than glad he'd agreed to the steak. She hadn't realized it until that very moment, but she was absolutely *starving*!

6

"You've got to believe me, Kit-Cat. Would this face lie?"

Ed plucked two breadsticks from the wicker basket in the center of the table and crossed them under his chin, batting his eyelashes at her. He looked about as honest and trustworthy as a late-nineteenth-century snake-oil salesman.

Cat gurgled the mouthful of beer she'd been trying to swallow back into its mug.

"Seriously." Ed uncrossed the breadsticks and stuck them into his ears.

Cat hiccuped another few drops and set the mug down harder than she'd wanted to. The couple at the table closest to them—business types who had already taken more calls on their cellular phones than Cat usually got all week—frowned at the auditory intrusion. Until they focused on Ed. And the breadsticks. Then they picked up their bill and hurried through the dwindling lunchtime crowd to the cashier.

Ed watched them go with a look of disgust, then turned back and shook his head sadly. The breadsticks quivered like horizontally placed antennae as he reached over and moved the mug away.

"My God, I just can't take you anywhere, can I?"

Cat tried to slap his hand away and missed. "Oh, like it's my fault. Will you get those damned things out of your ears."

Ed cocked his head to one side and cupped one hand around a breadstick.

"Eh? Speak up, little girl. Gittin' a mite deef in m'old age, dun't cha know?"

Leaning across the remains of their shared "Carnivore Special" pizza—pepperoni, sausage, Canadian bacon, and strips of marinated flank steak—Cat grabbed a breadstick in each hand and pulled them out herself. And a look of wonderment filled Ed's face.

"It's a miracle. I can hear! I can hear!"

"Shhhhhh!"

Cat dropped the breadsticks atop the unwanted crusts and quickly glanced at the lunch-hour crowd that packed the tiny Vietnamese-Italian restaurant. With the exception of the upwardly and literally mobile couple who left, none of the other diners seemed to notice Ed's antics. And for that Cat gave a small prayer of thanks. Despite the fact that she knew (without a doubt in her mind) that she would (one day) be an important enough journalist to curry the stares of complete strangers, Cat figured she still had a little time to work through her natural shyness.

Of course, if . . . no, *when* her story on the Denver werewolf brought her that attention, she might not have any choice about being stared at. . . . There'd be talk shows, maybe even a book contract and—

"Earth calling Space Cadet Moselle . . . do you read me?"

Cat blinked the current world back into focus. "Huh? Oh, I'm sorry, I was just thinking about . . . my article and hoping Tanner likes it. Did you say something?"

Ed's milk-chocolate brown eyes darkened to semisweet drops while he twisted his sauce-stained paper napkin between his fingers.

"You're a perfectionist," he said, "and that's a rare thing nowadays. But I don't think you have to worry, Tanner Boswell may be a tight-ass, but he knows what sells. I haven't read your piece yet, but, like I said before, you had me convinced that print had supernaturally transformed from beast to man." His mustache bristled around the edges of a wide smile as he picked up his mug of cream soda in a toast. "To you and your werewolf . . . may you find eternal bliss with one another."

Cat lifted her mug of microbrewed rice beer and took a sip. *He still doesn't believe me, the old coot!*

"Ah, perfection," Ed sighed, sucking the creamy lather from the edge of his mustache. "Just like you."

Cat rolled her eyes toward the open-beamed ceiling where garlands of plastic grapevines and white fairy lights tried to camouflage bare water pipes. He was still a smooth talker . . . for an old guy.

"Okay, okay . . . I'll stop with the compliments. At least until we get to know each other a little better, deal?"

Cat lowered her gaze back to his face. He looked semiserious. "Deal . . . and I'm sorry about picking this place. I know we talked about grabbing a steak."

"Hey, this was the best pizza I've had . . . in at least a day." His smile was contagious, and Cat gave in to it fully. "But seriously, I suspect you had your heart set on a nice, thick center cut . . . about three inches thick and so rare it's still mooing in protest. Am I right?"

Although she felt like she'd just swallowed a rather substantial bowling ball, Cat was surprised to find her mouth watering.

"Well?"

"Uncle," Cat moaned, hands raised in surrender.

"Ah, I knew it. Y'know, that was part of the reason I decided to move out here. I kept hearing people say that Colorado was prime meat country, and I wanted to find out firsthand." Ed picked a sliver of marinated steak off the pan and winked at her when he popped it into his mouth. "Florida was okay, if you're into fish and old people. Personally, I never developed the taste for either."

Cat burst out laughing. "You're horrible."

"Yup. And I think you're cute, so here we are, the perfect couple. Now, take these napkins and wipe your face. We can't have one of *QUEST*'s rising stars going back to work with marinara blood on her cheeks, can we?"

Cat set the beer down and took the napkins, dabbing where he pointed, and came away with a dollop of sauce the size of a half-dollar.

"And you let me sit here with this on my face?"

Ed leaned back against his chair and shrugged. "Hey, what are friends for?"

Cat couldn't really remember what friends were for. All her friends were back East and, aside from the few, and less than fabulous, "I'm-Going-To-Die-Alone" panic-inspired dates she'd gone on, there'd been no one in Denver she'd gotten close to.

Until now.

She shook her head and fixed him with what she hoped was a withering stare.

"You're so funny."

"Yeah, that's what all the girls tell me. You know, back in the sixties I knew I lot of girls who rinsed their hair in beer. It was cool, man, really cool. The best of both worlds, sex and the heady aroma of hops. Ah, them were the days, my friends."

Ed moved the pizza pan out of the way and leaned his elbows on the table, getting as close as he could to her. "Now, about what we were talking about earlier . . ."

Cat crumpled the stained napkin and dropped it into the pan. That was another thing she'd missed about not having close friends. Even if they didn't believe you completely, friends were willing to give you the benefit of the doubt.

"About tracking down the Denver Werewolf."

"Yeah," Ed said, "about tracking down the Denver Werewolf. Kit-Cat, this would be something that none of the other tabs would even consider doing."

His voice was too loud, given the narrow distance that separated them, but at least he wasn't shouting like he'd been the first time he brought it up as they walked up Blake toward the ballpark.

Cat lowered her own voice in the hopes that he'd take the hint.

"That's because what they write about isn't . . . real."

"That's exactly what I mean," he said just as loudly as

before. "Listen to your uncle Ed. I've been in this biz for a couple hundred years, so I know what I'm talking about, okay? This is real. At least to the guy in the rubber wolf mask, right?"

Cat didn't feel up to arguing that particular point at the moment. "Right."

"And to all the nice people who read *QUEST* and the other tabloids. Do you really think, and I mean *really* think in your heart of hearts, that anyone out there truly believes that Elvis is alive and well and living as a happy housewife in Encino?"

Cat was about to nod, or shake, or shrug when Ed took the opportunity back.

"Of *course* they do. Some of them, anyway. And it's them you have to write to. Them who'd give their canines—pun intended—to hear what the living and breathing Denver Werewolf has to say."

"But Ed . . . ?"

He waved the ounce of prevention away.

"Of course they would. Dammit, even Ol' Tannenbutt'll think you're a genius if you get an interview with this guy. Come on, honey, think about it. A real-life, face-to-goddamn-face interview with a werewolf. You'll be the Buba Wawa of the supernatural."

He reached over to take her hands in his. Cat shivered at their warmth and didn't mention that his forearms were resting in the two slices they'd left in the pan.

"Serious. This'll make your career, Kit-Cat. There won't be a real newspaper or TV news show that won't jump at the chance to get you on their team after this breaks. And, of course, you'll need your loyal photographer and sidekick to climb the ladder of success with you."

Cat pulled free and sat back in her chair. Without being obvious about it, she folded her hands in her lap and squeezed until the trembling stopped.

"Yeah, I know," Ed went on when she still hadn't said anything after a minute, "the guy's a nut, your typical fruit-cake with delusions of grandeur . . . or, in his case, delusions of Le Grand Guignol . . . but you gotta admit, it will sell papers.

"Now, all we've got to do is find him and the rest will be, as they say, history."

Cat felt her head nodding before she realized what it was doing.

"Ed, he's more than a nut. He killed that boy last night. He's a"—she dropped her voice to a harsh whisper—"fucking murderer."

Ed finally noticed the pizza slice attached to his arm and pulled it off. He took a bite and chewed.

"Yeah. So?"

"So? So the police are looking for him, Ed. How am I supposed to find him if they can't?"

The smallest twinkle worked its way into his eyes. "After that story comes out, I have a feeling he'll be finding you."

Her stomach did a tuck and roll and aimed for her shoes. It must have shown on her face, because Ed suddenly stopped eating and frowned.

"Kit-Cat?"

She shook her head. And Ed let the rest of the pizza drop to his plate.

"Oh," he said as if she'd just explained each gory detail. "Hey, you think I'd let you go alone on this? Cut me a little slack here, okay, hon. I might look like I fried my brain in the City by the Bay back in the way beyond, but I do still have a few marbles. When—and you'll notice I said *when*— this nut contacts you, all you have to do is set up the meeting, and I'll be right there within shrieking distance.

"Not that you have to worry. I don't think he'll hurt you."

"Easy for you to say." Her voice sounded like it belonged to a very small, very frightened, and not at all convinced five-year-old.

Ed's smile was back. "You're forgetting something. He saved your life last night. Do you really think he'd hurt you now? Hell, there's no way Mister Werewolf would harm one hair on your head even if his life depended on it."

"Uh-huh."

"Uh-*huh*! Believe me."

Cat nodded even though she didn't believe any of it. Not him or the fact that the man . . . *werewolf, it wasn't a mask and he wasn't wearing gloves, it was real . . . real . . .* would be willing to be interviewed. And, of course, there was another faction to consider.

"What about the police?" she asked. "If they find out I've interviewed him, they're going to put me in jail for aiding and abetting or something, aren't they?"

Ed picked up the last pizza slice and stuffed it into his mouth.

"Will you do us both a favor and stop watching reruns of *Law and Order*? Once you get the interview . . . or interviews if wolfie boy is cooperative . . . then we pull the plug on this nut. Set him up so tight the cops'll be sending us thank-you notes for the rest of our lives."

He swallowed and belched contentedly.

"So, whadda ya say, Kit-m'Cat?"

"Yeah, I guess it would make a better series than the Beauty and the Beast stuff Tannebutt . . . I mean, Mr. Boswell wants me to write. *If* he, you know, the werewolf, contacts me."

"He will, Cat," Ed said. "He will. And if anything does get a little hairy—*hah,* didn't even see that one coming, myself—I'll be right there to protect you."

Cat watched him suck pizza sauce off his mustache and wished she felt a little more positive about the whole thing.

7

Day. Then twilight. Then night and moonrise.

The Silverback lifted his head to sniff the air. The snow scent was stronger than the night before, the taste of winter's lean time coating the blood on his tongue with frost.

Day. Then twilight. Then night and moonrise and the kill.

And still he could not get the scent of her from him. The rich, hot, *ripe* lingering smell of her.

The Silverback snapped his jaws shut in frustration, the sound sending two of the Juveniles belly flat against the gore-splattered ground.

He ignored the show of submission and lowered his head back to the remains, snipped a morsel of flesh off a broken rib with his front teeth, and swallowed without tasting. His hunger had long been satisfied, but he ate from instinct.

A kill was meant to be eaten.

A bitch in heat, to be taken.

A pack, to survive.

Instinct.

But all he had was the scent that clung to his mind and body like pine sap. Her scent. Her ripe, wanton scent.

The Silverback lifted his head and howled softly to the

night sky. The instincts had been strong, urging him to en-
sure the pack's survival by bringing in a fertile Alpha Bitch.
And yet he let her go.

This time.

A second, deeper voice-song joined his and the Silverback
turned his head toward the scar-faced Beta. The big male
had smelled the bitch on him and grinned, black lips curled
back from battle-broken fangs in a challenge that went unanswered.

If not unrecognized.

Though they had fed only the night before, the Silverback
led them into another hunt to break the tension. And it
worked even better than he'd hoped.

The scent of the female the pack brought down had its
own ripe wantonness, one that was touched with the deli-
cious undertones of rot and rebirth. The menses blood had
been a pleasant surprise and driven the Juveniles into a feeding frenzy. They had gutted the female and fought each over
the blood-gorged uterus while she screamed and struggled.

It had been a glorious thing to watch, a reminder of times
past, and the Silverback had regretted having to stop the
sound and the struggles. But this was not times past and not
a place of solitude. He let the howl die in his throat and
licked the blood from his muzzle.

The Beta's song ended a moment later. In a growl.

Skin and fur stretched tight against food-swollen bellies,
heads low beneath spiked hackles, the pack turned as one.

And glared at the MAN standing in the shadows.

The MAN's breath came in ragged gasps that clouded the
air and made a moonbow around the small flashlight he held
in his hand.

Words came with each breath—"Oh God. Oh God. Oh
God."—as regular and steady as the beating of a heart.

The Silverback shifted his weight to his back legs and
regurgitated. The chunks of meat steamed in the cold night
air, leaving vapor trails that twisted and curled like restless
spirits among the whore's discarded bones.

Taking a step toward the MAN, the Silverback curled his
lips back from his fangs as the rest of the pack disgorged

the contents of their bellies. The weight of the meat, as sweet and tender as it had been, would only slow them.

And would, in very little time, be replaced. He had picked well, the Silverback thought as he felt the Beta Male's hot breath against his flank. This was the best hunting ground yet.

run him

One of the Juveniles darted forward in a long arcing path that was meant to startle not savage, and the MAN reacted. The words condensed into a single sound that lifted the hair along the Silverback's spine as the MAN turned and ran, the beam from his flashlight illuminating him, as well as the tracks and gravel beds of the rail yard.

When the Juvenile got too close the MAN swung the flashlight down and caught the inexperienced male on the side of the muzzle. The lens shattered and the Juvenile yelped and stumbled, his forequarter going out from under him in the loose shale.

The MAN had a weapon and knew it. His scent changed— adrenaline eclipsing fear—as he took a step forward and lifted the broken flashlight like a club. The MAN yelled, low and guttural and without meaning, to frighten them.

It was a mistake.

Head lowered, the Silverback advanced.

Den O'Brien's right hand and wrist felt as if he'd just gone three rounds with a brick wall. And lost. The animal hadn't looked that big, but by God Almighty, it was solid.

And a killer. Shit, but he'd never seen dogs do something like that . . . kill and eat . . .

Bile surged into the back of his throat. *JesusMaryand-Joseph.* He hocked up the burning gob and spit it at one of the smaller dogs. It slunk away, then turned and bared its fangs—white beneath the black, glistening stain on its muzzle.

Den tightened his grip on the flashlight's billy-thick handle and felt a drop of fear sweat roll slowly past the corner of one eye. These animals weren't going to be intimidated.

"YA!" He swung his arms and stamped. The dogs stood their ground, and the biggest one, pale gray in the backwash of the yard's security lights, yawned. "You mangy, louse-ridden son of a bitch! Get out of here!"

His voice was still loud and strong and filled with the bluster forty-five years of walking God's Green Earth without bending a knee to any man could produce. And that surprised him almost as much as what he'd seen the animals doing.

Eating . . . God Almighty, they were eating *someone.*

Shit, but he'd never seen dogs do something like that. They might bite or maul, Christ, they might even go so far as kill a man if they were rabid like the one in the movie; but even the worst-beaten, mean, slat-ribbed, junkyard dog wouldn't *chow down* on human flesh.

Not like these.

These were killers.

And they were looking at him like he was the next course in the all-you-can-eat human buffet.

"Like fucking hell!"

The pale dog backed up three steps when Den charged, swinging the broken flashlight like a club, but it wasn't fast enough. It went top over teacup, yelping in what sounded more like surprise than pain.

Den didn't wait to see if the dog was injured or not. Wrist, arm, and shoulder throbbing, he turned and ran for all he was worth toward the small security/maintenance shed in the center of the switch yard. Once there—and after a long pull on the bottle of medicinal Cutty Sark he kept to combat the cold of winter and heat of summer—he'd speed dial 911 and let them handle the mess.

And mutts.

Quick and easy shots—*blam, blam, blam*—and scrape up the remains of whatever hapless homeless type they'd been munching on, and Den O'Brien would be happy.

Happy? God Almighty, he'd be fucking out-of-his-mind thrilled.

He heard them, heard their claws on the gravel not two

seconds before he felt pain shoot up his leg. Den hit the ground like a sack of shit.

The pale dog was right there when he turned over, grinning around the shred of pant leg in its mouth. The rest of them were sitting in a semicircle behind their leader: tongues lolling out of the corners of their mouths, rumps flat against the uneven ground. All prim and proper and waiting for their supper.

"Goddamned bastards!"

Den kicked straight at the big mutt's head and watched as the animal parried it with one paw. If he needed more proof that this wasn't any ordinary killer dog, Dennis Louis O'Brien got it when the animal spit the cloth out of his mouth and laughed.

In a rich, deep, human baritone.

The back of Den's legs scraped loudly across the ice-frosted tracks as he pushed himself away.

"What the hell are you?"

The dogs cocked their heads in unison to the left, tongues going a mile a minute.

"What the fucking hell are you?"

Palms bleeding, legs shaking against the seeping wound in his calf, Den crawled backwards over two more rail junctures. The dogs didn't move, didn't stop laughing like a bunch of drunken high-school boys, until he'd gotten a hundred yards away and there'd be some sport to the chase.

For sport it was, Den realized, as he managed to lift himself onto his good leg, like a cat torturing a mouse before it gobbles it down.

Just like the other poor bastard, whoever he was, may his soul rest in peace.

Den balled his bleeding hands into fists and scanned the murky half-light for another makeshift weapon, when a whistle from one of the big diesels suddenly tore the night apart. He felt the train against the soles of his shoes, a bone-grinding rumble, before he saw it. And when he did, the white halogen light was like the door of Heaven opening up and shining down on him.

"Looks like you're gonna miss the blue plate special,

boys," Den yelled through another whistle blast, but when he looked back across the tracks the dogs were gone. No doubt frightened off by the advancing train. *Thank God.*

There was nothing in front of him but track and shadow and the ice-blanketed hulks of empty boxcars and oilers. Nothing skittering, belly low, through the almost bright pools beneath the security lights. Nothing out of the ordinary at all.

But that didn't stop Den from picking up an egg-sized chunk of gravel and pitching it at the spot where the dogs had been sitting. Waiting patiently.

The diesel was rumbling on, getting closer. He could feel the vibrations in the small of his back. It was a good feeling. A *safe* feeling. And it shook the fear out of him.

Den hawked up a double-lung loogie and hurled it along the same path the stone had traveled. He wasn't afraid of any goddamned pack of dogs. And just as soon as he called Animal Control they'd know it.

"Fucking mutts." He wiped his mouth off on the back of his jacket sleeve and turned into the glare of the approaching train.

The engineer blasted him a warning—like he thought Den was blind or drunk or maybe both—so Den waved him an answer. And the shadow of his one, extended finger raced ahead of the train, leading the way.

Den stepped back and stumbled, the heel of one boot slipping from off the icy tie. The engineer tooted him a longer blast.

"Yeah, yeah," he shouted into the white light. The train was so close he couldn't see the engine through the glare, couldn't feel his own heart through the rumble of steel against steel. "Keep your pants on. I'm moving."

He got as far as the edge of the rail ties when the exhaustion hit him.

And was just about to raise his hand in a friendlier greeting when the dogs hit him.

When he hit the train, Den O'Brien smeared himself across three hundred yards of track and tie and gravel before the shaken engineer could stop the diesel.

The high-pitched scream of metal against metal sent ribbons of agony through the Silverback's skull. Cringing, the big male pressed his ears flat against the sides of his head and trembled until the sound became almost bearable.

When he was finally able to move, he sniffed in the steaming aroma that rose from the ground chunks of meat that lined the tracks and licked his lips.

Oh, the things he did for fresh chopped liver.

Lucius Currer's hand stopped short of the hanging display of buffalo jerky and curled into a fist.

WEREWOLF SAVED MY LIFE

Usually he paid as much attention to the tabloids as he did to the racks of "impulse items" placed seductively at the entrance of the check-out lanes—either chuckling to himself over the lurid headlines or rolling his eyes at the unmitigated gall of the so-called publishers.

Or ignoring them.

Which wasn't hard to do.

Usually.

Lucius unclenched his fingers and set them against the plastic-covered "teething rail" on his shopping cart. It was pathetic, it really was.

The cover was right out of a 1930s pulp novel, complete with terrified young woman—hand held backwards against her lips, blouse opened just enough to impress—and slavering man-beast.

It was amateurish at best.

> WEREWOLF SAVED MY LIFE
> EXCLUSIVE —BY C. K. MOSELLE

Lucius hoped the experience was at least a memorable one.

Sighing, he shifted his weight from one foot to the other and glanced purposely at his watch and then at the "Sixteen Items or Less" sign posted above the aisle.

He could have saved himself the effort.

The cashier was still arguing with the shaggy haired Mom-

and-papoose combo that three six-packs of Pepsi could not be counted as one item just because they were all the same thing. Lucius wasn't surprised to see a copy of the same tabloid tucked in among the other items waiting to be rung up once the initial numbering dispute had been settled. The man-beast snarled at Lucius from over the rim of a "Just Like Take-Out" pizza carton.

He snarled back and pulled one of the papers from the rack. Might as well enjoy himself while he waited.

One page in was an editorial apology on the story *QUEST* had run the month before. The idea that a tabloid would apologize for anything intrigued Lucius to the point of a quick scan. And quicker smirk. Apparently, the article in question had listed the space aliens who'd met secretly with Rush Limbaugh as being from Alpha Centauri. They were, in fact, from Vega as the late Carl Sagan had postulated. We apologize for any inconvenience this may have caused.

Lucius shook his head and turned the page. Space aliens travel all the way from Vega, with or without wormholes, just to meet with Rush Limbaugh. That should have been more than enough proof there wasn't any intelligent life out there.

There were items on each page that Lucius had never seen on the six o'clock news. ELVIS ALIVE AND WELL—SEX CHANGE MAKES THE KING A QUEEN. DOG COMPUTER WIZARD—GETS STRAIGHT A'S IN PHYSICS. MADONNA'S SECRET SHAME—"THERE WAS THIS ANGEL . . ."

But his favorite had to be: AMAZING DISCOVERY — LOSE 100 POUNDS ON THE ALL BEER DIET!

"Yeah, all through piss," he said out loud, and glanced over the edge of the open paper to find the cashier, the mother, and the son all staring at him. He cleared his throat and quickly looked down as he turned the paper to the featured story.

Two grainy black-and-white photos, side by side, dominated the centerfold. One obviously faked, although Lucius doubted that anyone, except himself, would have known; the other . . .

"Transformation proof," the caption read. "Paw and handprint of the Denver Werewolf." Transformation occurred while photographer watched in horror.

"Signed affidavit on file."

How nice, Lucius thought. A signed affidavit just in case anyone actually questioned how they'd gotten both the before and after pictures. He clutched the edges of the paper, fighting the urge to lay his hand against the life-size print.

The Denver Werewolf print. After transformation.

How was it possible?

Lucius followed the page down to the article.

> WEREWOLF SAVED MY LIFE
>
> A *QUEST* EXCLUSIVE
>
> —BY C. K. MOSELLE
>
> DENVER, COLORADO—
>
> I never expected to meet a monster on a predawn bus ride through the silent streets of Metro Denver, but I did. In fact, I met two—one human, driven to monstrous acts by drugs, the other real, a creature I once thought only existed in movies and myths. A werewolf. A real "monster" that saved my life.

Lucius felt the paper shred beneath his nails.

> Marcus Friebert was only 15 years old, but he'd already lived a life hardened by drugs and criminal—

Fifteen. Still a child in human terms. But he would have killed her.

"Hey!"

Her. C. K. Moselle. The woman on the bus. The woman he'd saved. Her face

"Hey, mister?"

pale and terrified as she looked past the gun and saw him. *"Mister!"*

The monster.

Lucius blinked and met the cashier's eyes. She was glaring at him and the Mom-and-Baby were gone, remedial math problem resolved. He caught a glimpse of them, M-n-B, as they raced the shopping cart through the electronic doors toward the parking lot.

"What?"

"You're gonna have to buy that, you know," the cashier said, nodding toward the paper in his hands. "You tore it. We can't sell it if it's torn."

Her voice was making the red-gold fur on Lucius's arms stand up.

"I gotta charge you, anyway, so you want it or not?"

Lucius folded the paper closed and tossed it in with the butcher-wrapped items already on the rubber conveyor strip. Blood from the weeping chuck roast added its own dramatic touch to the cover.

"Sorry," he said, when she began dragging the chunks of meat over the laser scanner. "It's just that sometimes it amazes me what gets into these papers. I mean, how much do they actually think the reading public will believe?"

"I wouldn't know." The cashier's icy tone told Lucius that she never had *any* trouble believing. She was the kind of person who would not only believe the story about the Denver Werewolf, but would actively go look for him each and every night of the full moon.

And God only knew how many more would do the same. Women looking for a *real* beast with a heart of gold, and men with guns looking to score another point on the Machismo Scale. It had happened before.

Worst case, the lookers would find each other in the darkness beneath the moon and the metro-area crime rate would go up.

Again.

Either way, C. K. Moselle was going to have a lot to answer for.

Unless the story died a natural one-issue death.

Lucius was about to offer a prayer for just that when the bag of soup bones he'd bought as a special treat thumped against the metal scale and drool filled his mouth. He coughed and swallowed loudly.

It seemed to be the opening the cashier had been waiting for.

"This sure is a lot of meat," she said, tipping the family-sized package of chicken gizzards on its side in order to scan the bar code. "You know you can get more than enough protein from lentils, and that way no animal has to die."

Lucius smiled and nodded. *Damn, not only a believer, but a* politically correct *true believer.*

"I know," he said and leaned forward over the raised courtesy ledge, "but I'm on the Atkins diet . . . and it's doing wonders."

The cashier's face hardened. "But with lentils . . ."

"Actually, I just read an article about lentils in last month's issue," he said, nodding to the tabloid. "It was about how botanists have discovered that modern organic fertilizers have actually begun producing lentils that show signs of rudimentary intelligence. Apparently they feel more pain when they're processed than meat animals do. Isn't science amazing?"

The Cashier looked a little sick after that and let the rest of the conversation devolve to "Paper or plastic?"

Day. Then twilight. Then night.
And moonrise.

8

"Scooter?"

Lucius paused just inside the doorway and let the ambient streetlight spill into the warehouse ahead of him. Nothing but dust moved through his elongated shadow and nothing but silence reached his ears. The building was as empty and abandoned-looking as the "Condemned-Keep Out" sign would have the casual passerby believe. The Family had gone to a lot of trouble to make sure it looked that way.

Abandoned. Empty. An outrageously large check sent each month to an official of the city planning board to make sure it stayed condemned. And patrolled. Although not closely.

That's the way Scooter wanted it—all cobwebs and dusty tarpaulins half-concealing empty crates and boxes consigned but never delivered to imaginary destinations. It went, he said each time Lucius offered to find him a better place, with his lifestyle.

The one ordained and ratified by the Family.

Under Mother's orders.

Lucius leaned back against the dry rot of the doorframe and sniffed the air. He didn't need light to find his brother, the scent hadn't changed since the last time he'd stopped by "to visit" . . . equal parts of musk, sweat, rush, and urine.

With just a soupçon of rancid meat for spice.

Lucius snorted and rubbed his nose on the sleeve of his sheepskin jacket.

"You know, taking a bath every now and then isn't a criminal offense anymore."

His voice echoed through the darkness.

The waiting, the hovering at the threshold until invited in, and the silence were all parts of the dominance game he allowed Scooter to play.

That his brother allowed *him* to win.

"Come on, you know I only get an hour for my dinner break."

"That's what you get for trying to be human, little brother. An hour for dinner and regular hygiene habits. Tell me . . . do you floss after every meal or just chew Dentine to keep the ol' choppers tartar-free?"

Lucius lowered his chin to the fleece collar to hide the snarl that tugged at his lips at the same time he held up the bags of meat. The blood had seeped through the butcher wrap in enough places to stain the inside of the plastic.

"Hey, if you don't want this, just say so. I've got better things I could be doing."

"Oh? Like what? Sniffing after the old bitch?"

Lucius bit back the answer as his brother slowly wheeled himself out from behind a water-damaged crate of plumbing fixtures. The grating of the coasters on his handmade sled against the rough-poured concrete flooring made Lucius's skin crawl.

That was another part of the dominance game. Another part of his chosen *lifestyle*. A wheelchair wouldn't have been as . . . pathetic.

His brother stopped in the center of Lucius's night-cast shadow. And smiled. He was shaggy hair and matted beard, torn clothes and wild-eyed. Lucius's identical twin.

And the firstborn.

"How you doing, little brother?"

"Fine, Darce. How are you?"

His brother frowned, then leaned across the withered

stumps that ended a few inches below his hips. His fingers
toyed with one of the oversize safety pins that held the ends
of the cutoff jeans closed. Lucius knew Mother had clothing
sent each month, but God only knew what Scooter did with
it. He'd been wearing the same grime-stained jeans and ratty
Avs sweatshirt since the first whiff of snow in the high country.

"Scooter's the name and scootin's the game, you know
that. The other was just for the Family album. Darce for dark
and Lucius for light. The old bitch decided the minute we
were born who was going to be the fair-haired one of the
family. No pun intended. Yuck, yuck."

Scooter never missed the opportunity to remind him of the
genetic hiccup that literally saved Lucius's life. There
couldn't be two Alpha Males in a pack. Had Scooter been
born with legs instead of useless folds of muscle and skin,
Mother would have had no choice but to kill the secondborn.

Him.

As it was, she'd shown unusual kindness by allowing her
crippled offspring to live. Unless you asked Scooter his opinion on the matter. Which would have taken longer than Lucius had time for that evening.

Or ever.

Lucius stepped into the warehouse and closed the heavy
door behind him. Without the natural ambient light to diffuse
it, his night vision turned every inanimate object in the building, as well as the building itself, a dull green. Scooter, and
a small mouse poking its head out from beneath a pile of
tubing, glowed bright chartreuse.

His boots made hollow thumps against the concrete as he
walked toward his older brother.

"Cut the crap, Scooter," he said as he dropped the gurgling
bag in front of the sled and kept walking. He stopped when
he got to a crate of machine parts and sat down. "Besides, I
thought you'd be starving."

"Aren't we street people always?" Scooter grinned as he
began rifling through the contents. "Let's see . . . Ooooh,
chicky parts. You got me chicky parts. I love chicky parts."

Scooter tore the plastic wrapping open with claws he no

longer tried to conceal and popped a gizzard noisily into his mouth.

"Thanks, bro. And I can tell by the utter look of disgust that you're still eating your meat cooked. Am I right?"

"Sometimes," Lucius admitted. "When I'm out."

"On dates, you mean." He didn't wait for the confirmation. Grabbing another chunk of chicken guts, Scooter tossed it at Lucius the way a man would toss a favorite dog a treat. "You're not out now, boy. Enjoy yourself."

Lucius snatched the meat out of midair and held it up to his face, letting the sweet, gamy aroma fill his head. That was a drug—the blood scent, not the meat. Meat sustained the body, but the scent, the smell of blood invoked memories that went deeper than flesh and bone. Closing his eyes until they were no more than slits, Lucius rolled the cold entrail between his hands until it warmed to the semblance of living flesh and then snapped it into his mouth. Shivered as he crushed it between his back molars and felt the blood ooze down his throat.

One bite was all he allowed himself before swallowing. Before *wolfing* it down.

"Thanks." Lucius wiped his mouth clean with the back of his hand, and then wiped the stain off on the cuff of his pants. He could tell that his brother was a little disappointed by his self-control.

"Hey," Scooter said, "we're brothers, right? And brothers gotta share. Let's see what else your guilty conscience brought me. Oh *ku-wel* . . . dessert!"

His hand snaked inside the bag almost too fast for Lucius to follow and reappeared an instant later with a knobby shoulder joint half the size of his fist.

Even though Lucius had never developed a taste for re- frigerated marrow, his mouth filled when Scooter dislocated his lower jaw and cracked the bone open. The slurping sounds made him wish he had stopped to grab a burger be- fore fulfilling his fraternal obligations.

Scooter finished the joint in less time than it would have taken a man to eat an apple and tossed the emptied bone over his shoulder. The pieces shattered when they hit the concrete.

"Man, I needed that." Scooter wiped the bone grease into his beard and sighed contentedly. "Today was a real ball-breaker . . . one business meeting after another. And on the social side, there was coffee and bagels with the mayor and then a late brunch at the Brown Palace with Billy Gates to discuss a high-tech merger. Oh . . . and then there was that little tête-à-tête with some psycho cop who didn't, quote, 'like my looks,' unquote and wanted to do something about them."

Lucius stood up.

"Oh, don't get your hackles in a knot, little brother. Nothing happened. All I did was convince him that touching me in any way would be a bad idea."

"How?" The question came out as a snarl.

"Oooh, how *Alpha* of you. But not to worry. I just double-lunged a couple of wet ones and told him I had a class-A case of the creeping grunge and if he didn't want to catch it, it might be a good idea to leave me alone. Normal street person stuff, but you'd be surprised at how well it works."

"Glad to hear it." And part of him was. Rolling his shoulders to release the tension, Lucius nodded and looked longingly at the door. Regardless of Scooter's familial displacement, he was still firstborn. "I should be getting back to work."

"How 'bout a beer before you go?"

Lucius turned toward his grinning twin. "You have beer?"

"Well, of course. What do I look like? A complete barbarian?"

"Where'd you get it?"

Scooter leaned forward, protectively over the bags. "You accusing me of something, little brother?"

"No. I just asked you where you got the beer."

For a moment the two stared at each other through the bright green aura, the silent challenge hanging in the air between them. Alpha versus Rogue. Scooter backed down with a smile that made Lucius feel he hadn't won any victory at all.

"A friend brings it to me," he said, sitting up and stretching.

"Who?"

"You don't know her." *Her.* "And before you say anything that both of us might regret, let me put your mind at ease, Alpha. I'm not fucking her. She's a friend and you don't fuck friends if you expect to keep them. Volunteers at the shelter a couple times a month . . . and she likes my attitude."

Scooter dropped his hand back into the bag. "What can I say? To the right people I can be a lovable old cripple. Now, do you want that beer or not?"

Lucius stuffed his hands into the jacket pockets and nodded. "Sure. Where do you keep it?"

Scooter jerked a thumb over his shoulder. "In the 'fridge. Where else would somebody keep beer?"

Lucius walked without hesitation to the chicken-wire-enclosed "office" that Scooter had made into his den. The beer wasn't the only new addition to the "found urban art" Scooter was forever hauling back with him. A rocking chair, sun-cracked and missing one rocker, slumped next to the dented metal bookcase that lined one wall. There must have been hundreds of books, mostly paperbacks but some New York Times best-seller hardbounds lined three deep in places.

There was a water-damaged copy of *The Horse Whisperer* lying open on the rocker. An empty and crushed beer can on the floor next to the rocker less one leg.

Lucius got two beers from the tiny dorm-size refrigerator Scooter had decorated with cutouts from some of the raunchier men's magazines, and had his half finished by the time he walked back to find his brother buried nose-deep in the bloodstained tabloid. He finished the rest before Scooter looked up.

"My, my, my . . ." he said, accepting the beer from Lucius and popping the lid. "My, my."

Lucius crushed the can into an aluminum ball and hurled it into the green-tinted clutter. Scooter was smiling at him over the top of the can.

" 'Denver Werewolf,' huh. Anybody we know?"

Lucius looked at the door.

"Word was all over the street this morning about what happened . . . but no one mentioned anything about a were-wolf." Scooter tipped the can to his lips and took a long swallow before continuing. "And you'd think that'd be something someone would notice. Someone besides a fucking newspaper reporter.

"You're in deep shit, little brother."

Lucius shifted his gaze from the door to his twin. "Give me a break, Scooter."

"What? You gonna stand there and try to tell me it *wasn't* you who did this? Shit, Lucius, I could smell what happened on you the minute you walked in."

Scooter finished his beer and tossed the can into a closer pile of garbage.

"Not that it matters to me. Shit, what's one less juiced up gangbanger gonna matter? Happens all the time around here. But the story, little brother . . . somebody saw you. Hell, and here I thought I'd be the one to blow the Family's cover."

Lucius's skin suddenly felt too small again, too tight for his body. He lifted his hand to the silver squash blossom at his throat. But the sensation didn't go away. Unless he was very careful and concentrated, the beast lurking beneath his flesh would tear its way out.

Again.

He began pacing, stiff-legged, back and forth in front of his brother.

"You're making a dangerous accusation, Scooter."

"Maybe." Lucius watched his twin fold the tabloid over his stumps and lay his hand on top of the *after* handprint. "Of course I guess a new Lycanthrope could have snuck into the neighborhood without any of us knowing it."

Scooter lifted his hand and read the caption directly under the photo " 'Staff members watched in horror while the blood-stained paw print they had just photographed transformed into the print of a human being.' Not what you'd call high journalism, but I think it gets its message across. Don't you, Alpha?"

He looked up, black eyes following Lucius.

"Looks like you literally screwed the pooch, bro. What *will* Mother say?"

The beast snarled in pain as the edge of a silver leaf cut a searing path across Lucius's palm, but it wasn't enough to stop the lunge.

The impact lifted Scooter off the sled, sending it, and them, careening in opposite directions. Scooter might have been crippled, and therefore unsuitable to lead the Family, but he more than matched Lucius's speed and strength.

They had been dominate and subordinate while still in the womb. Lucius hadn't been Alpha then and was in danger of losing that position now.

A quick sucker punch to the gut shifted the advantage, and Lucius took it, his hands closing around the soft flesh hidden beneath the matted beard. The beast under his skin howled in pain when his fingers closed around the silver choke chain Scooter wore.

When Lucius rolled onto his back, eyes staring at the dull green ceiling some twenty feet above him, the beast was gone, cowered back into restless sleep by the minuscule particles of silver that had entered his system through the cut on his palm.

Lucius closed his eyes as he listened to his brother push himself into a sitting position next to him.

"Now, was that very nice?" He wasn't even panting hard. "I thought Alphas were supposed to stay in control at all time. And just look at the mess you made. Tsk, as they say on the British Comedy Network, tsk."

Lucius lifted his head and opened his eyes, noted the positions of each bleeding chunk of meat and that the sled had bounced off a small crate and overturned, casters spinning, before closing his eyes and lowering his head back to the cool concrete floor.

"Sorry," came harder than Lucius thought it would.

"No problem. It's just nice to know you're human, little brother." From behind his closed lids, Lucius heard Scooter take a deep breath and smack his lips. "*Very* human, in fact."

The scent made him open his eyes and grab for it. Scooter knew it was coming and rolled out of reach, waving the small mitten at him. In hunting-sight, the rich purple looked gray-ish green.

"Purple's not your color," Scooter said, sniffing it openly. Obscenely lifting his top lip to work the scent farther into his memory. "But I have to admire your taste in . . . hand-wear. Have you found someone willing to fight the old bitch for the position of Alpha Female?"

Lucius felt the ground shift uneasily under his boot as he stood and hunched his shoulders forward.

"Give it to me, Scooter," he said, holding out his hand. The thin cut was still oozing clear liquid, but the pain, at least, was lessening. "Now."

Scooter smiled and sank his nose deeper into the wool.

"Hmmm, nice little bouquet—sort of a subtle blending of pheromones and diesel fuel." He draped the mitten over one stump and covered it with his hand. "Is she the one from the bus? The reporter?"

Lucius took a step forward. Then another. Before he was able to take a third, Scooter tossed the mitten into the air.

"That's none of your business," he said as he caught it, folded it over on itself, and tucked it carefully back into the pocket of his jacket.

"Maybe not, little brother," Scooter said, leaning back on his elbows and smiling up at Lucius with a shit-eating grin, "but I'm pretty sure Mother will think it's her business, don't you?"

This time it was Lucius who laughed. "Hell, do you really think the old Bitch will believe this shit?"

She did.

MOTHER believed.

MOTHER was not happy.

And MOTHER let him know about it.

The phone call came while he was slipping the black-satin bar vest over his head. Although his "discussion" with Scooter had made him almost a half hour late for his shift behind the bar, the night manager had blown it off with a wave across the half-empty bar and a shrug. The Broncos weren't playing and temperatures that had fallen into the near-freezing range had kept most of the regulars home.

It was so quiet that the dozen or so customers scattered around the room jumped when the phone rang and the night manager slopped a good portion of his Irish coffee on the bar.

Lucius tossed his boss a bar towel and grabbed the phone on the second ring. "O'Connell's."

The electronic ocean hissed in his ear. *"lucius."*

MOTHER. She was on one of the speaker phones, most likely the one in her private sitting room. And she was pacing. He could hear the sound of her nails tapping against the polished marble floor as she moved, back and forth, the way she always did when she was upset.

"I'm working . . . Mom," he said, cringing at the familiarity but still using it by way of explanation when his boss lifted one eyebrow in question. "Is there something wrong?"

The sound of pacing stopped.

He could just picture her, silver-white pelt shimmering pale against the night she would have filled the room with before calling, staring at the phone as if it was responsible for the words that had come from it.

Fortunately, he was probably the only one in the bar who thought anything was wrong with a full-grown man calling his mother "Mom." The manager rolled his eyes and smiled, nodding as he tossed the damp towel into the small sink under the bar.

And Lucius played along. He frowned and let his shoulders slump. *Moms*, he mouthed again and sighed.

MOTHER growled at the sound.

"it seems i am disturbing you, lucius, but i would have thought this particular matter would take precedence over pouring beer."

Lucius took a deep breath and held it for as long as he could. Scooter must have speed-dialed the Family about the article the moment he left. Damn him.

Turning his back to the room and curious eyes that had nothing better to stare at, he let the air out of his lungs and pressed the receiver tighter against his ear.

"And what matter would that be, Mother?"

The howl that filled the line was so ancient a sound that it hadn't any words. Only meaning. His free hand reached for the silver-and-turquoise necklace without him even realizing what he was doing. Until his fingers closed around the familiar, numbing tingle.

"don't play the fool with me, alpha. you were whelped to protect our family, not endanger it."

"Look, you're blowing this way out of proportion. Everything will be all right."

"will it? you killed a man without cause."

A woman sat down at the bar opposite him and smiled at his reflection in the bar mirror as she slipped off her coat. The sweater underneath was too thin for the winter chill. Her nipples tented the soft wool. Lucius quarter-turned away from the image and lowered his voice another degree, knowing the old bitch would have no trouble hearing him.

"There was a cause, Mother. You'll have to believe me on that."

"oh yes, i know." Lucius heard the sound of paper being shredded. *"you saved a woman's life. the woman who wrote about you. about us, alpha."*

He forced himself to chuckle. "Come on, can you honestly tell me that you believe anyone in their right minds is going to believe . . . that? Hey, this is the same paper that has a monthly column written by space aliens."

He didn't know that, of course, having never picked up a copy until that night, but it sounded like something a paper that would write about *Werewolves* and *Elvis* would do.

And, better yet, the lie pacified MOTHER.

"you're still such a child, lucius. you still believe that man is a rational creature but i don't because i've seen what fear can do to them. and lived through it. man is more beast than we can ever hope to be, lucius."

It always amazed him just how sweet and maternal her voice could be when she so desired, and he pictured her standing in the darkness of her sitting room, naked, the long silver tresses caressing her bare flesh.

He cleared his throat to mask the groan that the sudden

pressure of his erection had caused and saw the woman in the mirror smile. It wasn't the right face or scent, but she would do as a diversion.

Lucius turned around, receiver cupped between his ear and shoulder, and motioned the standard question, "What'll it be?" with his hands.

"Vodka Cosmopolitan," the woman said just loud enough to make sure she'd take precedence over the phone conversation. "No cherry."

Lucius pretended he hadn't heard the subtle come-on before and winked. MOTHER mumbled something as he began pouring vodka and cranberry juice into a chilled martini shaker.

"What?"

"i said, i hope, for all our sakes, that you're right about this."

She hung up without another word. The way she always did.

Lucius poured the drink before replacing the receiver.

"Shaken," he said with as much of a British accent as his native tongue would allow, "not stirred. And no cherry."

The woman giggled on cue and took a sip. Her eyebrows arched at the first taste. Also on cue.

"Hmmmm," she purred. "That's the best I've ever had."

Lucius accepted the compliment with a smile. Suddenly, the idea of a diversion didn't seem all that important.

"Thanks," he said, and walked down to the opposite end of the bar. "Hey, Fred, mind if I turn on the tube?"

Fred, the night manager, yawned as he looked up from his Irish coffee and shrugged one shoulder.

"There a game on somewhere?"

"Naw," Lucius said as he picked up the bar's remote and aimed it at the nineteen-incher mounted to the ceiling behind the bar. "The news. One of the cousins told my mother there might be more reparations made to our tribe. Can't hurt to check it out."

Fred accepted the lie with a nod and went back to warming the cockles and mussels of his heart. As far as everyone in the bar was concerned Lucius was one of Colorado's more fortunate half-breeds—one who'd gotten off the reservation on a football scholarship and his white daddy's good graces and found suitable employment dispensing firewater instead of consuming it when he flunked out a year later.

No one ever asked what school he flunked out of or what reservation he was from. Proof positive that the lie worked.

The screen brightened around the 10:00 news team sharing a private joke over the last story, which apparently had something to do with a poodle shooting its owner. Hah. Hah.

Lucius checked the bar, noticing the woman in the tight, thin sweater's pout at being abandoned, before turning his attention back to the screen. A few eyes watched along with him, the same way they'd watched him while he was on the phone—because there was nothing else to watch.

The laughter over the man-hunting poodle ended when the anchor began reciting the details of the "killing on a Metro bus early this morning."

"I don't know what the city's coming to," the woman from the mirror said as she slipped onto the stool catty-corner to where Lucius was standing. "I'm sure glad I drive. Another, please." She handed Lucius the empty martini glass. "And make it a double."

A double, after telling him that she drives. He was glad that made her feel safer.

Lucius started on the double while the news commentator mentioned a possible gang involvement—*What else was he going to say, given the dead kid's age?*—over the killing, citing the use of "a Halloween mask similar to the ones used by gang members in California during a bank holdup."

A Halloween mask.

He added an extra quarter-shot to the glass before setting it in front of the woman. Her eyes sparkled blue in the backwash from the television screen.

"And no cherry," he said.

She laughed another *funniest-thing-I've-ever-heard* and swatted his hand before he could get away.

"Good memory."

He nodded as the news story segued into the standardized

demand for stricter rulings on juvenile offenders and then droned off in another direction, that of a suicide in the train yard.

Messy.

"Got to have a good memory in this business," Lucius said, filling a bowl with dry-roasted peanuts and sliding it in front of her. "Or no one leaves you a tip."

More laughter.

Lucius leaned back against the counter that held the blenders and stuck his hands into his pockets. Closed the fingers of his right hand around the small glove and held on for dear life.

"there is another."

The pack gathered around him, bellies still swollen from the night's hunt but hackles stiff and tongues lolling.

"where?" Beta growled. He was standing away from the others, tucked into a corner of the den the Silverback had found for them. Apart, always apart.

The Silverback turned to look and felt pressure from the wound on his muzzle force his eye closed. He opened it quickly, lest the big male take advantage.

"unknown, but close . . . very close."

"danger?"

This was from one of the Juveniles, naturally. And just as naturally, the Beta snapped at him in anger. The Silverback chose to ignore the reprimand. This time.

"unknown . . . but this hunting place is his . . . he will defend it."

"alone or in a pack?"

The Silverback snorted. *"i only know there is another and that this is his place . . . and that he will defend it against us . . . but . . ."*

He waited until all eyes, including those heavily hooded ones of the Beta, were focused on him.

". . . the other does not know about us."

Lips curled back from glistening fangs in what passed

among them as smiles. They had fed well in this new hunting place and they would defend it against any interloper.

With one last look at his Second, the Silverback turned and began climbing the stairs out of the basement. The transformation was complete by the time he reached the heavy wooden door that led into the kitchen, but the minute his bare foot hit the cold linoleum he realized he should have planned it just a little better.

He never felt the cold. Except on the bottoms of his feet. One day he'd have to ask someone about that.

The slippers, worn thin but still smelling of the sheep they'd been cut from, were right where he left them—next to the refrigerator. He stepped into them and popped open the door, then freed a can of Coors from its plastic six-pack noose.

Nothing like cold beer on a cold night, he thought, finishing it off in one swallow and tossing the empty into the dark fireplace. The real-estate woman had gone on and on about how "cheery" a roaring fire would be during the winter while he busied himself signing leases and promises of upkeep on the rental property.

There'd never be a fire, he knew, unless it was to burn the place down . . . when they decided to move on.

If they decided.

Scratching his naked belly, he belched and smacked his lips on the taste of fresh beer and digesting meat. Damn, but it was good to be alive. Part of him hoped the other would want to fight. They hadn't had a good territorial war for generations now . . . and it was long over due.

Besides, the *other* couldn't be alone. True or were, wolves were creatures with strong family ties—and family meant females.

He smiled as he scuffed his way to the front window and pushed back the curtain. The historic district he had rented the house in was quiet, fast asleep and dreaming beneath the skeletal cottonwoods that lined the narrow street. Yeah, he really hoped the *other* would want to fight.

Tilting his head back, he closed his eyes and howled. The

pack answered him from the basement and filled their new canyon with the song of joy and homecoming.

Day. Then twilight. Then night and moonrise.
And day again.

9

The Denver Werewolf stalked her from midnight to an hour before sunrise, howling from the darkest corners of her imagination each time it seemed that she might actually fall into dreamless sleep. Halloween masks and black dusters; red fur and god-awful Hawaiian-print shirts that glinted with tiny silver spaceships.

When she finally gave up the struggle and shuddered herself awake, the sky outside her bedroom window was just beginning to brighten beyond the city towers to the east, and the Denver Werewolf was still very real.

Of course, two hours later, fully dressed and filled with coffee and Special K, Cat was able to finally see Ed's side of the argument and relegate the Denver Werewolf to the ranks of: *Nut, disgruntled with mask.*

The *paw print into handprint* was a little harder to explain, but by the time she'd gotten off the bus *(a nice safe bus filled with nice safe, sleepy people)* and jaywalked against traffic on Market, Cat had convinced herself that excess adrenaline, terror, poor lighting, and an overactive reporter's sense of story had added real fangs to a cheap plastic mask.

ELVIS IMPERSONATOR REALLY DENVER WEREWOLF

No, too silly. Besides, she wouldn't want to lessen the impact of her journalistic creation with one that, she personally hoped, was reaching the end of its after-life span.

ELVIS DEAD . . . DENVER WEREWOLF ALIVE!

Smiling to herself, Cat began to hum along with the elevator's Muzak rendition of Alice Cooper's "House of Fire" when the doors opened onto the Editorial Department and she came face-to-shirt with Ed.

Or at least face-to-opened newspaper. "Ed" was more of the conclusion she'd jumped to when she saw the edge of the orange-purple and pink flamingo Hawaiian shirt peeking out from under the paper.

The twinkle in his eyes was slightly overshadowed by the angry red-purple-green bruise on his right cheek. She'd never before met a man who tried to coordinate his injuries with his outfits.

"Oh my God! What happened?" Cat asked, pointing as if he wouldn't know what she was talking about. No less than three heads poked up over the tops of cubicles to find out. *Nosy, story-hungry bastards!*

The paper rustled when he lowered it. "What? Oh, you mean *this?*" He shrugged and grinned, bunching the bruised skin into wrinkles. Cat flinched in sympathy. "When I was driving in this morning I saw this homeless guy who was the hunka-hunka-spitting image of the King hisself, so I grabbed my camera off the passenger-side seat and . . . forgot the driver's side window was closed. Ah, the things we suffer for our art. Literally, sometimes.

"But enough about my stupidity . . . You, my dear, have hit the big time, and I am humbled by your presence."

The elevator doors, not so humbled, began to close between them, and they both reached out to hit the cushioned safety bar. Ed reached the bar first, then continued along the same line and grabbed her wrist.

Cat could feel the heat from his hand through the sleeve of her coat and sweater.

SECRET OF ABOMINABLE SNOWMAN REVEALED (?)

"You have any idea what I'm talking about?" When Cat shook her head, he sighed and tucked her hand into the crook of his arm, leading her through the cubicle maze back to her personal cubbyhole. The onlookers quickly lost interest. "Whazza matter? Don't you read the *real* newspaper?"

She nibbled a flake of winter-chapped flesh off her bottom lip. "Usually when I get home at night. Why?"

"Why, she asks." Ed rolled his eyes above the bruise and wrinkles and released her to shrug off her coat and toss it over her one allotted filing cabinet. When she was finished and sitting at her desk, he snapped the paper open to the front page and held it out for her to read. "De ol' Denber Werewolf hass bean a busy hombre, ah teenk."

Cat read the headline above the grainy color photo showing two grim uniformed police officers in the background standing next to three, no *four* blanket-draped piles.

TRAIN KILLS TWO

She shrugged. "So?"

"So," Ed said, eyes twinkling as if he was Santa Claus's slightly demented twin, "if you read the news item itself you'll find that one of the victims showed signs of being moved onto the tracks *after* being killed."

"Then it was a homicide." Cat nodded. "So what does that have to do with my Denver Werewolf?"

Ed's bushy grin completed the Santa impersonation. "Ah, how quickly they grow up and become possessive. Good! Stay that way."

"But—"

"But you still don't understand. Oh, my sweet, innocent child. If you read the news item itself, it mentions that one of the bodies . . . the body that was *moved* . . . had certain anomalies that were inconsistent with being turned into ground round under a train."

The Special K Cat had for breakfast twisted uneasily beneath her belly button.

"Ed," she whimpered. "Please?"

"What? Oh . . . anyway, they were pretty careful not to mention anything, especially after our . . . excuse me, *your* masked friend last night, but the reporter managed to slip this in past his editor's nose. Let's see, where . . . is . . . it . . ."

Ed lifted the paper and disappeared behind it, muttering to himself as he scanned the newsprint. Cat busied herself by reading that JC Penney was having a 25 percent off sale that coming weekend while her breakfast slowly began to settle. She jumped when Ed hooted from his side of the paper.

"Here . . . listen to this: ' . . . *despite the trauma, the body showed obvious signs of animal interference.*' Translation: They were being chewed on before they died. How 'bout them apples?" he asked, lowering the paper. "Now it'll take a little doing to get our illustrious boss to run a supplemental insert that'll connect your puppy with the ones that were chewing on this guy before he got creamed, but if you just show him the—Cat?"

She was a little too far from the cubicle to answer. Not that it would have been any better if she'd been still sitting there. She didn't even think Ed would have been able to understand her with her head in the wastepaper basket.

And thanked God that she hadn't had a chocolate chip bagel with cream cheese for breakfast.

The newspaper was tucked into the basket below his mailbox just as it was every morning. But this morning it was tied with a frayed and oil-stained red ribbon.

Snapping the ribbon, Lucius glanced through the key-locked glass doors just beyond the Security/Reception Desk and wondered how the hell his brother had gotten in. It wasn't the ribbon, even though that was the sort of sick-joke thing Scooter loved to do, or the note that had been scribbled on the back of a used bar napkin and Scotch-taped to the front of the paper. He'd *smelled* his twin the moment the elevator doors opened onto the lobby.

"Just thought you'd like this for your album. My but we've been a busy little brother, haven't we? And I bet you didn't even save me a rib. By the way, I copped this from a cop. Get it? No? Well, I'm sure Mother will. Take care, little brother.

—S"

Lucius read the front-page story on his way back up to his apartment. And wasn't at all surprised to hear his phone ringing off the hook when he opened the door.

"Shit!"

At that same moment, ten miles away at the Jefferson County Sheriff's Department, the Investigation Division knew it wasn't going to be a good day when one out of every three incoming calls was about the "Denver Werewolf."

Half of which were hunters volunteering to help hunt it down and skin it.

By eleven o'clock, the entire Investigation Division was wondering if there'd been some kind of psychotropic drug leak in the Greater Denver Metro area that they hadn't heard about.

It wasn't until one of the techs working in the Criminalistics Unit came back from lunch with a copy of *QUEST* that the mystery was . . . if not solved, then at least relegated to the hysteria files where it belonged.

"Shit."

10

GRISLY DEATHS IN RAIL YARD
IS THE DENVER WEREWOLF RESPONSIBLE?
—*Supplemental by C. K. Moselle*

Cat arched her back and listened to the soggy snaps and pops of her backbone realigning itself. Or trying to.

It didn't do much good, but it did help to remind her that her butt and feet had fallen asleep sometime during the last edit/rewrite/damning self-analysis.

Being your own worst critic could be a burden at times.

Letting her back return to its most comfortable curve, Cat yawned and allowed herself a brief diversion from the woes of pressure-cooker creativity, to pluck one of the many pink "While You Were Out" notes that ringed her monitor like twining morning glories.

In truth she hadn't left her cubicle since returning—pale and shaken—from the ladies' room, but the constant phone interruptions had begun to cut into the already minuscule amount of time Tanner had (begrudgingly) given her to write, edit, proof, and deliver the Werewolf Update Supplemental Ed had talked him into running.

"Hell, no tabloid has ever run a supplement on a story while the first issue was still in the stands," he had bellowed when Ed first pitched the idea and she stood, meek and mild, behind the camouflage pink flamingos. "It's unheard of. We'll be the talk of the industry.". . . . "I like it! Have it on my desk in an hour."

The department secretary had been easier to convince. She'd succumbed to Ed's charm almost immediately and agreed to hold Cat's calls and play message monitor for the rest of the day on only the promise of coffee after work.

Cat picked through the stack of memos and smiled. *Woman thinks Den-Were* (Denver Werewolf) *is ex-boyfriend. Wants you to call her back for possible interview. Group called "Avenging Ethical Treatment of Animals Guardian Angels" confesses to killings, wants interview.*

Man has pictures proving his brother-in-law is Den-Were and space alien. Willing to negotiate price of pics. Wants interview.

"I love this business," she mumbled, and began sorting the messages into two piles: left-hand side of desk, "too crazy even for *QUEST*," right-hand, possible story ideas.

Man confesses to being werewolf. Blames it on Viagra overdose. Another winner.

There were also a couple of hand-drawn cartoons that had come through the fax that Cat pinned to the "wall" above her monitor. One showed a smiling werewolf sitting in the classic "Thinker" pose, contemplating a bottle of Nair. The second depicted a werewolf that had just been run over by a mobile-home full of tourists. Its caption read: Transylvanian Roadkill.

The populace was already seeing werewolves behind every construction barricade "cone zone" sign even without her supplemental.

Sweet!

Cat read three more notes, two more that attempted to connect the Denver Werewolf with government conspiracy plots and recent UFO sightings, and another confession, this one from a dermatologist in Longmont, all of whom wanted interviews, before thinking she really should be getting back to work on the supplemental. But it was like eating cheese puffs . . . you just couldn't stop until the bag was empty.

"No," Cat told herself as she pushed the stack of unread messages to the farthest edge of her desk, out of harm's and arm's reach, and turned back to her monitor screen. "I'm a professional with a job to do. And I'm going to do it. I'm going to—"

Ah . . . just one more. What could it hurt?

Cat leaned backwards and let Fate pick the next entry into the possible story contest.

"And the winner is—"

I have your mitten. Call me.

Ice formed in the pit of Cat's stomach and worked its way up along her ribs to her heart. She hadn't even thought about her missing mitten since . . .

Denver, we have a problem.

Cat reached for her desk phone and punched access to an outside line. There was a name below the message, *Lucius*, and a phone number, the prefix putting it somewhere east of the office's own Curtis Park location.

An eternity passed in measured, electronic tones before a voice answered.

"Hello?"

A man's voice, so deep that it tickled Cat's ear with its vibration. She heard herself gasp, the sharp intake barely making it through the sudden constriction in her throat.

"Hello? Is there someone . . ." He paused for only a moment. "It's you, isn't it? C. K. Moselle."

UPDATE:

DENVER WEREWOLF PSYCHIC

KNOWS ALL . . . SEES ALL

kills all

Some part of Cat, a *very* small part, was all ready with the standard glib comeback—*"That's my name, don't wear it out."* She was very glad it didn't get a chance to speak.

"We have to meet," he said. "So I can give you back your glove. From the other night."

That same, previously unheard part, fainted. "You're . . . I mean . . ." Cat licked her lips and saw herself reflected in the monitor's black screen. The white lines of words looked like prison bars.

"Yes."

One word. Only one. And Cat watched her reflection shake its head. *No, no, no. Not possible. No one in their right mind would call up and confess to a murder.*

Except a nut.

And that made her feel better.

Cat leaned back and exhaled. Nuts she could deal with, even nuts who wore Halloween masks and killed drugged-out kids. And left behind bloody pawprints . . . *hand*prints.

And knew about her mitten, which meant . . .

The internal chill instantly evaporated in a rush of journalistic furor. If this guy really had her mitten, then she had a story that was worth its weight in Pulitzers. Cat sat up so slowly she felt the muscles in her back tremble. The last thing she wanted to do was frighten him off.

Right . . . me frighten him.

QUEST EXCLUSIVE

DENVER WEREWOLF REALLY SCAREDY-CAT

"Look, I can help you."

He chuckled soft, and the sound constricted the flow of blood to her brain. *Damn him!*

"Oh, I think you've already helped me enough, don't you? Until you printed that damned story, no one knew I existed . . . and believe me, I liked it that way."

"I'm sure every murdering son-of-a-bitch says that."

Whoa, where did that come from?

"I'm not a murderer," he whispered, "and you know that as well as I do."

"All I know right now, for certain, is that you picked up my mitten, but you could have found it when they were cleaning the bus. That isn't enough to convince me you're the Denver Werewolf." Standing up on legs that would have preferred she remained sitting, Cat snatched the right-hand pile of messages and shook them against the receiver so he could hear the rustling. "So far you're only one of about a hundred guys who've left me messages claiming that *he's* the heir to Junior Chaney's legacy."

"That's Lon Chaney, Junior," he corrected.

"Whoever, but the fact remains you're just one of the many nuts who wants an interview."

Silence.

"And how many of the others nuts did you call back?" the voice asked.

Silence again, this time from her.

"All right, let's just say the item about the mitten intrigued you. Good. And believe me, I'm sorry I took it after I'd ripped that boy's throat out to save your life." She heard him take a long, ragged breath. "But I supposed not even that confession is enough proof for you, is it?"

The message slips fluttered to the desk like autumn leaves. "N-no."

"Then how am I to convince you, Ms. Moselle?"

Cat was trying to think of an answer when Ed came barreling into her cubby, Hawaiian shirt fluttering at the sides of his belly like flags. His sudden appearance made her gasp, she couldn't help it.

"What's the matter?" The voice in her ear had dropped to a rumbling growl. It barely sounded human, and she wondered if it ever had.

Ed, on the other hand, hadn't seemed to notice the panic he'd inspired or that she was on the phone.

"Hey, Kit-Cat, I was wondering if you'd like to grab something to gnaw on."

"Answer me," the voice growled at her. "Are you all right?"

"Fine," Cat shouted, and realized she'd answered both questions. Lifting her finger to her mouth, she looked at Ed and pantomimed a request for silence. He nodded and slumped against the side of her doorway. "I'm fine."

His voice had a more human quality when he spoke again. "I'm sorry I snapped at you, Ms. Moselle, but you can imagine that I've been under a lot of . . . stress of late."

"Of course," Cat agreed.

Clearing his throat to get her attention, Ed pointed to the phone and mouthed *"who"*. Not wanting to make the call appear to be more unusual than any of the other calls she normally got, Cat leaned back and twirled her index finger in a tiny circle above her ear. It was a universal sign that Ed understood immediately.

"So tell me, Lucius, why did you call? I mean, if you are who you say you are, then isn't it a little dangerous to expose yourself like this?"

"You talking to a flasher?" Ed whispered.

Cat shook her head and waved him into silence.

"As I said in my message, Ms. Moselle, I have your mitten and—"

The line went dead.

Cat pulled the receiver away from her ear and stared at it. "No," she said. "Oh, please no."

Ed cocked his head and wrinkled his brow. "What's wrong? You look like you just ran over your best friend's puppy."

Cat looked at him. "He . . ." And then looked back at the phone. "I . . ." And then back at him. "I was talking to—" *What did Mr. Boswell just tell you about keeping your leads to yourself?* "—someone and we got disconnected. Oh, God, Ed, what am I going to do."

Ed stopped looking concerned and smiled. "You have his number, right? So why not just redial it?"

"Oh." She looked at the memo. "Yeah. Good idea. Thanks."

If Human Combustion was possible, and according to at least three dozen *QUEST* articles it was, she should have been a smoldering pile of ash right about then.

Cat replaced the receiver and picked up the memo. *I have your mitten. Call me.* Nodded at the phone number she'd just called and felt the blush crank itself up to *broil*. Damn, damn, damn! One phone call from a man claiming to be the Denver werewolf *(Without proof, Catherine, let's not forget that small point)* and all her training and self-reliance goes right out the window. One frigging phone call that gets disconnected and suddenly she turns into some helpless, hapless, befuddled female stereotype who—

The incoming call startled her, but she managed (just barely) not to gasp.

Or swoon.

"QUEST NewsJournal," she yelled into the phone, "C. K. Moselle."

"Ah, just the person I wanted to speak with."

The voice *sounded* the same. Sort of.

"Are you the man I was just talking to?"

"And who might that have been?"

Cat looked away from Ed whom seemed completely happy to stand there and eavesdrop.

"You *know*."

The voice dropped an octave. "I have no time for games, Mzzzz. Mozzelle, but maybe this will answer the question of who I am."

The inhuman howl cut a path through her head and leaked out into the main room. At least that's what Cat thought probably happened from the look on Ed's face.

"The Denver Werewolf?" Ed hissed.

Cat nodded and was surprised to find that she was still able to hear. Somewhat.

"Are you still there, Mzzz. Mozzzelle?"

"Y-yes."

"Very good." He chuckled. Not the same chuckle, but close enough. "I think we need to meet, don't you? I mean, after all, if you're going to talk about me, I'd like to have a chance to give my side of the story . . . so to speak."

Cat leaned back in her chair. "All right," she said. "When?"

"Let's say tonight. Midnight. Nineteenth and Bassett. Do you know where that is?"

"No," Cat confessed, "but I can find it."

"Very good. When you get there, walk to the end of Bassett . . . but walk alone, Mzzzz. Mozzzelle, or you won't like what happens next."

"No, of course not. You can count on me t—"

This time Cat was relieved when the connection was broken. Turning, she picked up a pencil from the coffee-mug holder on her desk and wrote *19th and Bassett* on the back of a used envelope.

"What the hell's at Nineteenth and Bassett?" Ed asked,

looking over her shoulder. Regardless of his offer of food, she could smell pastrami or some other cured meat on his breath.

Cat was about to answer him when she noticed that there were a half dozen heads, or more, peeking around, or over, the maze walls, ears pricked toward their conversation.

The Denver Werewolf story was hers . . . but that didn't mean another of *QUEST*'s "industrious" reporters wouldn't try to scoop her. She was still the new kid on the block, but gaining ground fast.

Maybe too fast for some.

"What *is* at Nineteenth and Bassett?" she asked, lowering her voice.

"How the hell would I know, I'm new in town remember. Why?" The light began to brighten behind his eyes. And it wasn't a pretty sight. "Why?"

Cat offered him her most beguiling smile—the one that always worked on her father—as she reached over Ed's shoulder to rescue the copy of *Denver Regional Street Atlas* from beneath the stack of file folders, and flipped it open to the index.

"Because I'm getting the interview of a lifetime," she said, running a finger down through the Bs. "And I thought you might like to come along to take pictures. He said to come alone, but I really think . . ."

The smile finally faded when she found the "intersection" of nineteenth and Bassett.

Cat looked at him from over the page. "How far away is this from where . . . those people died last night."

Ed stood up and noticed the location, then gently took her arms and danced her around to the chair he'd just vacated.

"The Denver Werewolf wants you to meet him here?" he asked.

Cat nodded, not yet trusting what she might sound like if she tried to say anything at that moment.

"And he wants you to meet him here . . . I mean there. Tonight?"

Another nod.

"Shit."

Cat nodded a third time.

QUEST EXCLUSIVE

"SHIT HAPPENS," SAYS DENVER WEREWOLF

When the man was right, he was right.

Lucius looked at the silent phone for a long time after he hung up, her voice still echoing in his ear. Until a rumbling *"hey, asshole"* displaced the gentle sound.

He turned away from the pay phone and glared the man, one of the city's pedestrian Kamikazes, into silence.

"Sorry," Lucius said, sidestepping away from the molded-plastic housing. "All yours."

He walked away without listening to the muttered reply, knowing that if he had he'd probably be forced to confront the man . . . and that was something he didn't want to do.

Not now.

Not while her voice—*her voice*—still sang to him; deepening the color of her eyes, the ebony sheen of her hair, the white marble of her skin. Marble white but soft and warm and yielding to the pressure of his flesh against it. As he touched her. Tasted her. Took her.

A woman and her cellular phone darted across the sidewalk in front of him and stopped him in his tracks. Which was just as well. The growing pressure at the front of his jeans had been making it more . . . difficult to walk.

Lucius watched the woman yell into her phone and make her way through the stalled traffic on Blake until his erection returned to a manageable state.

But just to make sure, he reached up and laced his fingers around the silver squash blossom at his throat. He shuddered at the familiar, and thankfully brief, loss of equilibrium, and took a deep breath of the carbon-monoxide-scented air.

The wind swept up on his blind side, curled around him like a cat and whipped strands of hair loose from the thick braid at the back of his neck. He let go of the necklace to brush the hair out of his eyes and started walking.

East. As good a direction as any.

His car was still in the parking lot behind the brew pub,

all but forgotten when he rode the bus back into the downtown area. Hoping that somehow she'd be there . . . even though he knew, thanks to Scooter's lunchhour update, that she was still at her office.

He'd left the message about the mitten because he knew she was there. And he wanted to hear her voice.

A raven cawed from the top of a lamppost as he passed. He hissed up at it and pulled the sides of his duster in tighter around himself. The sight of the carrion bird made Lucius's skin crawl.

He got the same reaction when three teenagers—virtually and visually indistinguishable—poured out of a giant CD/computer/book store, giggling over a copy of *QUEST*.

Lucius felt the hairs at the back of his neck bristle when one of the teens suddenly lunged at its closest companion, snarling, fingers curled into makeshift claws.

"Hey, like I'm the Denver Werewolf, dude," he/she/it shouted. "Arf, arf."

The other two growled back at their friend and then started taking pot-growls at passersby. When they got to Lucius, he growled back and let his lower canines slide up just enough to say howdy.

It wasn't the smartest thing he'd ever done, given the number of people—and patrol cars—in the general vicinity, but it *felt* good. In fact, he had to admit when the teens already pale Goth complexions faded to winter white, that it felt wonderful.

Lucius sucked his canines back into his jaw and continued down the street. He could smell the fear on them but part of him didn't care.

No, that wasn't entirely true. *None* of him cared.

He carried the lie for another two blocks before dumping it in a trash bin next to another pay-phone kiosk. The line rang fifteen times before Scooter picked up.

"One Hung Lo's Chinese Restaurant and Pet Shop. Ask about our crate 'em and cook 'em specials. One Hung, speaking."

"I need you to do me a favor, Scooter."

His twin didn't even try to hide the venom in his voice.

"Well, of course, Alpha. How can I help you?"

"I need you to follow someone."

"Ah, a little reconnoitering, huh? Good, I haven't wrecked a noiter in months. Hate the little bastards, always sticking their tiny, wet noses in other people's butts."

"Scooter."

"For fifty, I'll follow," his brother said. "For one hundred, I'll call if I feel something might go down. For two, I'll get involved. For five hundred I'll kill the noiter and eat the evidence."

"I'll have the hundred and a pager at your place in twenty minutes."

"You're one of the last of the big-time spenders, bro."

The line went dead.

Midday. Then twilight. Then night.

Finally, moonrise above the canyons of steel and glass.

11

Cat zipped up the last two inches on the parka's collar and leaned back against the driver's seat, staring through the fly specks and dust streaks covering the windshield at the empty lot where Bassett Street ended.

Empty, that is, except for the silent earthmovers that had been left to defend the site. What they were moving was obvious, even in the reflected light from the city and the one dim streetlamp.

Dirt. Mounds of dirt.

What they would be putting in its place was anyone's guess.

Cat suggested another warehouse, since that seemed to be the prevalent construction d'choice of the windswept rise that was bordered by the South Platte to the west and railroad tracks to the east. Ed, scrunched down among the litter in the passenger-side foot well, he and his camera hidden beneath a rancid-smelling army blanket he'd had in the trunk, agreed even though he hadn't actually seen the area.

"Anything?" he whispered through the heavy wool.

"Nuh-uh."

"Well, if he doesn't show soon, I say we leave and go

back to the Chop House for dessert. I mean . . . it's the only place you seem to know how to get to."

Boy, that was the truth.

After confronting Tanner with the plan (who had agreed even though he'd turned into the tyrant Old Tannenbutt half-way through her plea),

MORE MONSTERS IN DENVER

EMPLOYER TURNS INTO ASSHOLE BEFORE REPORTER'S EYES!

Cat had quit two hours early and gone home to prepare for the midnight interview. Her original plan was to sleep, shower, and make sure the batteries in her minicassette recorder were working.

But instead she spent the next nine hours wandering around the apartment looking for stray cobwebs to dust away, too excited and keyed-up to rest.

Ed had shown up early—showered (he said), combed (which was obvious), and sedately dressed (for him) in faded black jeans and a Hard Rock Cafe/Niagara Falls sweatshirt. He'd come early so they'd have more than enough time to find the intersection of Bassett and Nineteenth before the appointed hour.

It proved to be a wise move.

Finding Nineteenth was not the problem. They found it. A number of times. Each time ending in the parking lot of the Denver Chop House.

After the sixth "Are you *sure* you said turn here?" tour of the LoDo district, Ed pulled the rusting, rattling Volvo into a parking space vacated by a Lexus and suggested that the Gods of the Night were trying to give them a hint.

With another couple of hours to kill, Cat decided dinner would be a good idea—until the stuffed potato skins arrived and she discovered that her stomach had twisted itself into a quivering mass of nerves.

She only managed a few stray nibbles, poring over the map while Ed consumed enough red meat to make the waiter's eyes shine in anticipation of an equally juicy tip.

The quivering nerves stayed with Cat throughout the rest of the meal and the impromptu map-reading lesson from their waiter (*"Take Twentieth to Lipan over to Bassett."*), and caused just a minor scream fest when she thought she saw *something* dart into the shadows as they crossed the parking lot.

Ed had laughed and tossed an arm over her shoulders. Paranoia happens, he joked . . . but that still hadn't stopped him from watching the shadows as he tossed her the keys and climbed into the passenger-side seat.

There'd been something in the parking lot . . . watching them.

Just like now.

Something.

Cat squeezed the tops of her arms through the jacket's insulated padding and looked over at the glow-in-the-dark dash clock:

11:49,

11:50,

11:51.

"One-Mississippi, two-Mississippi, three-Mississippi, four—"

"What?" Ed's muffled voice asked from below.

Cat covered her mouth with her hand and watched the shadows.

"Just counting," she whispered. "Nine . . . eight more minutes to go."

"Oh." She heard him shift his weight and groan softly. "Do you know how stupid this is? I mean how friggin' stupid?"

"Shh." Her breath warmed her palm, sending reverse shivers up her spine.

"Come on, Kit-Cat," the lump in the darkness whispered. "You've done great so far without meeting the man . . . why risk serious complications now?"

Cat sat up, pretending to work a kink out of her back, and patted the tallest point of the lump.

"Because he might be the real thing, Ed."

"Real. As in a *real* werewolf? Hey, come on, kid, now you're starting to scare me."

Now? "SHH!"

His voice returned to a muffled roar. "Are you listening to yourself, little girl? You don't really think he's real, do you?"

Something brushed against the back of the car. Not wind. Not dust. *Something.* Cat felt her back go rigid.

"Look, Cat," Ed continued, unaware, "I admire the hell out of you and all you've accomplished with this story, but that's all it is . . . a story. You start believing the stuff you write and pretty soon you'll be adopting litters of kittens and wearing an aluminum-foil hat to keep the government from reading your thoughts. Listen to your uncle Ed, okay—"

Cat could feel it. The *Something.* Watching her. Close. So very close now.

"—you're planning to meet some guy who already has a few screws short of a gross. Alone. In the middle of the night. The *best* you can hope for is that you'll only get raped and I'll only get beaten into a bloody pile. C'mon, baby, it's still not too late, let's get out of here."

A shadow broke away from those huddled around a giant crane, and beckoned.

Cat's fingers found the steering wheel and tightened around the cold plastic as she glanced at the dash clock: 12:00. Midnight.

"It's too late," she whispered.

She felt Ed's body go tense under the blanket. "He's here?"

"Mmm-huh."

"Okay, remember the plan . . . we both pop the doors at the same time. And leave your door open . . . just in case you need to make a fast exit. Give me a sec to find the handle. Shit—"

The car shook while Ed tried to find the door handle from under the blanket. And the shadow beckoned again.

"Hurry it up," Cat hissed, nodding and turning toward the driver's side door. "Come on."

"Okay. Got it. On the count of three. One . . . two . . . I'll be right behind you . . . three!"

The sound of one latch screeching covered the sound of the second. Ed had made sure the dome light was off before they left the Chop House. He wanted to make sure he wouldn't be spotted, but stepping from the dark car into the darker night took most—if not all—of Cat's resolve.

This is stupid. This is crazy. This is absolutely nuts.

"Mzzz. Mozzelle, I presume."

The voice sounded different without the walls of distance and anonymity between them. It sounded *real*. Was real . . . and she was walking right into it.

The ground crunched under her boots, and ice glistened in the weak light. There was the smell of snow in the air . . . and something else, something vile and rank. His smell.

Cat slipped her hands into the pockets of her parka and curled her fingers around the objects they found there—the minicassette recorder in the left, the pocketknife in the right. All other shortcomings aside, her mama didn't raise no idiot.

"Yes," she said, hoping her voice would cover the sounds of the recorder turning on and the knife snicking open, "I'm C. K. Moselle."

"But you're so small," the shadow man said without moving closer, "barely a mouthful."

The laughter that followed was hard and humorless. Inhuman.

Cat backed up as warning bells, sirens, and whistles went off inside her head. Whoever . . . whatever the man was standing in front of her, he wasn't the Denver Werewolf. He hadn't recognized her.

"STOP!"

She did. *What?*

"You will follow me. Now."

No way! And her body ignored her and followed the instructions it was given without hesitation.

MIND CONTROL IN DENVER

"THE DEVIL MADE ME DO IT"

He was waiting at the edge of the graded stretch of ground, his back to her. *She could turn and run back to the car without him seeing or even noticing. She could get away. Now.* Cat stopped when she reached the end of the hill they were on and looked down. The South Platte flowed through the darkness below, rumbling softly. She kept her eyes lowered to the narrow valley, watching the occasional flash of light reflecting off the black water.

"Before your kind came, this was a place of animals and trees," the shadow man beside her said. "But you just can't stand letting animals and trees live on prime real estate, can you? Nope. Your kind has to be in charge of everything it sees, isn't that right?"

Cat swallowed with some difficulty. "M-my kind?"

"Humans," the shadow said, and turned, just as the waxing moon slipped from behind a cloud.

It isn't him.

The wide, drooping mouth curled around a broken-toothed smile as he ran grime-blackened fingers across the dark stubble on his head. A tiny swastika formed the pupil of the crudely drawn third eye in the center of his pimpled forehead.

Cat backed up in time with the strange man's advance. *It isn't the man from the bus, the man with red hair. It isn't the werewolf.*

The knife tore open a seam as she pulled it out. "Stay away."

The smile widened. "You think that will hurt me? *Me?* You don't understand . . . none of your kind does. You can't hurt me. I was created decades ago. By the only true God."

He touched the swastika-etched eye and howled. The moon slipped behind another cloud, casting them into darkness.

"I am *Jungend Wulfen*. Do you know what that means, bitch? No, of course you don't . . . you wouldn't. It means, *young wolf*, and that's just what I am. One of Hitler's Elite, created to slaughter the weak and genetically inferior. Just like you."

HITLER ALIVE AND WELL AND LIVING IN LO-DO

Stop it! Cat's left hand closed around the mini-cassette recorder and pulled it into the open.

"Is that what you want to tell my readers?"

The question seemed to surprise him less than it had her. "What?"

"Th-the interview," she stammered, holding the recorder

out in front of her like it was a crucifix and he was a vampire instead of a . . . "Remember, I'm going to interview you for *QUEST*? You are the Denver Werewolf, right?"

"Of *course* I'm the Denver Werewolf. Who else would I be? But do you think I want anyone to know that?"

Cat screamed as he slapped the recorder from her hand. She heard it strike the ground at her feet a moment later, but in that moment she was already fighting for her life.

The knife fell, as useless a diversion as the recorder had been, when he grabbed her throat and squeezed the scream quiet.

"Shhh," he told her, one hand sliding across the front of her parka. "Hmmm, nice. I may have to play with you a little first."

Cat's stomach lurched at the feel of his erection against the front of her jeans. *God, Ed was right. The best I can hope for is just getting raped. Where is Ed?*

"You think I was ever going to let you interview me? Me . . . the Denver Werewolf? You aren't anything but food."

Then, as if to prove just that, he wrenched her mouth open and filled it with his tongue. His hands tore at the zipper on her jeans as he pushed her down onto the ice-frosted dirt, his legs spreading hers as the scream that was trapped behind the probing plug of flesh grew until it echoed through her body.

Noo

"—oo!"

Her scream was joined by the neo-Nazi *Wulfen* as he sailed backwards through the darkness, a vapor trail of sound that etched in the air and encircled the shaggy head of the creature that stared down at her. At first only a vague silhouette against the cityscape backdrop, it lifted its head as the moon broke the clouds' embrace a third time.

His fur was bleached monotone gray in the moonlight, but somehow Cat knew it was red. The color of a fox in autumn. The same color she'd seen on the bus the night before. First on the genetic mismatched Native American. Then on the werewolf.

"You're . . . real."

The whisper was barely audible even to her, but the creature heard it and dropped from the upright ... *man*like stance to all fours. It wasn't a natural position for him any more than being sprawled flat on the ground with her jeans unzipped was natural for Cat.

And both of them seem to know it. But accepted it.

"Are you all right?"

The voice was low, the words little more than muffled grunts, slow in the forming; the elongated muzzle and almost nonexistent lips chewed each syllable as if it were a stringy piece of meat.

The image didn't sit well with Cat.

When it sat back on its narrow haunches and reached out to her with a paw the size of a dinner plate, the print of which was even then gracing God-only-knew how many homes ... the print that had been etched into her memory ... Cat pulled her legs up to her chest and kicked. As hard as she could. Straight at the fur-covered genital sack.

He caught both of her legs in one hand ... *paw* ... and cocked his head, ears pricked forward. A large, toothy grin split the muzzle in two.

Cat's legs felt as though they'd been encased in warm concrete. She couldn't move. Couldn't kick. But she sure as hell wasn't just going to lie there and become a midnight snack.

Filling her lungs, she prepared to scream as loud and as long as she could.

The werewolf leaned forward and pressed a clawed "finger" against her lips.

"Shhhhh. I won't hurt you."

Cat let the air out of her lungs slowly, the breeze it created stirring the scent of him into her nostrils when she inhaled again. Beyond the animal musk, he smelled of Scope and Canoe aftershave. Just the thing a *man* would use before going out on a date.

And, for some reason, that almost made sense to her.

"You're ... You called me this afternoon about my glove, didn't you?"

The werewolf's paw dropped from her face as he leaned

back on powerful hind legs. He stared at her and for a moment, only a moment, Cat thought she saw the wolfish countenance flicker . . . the shimmering fur melting around high cheekbones and hooked nose.

"Lucius?" Cat sat up, closing the distance between them. This time she reached out to run trembling fingers through the thick pelt on his chest. Just to make sure he was there . . . and real . . . and . . .

His paw closed over her hand, held it against the slow, strong pounding of his heart.

"Yess."

And then something terrible happened. Cat transformed as the moon drifted into a cloud bank—from terrified near victim to born-again reporter.

Using modesty as a cover, Cat pulled the front of her parka down to cover the open fly and looked up from beneath her lashes.

"Please?"

He nodded and looked away—a gentleman in werewolf's clothing. Watching to make sure he'd stay the gentleman, Cat reached down and picked up the mini-recorder. *A miracle, it was still running!* Thank God for the indestructibility of modern plastic and microcircuits. A deep breath later and Cat slipped the recorder into the pocket of her parka and zipped up.

"Thank—" The snap closure on her jeans was apparently all he needed to hear. He turned back toward her at the sound and Cat's breath momentarily caught in her throat. "Ah . . . you. Thank you." *Come on, girl. Speak!* "Um . . . Were you always a werewolf or did you get bitten like in those movies . . . you know, *An American Werewolf in London* and *Wolf*? And does the full moon really turn you or . . . No, wait a minute, moon's not full tonight, is it?"

Cat looked up into a furry, furrowed brow. "What?"

"The moon. I guess that's just part of the Hollywood legend, huh?"

The werewolf sat back on his haunches, sinewy arms laced over the knobs of his knees, and stared at her as if *she* and not it, was the monster. A moment later he shook his head and stood up.

"You have to stop it."

Cat's ascent to her feet wasn't nearly as easy or graceful.

"What do you mean?"

"You have to stop *writing* about me. The Denver Werewolf."

"But . . ." *Think, girl.* "But no one really believes it. Really."

Lame. Very, very lame.

"Some do." His jaws stretched out into a toothy parody of a grin. "Don't they, Ms. Moselle?"

Cat cleared her throat.

"Exactly." He reached out and brushed the hair out of her eyes. "Stick with writing fiction. You may live longer."

Whatever else it was, his last statement wasn't a threat. There was no anger, no demand that she stop. It was more of a suggestion . . . a very *good* suggestion.

However . . .

"Look," she said, "we both know *QUEST* isn't exactly the *News* or *Post* . . . or much less the *New York Times*, so I don't think you have very much to w—What's the matter?"

The werewolf's entire demeanor changed as she was babbling. Standing nearly as erect as a man, he stared over the top of Cat's head. She could feel the hairs on the back of her neck rise in sympathy with the hackles across his shoulders and spine. Childhood memories of scaring friends by staring over their heads (only to scare herself in the process) came flooding back.

Cat spun around and stared into the windy darkness.

"What is it?" she hissed to the *real* monster standing behind her.

He sniffed the air in a way that dislodged her heart from its normal place and sent it into exile at the back of her throat.

"What?"

"We have company."

Ed. Shit . . . she'd forgotten all about her erstwhile protector.

"Who is h—"

The rest of the question was lost, or swallowed, or didn't need to be answered when a single, deep-throated howl filled the darkness above them. He answered immediately. And Cat just stood there, silent, listening to the challenges echo across the river valley and wondering what the hell she was getting herself into.

What she'd *already* gotten herself into.

"That wasn't just a dog," Cat asked, looking over her shoulder at him. "Was it?"

His silence was worse than any answer he could have given her.

Cat backed up until her spine was pressed against the hard, fur-covered ridges of his belly. She trembled only for a moment when he gripped her shoulder, and then only because of the heat that penetrated the thermal lining. *He was so warm . . . so warm.*

QUEST EXCLUSIVE:
LOVE AND THE PROPER WEREWOLF
—BY C. K. MOSELLE

"Leave," he whispered to her, his breath tickling the side of her neck, the coarse hair on his muzzle almost touching her cheek. "Now."

Cat looked into his eyes as she turned—twin spheres of cut hematite that followed her every move.

"Lucius . . ." She liked the way his name felt against her tongue. "Lucius, I—"

He lowered his head toward her just as the night exploded in a blinding blue-white flash of light and sound.

"Holy-Mother-of-Pearl-Jesus-Save-Us-I-don't-believe-it-My-God-damn-Would-you-look-at-that-MOTHER-Shit!"

Ed.

To the rescue with camera flashing.

Cat rushed at him, arms waving—"No. Don't!"—but was about three seconds too late. The werewolf brushed past her as though she were standing still, knocking Ed, and his camera, back into an eight-foot mound of dirt.

Surprisingly, neither the camera nor Ed seemed any the worse for the experience when Cat reached them. Ed, in fact, was grinning ear to ear, mustache bristling.

Cat could have killed him.

"Where *were* you?" she screamed.

Ed looked up at her and blinked, the grin fading just a bit. "Huh?"

"Huh? *Huh?* How can you ask *huh?*" She was breathing harder than Ed despite the fact that he'd just been the victim in a werewolf Hit-and-Run. And trembling a lot harder, too. "Where were you, Ed? I was almost raped."

The last of Ed's smile disappeared. Sitting up, he touched a mark just above his left eyebrow that Cat hadn't noticed. Her first thought was that it was a shadow or smudge ... until she saw the blood.

"What happened?"

"When I saw what that pervert was trying to do to you, I put down the camera and was halfway to the door handle ... when I knocked myself out on the door frame." He touched the wound and grimaced. "Some superhero I turned out to be. It's a good thing our boy showed when he did, isn't it?"

Cat took a deep breath and turned to scan the restless shadows that surrounded them, but he was gone. *Lucius* was gone.

"Yeah, it was."

"Here, take this and be careful," Ed said, handing her the camera when she turned around. "I don't know how many more tumbles that thing can take. Now, as for myself ..."

Once free of the camera, he vaulted to his feet like a bronze-medal gymnast. "Oh my God, this is fucking unbelievable! Shit, what a shot. That *real* Denver Werewolf ... and I mean *R. E. A. L!* Christ, if Tanner doesn't cream his jeans on this one, I'm going to think about getting that sex change I've always wanted." Concern played on his face now as he reached out to take her arm. "But how about you? Are you okay?"

Cat licked some moisture back onto her lips. "Yeah. I'm fine."

"Good girl." Concern gone, joy returned as he took back

his camera and danced a jig with it. "Jesus, what a shot. What a shot! You get anything?"

Anything? Cat frowned. "What?"

Concern again. "On tape. Aw, geeze, Cat, don't tell me you forgot about the recorder."

No, she didn't forget about the recorder . . . nor about the man who'd tried to rape her and was tossed away into the river like just so much garbage. Cat didn't forget anything. But neither did C. K. Moselle when *she* reached into the pocket of Cat's parka and pulled out the minirecorded.

If either of them—Cat or her professional alterego—reported the attack—and rescue—to proper authorities (like good citizens) they'd both end up spending the night in a dingy Interrogation Room trying to explain.

And that wouldn't do either of them any good.

"I think it picked up," *C. K.* said, punching the PLAY button.

Lucius's voice sounded even less human on the recording, but she'd be able to transcribe it without too much hassle. It was, after all, just part of *her* job.

"Got it."

"*Yes!* Way to go, Kit-Cat m'wee love." Ed's grin reattached itself to his face. "God, we got it, you know that? We've got proof that this guy . . . excuse me, this *monster* really flippin' exists! Shit, a Pulitzer is just the beginning! We could get our own *National Geographic* special out of this! WoooWHOOOO!"

Ed threw back his head and howled. And even though it didn't sound anything like a wolf . . . *or Lucius* . . . Cat fainted.

And took C. K. Moselle down with her.

12

Cat woke up slumped down across the Volvo's front seat, staring up through the fly-specked, dust-streaked windshield at a grinning blond man.

The man smiled, showing teeth that would make a horse envious.

And Cat screamed.

"LUCIUS!"

The man wasn't taken aback at all by the scream.

"Carmine," he said, coming around to the open window on the driver's side. "I'm Ed's . . . cousin."

Blinking, Cat pushed herself up and over, molding her hip and shoulder into the passenger-side door. There was enough ambient street light for her to see the scars that crisscrossed the man's face.

Cat pressed closer to the door when the man reached in and offered his hand. He was wearing a black, muscle tee, his arms bare except for the dark tattoos embedded in the flesh.

"And you're Cat. Pleased to meet you."

Cat jumped when their flesh met. He was even hotter to the touch than Ed was. Than Lucius—

"Hey, cut the charm before she starts screaming again, will you?"

Carmine dropped Cat's hand instantly, a glimmer of guilt and something darker crossing beneath the scars on his face as Ed came bounding up to the passenger-side door, a steaming mug of something sloshing in his hand. Tapping the window glass with a knuckle, he motioned for her to roll it down and slipped the mug in. The scent of hot chocolate filled the car.

Cat took a timid sip, but was ready to spit it out if it turned out to be anything like Ed's "tea."

He noticed and chuckled. "I swear, it's *only* instant cocoa. Not even with marshmallows. Carmine suggested it. Said you probably fainted because of low blood sugar." Ed winked past her. "Carmine was a medic in 'Nam. Knows all about that kind of stuff."

Cat nodded at the ex-soldier over the rim of the mug. The hot chocolate seemed to be just that—hot chocolate, rich and creamy. "Thanks."

"No problem. Any . . . friend of my cuz is a friend of mine."

"And with that," Ed said through the open window, "he departs."

The dark look flickered again as the man stood and walked around the front of the car to the curb and stopped. Although he was talking too softly for Cat to catch more than a word or two, the tone was definitely not friendly despite the grin on his face.

". . . sure you want . . . to go?"

Ed, on the other hand, remained his usual, boisterous self.

"Sure as snow falling on little green apples, *cuz*," he said as he popped open the driver's side door and folded himself in behind the wheel. "My Kit-Cat's a lot stronger than she looks. Aren't you?"

"What?" Cat looked first at Ed and then at his cousin. The man was a lot bigger than Ed, all muscle where Ed was mostly sinew, but there was something about the way he stood there, hunched ever so slightly at the shoulders, that gave her the impression he wouldn't have challenged the older, smaller man if his life depended on it. "Oh. Yeah."

"See!" Ed yelled through her opened window as if she'd answered him. "I told you. Now, you and the boys have fun and I'll be back as soon as I drop my fair damsel off at her castle. Okay?"

Even Cat caught the dismissal in the last word. Pretending to study the top of the mug, she watched the man turn away from the car and walk stiff-legged up the narrow walk of a two-story brick Victorian. Ed just didn't look the type for wrought-iron railings, window awnings and a brace of stone lions guarding a stained-glass door inset.

"You live here?" she asked. And cringed at the incredulous tone in her voice.

He apparently heard it, too, but laughed.

"Renting," he said as he started the car and pulled away into the empty street. "We got a real good deal on it."

"We?"

"Yeah." He glanced back at the house, smiling. Cat did the same just in time to see the curtains in the front and upstairs windows flutter back into place. "Got a lot of mouths to feed and so far I'm keepin' 'em that way. Knock on plastic."

Ed thumped the Volvo's steering wheel and Cat laughed.

Kids. She never would have thought of Ed as a family man.

"Shit!."

It was the one word that described the situation he currently found himself in. *Shit!* But the cold and clammy kind that seeped into your jeans and sucked the warmth right out of you all the way down to the bone. Not the good, hot, steaming kind that came out of a genetic throwback after you'd beaten him to within an inch of his death and left him in the gutter.

No. It wasn't the good kind. Especially since he was the one crumpled facedown, his nose crushed against concrete while somewhere in the distance, water gurgled past.

Where am I? And why am I lying facedown in cold shit?

Good questions, but ones that weren't just going to answer themselves.

He opened his eyes as he lifted his head. Lights from the city danced across a wide swatch of dark water just a few inches from him, keeping time to the pounding behind his eyes and throbbing in his nose.

Still in pretty much of a daze, he pushed himself up to his knees and forgot all about his crushed nose until he ran a good portion of his muck-soaked arm under it.

"SHIT!"

But, if nothing else, the pain did wonders to clear his mind. While the Platte raced by, lapping gently against the concrete lip of the channel, the pieces of the evening's events began to sort themselves out.

He'd just been about to take revenge for all the injustices that had been heaped upon the Great Aryan Race by sticking it to that obviously inbred reporter when . . .

When . . . *what?*

Something had happened. Something not exactly as he'd planned.

He looked down at the front of his pants. Although hidden behind a layer of muck and mud, his zipper was open and his jockeys pulled down right where he liked them. But his dick, shriveled and cowering against his belly, didn't feel like it'd gotten any.

Damn.

It took three tries before he managed to get to his feet . . . but when he finally did and zipped up, he remembered *everything* that happened.

The bitch had teased him, lured him into trying to get him to divulge the truth about himself. About being the *Denver Werewolf.* And he was about to . . . by God, he was about to show her *exactly* what a werewolf was like when her partner had jumped him from behind . . . or maybe partners. Yeah, had to be more than one. A single man couldn't take a werewolf in a clean fight.

She'd set him up.

She'd humiliated the Aryan Race.

And she would pay.

In flesh and blood and bone.

He'd only been planning to rape her, stick it to her so hard she'd be walking bowlegged for a month, but now . . . now he was going to tear her apart.

Closing his eyes he lifted his chin to the cold, cloud-scudded sky and howled.

And was answered. In six-part harmony.

He opened his eyes to see a large pale wolf staring down at him from the edge of the embankment above. The scars on his muzzle crinkled as he pulled back his lips in what looked to be a smile.

Lucius watched from across the river as the pack tore the man apart. He felt no responsibility for the man's death. Nor did he feel remorse.

The man deserved to die. If Lucius hadn't stopped him, he would have raped her, possibly even killed her when he was done.

But no man deserved to die like that.

They were efficient hunters. The big Alpha Male had distracted the would-be rapist while a smaller, darker male scrambled down a shadow-thick culvert. At a silent, prearranged signal, the smaller male darted forward and slashed at the man's ankles, hamstringing him.

The scream that followed—high and sharp—filled the night, but Lucius doubted if anyone heard. Or, if they had, cared.

The city was, in its own way, as savage as the beasts across the river. And as heartless.

Other sounds replaced the screams almost instantly—growls and gurgles and snap of bone. Lifting his chin, Lucius turned his face into the wind and breathed their scent into him. They were animals, only partially hidden by the man skins they wore during the day. And *man* skins only. They had no females with them.

A pack of bachelor weremen. He'd never heard of such a thing.

A series of low, mewling whines pricked the loose hairs

at the back of Lucius's neck. Hand lifting to the heavy silver at his throat, he watched another wolf, his silver pelt shimmering in the darkness, walk stiff-legged from the shadows. The others gave way at the Silverback's approach, cowering as he approached, then turning onto their backs to expose the soft flesh of their throats.

His scent was familiar.

Lucius tightened his grip on the necklace. *His scent was familiar. The same that filled the air right before the man appeared with the camera. Right before. Her friend. The man with the camera.*

Only the big male Lucius first mistook for the Leader met the newcomer face-to-face, one paw resting protectively on a denuded section of rib cage, hackles going to points along the back of his neck.

Testosterone bled into the cold wind, but the challenge was neither given fully nor accepted. It was, Lucius decided as he watched the males snap and snarl at each other, a longstanding debate that would, one night, come to a head.

But not tonight.

The tension was broken when the Beta Male lifted his paw off the dead man's ribs and moved away. Even at the distance that separated them and without willing his eyes into hunting vision, Lucius could see that the pack's bellies were all full. Fighting and reestablishing loyalties were things for lean times . . . at least that's what MOTHER always said.

Lucius watched the pack of weremen devour every last scrap of flesh there was and then snap open the bones for the sweet, buttery marrow.

It was disgusting and a sin against all his kind had become.

And he almost choked on the drool that filled his mouth.

13

The Silverback belched contentedly and wiped his muzzle against a fan of ribs. They'd done a good job with this one, he thought, a nice quick kill without rupturing any of the internals and enough choice meat for a light nosh.

He'd have to remember to buy them a round of beers come happy hour.

Muffled huffs and muzzle snaps pulled his attention from thoughts of celebration to the Juveniles tussling in the blood wash that covered the sloping ground. Caught up in their excitement, the Silverback lowered his head and carefully nuzzled the sloshing bladder sack away from the gut pile. Although the man had pissed himself profusely as he died, there was still enough left to play with.

Rolling downhill, the bladder ruptured against a shard of glass and spilled its perfume into the cold night. The Juveniles were on it in a second, rolling in the wonderful richness of the scent and snapping at the steaming clouds that now trailed from them and the ground.

The first snowflakes began to drift down while the Silverback clambered up the embankment to stand next to his second-in-command.

The Beta was watching the man across the river.

"is that him?" the scarred male asked.

The Silverback decided to let the slight go . . . for the moment . . . and looked across the black-green of the river to the tiny, shimmering flame that glowed in the darkness. Surrounded by shades of green, the werewolf was the color of fire.

"that's him, boys. the denver werewolf."

The Beta Male lowered his head and growled softly. But there was no anger in the sound, no challenge. It was fear, pure and simple. There had been stories about werewolves, *real* werewolves, but that's just what they were supposed to be.

Stories.

Just like the kind his sweet little Kit-Cat writes. Wrote. Before this.

Thinking about her—the touch of her skin and the secret invitation that wafted up from between her thighs—pushed his cock, hard and hot, from its protective sheath of skin and into the cold night. The shock, although pleasant, was enough to bring the Alpha Male back to the more immediate problem.

"he doesn't look so tough," the Beta sneered through the frost gathering on his muzzle.

"he's tough enough."

Lifting his head, the Silverback tried to catch a faint whiff of the scent he'd smelled right before the big redback had jumped in to save his Kit-Cat; but the wind was coming in from the north, playing favorites—delivering their scent to him, but not the other way around.

The snow began to fall harder, covering the night and the activities that had taken place in it with a soft, cold blanket. There'd be more snow before morning. Much more, freezing the city solid.

But across the black river the flame still burned bright.

"blizzard's coming," the Silverback said to no one in particular but everyone in general. *"let's get home."*

The older males instantly began trudging up the embankment, but the Juveniles—like kids everywhere—ignored the command and continued playing. Even though there was little left to play with. The neo-Nazi had been reduced to little more than chewed bones and regurgitated piles of sinew glistening in the snow.

One of the younger Juveniles had ripped the man's face from its skull and had it draped over his muzzle in a parody of the ghoul mask he'd worn a few months back for Halloween.

Frost clung to the shredded cheeks and scalp and ringed the eyeholes and gaping mouth. What a waste.

"either eat that or put it down," the Silverback barked. *"and the rest of you haul tail or i'll do it for you."*

Haunches tucked down nice and tight, the juveniles headed uphill, the MAN mask discarded, facedown, in the snow.

The Silverback watched them join the older males and head toward the small park just beyond the construction site where he'd left the car.

What he told Kit-Cat was right . . . they hadn't been that far from the house they had rented from a lovely old couple who'd been their first meal after crossing into Colorado. The pack had made the run in less than ten minutes. He'd driven because, as he liked to remind the young, rank did have its privilege.

He stopped the Beta Male before he turned to follow.

"you go ahead," the Silverback said. *"we'll meet you back at the house, and you youngsters make sure to shower before climbing into bed. I just did laundry yesterday and I don't want those sheets smelling like you do now."*

There was a chorus of groans and moans and mutterings, but none of them complained loud enough to warrant a reprimand across the muzzle.

"Myron," he called out to the dark gray adult bringing up the rear, *"you make sure they wash."*

A jet of steam trailed from the male's muzzle as he nodded and urged the pack into a slow lope.

"what is it?" the Beta Male asked when they were alone.

The Silverback met the lesser male's eyes and then jerked his muzzle to the opposite side of the river. The werewolf was still there, a thin mantle of snow marking the fiery line of his shoulders and head.

As he watched, the werewolf lowered his arm and a bright white flash erupted from the glow above his chest.

"do you see what he's wearing around his neck?" he asked.

"no . . . it looks like . . ." The Beta Male's jaw snapped shut, the sound made louder in the gathering white silence. *"it can't be."*

"what can't?"

"it looks like . . . silver but it can't be."

"why not?"

"because silver's the only thing that can kill."

The Silverback turned his head and looked at the lesser male through the swirling flakes.

"when are you going to stop believing in fairy tales?" he asked.

Moonset.

And darkness before the dawn.

Then dawn and darkness again.

And in this way a week passed unnoticed.

14

The blizzard that everyone, with the exception of the
local weather-guessers, had predicted, came and buried the
city in eighteen inches of snow.

Trees that had stubbornly clung to the last of their foliage
were snapped and broken for their vanity. Branches the size
of telephone poles poked out of blue-tinted drifts like skeletal
hands pleading for salvation.

More than one car trying to traverse the downtown diag-
onals found itself spun around like a top on glass and added
to the snow-covered landscape.

People slipped, power went out, schools began accumu-
lating snow days, gangs declared truces until the spring thaw,
and water mains burst; but Denver didn't shut down.

The Queen of the Prairie had weathered worse storms than
this one.

Newspaper vans, ambulances, police cars, and buses followed the paths made by snowplows and gravel trucks, and
life continued much as it had before the blizzard.

And the Denver Werewolf.

Lucius rolled his shoulders beneath the dinner jacket he was obliged to wear while in the Family Home and watched MOTHER's reflection in the frosted windowpane. The wine in her goblet, identical to the quickly depleting collection back at the apartment, glowed red in the firelight behind her.

Raising his, Lucius sipped at the aged Merlot and exhaled the bouquet through his nose. He watched MOTHER watching him in the glass.

And she would continue to watch, in volatile silence, until he turned or made some other motion to indicate that he was ready to continue their little "discussion."

No matter how long it took.

Not that he had to be anywhere that evening.

The second night of continuous snow had taken care of even the most loyal of O'Connell's clientele, turning the pub into a brightly lit, hops-scented mausoleum. The third night burst the water main and flooded out the basement.

Since then, Lucius and the rest of the staff had been on "leave." All of which he spent standing at the balcony window, staring down at the snow-covered garden. Thinking . . . although MOTHER had another name for it.

"If you're finished brooding," she'd said that morning over the phone, "the Family needs to speak to you."

Needs, Lucius thought watching her reflection watching his. *Demands* was more like it. Hers . . . not the Family's.

It had taken almost an hour to drive the three miles from his apartment to the Family estate in Washington Park. University Boulevard was a skating rink but deserted. Hunched over the wheel and praying under his breath each time he skidded through a red light instead of stopping, Lucius felt the muscles in his back and arms tense long before he came to the ten-foot-high stone fence that surrounded the home in which he'd been born.

He hated coming *home* even in decent weather.

Lucius twirled his goblet slowly between thumb and forefinger as he turned to face their silent stares. Silent, that is, except for Scooter.

"Ah," his twin said from the pile of velvet pillows in front of the roaring fire, can of Coors raised in salute, "the great man turns. So what do you think about the article, Alpha? Did the little lady capture your *true* essence?"

MOTHER slapped the arm of her chair, demanding, and getting, silence. Light from the fire wove new textures across the already intricate design of the silver necklace she wore.

Lucius listened to the fire snap and sizzle as he crossed the room to the small table where the newest issue of *QUEST* lay.

The cover photo beneath the headline was a retouched publicity shot from the old *Beauty and the Beast* television series. In this picture, however, the Beast looked less like a tormented Man-Lion than a cross between a sheepdog and scarecrow.

> LOVE HATH NO FURY
> FORBIDDEN LOVE OF THE *DENVER WEREWOLF*
> — BY C. K. MOSELLE

It might have been for the best if he'd let the boy shoot her on the bus after all.

"So what's she like in the sack, Alpha? You do all the howling or does she?"

Lucius ignored his twin and met his mate/MOTHER's eyes.

"I honestly don't understand why all of you are so concerned about this. This . . . *paper* regularly does columns devoted to Elvis sightings. Not to mention their contention that AIDS is actually a government plot to deal with overpopulation."

To better illustrate his point, Lucius set the goblet of unfinished wine down and picked up the paper. LOVE HATH NO FURY indeed. Taking a deep breath, he held the paper in one hand and thumped one of the juicier subtext teasers with his finger.

" '*Woman impregnated by chemicals in her drinking water.*' Or, if that doesn't do it for you, how about '*Man born without head graduates college with perfect 4.0.*' " He chuckled when no one else did and shook his head. "These are comic books for the unimaginative, MOTHER. These particular stories are only interesting because they're local. In another month or so something else will be the hot new item."

"Another *month*?" The muscles in MOTHER's arms and back stiffened as if she'd suddenly been transformed into marble. "Do you honestly think that I will allow this to go on for one more *day*?"

"Forgive me, MOTHER," a soft voice said, "but Lucius is right. No one really believes these stories."

Silence, heavy and cold, slithered into the room and curled itself around the chair in which Cybil, the Family's Beta Female, sat. Pale and blond, nordic in look and size, she was the only fertile female allowed to consistently challenge MOTHER'S authority.

At least in minor matters.

Like this.

Lucius glanced over at her and winked. She smiled back, then quickly looked down to shush the two Juvenile females sitting on cushions at her feet. Only the younger of the two, the one she was still wet-nursing, took the hint; the second, Halona, continued to giggle into her cupped hands.

Halona was his first female whelp—his and the Bitch's. The pack's next Alpha Female. Hair the color of spun copper and eyes as pale as his were dark, she possessed the best qualities of himself and their MOTHER. There was no question in Lucius's mind that she would be the Family's next Alpha Female. All indications pointed to it. At the moment her scent was still that of innocence, but under the surface he, and all the other males, could smell the ripeness they'd come to recognize as that belonging to a Free Breeder.

When her time came, she would find a HUMAN mate.

To keep the hybrid line strong.

After Lucius had taken her virginity and produced the next Alpha Male.

As was tradition.

Cocking his head to one side, Lucius raised one finger to his lips and smiled as she fell silent and lowered her eyes demurely to her lap.

It wouldn't be long now . . . a year or two at the most and he would carry her one night, to the secluded bower of trees behind the house, to produce the next generation of leaders. Father and lover, a bond so strong that it made him dizzy.

"Is it true?"

The paper rustled in Lucius's hands as he looked at his MOTHER/mate over the top of it.

"Is what true, MOTHER?"

A soft *ping* answered his obviously stupid question. MOTHER held the goblet's bowl clenched in her fingers while the narrow stem lay across the folds of her velvet gown. Lucius almost smiled, knowing at last, where he got his penchant for crystal destruction.

"Don't play the fool, Alpha," she said as calmly as before. "That's your brother's position. I asked if there was any truth in the article. Is there?"

"That I love her? No," Lucius answered honestly. "I don't even know her."

MOTHER snorted angrily though her thin, aristocratic nose.

"Then why didn't you let her die? She's only human."

Eyes that were the genetic source for Halona's burned into his.

"No," he said again, "she's not."

New sounds whispered through the firelit room. Tucked into the far corner, beneath the mounted heads of their ancestors, the bachelors huddled around Kieran, their chosen leader, their voices low and rumbling, their excitement at the promise of a possible new breeding source evident by the almost visible waves of testosterone that filled the air above them. Their eyes glowed green in the flickering firelight.

In their own corner directly opposite their male counterparts, the nonbreeding females stilled children that were not theirs except to raise while offering their own, darker thoughts on the subject. Their scent was bitter, tainted with envy and regret.

At Cybil's feet, Halona yawned . . . unimpressed by his announcement.

MOTHER didn't appear any more enthusiastic. There was

nothing in her scent to indicate any of the emotions she might have been feeling.

"Are you sure, Alpha, or is this just wishful thinking on your part?"

Lucius fought the urge to hurl his goblet across the room, settling instead to open the paper to the indicated page on which the article began. There, below the secondary bold-faced heading I KNOW HE LOVES ME was her picture. C. K. Moselle's.

He could still smell her . . . the pungent, spicy animal hidden beneath the thin layer of human flesh and Vanilla Fields.

"She's a breed, but I don't think . . . no, I'm positive she doesn't know it."

"Breed or pure," MOTHER said, "you should have killed her to protect the Family."

Lucius set the paper down on the table and lifted his glass, drained the contents, and felt the small tingle at the back of his throat from the aconite-laced mulling spice.

"She's the least of the Family's concerns," he said, watching the firelight that seemed, for the moment, trapped within the goblet's bowl. "A pack of weremen has moved into the area. I've seen them. One of them was . . . with her."

The goblet's stem shattered like ice against the marble floor when MOTHER stood. Her flesh had become the same shade as her pelt, ghostly white in the firelight.

"That's not possible," she said, and for the first time that Lucius could remember, sounded her age. "Our kind destroyed those mutants centuries ago."

Lucius let her get to the mantel, above which the head of the Family's patriarch hung. Lips curled back from fangs the size of a MAN's finger, glass eyes shining, the great gray wolf smiled down at the generations of his progeny. Family legend said that MOTHER had been his firstborn. But even the cubs didn't believe that story.

Her own mounting board, however, hung empty to the great wolf's right. Lucius's mount hung at the left.

Looking at it, at where his own head would hang someday, had never bothered him.

Until now.

Lucius watched his MOTHER reach up and clasp the silver necklace. And she wasn't the only one. Around the room, hidden in shadows, hands slowly reached toward the silver lockets and collar that embraced each throat. Lucius balled his hands into fists.

"It's not possible," MOTHER repeated.

"Yeah," Kieran said, leaving his place of protection, white-blond shoulder-length hair streaming behind him. He'd gotten his looks from his mother, Cybil . . . his temper from Lucius. "We've all heard the stories about Viktoras's killing every weremen to avenge his mate's death. There aren't any weremen."

He stopped on the opposite side of the table, a smirk on his thin lips. At six-feet he only had another two inches to grow before they'd be looking at each other eye to eye.

If he lived that long.

If *either* of them did.

Lucius grabbed the boy's throat just above the silver-spiked dog collar he wore.

"Just like there aren't supposed to be any werewolves, isn't that right, boy?"

He released his hold with a backward thrust and watched the adolescent stumble a step before regaining his footing. And dignity. Lucius watched the younger version of himself stalk back to the fawning words of his lessers as his own flesh begged for transformation.

It was like an itch that couldn't be scratched.

"Where are they from, Alpha?" Griffin, one of the middle-rank males asked. He held his mate, a quarter-breed named Alana he'd found on a business trip.

All eyes, with the exceptions of MOTHER and Scooter's, converged on Lucius.

Without warning, the beast living in his skin ripped the silver from their throat and hurled it across the room. The pain where the necklace had cut into the back of his neck dissolved beneath the exhilaration of metamorphosis.

"Until a week ago," Lucius said through an elongating jaw, "we thought we were the only true Lycanthropes in Denver. Now we know better."

"Or worse, little brother," Scooter said softly. The flames behind him turned his shaggy mane into a fiery halo. He looked like a rather shopworn Avenging Angel.

"Or worse," Lucius agreed.

MOTHER cleared her throat and turned from the frozen gaze of their most noble ancestor to meet Lucius's eyes. Her fingers played across the silver at her throat.

"Could she . . . this woman be of our line? Could this be what made you . . . protect her?"

Lucius felt his shoulder blades rise to the back of his skull as his pelvis reshaped and tilted him forward. The seams of the turtleneck sweater and jeans he'd chose to wear reached their limits and burst around the newly formed musculature.

A moment later, Lucius stood before his Family clad only in the dinner jacket, carefully tailored with hidden pleats to accommodate any instant change on the part of its wearer.

"I don't know, MOTHER. I never thought of that."

"I want to see her," MOTHER said. "Arrange it."

Then without another word and with the ease of a practiced courtesan, she unhooked the silver from around her neck and placed it on the mantel beneath her supposed FA-THER's head.

"We've become careless," she growled, as the flesh tightened the wrinkles around her mouth and nose. "Thinking we were the only runners of the night."

HER voice deepened with each inch her silver-white muzzle extended.

"And now frightened. No more. Tonight my *children, we run again. and god help those mutants if we happen to run into them.*"

When SHE opened her voice into the darkness, Lucius was the first to answer the call.

Not because he wanted to.

But because he *had* to.

15

"Oh-God-Oh-Jesus-Oh-shit, oh-God-oh-Jesus-Oh-shit, oh-God-oh-Jesus—"

That had become the morning's mantra, repeated soft and frosty by the two uniformed officers who'd originally answered the call, the suited investigators, and her own team of overall-draped techs.

Criminalist technician, Helen MacEwen, however, kept silent and busy and tried to remember if she'd ever seen a crime scene that compared. Even the double smash and bash at the train yard had been less . . . *interesting*.

Usually she took spiteful joy by trying to nauseate at least one uniform by giving a play-by-play, *detailed* description of what she was doing: snapping picture of the deceased, taking fingerprints of the deceased, bagging the remains of the deceased and even, like in the train yard, *scooping up* the deceased.

Uniforms were three points, seasoned investigators were ten.

Her own people didn't count.

This morning the number of nausea points added up to a big, fat zero.

Which was pretty close to the amount of viable evidence she was going to get off the scene.

"Fuck," she muttered as she stood to look down at the pile of bones which was all that was left of *the deceased*. No new piece of evidence, or even an old one, suddenly jumped up and waved at her.

Her team had done all it could—chopping out as much of the frozen sheets of blood as they could, gathering up the shredded remains of what might or might not be the deceased's clothing, and, of course, what might or not be the deceased himself.

That much Helen was sure of. That the deceased had been male. They had the remains of the face on ice.

"Those two kids still here, Ross?" Helen called as she looked up the steep embankment where the brace of detectives were trying to look unaffected by the morning's events. Helen only knew one of the men, the bigger of the two. They'd worked together on a number of cases and although he could be a demanding son of a bitch at times, Ross Brown never once asked for anything she couldn't deliver.

His partner on the other hand . . .

"Last time I checked they were working on their third candy bar. EMT says they're pretty much in shock, so I don't think we'll get much more out of them than we already did."

Helen nodded and looked down at the glistening skull at her feet. The boys, brothers, had sneaked out early, determined to get in a few good sledding runs before their school reopened later that morning. Their parents hadn't even known they weren't in bed until they came screaming back into the house . . . the younger of the two, a fourth-grader, holding on to the thing he originally thought was a discarded Halloween mask.

After taking another file photo, Helen marked down the time and looked back upslope to find Ross's new partner, ferret of face and red of hair, absently kicking at a frozen clump of blood.

"Hey, Ross," she shouted, "keep your man on a leash, will ya? He's probably destroying valuable evidence."

The new cop jumped back, looking shamefaced.

"Hey, Helen, cut him some slack," Ross shouted back through the cloud of frost his breath had created. "Guy just transferred here from Kissimee P.D. a week ago. Poor guy's never seen snow before let alone a skinned face."

The new man dropped the look of shame and smiled, winking in Helen's direction. "Not true."

"Oh?"

"Yeah, I saw *Gorky Park* three times."

"Those were skinned skulls, not skinned faces."

A puzzled look crossed the man's face. "Isn't that the same thing."

Ross looked down at Helen and sighed before turning his attention back to his new partner. "And this is what they call a detective down in the Sunshine State. Christ, I would have thought they taught you guys the difference between a skinned skull and skinned face."

"Well, maybe not, but I think I could tell you the difference between a baboon's butt and your face. Want me to tell you?"

Helen burst out laughing. The new guy might look like a ferret, but he was human after all.

Which was more than she could say for the kid's mom.

Word was that the mom had been more upset to discover the boys had been sledding across the frozen Platte than in what they actually found.

Until the first news reporters showed up. And then it was all hysterics and Oscar-quality dramatics.

"It was the Denver Werewolf?" the mother had said into the camera as she clutched her sons amid the frozen blood and dismembered bones. "Oh God, it was, wasn't it? I just read this morning's supplement, but I didn't think it was this close. Practically right in our very own neighborhood. See, I *told* you boys he was real. And if you two ever pull this kind of stunt again, I swear I'm going to call him up and have him tear you apart, too!"

If the kids were in shock, *that* little statement was probably what caused it.

Some people, Helen thought, *just shouldn't ever become mothers.*

MOTHER had let them run, all right. Twice around the estate and then—*wonder of wonders!*—out into the great wild world! For an hour.

The youngsters scrambling across the ice on Smith Lake, using their hind claws as makeshift skates while the rest of the Family was content to watch.

MOTHER had stayed on alert—ears pricked forward, nose constantly working the wind, ice-blue eyes watching the shadows.

It was the cold that finally drove them back to the warmth of the great hall's fire. That and bed. Even though none of his adult siblings had jobs outside the home, there were still the many Family investments to watch and care for.

He'd been the only one to leave. The black sheep . . . in wolf's clothing.

Lucius stretched on his way to the front door and listened to his spine creak. Just a little past one in the afternoon and the soles of his feet still tingled from running on the ice. Hell, his entire body still ached.

Alpha or not, he should have known better than to try and show off. Even though he was showing off for Halona. And everyone knew it. She had teased him, raising her soft hackles and growling only to turn and skate away the moment he took notice. Her little rump twitching. Her scent luring him onto the ice.

The third or fourth time she'd skated in close, he took the bait and leapt after her, his hind claws digging deep, leaving star-shaped wounds on the ice.

The adolescents had cheered him on. Then cheered all the louder when he lunged at her and missed. He landed, head-first, in a snow-covered hedge as Halona, and everyone else, howled with laughter.

When he'd finally untangled himself, MOTHER only glared at him, and barked that he should really act his age.

Yeah, maybe he should. And maybe she should act her age and die.

The low rumbling of his stomach accompanied Lucius as

he stepped from the carpeted living room to the cool marble tiles of the foyer of his apartment and he promised to get it something to eat just as soon as he checked how well the Broncos were doing. He had a side bet going with one of the building's security guards—each time the Broncos won by more than two touchdowns, the man could count on getting an equal number of free drafts. If the Broncos lost, Lucius would have his afternoon newspaper hand-delivered to his door.

Lucius opened the door and smiled down at the neatly folded paper.

A yawn began to work its way around the corners of Lucius's smile as he bent down. Both the yawn and smile stopped in mid-snarl.

"I should have killed her when I had the chance," he whispered.

"I should have married her when I had the chance!" Tanner Boswell said as he puffed and strutted back and forth behind his desk. Cat had never seen her boss as . . . enthusiastic before and couldn't decide if she liked it or not. "Now just you watch—she's going to take the first offer that comes her way and leave."

He stopped strutting long enough to sigh.

"To be honest, boss, I don't think you would have had much chance with Kit-Cat," Ed said as he reached over to take her hand and pat it. He was dressed almost as conservatively as the night before—dark jeans (possibly the same ones) and a white Ozzy Osbourne sweatshirt. "Besides, if anyone's going to marry her it's gonna be me. Ain't that right, Ms. Moselle?"

Cat was saved having to answer when Tanner clapped his hands together and whooped.

"You really are delusional, Mr. Ed. Now, let go of my star reporter's hand before I have you arrested for indecent propitious behavior." He waited until Ed had done just that before dropping into his chair. The squeal tore through Cat's head like a rusty spike. "Honey, you just put us on the other side of the sheets!"

Cat shook her head. "What?"

"He means you just made us legitimate," Ed translated. "We're on the same level as the big boys now, thanks to you and Mister Werewolf."

"Oh."

"Oh, she says . . . the biggest thing to ever happen to *QUEST* and all she can say is 'oh.'" He was still smiling as he ran his hands over the two front pages on his desk. Although they differed slightly in story content, both afternoon editions of the *Post* and *News* held the Denver Werewolf responsible for the" ' . . . killing of a homeless man on the banks of the Platte' . . . God damn, children, it looks like we got the jump on the big boys this time."

Cat watched his hands slide from the newspapers to the thick manilla envelope that Ed had red stamped AREA 51-AUTHORIZED PERSONNEL ONLY. Inside were the minicassette's tape and the photos they hadn't used in her last article. Photos that were too dark and grainy to be used, because, Ed said, he hadn't wanted to give himself away by using a flash. Dark, yes. Grainy, very much so. But still clear enough for her to make out the vague outlines of herself and the would-be rapist. Of herself and the huge dark shape that had suddenly appeared behind the rapist as he tore at her clothes. Another shot, focused in tight, of fangs bared in what might almost look like a grin as he flung the rapist into the night.

And one more—Cat cringing on the cold ground while he knelt at her side, one clawed hand reaching tenderly toward her face.

He.

Him.

The Denver Werewolf.

Lucius.

Photos that couldn't be used, but that proved Ed had lied to her. A bit. He'd waited, taking shot after shot of her near rape and only decided to come to her rescue—before knocking himself out *(with the wound to prove it)*—after she was safe. Saved.

C. K. Moselle wanted to ask Ed about that, about why the hell he'd been sitting there, in the dark and taking pictures, while she was being assaulted. And *why* he'd suddenly decided to switch to flash? To scare away the big, bad wolf?

C. K. wanted answers. Cat was afraid of what those answers would be.

So neither of them asked.

"So, you think he did it?"

Cat's breath caught in her throat as she watched Tanner's fingers close around the envelope.

"Who?"

A look passed over Cat and landed on Ed. "Who? Who have we been talking about for the last couple of weeks? Your werewolf. You think he came back after rescuing you and killed the guy they just found?"

"Gee," a new voice suddenly asked, "we were just wondering the same thing."

Cat turned to look over her shoulder as two men, followed by the rather frazzled-looking receptionist, walked into Tanner's office.

"I'm sorry, Mr. Boswell," the receptionist said, hands fluttering uselessly in the air, "but they wouldn't wait for me to announce them."

"We find we get much better reactions that way," the first man said. He had red hair.

Cat stood up as he lifted his hand and smiled at her.

She knew fainting was a temporary loss of consciousness resulting from a decreased flow of blood to the brain and not, as many writers of bad romances would have readers believe, the product of overzealous emotions or hormones. Not that she had never used it as a convenient device if and when a character found herself trapped between the proverbial rock and hard place, or when nothing else seem likely to work.

People just didn't faint on cue, but lines like *"and then she fainted"* had saved Cat's editorial rump on more than one occasion. Fainting allowed the reader to add in the details—like what happened *after* Bigfoot's teenage love interest fainted at the hulking brute's hairy feet—without the writer having to go into details.

Ellipses were useful too. *And then she fainted* . . .

"C. K. Moselle?" the tall red-haired man said. Something flashed in his hand. Something silver.

People don't faint for no reason. But Cat had a reason.

So she fainted . . .

Again.

. . . this any more than you do, but her last article puts her . . . same place as the victim . . .

. . . listen? I said SHE coulda been the victim instead if he . . .

. . . mean he's real?

Cat tried to turn away from the noise, but when that didn't work she threw her arm over her eyes. The darkness seemed to help a little even if the noise on the other side of her arm continued.

"Hey, I think Sleeping Beauty is waking up. You okay, Kit-Cat?"

Cat lifted her arm just enough to see past the bulky sleeve of her sweater. Ed's face came into focus slowly, surrounded by cold white fluorescent light. He looked like a cut-rate Christ.

"What happened?" she whispered when a darker, less focused shadow stepped in to eclipse the light.

"You took one look at Mr. Detective over there, screamed, and hit the floor like a sack of manure," Ed said as he reached down to brush her cheek. His fingers were burning hot. Or maybe she was just cold.

"I screamed?" Cat asked while Ed helped her into a semisitting position. They—whoever they were—had moved her from Tanner's office to the employee lounge and laid her out on the futon/couch. The smell of stale espresso hung heavily in the air.

"Like a banshee with her bloomers on fire." Mustache bristling around a grin, Ed leaned forward and lowered his voice. "Not that I can blame you. The guy looks like a card-carrying member of the IRA, if you ask me. Probably NRA, as well. With maybe a little IRS thrown in to complete the alphabet soup."

Cat was about to smile when the tall, red-haired man tapped Ed on the shoulder and jerked a thumb in a not-so-subtle hint for them to switch places.

"Chin up, shoulders back, and don't forget the suicide pill we've secured in your molar. Good luck, 007."

Ed saluted as he stood up. Cat tucked her legs in under her as the man sat down, red hair shining in the light, silver *badge* gleaming.

It wasn't him. She didn't know who it was, having missed the introductions, but it wasn't him . . . it wasn't Lucius.

"Are you feeling better, Ms. Moselle?" the detective asked. There was the tiniest bit of an Irish accent beneath the Midwest twang in his voice. Cat bit the inside of her cheek to keep from smiling.

"Yes, thank you."

"I'm glad. So, from the beginning . . ." He smiled at her. The man who wasn't Lucius smiled at her and winked. He wasn't bad looking, in a pinched sort of way. "I'm Sergeant Freeland of the Denver Police Department and that's my partner, Detective Ross Brown. Do you think you feel up to answering a couple of questions for us?"

Cat heard Ed's growl from across the room.

"Hey, Kojak," he said, "shouldn't she like have a lawyer present or something first?"

The man's expression didn't change except that his thin-lipped smile got a little thinner.

"Do you feel you need a lawyer, Ms. Moselle? Because if you do, you may certainly have one . . . in fact, we can even obtain one for you if you can't afford one. But, if that's the case, I'm afraid we'll have to continue all this down at the station . . . right after I read you the rest of your rights. So what'll it be, hmm?"

"Jesus pal, when are you gonna bring out the rubber hoses?"

The man's expression finally changed when he turned to look at her long-haired protector.

"Back off, pal—"

"Pal?" Ed's eyes widened in mock horror.

"—and let the lady talk, okay? But don't worry, we still have a couple hundred questions we can ask you about your part in all this, and right now I don't care who I talk to. You or Ms. Moselle here . . . as far as we're concerned you're both in this up to your necks."

Cat was about to play her "poor dumb little me" routine and ask what exactly they were up to their necks in when she saw the AREA 51 envelope in the second detective's hand.

Their eyes met briefly, hers and Ed's, before he looked away. She was still looking at him when the red-haired detective turned his attention back to her.

"You and your . . . *friend* over there are already implicated in this last homicide, Ms. Moselle. But considering what those pictures show, if you cooperate I can promise you won't serve any time."

"Serve time?" She hadn't meant to be so loud, but apparently she was. The lounge door burst open and Tanner charged in, hands clenched, head swinging from side to side like a bull trying to decide which way to charge.

"Who's gonna serve time?" he bellowed. "And for what?"

The second detective, a nondescript dark-haired man in a matching nondescript suit, stopped the charge before it got halfway across the room.

"How about accessories after the fact for starts?" he bellowed back at Tanner. "You were all aware that a crime had been committed . . . hell, that *two* crimes had been committed, and you didn't do anything about it."

Tanner Boswell's rage melted like a chocolate chip on a hot stove.

"Hey, Ross, calm down," the red-haired good cop said to his partner's bad cop. It was a standard, time honored tradition that Cat had seen in every police series . . . but it was still amazing how well it worked in real life. "Those pictures you're holding are pretty good evidence for that case, but they also show Ms. Moselle here in danger. So, if you cooperate like I said, I'm sure we can work this all out without having to get the D.A. involved."

"Yeah, *Ross*," Ed added, "and let's make sure we all remember that she DID cooperate with you boys after the bus accident and you thanked her and sent her on her way. Or did we forget that little part of history?"

Color, deep and red, bloomed in both detectives' cheeks. Cat didn't think they'd forgotten that, but she was certain they didn't like to be reminded of it. Especially by someone who looked like Ed.

"Okay."

The good cop recovered first. "Okay what?"

"What do you want me to do?"

"Thank you, Ms. Moselle. Okay, let's go for the obvious—this guy really isn't a werewolf right?"

Cat looked at Ed who was still busy contemplating the lounge carpet. If she cooperated and told the truth, chances are she'd not only wind up in jail, but in the psycho ward of that fine facility.

"No," she said and watched Ed's gaze swing up to hers. "It's a costume. A really good costume."

"But he *thinks* he's a real werewolf, right?"

Cat nodded, and the dark detective clapped his hands, the envelope rattling.

"Okay, Ross," her detective mumbled, "you win. I owe you twenty. Now, Ms. Moselle . . . did you actually see this *man* kill the guy in those photos?"

Cat shook her head. "No, Lucius wouldn't d—" *Shit!*

A small notebook and pen instantly appeared in the man's hands.

"What's his name?"

shit shit shit shit

Cat leaned back against the futon and wondered if she could manage another impromptu faint.

"You might as well tell them, Kit-Cat," Ed said, arms folded across Ozzy Osbourne's wrinkles, "they'll find out anyway. His name's Lucius."

"Ed!"

He shrugged. "Can't protect a murderer, honey."

"Any last name?" Red-haired good cop asked.

"No." Cat sank her nails into the palms of both hands and glared at Ed. *How could he?* "And I don't even know if that's his real name or not."

The cop made a note of that in his notebook. "Probably not, but it gives us something to go on." He looked up at Cat and smiled. "You're being very helpful. How do you feel about going on television?"

A terrible coldness settled in the pit of Cat's stomach. Shivering, she pulled her legs up to her chest and wrapped her arms around them.

"Why?"

"Well," redhead said, "from your articles and . . . those pictures, it would seem that this Lucius has a special interest in you. One that we can exploit."

The coldness moved upward, freezing everything in its path.

"I don't understand what that has to do with my going on television." Cat tried to make her voice light, tried to smile, only to find that the cold had numbed her face.

Redhead smiled for her. "We're going to try and catch a werewolf, Ms. Moselle. And you're going to be the bait."

"Lucius. Yeah, that's right. L. U. C. I. U. S." He listened for a moment then shook his head as if the person on the other end of the phone could see him. "No. No last name, but we can get Jack to see what he can do.

"What? Yeah, I wouldn't have thought he'd be that stupid either, but hell . . . you know how it is when the scent is in the air and the ol' blood is pumping. Okay . . . so you *remember* what it's like."

He listened again, frowning.

"Look, trust me on this one, will you? If what I think about Big Red is right, we're all going to be swimming in bitches soon enough."

The sigh that echoed into the receiver tickled his ear. Christ, it had been a long time. Smiling, he plucked a pencil from the skull mug he'd picked up at some genre bookstore in California and beat a riff across its ceramic forehead.

Prominent among the clutter that covered the top of his desk were copies of the photos the dickheads had taken with them.

Kit-Cat getting saved from the Human Turd by the WereTurd.

Flipping the pencil end for end, he tapped the pink-rubber eraser against the WereTurd's left eye. Big Red. Lucius.

"The friggin' Denver Werewolf in the pelt. Asshole."

He tossed the pencil into a lopsided pile of file photos and started a minor avalanche. The remains of a baloney-onion-and-mustard sandwich disgorged itself from somewhere near the bottom of the pile and slid into view. There was only a little mold growing along one edge of the hardened crust.

He picked it up and sniffed it. Swallowed it whole without chewing only because it was wrong to waste food.

The resulting belch tasted even worse than the man-processed meat had.

"Huh? What? No Carmine, you don't have to do anything. Let Jack handle it, okay? I . . . What?"

He could feel the hairs prick at the back of his neck.

"No . . . repeat what you just said."

Silence pounded in his ear while the owner of the voice built up the nerve to repeat out loud what he'd mumbled a moment before. While he waited, his fingers found another pencil and broke it in two.

"What? Oh, I see. You don't like the idea. Well, when I start worrying about what you like or don't like, you can rip my throat out and pee in the hole, okay? Or is this whole thing a challenge? Is that the trip you're laying on me, dude?"

The whining sputter coming through the line was music to his ears. Carmine wouldn't offer a challenge until he knew what the score was . . . and that was something he wouldn't be figuring out for a while.

None of the pack would.

He hadn't stayed Alpha for this long by letting his people know which of his sleeves held the aces.

"Okay then," he said magnanimously, "chill and stay

loose. The cops are gonna do us more good than themselves
in this. The minute I have a name, Jack'll be able to run a
make. What? Yeah, right . . . even a monster has to have a
paper trail nowadays. And not just to line his cage. HAH!
C-man, you are a card and a half."

Jerk.

"Yeah, I'll be going with her for immoral support . . .
right, best-buddy status and all that." He forced himself to
chuckle at the lame joke just to show everything was back
to normal between them.

"Right, if everything goes as planned we'll be humping
more than street trash." *Or,* he thought, *I will.* "You too, bro.
Ciao."

He hung up without waiting to hear if the Beta Male had
anything else to say. Not that it mattered if he did or not.
Time was getting short, and there was a hell of a lot to do
before Kit-Cat made her television debut.

But that didn't stop him from picking up the lower half
of the busted pencil and begin scribbling the name of his
rival over and over and over across the front of the rescue
photo.

   lucius
   Lucius
   LUcius
   luCIUS
   LUCIUS

Ed decided it was a really stupid name. But one that would
look *marvelous* carved in marble.

In the middle of a tombstone.

16

Channel 4 thought the idea had merit, but didn't have an available "On the Spot" reporter they could spare to cover the story. So *very* sorry.

Channel 9 asked if it was some kind of sick publicity stunt.

Channel 7's receptionist was still laughing when she hung up.

The local FOX affiliate had their viewers to consider. Of *course* they would do the interview. After all, hadn't they already proven the existence of a government conspiracy concerning the Extra-Terrestrial autopsy?

Two and a half hours later, Cat found herself made-up and miked while she watched one of the *Nightly News* anchors strut and fret his part upon the tiny interview stage in one corner of the studio.

The questions—and answers—had been hastily written by a police psychologist who guaranteed they would bring the killer *(Lucius)* out in the open. She was to be portrayed as a victim, trapped by her own submissive tendencies and the delusion that he, the killer *(Lucius)* really was a supernatural monster.

All she had to do, they told her, was read the cue cards and look frightened.

Looking frightened hadn't been a problem, but Cat refused to go through with the interview when she first read her "answers" and no amount of coercion was going to change her mind. Period. End of discussion.

Until Ed talked to her.

If the police made good with their threats to put her in jail as an accessory, Lucius might get himself killed trying to rescue her.

No. There were no "mights" about it. He would get himself killed.

It was the way Ed said it, slow and calm and so utterly sure, that sent chills racing beneath her skin. Lucius would get himself killed if he tried to rescue her.

She had no choice but to play their word game and pray he wasn't watching the FOX network.

The interview lasted fifteen minutes, and by the time it was over Cat felt drained from the hot lights and her own fears. It was all she could do to thank the interviewer and his crew and get back to the makeup room without passing out.

She had just closed her eyes, face throbbing under its thick mask of foundation and blush, back pressed against the unforgiving canvas of one of the makeup chairs, when she heard footsteps in the hallway outside. The steps were slow and deliberate, as if someone was trying not to be heard.

Lucius.

She was sitting up, hands grasping the wooden armrests, eyes open and staring at the door's reflection in the table mounted mirror in front of her as the red-haired detective walked in.

"I thought you were asleep," he said by way of explanation. "Feel like talking a little?"

Cat nodded and watched his reflection take the seat next to her. It was easier, she decided, to look at the reflection of the man instead of the man himself. Would have been easier still if he'd just leave her alone.

Leave them both alone.

Her and Lucius.

Cat stared at her own reflection, all made up and with

nowhere to go. She looked just like a little girl who'd gotten into her mother's makeup. A little girl who was pretending to be all grown up.

Neither the detective nor his mirror image seemed to notice as "they" handed her a Styrofoam cup.

"Hope it's okay," the man in front of the mirror said. "Your friend said this is the way you take your coffee. Real cream and two sugars?"

Cat looked up to catch Ed's reflected nod before he stepped away from the door. He'd been hovering around her since they got to the studio . . . hell, *before* they got to the studio and she was certain he'd be waiting to drive her home through the icy streets when her little "talk" with the detective was done.

"Thanks," she said, taking the cup and sipping to show her gratitude. The coffee was perfect even though she couldn't remember telling Ed that was the way she liked it.

"You did great out there," the detective said, lifting his own cup toward his lips and stopping short to salute her. "It must be hard for you and I . . . we appreciate it."

Cat shrugged at his reflection.

"I think it'll get results."

Another shrug. What kind of results was the question. C. K. Moselle—not her—had pleaded with Lucius (they'd wanted her to repeat his name as often as possible) to turn himself in before he got hurt.

It was very tender and heart-wrenching.

For something done with very little rehearsal.

And it probably would work . . . unless he didn't watch the early-evening news on FOX or was stuck in rush-hour traffic somewhere or was busy doing whatever werewolves did when they weren't protecting poor, defenseless (*occasionally stupid*) tabloid reporters.

Cat swallowed the mouthful of coffee with an audible gulp.

"You know," the detective said, "I really am sorry about frightening you like that this morning. I mean, I never had a woman faint on me like that . . . at least not until after I asked her out."

Cat chuckled softly. "It's kind of embarrassing. I usually don't faint—" *Liar, liar, pants on fire!* "—much."

Now it was his turn to chuckle and he did; a low, slow sound that seemed to start in his toes and work its way up in echoes.

"Well, that's a relief." Shifting his cup to his left hand, he held out his right. "So why don't we start over . . . and please, if you feel like fainting let me know and I'll stop. Okay? Not getting light-headed, are you? Great. My name's John. Freeland. But everyone calls me Jack."

He kept his hand out until Cat, still chuckling, slipped hers into it for a quick snatch-and-pump. His fingers were still hot from holding the cup.

"Pleased to meet you, Ms. Moselle."

"Likewise, I'm sure," Cat answered, then quickly brought her hand back to the safety of her own cup. He seemed nice enough for what Ed had assured her was "your typical tight-tassed, narrow-minded flatfoot with self-deceptions of superiority." True or not, Jack Freeland would do well to try another brand of cologne. She caught the scent on her hand. It reminded her of sun-spoiled fruit and mildewed wool.

And Lucius.

Without being obvious (she hoped), Cat dropped her hand to her lap and rubbed it against the paper napkin in her lap.

"You know," *Jack* Freeland said, "I can understand why he's so taken with you. You're one of a kind . . . very special."

"He?"

"The Denver Werewolf." Freeland leaned forward, narrowing the distance between their chairs, his reflection shifting as he got closer . . . changing . . . the thin-lipped smile widening. "You're very special, indeed, Kit-Cat."

Cat screamed when Ed's reflection suddenly appeared between them. *Jack* got off his chair and backed away quickly. The smile had come and gone as if it never existed.

"Smooth move, Ex-lax," Ed said, smiling at them from the mirror. "This how you get a date? 'Cause if this is the best you can do I wanna grab a seat and see if it works. I'm always interested in new techniques. Even pathetic ones."

Cat watched their eyes in the glass with little concern until Jack Freeland reached into the inside pocket of his suit coat.

She was almost disappointed when he brought out a small white business card instead of a gun. After all, how many times does a girl get the chance to have two men fighting over her.

Two *men*. Werewolves excluded.

Ed snatched the business card out of the detective's hand before Cat could move.

"Oooo," he said flipping the card over, "and I'll bet this is your *private* number, isn't it?"

A number of emotions trickled across the man's face.

"Yes," he hissed, "and that's standard police procedure. Just in case she . . . wants to talk to me about . . . the case."

"It's so good to know you care," Ed said and slipped the card into the back pocket of his jeans. Which was just as well. Cat didn't think she'd be asking for it anytime soon.

Especially now.

"We'll keep in touch," Ed promised.

There was another moment of impotent glaring over the top of her head before the detective dropped his gaze to Cat.

"Just let me remind you, Ms. Moselle, that if you do hear from this . . . man Lucius and don't contact us, I will run you in as an accessory after the fact."

Ed winked at her from the glass as he stepped around and began massaging the stiffness from her shoulders. Old though he might be, his hands were strong, and in a moment Cat felt the tension begin to dissolve.

"I'm not sure, but I think I heard that same line on a rerun of *Law and Order* the other night. Or was it *NYPD Blue*? I get confused . . . they all sound alike. Oh *I* know—*Car 54, Where Are You?* Loved that show."

"Ed," Cat scolded as nicely as she could. "I promise, Detective Freeland, I'll let you know if anything happens." She held up three fingers. "Reporter's honor."

"Excuse me, Miss Moselle?"

Three sets of eyes stared into the mirror at the skinny young man standing in the door. He jerked a thumb off to the right.

"Telephone," he said. "You can take it in the director's booth."

"Undoubtedly our beloved boss wondering what the hell happened to us. Want me to take it, Kit-Cat?"

Cat thought about it long and hard before patting his hands still.

"No," she said as she slid from the canvas director's chair, "it's okay, I'll talk to him."

Cat backhanded a wave as she followed the stage hand toward the glass enclosed director's booth. The phone was similar to the multi-lines back at *QUEST*. Cat lifted the receiver to her ear and pressed the slowly pulsating HOLD light on line four.

"C. K. Moselle."

"You'd make an excellent actress, Ms. Moselle."

It wasn't Tanner Boswell.

"I—I, um." It took Cat a moment to remember which muscles to use to wet her lips. "You saw me?"

"Did you think werewolves don't watch TV?" Lucius asked, then laughed softly. His voice was gentle. Human. "Can you speak freely?"

Cat turned and looked out across the busy studio. No one was looking in her direction. Except Ed. And Detective Freeland. Cat waved and pointed to the phone, mimed an exaggerated sigh and smiled. Both men started walking toward her. *Shit!*

"No, I can't," she whispered into the phone—a useless effort since she was the only one in the booth at the moment. "Look, none of this was my idea. Please believe me."

He didn't say anything for a moment. "I don't know why I should, Ms. Moselle, but I do. We have to talk. Alone this time."

A tremor, although not unpleasant, worked its way down Cat's spine. Ed and the detective were getting closer. She could almost feel the vibrations of their steps through the concrete floor as they walked. *This is stupid,* the voice of reason inside her said. Again. *This is so frigging stupid. He just heard you call him by name on television. You meet him and you're a dead woman.*

A dead STUPID woman.

Cat took a deep breath and nodded. Ed and the detective were less than six feet away.

"Where," she asked.

"O'Connell's," he said, "on Blake near the stadium. The roads are pretty clear, but you might want to take a cab just to be on the safe side."

And to make sure I really am alone, Cat thought. "Okay. When?"

"Is ten o'clock too late?"

Ed was the first one in the door, Detective Jack right behind. Questions in both their eyes.

"No. That'll be fine . . . Mom. See you then. Oh, one more thing . . . Mom. How am I supposed to . . . recognize this guy?"

"I'll be behind the bar, Ms. Moselle. Until tonight."

The line went dead, and Cat's little voice of reason was right behind it.

"Mothers." Cat sighed as she hung up the phone. "The son of a friend of hers who lives here in Denver saw the broadcast and called her. Live television, huh? Wow."

"And she called you . . . here?" The detective was only being a detective, but even Ed looked dubious.

"That's my mom," Cat said. "She said the guy sounds just like my type, so she set me up with a date. I gotta get home and change and . . . Oh God, I have to call Mr. Boswell and ask if I can get the rest of the day off."

Ed smiled and glanced up at the schoolhouse clock over the control panel.

"Honey, I don't know about you, but I quit work a half hour ago. C'mon . . . I'll drop you off."

There was a hard edge in Ed's voice that frightened her.

"No, honest, it's okay. The roads are pretty clear . . ." His words coming out of her mouth. Cat cleared her throat. "I can take the bus."

"And meet what very well might be your future Prince Charming with a runny nose? Nevah!"

Her laughter sounded forced and weak. Maybe she wasn't as good an actress as Lucius thought she was.

Lucius stayed near the phone after he'd hung up, re-turning to that spot after making the rounds to replenish drinks or make new ones. No one seemed to notice or care where he stood or how much time he spent watching the fat snowflakes drift past the windows—as long as he heard when they called for another round.

Which he did and had since the first wave of blizzard-deprived social drinkers stomped in.

Maybe they thought he was just watching for signs that another whiteout was on the way. More than once Lucius caught a mimicking glance out of the corner of his eye, but snow was the least of his concerns at the moment.

Any moment, he expected to see the drifting white flakes go crimson and sapphire as police cars screeched to a halt in front of the bar.

As Scooter would undoubtedly have said—had he been there when Lucius followed the crowd's giggling attention to the bar's television screen—he was guilty of being stupid in a No Stupid Zone.

The crowd had thought it was a joke, laughing and applauding when she, C. K. Moselle, pleaded with him, *by name* ("Hey, Lushush, she's talkin' about you, man. Hah, hah!"), to turn himself in . . . to come to her and be her love and everything would be all right. She promised. *"Lucius, if you're watching this, you have to turn yourself in and explain . . . how you were protecting me. Please, Lucius."*

They were using her as bait, and he had to admire them for that . . . even if it was the oldest trick in the book.

But old didn't mean it wouldn't work. Especially since it did. Outside the snow was still white.

"Hey, barkeep, what's a girl got to do around here to get a drink?"

The voice was soft and feminine and close. Too close. Too soon. It couldn't be her.

Lucius turned—too quickly—and sent an empty beer mug crashing to the floor. A half dozen barflies applauded as he grabbed the hand broom and dustpan from its place under the bar.

"Be with you in a minute," he told the woman who only wanted a drink. Who wasn't, and could never be, her. "Sorry."

The woman smiled around perfectly capped teeth and brushed back a swirl of ebony hair glistening with snow dew. There was a trace of the bitch in her almond-shaped brown eyes. She was another half-blood. Like C. K. Moselle. And neither of them knew it.

"Take your time," she said, plucking a honey-roasted nut from the small bowl in front of her. "I'm not going anywhere."

"Neither am I," Lucius said as he dropped to one knee and began sweeping up the broken glass. "At least not for a while."

17

Moonrise.

Moonrise.
Hidden behind cloud. But felt nonetheless.
A ripple beneath the façade.

Cat's skin felt as if it'd been trying to crawl off her body since she got home.

And no amount of lotion or long soaks in hot, bubble-topped bathwater or even the three glasses of white wine she'd consumed during the slow course of the evening seemed to do any good.

She wasn't even drunk. Pruned and slippery, but not drunk.

Or hungry . . . even before she forced down a can of Chunky Sirloin soup (straight from the can, unheated, and with a fork) between glasses two and three.

What she was . . . was nervous. And scared to death. And really, *really* cold.

Cat scratched the itch under her chin and stepped back into the closed travel-agency doorway. The sun-shaped sign on the door said they'd be open at eight the next morning,

PLEASE COME AGAIN. But right now, silent and dark, it was the perfect place to study the brightly lit bar across the street. Despite the snow and cold, the late hour and all the other microbreweries and trendy eateries that lined Blake from Coors Field to Fifteenth, O'Connell's seemed the most crowded.

Which was good.

Which was what she wanted.

Which was why she'd had the cab driver go around the block twice before allowing him to drop her off.

If the bar had been a dive or in a less-populated area, she would have told the cabbie to take her home. Agreeing to meet the Denver Werewolf, face to muzzle, was stupid enough, but . . .

But *what*? It was stupid.

Cat pressed her back against the agency's concrete wall and took a deep breath. Stupid or not, it looked safe enough. In an Irish fairy-tale sort of way. All rough stone façade and polished brass fitting, O'Connell's had enough harps and shamrocks etched into the Tudor-paned windows above the crisp lace café curtains to make any son of the Auld Sod feel right at home.

It was just the place a man would take a woman to impress her. Even if he was the bartender.

Cat took a deep breath and rolled her shoulders beneath the knee-length down coat she'd decided on at the last moment. The parka, as much as she loved it, wouldn't do with the dress she'd also decided to wear at the last moment.

A dress, for God's sake.

Low-cut in front and clingy all around. The color of fire. The color of blood. A dress she had bought for the office Christmas party last year and hadn't had the nerve to wear. A dress that had been sitting in its dry-cleaning shroud, pressed and ready, at the far left-hand side of her closet. Along with the two-inch, red-leather shoes, which were even now cutting off circulation to her toes.

Cat looked down and kicked a dollop of street gray slush from the top of her right shoe. Blood red. The perfect color for a piece of bait to wear. It was the shoes that made her opt to keep the promise she made about taking the cab. Women dressed like her just *didn't* take the bus.

Women dressed like her didn't stand in doorways across from bars either, unless they were waiting to transact a little business.

Turning, Cat looked at the neon-rimmed clock mounted on the agency's back wall: 9:45. She was still early. He said to meet him at 10:00, and it wouldn't take fifteen minutes to walk across the street even with slick leather soles.

Ten minutes was all she could hope for. Tops.

Laughter from the street turned her around in time to see a man and woman dressed in L. L. Bean outerwear pass her observation post and jaywalk toward O'Connell's door. Cat smoothed down the front of her coat. Her outfit looked as good as theirs. Better. She could pass.

She would pass.

She just hoped Lucius would like it.

Where did that *come from?*

Cat leaned back against the cold brick doorway and fumbled with the buttons of her coat. A hard lump met her fingers through the layer of down and made her smile. Ed's good-luck charm . . . a Day-Glo PEACE button he said kept him out of Vietnam and VD free for the last twenty-odd years. He insisted she wear it that night, as protection against the monster in man's dress, and wouldn't let her out of his rattling Volvo until she promised—Cross her heart and hope to die, Stick a needle in her eye—she would.

"A promise is a promise," he'd said after giving her a fatherly peck on the cheek as she reached for the door handle. *"And I'll know if you don't wear it, Kit-Cat. I really will."*

Cat pressed harder on the little button and exhaled slowly.

"I can do this," she whispered and hoped she was right as she stepped out of the doorway and followed the L. L. Bean couple's tracks across the ice-slick street. "Ready or not, here I come."

Tiny brass bells tinkled as she opened the door, not that anyone inside the cavernous bar would have heard it over the auditory melee of voices and contemporary Irish rock.

Cat's ears were ringing before she'd gotten two feet from the door.

A man in a black Stetson and cowboy boots smiled at her as she passed. He looked as out of place as she felt, but at least she could hide that fact. Cat ignored him and set her sights on the bar, opening the front of the coat and letting it slide back over the knobs of her shoulders.

Approving glances were everywhere, but none that belonged to the one man she wanted . . . to see. And be seen. It'd worked for the first Little Red Ridinghood, hadn't it?

Shoulders back, chest out, peace sign hovering at the point of the low-cut V, Cat sidestepped around two businessmen in pin-striped suits and was just about to go around a woman with much more bust than was harmonically possible, when a Celtic-knot belt buckle, with a man attached, stepped in front of her.

Cat looked up into six-feet-plus of perfect tanning salon-baked features, golden curls, and wide-set eyes that matched the kelly green of his turtleneck sweater. An Irish tweed sports coat completed the ensemble.

"An' what, may ah ask, is such a lovely lass doin' without an escort?"

The accent was more Nacogdoches than Belfast. Cat ignored the question and tried to go around the immovable hulk. Without success. Where she moved, he moved. *Christ.*

"You're ney bein' very sociable."

Cat gave up. "Look, I have an escort, okay?"

The big Irish-Texan's body eased in a bit closer as he scanned the room around them. "Well, I don't see no one an' besides . . . any man who'd leave a pretty wee colleen like yerself alone deserves to be bested. And I'm the best you'll ever see."

Oh Lord. Cat cocked her head to one side and smiled.

"That I doubt. Now, will be please fuck off, shithead? Thank you."

Tex-Mick mumbled something about ". . . must be a dike . . ." before wandering off to try his luck with another colleen.

Fingers clasping the peace button as if it was a holy medal,

Cat took a deep breath and continued to push her way toward the bar, heart fluttering each time she caught a glimpse of red hair.

Natural or bottled, red seemed to be the hair color of choice for the majority of the pub's patrons. A women in a tight leather jumper brushed past, long amber hair trailing over her shoulders. *Well*, Cat thought as she squirmed into the opening left in the woman's wake, *at least my dress matches.*

The bar was as crowded as the rest of the pub. Each stool was occupied and each space between stools filled to capacity. A small red-haired barmaid in a green O'Connell's T-shirt smiled an apology as she stepped in front of Cat and shouted an order to the man crouched behind the bar.

"I'll be behind the bar, Ms. Moselle."

Cat tightened her grip on Ed's good-luck charm as the bartender stood up and leaned toward the waitress. The bartender was dark and chubby.

"It's not him," she said out loud.

"Then how about me, baby?"

Oh shit!

Cat followed the oil-slick voice back to its source. Tall and gaunt, with thinning brown hair combed straight back over a high forehead, the man grinned and lifted the glass of beer he held. He smiled and Cat felt her stomach contract. There was something about the man that felt wrong. Dangerous.

"So, whadda ya think? Will I do?"

" 'Scuze me," the barmaid shouted to whoever might hear. "Drinks comin' through."

Cat stepped aside to let the woman pass, and then quickly took her place at the bar. The chubby bartender raised one eyebrow.

"White wine," Cat yelled as loudly as the waitress had just to be heard.

"You didn't answer me," the oily voice whispered over her left shoulder. "Won't I do?"

"Lucius?"

"Thadda be three bucks," the bartender shouted. "Want me to start running a tab?"

Cat nodded and downed half the glass before she felt the unmistakable sensation of a hand on her ass.

"I mean it, sweet-cakes," the voice continued, "I'm not like other men."

Cat tried again. Louder. "Lucius?"

"Sure. I'll be anyone you want, baby."

The hand on her ass inched its way toward the open front of her coat. Cat didn't think. Cat reacted.

The wine in her glass and heel of her right shoe caught the man in face and shin at exactly the same time. His howl of pain and surprise was nothing compared to that of a werewolf's, but it was nonetheless satisfying to hear.

His hand, however, seemed unaware of what had just happened to the rest of its body and remained glued to her ass.

Cat was about to remedy that with broken shards of wineglass if she had to, when the pressure on her ass disappeared.

"Is he bothering you, miss?" a low voice rumbled in the almost silence that followed.

Cat could almost hear the piped-in Celtic music above the pounding of her own heart as she turned and looked up into Lucius's eyes. He was holding the oily-voiced man by the collar, the way a wolf would hold a cub.

"I think apologies are in order, friend," Lucius said, shaking the man.

"S-s-sorry."

"No harm meant?"

"N-no harm meant."

"You were just being an idiot?"

"Y-Y-Yes. An idiot."

"And you won't ever come back here again," Lucius asked to the growing delight of the crowd who'd become eavesdroppers in the little human drama. "Will you?"

The man's head nodded enthusiastically with Lucius's help. And the crowd showed its approval when, after his release, the man left the pub. Quickly.

"Okay, folks," Lucius said, brushing off the front of his

green apron as if he'd just touched something unwholesome, "show's over. Sorry about the noise."

There were still a few perfunctory claps when Lucius turned around and took Cat's arm.

"Are you all right, Ms. Moselle?"

Cat looked up into his genetically mismatched features and felt the floor tilt slightly off center.

"Yes, I'm fine . . . Lucius."

How sweet.

Ed pushed the headphones off his ears and stretched against the Volvo's steering wheel. He could still hear them—voices whispering above the hiss of windblown snow, keeping him company in the small alley a quarter of a mile west of the bar.

Turning his stomach.

Releasing his grip on the wheel, Ed reached down and patted the Contra Army Surplus receiver he'd picked up, along with the tiny microtransmitter he had hot-glued to the pin Kit-Cat was wearing. It was amazing the things you could find in the Paranoid Classified section of his own beloved *QUEST*.

Landing that job was probably the best thing that could ever happen to him. Next best to having a grandson on the police force.

Maybe. The jury was still out on that particular issue.

The wind whipped snow across the frosted windshield as laughter purred against his neck. Getting her to wear the bugged pin was the easiest part of the whole operation. He'd suspected she'd try something like that long before the phone call actually came. And like the survivalist who sold it to him said, anyone who isn't prepared is food.

How true.

Pushing himself higher on the seat, Ed cocked his head to one side and listened. The laughter had a drunken edge to it, background noise to their cautious small talk. *Are you sure you're all right? Yes. He didn't hurt you, did he? No, he just frightened me.* More laughter and the clink of glass against glass and glass against wood. *I wasn't expecting you to be early. I'm sorry.*

Ed's fingers curled slowly back toward his palm, the nails tearing four grooves in the receiver's plastic housing. She was apologizing. To *him*! For being early.

His nails pierced the thick callus on his palms. If Kit-Cat had only confided in him about the phone call, had just come out and said, "Ed, I'm going to meet Lucius tonight. Follow me and tear out his throat," neither of them would be listening to that macho Alpha Male bullshit right now.

If she had just told. But she hadn't. She lied to him like he was just another single-gene reject walking around with his thumb up his ass.

Not that he hadn't given her the chance to come clean. Hell, the stink of the lie was so strong on her he'd almost choked to death. Even her skin tasted of deceit. It'd been all he could do not to vomit it back on her after he kissed her.

After she'd *allowed* him to kiss her.

Ed felt his cock stiffen against the front of his jeans but not from lust. His little Kit-Cat would need some learning in the fine art of submission before he got her with cub.

And get her he would.

Over Lucius's moldering corpse if need be.

More laughter trickled through the headset and this time it was them. Still cautious, but relaxing a bit.

Were you followed? No, I took a cab and made him drive around the block three times.

"My, my," Ed answered, "weren't you clever. Probably never knew a cop can find out a cab's destination without a written warrant, did you, Kit-Cat?"

Ed turned and looked at the silent figure sitting in the backseat.

"And I have you to thank for that info, man. I never would have known about half this shit if it wasn't for you. What can I do to show my appreciation?"

The survivalist didn't say a word. Understandably, since his tongue and throat were the first things Ed removed after making sure the receiver worked.

Sniffing as the snow continued to pile in around the car, Ed replaced the earphones and reached over the seat to grab another mouthful of meat. Surveillance work always made him hungry.

18

"I'm really sorry about all that," she said over her shoulder, as he steered her through the crowd toward a relatively quiet corner at the far end of the bar.

Her voice was thin and brittle as ice, the fear scent still strong on her breath.

"Don't worry about it." He smiled and let his fingers press deeper against the back of her coat. "If we have less than a half dozen altercations per night we'd be under investigation by the Irish Pub and Amateur Boxing Commission."

She began to laugh, forced and uneasy, then gasped when two men cut in front of her. She stopped and her back pressed against Lucius's hand. He could feel her body through the thickness of the down, the interplay of muscle against bone, the same way he'd been able to cut her scent from the hundred others the moment she entered the bar.

A sharp clean scent—a blood scent thick with estrogen and musk. A mating scent.

The animal in her was stronger tonight, closer to the surface. All he had to do was release it. One true touch and she would slip from her world into his.

Lucius moved his hand to encompass her waist and felt

her tremble. *Too soon.* His hand fell away as she moved out of reach.

"Here?" she called when she'd gotten to the far corner. There was still ice in her voice, still the bitter stench of fear on her breath.

A man and woman, not a couple but their scents giving strong indications they soon would be, watched from the bistro table they had laid claim to. Lucius smiled and offered the man a subliminal growl of dominance. The man bolted first, the woman following quickly . . . while C. K. Moselle stood back and watched.

"Perfect timing," he said and held the chair the man had vacated out for her. "Can I get you a drink? You look like you could use one."

She nodded her head, ebony tresses curling over her shoulders as she slipped out of her coat. The red of her dress almost blinded him.

"I'd love a drink," she said, pulling a small wallet from one of the coat pockets before tossing it over the back of her chair. Her hands were shaking as she tried to extract one of the crisp ATM twenties. "S-scotch. Straight up. Double."

Lucius covered both her hands with his one. "On the house. I know the bartender here. Now, sit down before someone steals our chairs."

She sat. A little too quickly. Lucius heard her teeth clink together and saw the sudden shock in her eyes.

"Be right back," he told her, and immediately felt her relax.

It was going to be a long evening.

She was calmer after her second double scotch.

"You're kidding? You're one of *those* Currers? The ones who keep showing up in the society page? With that big stone mansion and all that money? One of *those*?"

Lucius smiled and leaned back in his chair. The name and financial fame weren't lost on her.

"You mean you're all . . ." She lowered her voice. ". . . like you are?"

"Lycantropes? Yes. Although, we prefer to be called Metamorphosic Americans."

"What?"

He tipped his head to one side and for an instant, *only an instant*, Cat saw the animal beneath the thin layer of human skin. "That's a joke, Ms. Moselle."

"Oh." She wasn't sure he was joking but threw back her head and laughed nevertheless. Her laughter sounded better than her fear. She hoped. "So . . . how many of them . . . of you . . . of . . . You seem to have a large family."

The smile on his lips faded. "No, not anymore. We're not a wolf pack, Ms. Moselle, where the Alpha Male can mate only with the Alpha Female. We're human in that respect . . . actually quite Mormon in that respect. We've always practiced polygamy. By the laws of my ancestors, I should mate with every fertile female regardless of rank. But I have chosen only . . . the Alpha and Beta females to produce offspring."

The sudden dryness in Cat's mouth and throat made speaking difficult. The Scotch was a wonderful lubricant. "So, how many off— . . . children do you have?"

"Only six," he said as if he was telling her how many CDs he had. "Plus six unmated Juveniles. Not a large family at all."

"No." She took another swallow. "Not at all."

Shaking his head, Lucius lifted his hand to the collar of his green dress shirt and rubbed the silver squash blossom between his thumb and forefinger, waiting for her to notice. It took her a moment, but she finally did.

"That's silver, isn't it?"

Lucius nodded and held it out toward her. "Handmade."

"But I thought . . ." A faint blush touched her cheeks as she lifted the half-empty glass. "Aren't silver bullets supposed to be the only thing that can . . . stop your kind?"

"Bullets will generally stop anything that gets in their way, silver or lead. We . . . all of us wear something silver against our skins as a sort of safety valve. We can't change until we remove it."

"Oh. I must sound like an idiot."

Lucius shook his head and let the heavy silver blossom fall back against his neck.

"On the contrary, I think you're doing very well for someone in your position."

She nodded and lifted her glass. The animal under her skin grinned at him.

"Hasn't anyone ever told you about the effects of high-altitude drinking, Ms. Moselle?"

"Yesh." She giggled and carefully set the glass back on its damp cocktail napkin. "*Ahem* . . . Yes, I know all about how much faster alcohol gets into the bloodstream a mile above sea level, but I think under the circumstances it's okay. Don't you?"

"More than allowed, Ms. Moselle."

"Cat," she said. "C. K. is short for Catherine Kelly . . . which really kinda fits in with this place."

"Cat," Lucius repeated. "It suits you."

She smiled, embarrassed, and reached up to mimic his own fidgeting with the pink-and-orange peace button she wore. The pin was hideous but as a focal point for her breasts, it was beyond compare. Lucius wondered what they would look like, multiplied by four and covered in a silky black pelt.

He shifted his weight against the sudden pressure at the front of his jeans and watched her drop her hand back to her empty glass. A quick change in subject was needed.

For both of them.

"Cat, I didn't kill that man."

She didn't ask what man. They both knew who he was talking about.

"Then if it wasn't . . ." Her voice dropped to a whisper. ". . . the Denver Werewolf, then what killed him? Dogs?"

Lucius shook his head and motioned the roving waitress over. High altitude or not, she was probably going to need another drink.

"Could you bring the lady another scotch, Jeannie? Single, with a splash, this time. And put it on my tab. Thanks, hon."

Cat was staring at him wide-eyed when he turned around.

"There's another pack of lyc-shapeshifters in the area, Cat.

Weremen, not wolves . . . a subspecies that has always looked at MAN as food. They're much more dangerous than we are, Cat. And one of them is following you."

Her eyes, frozen gray-green pools, locked on to his.

"What?"

"Scotch," the waitress said as she picked up the empty glass and replaced it with the single shot. "With water. That's what you ordered, right."

"Right. Thanks, Jeannie." Lucius waited until the woman left before sliding the glass closer to Cat's hand. "Take a sip."

She nodded and lifted the glass to her lips, but the sip lengthened into one long swallow. Ice tinkled against the sides of the empty glass as she lowered it.

"What do you mean, one of them is following me?" Her voice was slow and steady, the fear stench buried beneath alcohol fumes.

Just as well, Lucius thought, and took her hand. She leaned forward at his touch. Anyone would think they were in love. Or about to be.

"I sensed him that night . . . the night you were attacked. He was watching us, and I'm pretty sure he's their leader." She was shaking her head, *no no no*. "Cat, they killed that man. I watched them do it."

"You . . . watched them?"

"Cat, I—"

The hair on the back of his neck sharpened to points as a new scent—*dark rank animal*—curled into the air in front of his face.

"Lucius?"

He let go of her hand and stood up, glancing from one alcohol-flushed face to the next. Smiles or frowns twisted features as the moods directed, but no one looked out of place. No one looked dangerous.

"Lucius . . . What's the matter?"

"He's here. And he's not alone."

Lucius heard chair legs scrape against the floor, and the soft *whoosh* of her coat as she pulled it around her shoulders. A moment later he felt her body heat against his back.

"Where is he?" she whispered.

"I don't know." Turning, he smiled and tossed an arm over her shoulder, pulling her close and ruffling the top of her head with his chin. "Do you think you can pretend that I just asked you out and you accepted?"

A smile, although somewhat lopsided and hesitant, curled her lips. It was only then that Lucius realized she wasn't wearing any lipstick, that her lips were naturally as red as the dress she wore.

"S-sure," she said. "Why?"

"Because we're going to leave," he answered, tugging the front of the thick coat closed. "And with any luck, your admirer will think the bar's too crowded to start anything. I don't suppose you disobeyed my instructions this time and told the police you were coming here?"

Cat looked up at him miserably. "No."

"Well, you sure picked a fine time to start listening to me."

He never meant to kiss her.

Not then. Not with the OTHERS so close.

But he did.

His mouth closed against hers. A moment later he felt her lips part and the tender probing of her tongue against his teeth.

"Hey, where can I get me some of that?"

Cat pulled back first and smiled at the tall woman in glasses who was staring at them with open envy.

"Better be careful," Cat told her. "This one's a real monster."

The woman sighed. "Ain't they all?"

Ain't they all? The words bounced around the inside of Lucius's skull as he took Cat's hand and began winding their way toward the front door. Even with the snow and late hour, there were still a number of cars on Blake. They'd have a better chance of avoiding a confrontation there than in the deserted alley behind the pub.

The OTHERS were still there. Lucius could smell them.

Ain't they all?

But which ones? The tall woman with glasses was talking to a dumpy little man in a surplus Army jacket. A man with red hair and cold eyes stared after them only until he found something better to stare at. Two men in matching gray suits argued over long-necks near the door.

Ain't they all?

He tightened his grip on Cat's hand until she yelped.

"Lucius, what's the matter?"

Instead of answering, he turned them away from the door and headed them back toward the small rest room/phone alcove on the opposite side of the bar.

"They're moving in. I don't think they'd harm you, but I'm not going to take that chance. Aim for the Ladies Room and then keep going. The Exit's the last door on the right. Here."

He fished the car keys out of his back pocket and pressed them into her hand.

"The silver Bronco's mine. Get in and lock the door behind you. You'll be safe in there."

"Lucius, I won't leave you. Come with me."

"Cat, look . . . I think I was wrong about the OTHERS, I don't think—"

Noise erupted from the crowd, but it wasn't typical bar-crowd noise. Screams replaced the laughter and conversation as a head—male, balding, and still the slightest hint of a smile in his glassy eyes—sailed through the air like a deformed volleyball and mashed into the mirror behind the bar. The gory backwash caught Cat across the face. Thick droplets gathered at her chin and rained down over the gaudy pin at her breast.

Peace no more.

Lucius grabbed a double handful of bloodied coat front and swung Cat into the alcove just as a deep, undulating howl, rose above the screams. His body convulsing, the OTHER dropped to the floor while muscles re-formed to be covered by a coarse red pelt.

Dark eyes glistened, surveying the panic.

"hello luuuu-cious."

Cat's fingers sank into the front of Lucius's shirt.

"Oh my God, it just said something."

She'd understood the Lycanspeak and it terrified her.

196   P. D. Cacek

Maybe she was more Blood than even Lucius thought. Perhaps even Full but never taught the ways.

"wanna play luuu-cious?"

Her nails pierced the thin fabric and found the hard flesh beneath. Lucius cupped her face in his hands.

"Don't worry. I won't let him hurt you."

"promises promises," the OTHER snorted and, farther back, anOTHER chuckled. The Alpha Male. The Silverback. Their leader.

"Trust me, Cat."

Without taking his eyes from hers, Lucius reached up and tore the necklace from his throat. He barely felt the pain of muscle and sinew stretching around rc-formed bone as he watched the transformation reflected in her eyes.

And saw the monster he really was.

"Take this," he said as he closed her hands around the silver necklace. "If anyone any*thing* tries to stop you, use it. Get to the car."

He pushed her toward the exit but it was already too late. Too late. Another monster filled Cat's eyes.

"too late."

The OTHER was smaller, faster. Dropping to all fours, he slashed at the back of Lucius's stifle, missing the joint but leaving a bloody gash in his wake. The pain was unlike any he'd ever experienced. Transformation seemed like a stubbed toe in comparison.

The beast in Lucius bellowed with rage, the MAN in him froze as he watched the OTHER knock Cat to the floor and stand, stiff-legged, over her.

"one bite, lucius, and i send the bitch to hell."

To prove he was telling the truth, the OTHER lowered his muzzle to Cat's throat and ran his tongue slowly over her skin.

"or maybe i should just mate with her. how would you like that, luuu-cious?"

Whimpering, Cat moved her hands to the top of her coat and pulled it closed. The OTHER watched, fascinated.

"she understands?"

"What do you think, fur ball?"

Before the wereman could answer, Cat swatted him across the muzzle with the silver necklace. Flesh and fur parted around the sizzling, blossom-shaped welt. Sneezing, eyes closed tight against the pain, the OTHER dropped his head and snapped where Cat's throat should have been.

But wasn't.

The beast under her skin reacted and twisted Cat to one side, knocking into the slavering wereman's left foreleg and throwing him off-balance.

"oh you like to play games, huh, bitch?"

The OTHER snapped at her head, claws scraping purchase from the emerald green/gold-flecked linoleum the owner had put in only a month before, and lunged at her.

"so how'd you like this ga—"

Lucius's clawed hand closed around the OTHER's windpipe and lifted him off the floor to pin him against the opposite wall like a bug on a mounting block. Unrestricted to only the lupus form as the lesser male was, Lucius straightened his spine until he stood as erect as possible. As MAN-shaped as possible.

He'd fought lesser males before, *many* times before, but those fights had always been for show and custom; ritualistic scuffles for dominance that ended when he—always he—lunged and held the challenger at bay.

He had never fought a *real* challenger.

"give," Lucius commanded.

The fear smell was strong on the lesser male, but he wasn't going to give up that easily.

"fuck off."

Whatever his ranking in his own pack, or in the world beyond, he wasn't going to give up without a fight. Lucius was almost impressed.

Almost. But not quite.

"who is the silverback?"

"what's the matter, wolfman, don't you understand the tongue of your own ancients? i thought i told you to fuck off."

Tongue lolling to one side, the OTHER tried to chuckle

around the constriction caused . . . until Lucius squeezed the sound to silence.

"answer me and i might let you live out the night."

Russet lips curled back from fangs riddled with decay.

"you might . . . but he wouldn't."

Claws raked Lucius's belly as the lesser male attempted to bite the hand that held him.

Instinct, coupled with the boxing lessons he was forced to take as a child, and Lucius balled his claws into a fist and punched a hole through the lesser male's diaphragm.

Family legend spoke of ancient challenges that wouldn't be settled until the beating heart of the vanquished was devoured before his eyes.

That particular legend had always sickened Lucius.

Until now.

Cupping the trembling heart in his paw, Lucius lifted it to his mouth and bit it in half. Blood spurted from the torn aorta at the same time it poured down Lucius's throat—rich and hot and satisfying.

A memory that was all but forgotten.

Of dominance over all living creatures.

Lifting his head, he crushed the remaining half of the heart and sang of his victory to the sky. Other voices in the night joined his—one close, one far, one farther still . . . the last echoing through the night bright canyons beyond . . . the voice growing louder and louder until he recognized it.

Sirens. A whole *lot* of sirens.

Lucius dropped the ruined heart and wiped the last of the blood from his mouth. Cat had stopped screaming, although she looked as if she'd start again without too much effort or warning.

The dead man lay sprawled at her feet, naked, a ragged hole where his chest had been. Lucius slid the remains of the heart behind him as he transformed. By the time he reached her, pulled her into his arms, he was almost human. Naked but human enough to pass.

She didn't seem to notice.

"You killed Detective Freeland."

"What?"

Cat blinked as he tipped her chin up. "Him. He was one of the detectives who talked to me today. You killed him."

Her lips continued to move even though no sound came out. For a moment. And then she screamed.

The back of Lucius's knuckles were still a bit hairy where they caught the point of her chin, although he doubted the thin layer of fur had softened the blow too much.

Stooping to retrieve the necklace and his car keys from where she'd dropped them, Lucius slung Cat over one shoulder and trotted to the exit.

To the sounds of sirens and Celtic rock pouring out through the open door, Lucius hit the cold night on a dead run and hoped he still had an extra set of clothes stashed in the Bronco.

If he didn't he'd have to drive home in werewolf skin . . . and at the moment, that definitely wasn't an option.

Ed watched the Bronco burn rubber as it took the turn onto Wazee and belched. He'd thrown the remains of his dinner companion in a near-by Dumpster to give the cops another little tidbit to pin on the Denver Werewolf, but then his idiot great-grandson had decided to go out and become the wereman's answer to Rambo.

"Kids," he grumbled to himself, and eased the Volvo slowly into traffic. He didn't have to rush. He had all the time in the world.

A soft *beep* echoed through the car's interior—soft and low, like the beat of a dying heart. Soft and low and in time to the flashing red light at the top of the receiver box. The light marked TRACE.

Yes sir, it sure paid to be a paranoid survivalist nowadays.

Ed smiled at the little black box before reaching under the dash for the cellular phone he'd mounted there—out of sight of prying eyes. It was bright and shiny and top-of-the-line . . . definitely not the sort of thing that went with a scruffy, antiestablishment, radical old hippie with a beat-up car and ancient ideas.

Very ancient.

He thumbed the first button and listened to the little computer inside speed-dial. A familiar whine answered on the third electronic ring. Shit, he'd forgotten Leon, half-wereman/half-pansy, was working phones tonight. Oh well.

Ed watched the parade of police cars swing the wrong way onto Blake—after all, one of their own had been killed—and forced his voice into his soberest tone.

"Leon . . . he killed Jack."

High-pitched wails instantly erupted from the phone.

"Yeah, yeah, Leon, I know. It's horrible, but what are you gonna do? I told the kid to wait for my signal, but you know how these cubs are . . . all gonads and no brains. No, you can tell Carmine."

Ed pressed the phone to his ear as the wails were replaced by sniffling sobs.

"What? Look, Leon, cut the waterworks for a minute, will ya? Yeah, I'm very upset, too. Right. No, I'll be home in a while . . . I've got something to do first."

Ed switched the phone off and tossed it to the seat next to the receiver. He wasn't worried about anyone seeing the equipment and attempting to break in . . . rusted-out Volvos just weren't the sorts of cars jackers were interested in.

Besides, he thought as he pulled the car into *QUEST*'s parking lot, that's what Ol' Tannenbutt paid all those Rent-a-Cops for. Security.

Ed waved to the night man as he walked to the lobby. The guy made Ed look like a teenager . . . even in dog years.

19

Someone was laughing. Soft and rumbling.

It tickled Cat's ears, and she smiled.

"Hey, little brother, I think you'd better get over here. Looks like your lady's waking up."

Cat opened her eyes and squinted at the shape looming over her.

"Hi, sweetheart. How's it going?"

Lucius had changed! Dramatically. And possibly with the help of a demonic-possessed Cuisinart. His hair was loose and tangled ... *all* of his hair. He'd either hadn't gotten around to a complete transformation back to human form, or he had the worst case of five o'clock shadow Cat had ever seen on a man.

Which, of course, was a moot point in this case.

Cat squirmed higher on what she discovered was a low couch upholstered in almost the same shade of peach silk that she was currently wearing. She let her hands verify the fact that she was still wearing underwear beneath the robe.

I WAS THE DENVER WEREWOLF'S LOVE-SLAVE REALLY!!!

Lucius grinned. A silver chain, with links as wide as her thumb, jangled as he sat back.

"You can thank Cybil for the loan," he said. "Personally, I didn't mind what you had on when Lucius brought you in. A little bright maybe, but red's always been my favorite color."

His eyes never left her face, and the leer never left his lips as he slid off the couch and dragged himself backwards toward the pile of cushions in front of a white-marble fireplace. Cat looked down at the stumps where his legs should have been and felt her heart tear in half.

"My God . . . They crippled you."

He flopped onto the cushions and scratched his jaw line through the matted beard.

"A long time ago, sweetheart." His black eyes caught the light as he shifted his gaze to a spot over her head. "I think she's got us confused, little brother."

"And I'm sure you didn't do anything to correct that impression, did you?"

Lucius stepped into the room through double doors that went all the way to the ten-foot ceiling and smiled at Cat's quick double take. There were two of them. Two Luciuses, but not quite. One lounging in truncated jeans and dirty flannel, the other standing ramrod straight in dark slacks and a loose fitting black silk shirt. One in a dog collar, the other wearing silver and turquoise. One clean-shaven, the other bearded.

Two genetic misfits with Native American features beneath Celtic bright hair.

Twins.

STARTLING NEW DISCOVERY

DENVER WEREWOLF'S TWIN REALLY BIGFOOT!

Minus feet. "Stop it."

"Pardon?"

Cat shook her head. "Nothing. Sorry."

"And I'm sorry, too. You'll have to forgive my brother, Cat," Lucius said as he crossed the room. "He likes to mislead people sometimes."

"What do you mean sometimes?" He leaned forward over the cushions and jerked a thumb toward the shadows beyond the firelight. "Just ask them."

Cat pulled the front of the gown tighter over her breasts and hips as she swung her legs off the couch and stood up. She hadn't noticed them while she was looking back and forth between Lucius and his brother . . . the dozen or so men and women in evening dress, silently watching her.

For a moment Cat thought they were painted on the walls, an artist's glorified tableau of a century long past—for they certainly "went" with the flocked wallpaper, parquet floor, oriental throws, and mounted wolf heads?—standing on either side of a small raised dais where an elderly woman in silver lamé sat upon a golden throne.

It was a bit overdone, even for a lasting tribute to the ancient matriarch of one of Denver's leading families . . . but then the ancient matriarch moved, lifted a pale hand to the silver strands around her throat, and growled softly.

At Cat. The society page's black-and-white publicity photos had not done Mrs. Regina Currer justice.

QUEST REPORTER FOUND DEAD IN WEREWOLF DOO

"Don't take it too seriously, little sister," Lucius's twin said, chuckling softly. "Moms never like their son's girlfriends."

"Can it, Scooter."

Lucius. To the rescue. Again.

Cat felt his hand on her arm and jumped.

"Oooo," Scooter said, not taking the warning Cat had heard in Lucius's voice, "looks like you got a live one there, Alpha. Might be more than you can handle. 'Course, I'd be willing to step in . . . so to speak."

Cat felt Lucius's fingers tremble as he stepped around behind her, putting himself between her and his crippled twin.

"I told you to can it, Scooter, and I mean it."

Scooter laughed without humor. "Like I'd be frightened of you. I'm firstborn, remember that little brother, and show me some respect."

His fingers stopped trembling. "You've never deserved any."

"Oh no? We only have MOTHER's word that I was born crippled. A pack can't have two Alpha Males, so maybe she just tossed a coin and I lost. Maybe you only get to strut your stuff because of chance . . . ever think about that, Al-pha?"

Whatever Lucius would have said next was silenced by a single loud clap.

"If you two are finished?" All eyes, including Cat's, fo-cused on the old woman as she lowered her hands back to the throne's carved armrests. "Thank you. Miss Moselle . . . how kind of you to visit." *Visit?* "Would you care to come closer? My eyes aren't what they used to be."

Cat doubted that last statement, but accepted Lucius's of-fered arm. The silken gown whispered against Cat's ankles, reminding her of just how *undressed* she really was. Cat studied the faces of the silent, watching women and tried to guess which of them was Cybil . . . who'd thought a bath-robe, regardless of the material it was made of, was a more appropriate outfit for a first impression than a low-cut, skin-tight, red . . .

Cat decided she'd have to thank Cybil once they met.

PROM NIGHT NIGHTMARE—A WEREWOLF'S WORST MEM-ORY

AS TOLD TO . . .

She hunched her shoulders when a teenage boy with long blond hair, smiled at her as he set a high-backed wooden chair down in front of Mrs. Currer's throne. Cat tried to smile back, but apparently didn't manage to pull it off.

He glared at her when Lucius wasn't looking and slunk back to the group of boys he'd just left. Cat reached up for Ed's pathetic little good-luck charm before she remembered it, and the dress, were no longer with her.

She sat down slowly, making sure nothing jiggled or thumped. And her attempt at decorum didn't go unnoticed. A little girl—red hair shimmering in the firelight—covered her mouth with one hand and giggled. Mrs. Currer lifted one hand, as if about to swat an insolent fly, and silence returned.

"My son tells us that you knew the other . . . the wereman who attacked him this evening. Was he part of your family?"

"My family? God no, he was a mons—" Cat licked her lips and started again. "He wasn't human."

Lucius's mother leaned forward, fingers curling into the

armrests, her pale eyes sweeping past Cat to her son.

"it would appear your little friend likes to play games, lucius. please tell her i do not."

The bitch! "You know you can speak directly to me," Cat said without thinking. "I am sitting right here."

Mrs. Currer looked at Cat and smiled. *"and i am talking to my son."*

Cat was all set to continue the argument when she realized the words . . . the *sounds* she was hearing weren't English. They weren't even words. The Grand Dame of Denver was snarling and growling like a junkyard dog. And Cat understood it. Just as she'd understood Detective Jack Freeland in the bar . . .

She turned to find Lucius staring down at her.

"I was going to explain," he said.

"Explain what?"

"Oh, don't take it personally, little sister," Lucius's brother said from his place by the fire, "full bloods sometimes forget the niceties when they're talking to breeds. Hell, sometimes MOTHER even forgets that when she's talking to *me*."

Cat shook her head, not wanting to hear what would come next, but needing to nevertheless.

"Lucius?"

"enough of this nonsense. look at me, breed!"

Cat stood up as she turned, holding Lucius's arm as if it was a life preserver and she, a victim of an angry sea. Mrs. Currer was on her feet, shoulders hunched forward as her spine rose above the knob of her neck. At her feet lay the silver necklace.

And I thought my *mother was a bitch*, Cat thought as the woman's society features elongated and reshaped while her salon-designed coiffure sprouted matching waves along her cheeks and chin.

The lamé gown puddled around the base of the throne as the matching silver-gray wolf jumped down from the dias and walked, stiff-legged, toward her. Lucius pushed Cat gently back onto the chair and placed a hand—*protectively*—on her shoulder.

"Tell MOTHER about the man in the bar . . . the detective."

Cat looked at MOTHER, lips curled back over yellow fangs, and swallowed.

"I don't know . . . I didn't know he was like you."

MOTHER lunged at her, jaws snapping shut an inch from her face. The scream caught in Cat's throat and almost choked her.

"Not a smart idea, breed," Scooter said, "now you got her mad. Look, why don't you save yourself some pelt and just tell Mama what she wants to know."

"I don't understand. What do you want?"

"how convenient your memory is, breed," the she-wolf snarled. *"where is the other pack? the one you're protecting by giving denver* my *son as their monster?"*

"What other pack?" Cat shook her head. "I thought . . . Lucius said something about others, but I didn't . . . This was all supposed to be make-believe, junk stories, the kind of thing no one thinks is real. It's not supposed to be real. It's not. Monsters don't exist."

She knew she was rambling, on the verge of hysterics or a nervous breakdown, but she couldn't stop herself. Cat watched as Lucius knelt next to the chair and took her hands. He was so warm, almost hot . . .

"You're not real, Lucius," she whispered. "You're not supposed to exist."

He cupped her hands, the heat of his flesh so comforting . . . so familiar. . . .

"Cat, listen to me," Lucius said softly. "Remember what I said in the bar? There are more than just our kind of Lycanthropes in the world. Werewolves and weremen. The creature you called Detective Freeland was a wereman. Did you tell him where you were going to meet me?"

Cat shook her head. *Weremen? Our kind?* What the hell was he talking about?

The she-wolf growled. No words this time, just emotion. But enough of the latter for Cat to still understand the message behind it.

"Could he have followed you, Cat?" Lucius asked. "Without you knowing it?"

"No. Why did she call me a breed, Lucius? I don't have any Native American in me . . . no offense."

Scooter clapped his hands and howled. "Jesus Christ, you didn't even tell her."

"Tell me what, Lucius?" Cat pulled her hands away from his, balled them against the tops of her thighs. "All of you keep hinting at something. What's going on?"

Lucius ignored the question. "If you didn't tell the detective, who did you tell?"

"No one."

"Who, Cat?"

"No one! Ed might have guessed I wasn't telling the truth about the phone call, but . . ."

His hands found hers again, but this time there was no gentleness in their touch.

"Who is Ed?"

Cat couldn't decide which hurt worse, his grip or the look in his eyes.

"No one . . . just this nice old hippie photographer who—"

"Was *he* the same man who took those pictures the night you were attacked?"

The puzzle—although one very important piece still seemed to be missing—began to fall into place.

"You think Ed's a . . . ?" Cat shook her head and would have laughed out loud if she'd had the strength. "Look, Ed's probably a lot of things, including a dirty old man, but I don't think he's a monster."

Oops.

"I mean . . . he's just a guy who knows how to fake pictures of monsters. No offense."

Cat sat back in the chair and folded her hands in her lap. Lucius was kneeling at her left knee, his MOTHER was dripping froth at her right. One way or another, she knew this would probably be the last night of her life.

She took a deep breath. "Now, what did you mean about me being a breed?"

A new headline was beginning to form across the back of

Cat's eyes when Lucius cocked his head to one side—it looked so different when he didn't have fur—and brushed the hair away from the left side of her neck.

STARTLING DISCOVERY:

"I'm sorry, Cat," he said and squeezed just inside her collarbone.

Air suddenly became the most important thing on Cat's mind. Not her burgeoning career and fame as a top-rated journalist, not Lucius, not even why he'd saved her life one night only to end it now—in front of witnesses. Air, and the process of getting it into her lungs, was all that mattered.

If she'd only take a breath, just one more breath, she would have been all right. Just one. Just . . . one.

"I AM ONE . . .

In the soft darkness that crept over her from her feet up, Cat thought she heard the muffled sound of applause.

. . . OF THEM."

"get her dressed and take her home," MOTHER growled as she turned and trotted toward the door. *"the rest of you get to bed. it's late and i have to be at a friends of the library brunch at ten."*

The rest of the Family followed her out of the room, the youngest transforming as if it was a game and leaving their clothes in piles for Cybil to pick up. She did, draping each piece carefully over one arm and pausing at the door just long enough to give Lucius an understanding smile.

She closed the door behind her to give the twins a moment of privacy.

"So," Scooter said, "how 'bout them Broncos? Think they'll make the playoffs?"

Lucius looked at his twin as he got to his feet. "Why don't you do everyone a favor and roll yourself under a bus?"

"Hey, is that a nice thing to say to your older brother? Besides, I thought buses were your field of expertise."

Lucius lifted the middle finger of his right hand.

"Whoa," Scooter gasped, clutching his chest, "I'm

shocked. Don't you know the walls have ears? Stuffed, though they may be."

Lucius looked at the heads of his ancestors, full bloods all. Like MOTHER. Like himself.

Like Scooter.

A line that went back through the centuries to Viktoras, full blood to full blood.

"I'd give you a penny for your thoughts," Scooter said when Lucius finally lowered his gaze back to Cat, unconscious and still—mercifully or not—unaware of the half blood she carried, "but since I probably already know what you're thinking, it wouldn't be worth it."

"Probably not." Bending at the knees, Lucius scooped her into his arms. She curled against him like a child, like Halona did each time he carried her up to her bed.

He caught the bitter scent of envy as he turned toward the door.

"So, you gonna do the right thing and make her the latest victim of the Denver Werewolf?" The scent changed abruptly when their eyes met. "No, guess not. But just so you remember, little brother, *she's* the one who started all this. Well, after you screwed up."

Scooter let him get all the way to the door before saying another word.

"You know, there's more than a fair chance that's she's already mated with this Ed character."

Lucius felt the silver cut into the back of his neck as he turned to look at his twin. If looks could kill, there would have been another head mounted on the wall, although at the moment he wasn't sure whose it would be.

"She hasn't mated with anyone," he said when the moment passed. "I would have smelled it on her."

Scooter leaned back against the pillows, hands over his head and stared into the fire.

"Suppose you'd know better than anyone else, sniffin' around her like you've been doing."

Ignoring the bait, Lucius grunted as he carried her to the door. She wasn't heavy, hardly more than Halona weighed, but the pressure and warmth of her body against his was

making it difficult—if not just a little uncomfortable—to
walk.

"Taking her back to her place?" Scooter asked. "Or
yours?"

The brass door latch bent slightly from the sudden pressure
of Lucius's hand. Even with the silver, he could feel his
claws begin to extrude from his fingertips. His brother was
pushing harder than he'd ever attempted before.

It was unusual, but not totally unexpected.

"If I take her to her place, Ed and his pack will be all over
her . . . and I don't think he's as nice as Cat thinks he is.
Right now, she's the only advantage that we have."

"Oh? And how do you figure that, little brother."

Lucius turned and nuzzled her cheek in full view of his
twin.

"Because he knows how I feel about her. If he gets her,
he knows I'll do anything to get her back."

And for once in his life, Scooter remained silent.

20

Ed popped an After Eight mint into his mouth and
crushed it between his back molars as he traced the carved
hunting scene on the door with his fingers. Beautiful. Expensive. One of a kind.

He extended his claws and added a few finishing touches.
Better.

"Not to sound crass or anything," Ed said, snagging another mint from the crystal candy dish as he turned, "but
how much did all this shit set you back?"

The question was met with an icy stare . . . an icy *one-
eyed* stare. Like it was his fault they decided to fight instead
of submit. *Stupid bitch.*

Ed peeled the foil off another candy and dropped it to the
floor. One more piece of litter wouldn't matter now, considering the mess.

Rubbing his bare ass against the ruined door in a modified
territorial display, Ed swallowed the candy whole and
smiled. His little business meeting with the very much
changed Mr. Tanner Boswell had gone better than he'd expected, but took less time than he'd thought. He'd gotten to
the Currers' very palatial estate just as the big red Alpha

Male was strapping Kit-Cat's limp little body into the passenger side of a gleaming silver Bronco. He would have charged them, right then and there; alone, no pack, *poue et poue*—which would have been painful if not downright suicidal—had the silver on the vehicle been just paint.

Which it wasn't.

Ostentatious bastards.

"So," he said, kicking at the shredded remains of clothing and paintings and shattered pieces of objets d'art that covered the gouged parquet floor, "you going to sit there like a lump on a log all night or are you going to be nice?"

Nothing. Not even a growl. *Shit.*

"Okay, have it your own way."

Shrugging, Ed walked to the fireplace and landed a solid, heel-first stomp on the bloodied, battered creature tied to the silver *(Christ, these people!)* fire irons. Despite the wounds and broken jaw, and the fact that the steel-reinforced toe of Carmine's biker boot had removed most of his teeth, Lucius's twin snarled and tried to bite.

The legless male spit a bloody incisor at Ed. In looks and deeds, he was a dead ringer for his brother.

Dead being an active noun in this particular case. Future tense. And counting down.

"I know compared to you guys we're just a bunch of mangy plebeian slobs," Ed said as he held his hand out to the fire, "but it does keep the ol' gene pool strong. Fer' instance, plebes that we are, we'd never have let anything as useless as you live."

Lucius's twin looked up at Ed and chuckled. It was a watery, half-choked sound.

"Then why are you breathing?"

Spunk. Ed liked that in a person. Sometimes. But not this time and not this person.

A sharp kick to the groin ended the discussion. Ed stood there for a moment, hands all warm and toasty, listening to the crippled male convulse and looking up at a mounted wolf head above the mantel. The room was lousy with mounted heads—*all the big bad Denver Werewolves*—but this one had to be Mr. Bad Ass Himself. Lucius's great-great-great-however-many-times-removed-grandpaw.

"If this isn't the sickest shit I've ever seen in my life. Damn." Ed dropped his hands to his bare waist and inhaled the musty scents of death, decay, and sawdust into his lungs. And sneezed. Loud and wet. "Why didn't you just devour them? Meat's meat."

"Because *we* rose above the level of beast," a quivering voice answered.

Ed rubbed his nose off on the back of one hand as he turned.

"Well, well," he said, "the Grand Dame speaks. I am honored beyond belief, Your Majesty."

He snapped his fingers, and one of his lesser males backhanded her across the ruined mask that had become her face. She growled and slashed back, but the loss of one eye had thrown off her depth perception, and she hit nothing but air.

"Myron . . . mind your manners," Ed reprimanded as he left the legless wonder by the fire and sauntered across the room to the lopsided fancy-dancy chair. One of the carved wooden legs had been snapped off in the first few minutes of the fight, but Lucius's mom still perched on its gutted cushions like a fucking queen.

"The old bitch is still the Alpha Female." He smacked his lips and let his eyes wander slowly over the line of females cowering against the back wall. Some of the younger, tastier ones were still in pajamas and sleep tees. The mature females were naked, bodies marked by tooth and claw. "At least for the moment."

"Touch one of my daughters, wereman, and I'll rip your throat out."

Ed howled with laughter. "Whoa! You guys listening to this? This old bitch got balls the size of Montana. Listen, Grandma . . . we won, you lost, so don't go trying any more of this dominant shit with me, okay? I don't particularly want a dried-up piece of gristle like you around, but I'm willing to let you live a while longer if you just shut the fuck up. Got it, Granny?"

Just to make sure she did, Ed swatted her lightly across

the nose. And waited to see which of her offspring would react.

He'd thought it be one of the Juveniles . . . and he was right.

A tall, lanky kid with white-blond hair suddenly lunged at Ed from across the room, silver chain around his throat still gleaming in the places not marred by blood. That was the part that had surprised Ed the most, that even during the heat of the battle, even when they saw how badly they were being beaten, very few of the Lucius's pack had stripped themselves of the hampering silver "charms." Maybe it was like the old bitch just said—*they* thought of themselves as MAN, not beast.

And thank the Lycanthrope God for that. If more of Lucius's pack had given in to instinct, the Currers' would be the ones cleaning up the mess in the blood splattered room . . . and not be the mess themselves.

"Like this one," Ed muttered as he caught the Juvenile just below the jaw. Keeping his fingers clear of the cursed metal, he lifted the teenager off the floor and held him there—no mean trick since the kid was almost a full head taller.

"How could you think that *this*," he said, shaking the kid until the chain rattled, "*this* was gonna make your kind more human? Shit, woman, I'm surprised any of your whelps stayed once they were weaned. You wanted to belong to MAN'S world so much you didn't even see you were changing your family into fucking were*dogs*."

Ed released his hold and watched the kid fall to the floor.

"What do they call you, boy?"

"You don't have to answer him," the bitch said.

The Juvenile looked up, fingers curling around the silver links until the bony knuckles went white. There was something in his eyes, something lurking behind the metal's influence, that told Ed this one might just make a decent fighter.

Given the right guidance. And initiative.

And once the old bitch was history.

"Kieran," he said.

Ed shook his head sadly. "First collars, and then names I

wouldn't give a gay poodle." He reached out, slowly, and ruffled the boy's hair. "Must have been rough."

The boy nodded, the movement almost imperceptible— *yes*. Ed smiled down at the boy and felt . . . absolutely nothing. It was too easy a victory. All the opulence, the manners, the *silver* had stripped the kid of his true nature. He'd make a decent pack number, true enough, but only until a bigger pack with a bigger Alpha came along.

There was no sense of loyalty in the boy.

"Must take after your father," Ed said, winking to show he understood as he helped the boy to his feet.

"From now on we're going to call you Killer, how's that?"

An ear-to-ear grin answered him. "Okay, Killer, you go stand over by Carmine and watch the bitches. But no sniffing."

A faint blush accompanied the boy as he hurried away to stand guard—straight and tall, narrow chest held high, puny little cock twitching—over his sisters and aunts.

Ed rolled his shoulders and leaned forward as his body transformed back into its natural state. A couple of the little girls cried out and hid behind their hands. *Better get used to it,* he thought as he trotted toward them.

"Leave them *alone*!"

One eye or not, the old bitch could still move. She was almost in full pelt by the time she leapt from the chair, claws extended and aimed at Ed's muzzle.

Just as he expected.

He let her come, straight at him while the members of both packs—his and hers—screamed or shouted. The silver in her coat was whiter than his, the pelt thicker and better cared for; but the muscles beneath less taut. High living was about to stop.

He swung his head at the last moment and caught her low, tearing out a chunk of meat along her shoulder. The pain made her react without thinking. She came at him again, snarling and snapping at empty air. Ed almost felt sorry for the old bitch as he drove at her wound a second time, worrying the flesh apart until he exposed the bone beneath.

The sound was lost in the horrified shrieks that rose from

her progeny, but she was beyond hearing it. Panting, she lay on her side, shivering in pain. Ed stood over her, the taste of her blood on his tongue. It was saltier than he liked.

Her eyes were already glazing over when he lowered his muzzle to the soft fur at her throat. Out of respect for her position in the pack, Ed crushed her windpipe before tearing her open like a piñata.

And gobbling down the goodies.

The snow was red.

And blue and white and then red again . . . bleeding across the sky hung with silver and crystal stars as Lucius reached through the bloodied/azure/crystal snowflakes to take her hand . . . her paw . . . small and tear-shaped . . . covered with soft, black fur . . . the nails ivory tipped in red . . .

Cat woke before the nightmare died, fighting the blanket that clung to her sweat-damp skin as she sat up. Wherever she was, it wasn't home. Home was Target "Some Assembly Required" furniture and a bedroom/living room/office/kitchenette bathed in the yellow glow of a streetlight. Here was a bedroom filled with *real* furniture that seemed to stretch forever beneath the glass-tiled ceiling. Soft blue light filtered into the room through the balcony window directly opposite the massive king-size bed.

Home was *never* like this.

Cat took a deep breath and closed her eyes.

"I'm dreaming," she whispered, and silently counted off ten on her fingers—giving herself time to wake up—before peeking out from under one eyelid.

It didn't work. She was either still asleep or . . .

Cat reached under the blanket and pinched her leg. Hard. Through the slippery satin pajama bottoms she knew she didn't own.

She was awake. This wasn't a dream.

Cat looked up at herself in the mirrored ceiling. The tiles directly over the bed had been laid out in the shape of a five pointed star.

A pentagram.

The sign of the werewolf . . . among other things.

"I WAS A TEENAGE GOTH WEREWOLF"

As Told To . . .

"Oh shit."

One kick sent the blankets flying and almost removed the pajama pants as well. Grabbing a double handful of the flowing material, Cat hauled the waistband up to her breasts but found she still had to walk on her tiptoes if she wasn't going to trip.

The question, however, was *where* she was going to walk.

A double-wide door, pin-striped yellow outline against the midnight blue wall, was to her left; the double-wide balcony window to her right. Door Number One, Window Number Two. Equal distances away, but it was what might be behind Door Number One that turned Cat toward the window.

The first snow-laced blast took her breath away, the second was barely felt as she walked through the shallow drifts. An enchanted garden filled with flowers made from lights bloomed in the icy darkness below. Cat leaned over the balcony's railing, snow melting against her arms and belly, and stared. In lieu of a traditional (and probably more expensive) office Christmas party the year before, Tanner had opted for a personally guided tour of the Botanical Gardens' Christmas spectacular, the "Blossoms of Light" and a paper cup of hot cider afterward.

Most of the staff had grumbled, but Cat loved it.

But it was nothing compared to viewing the fantasy of lights from where she now stood, despite the blowing snow.

Another light, soft and yellow, washed across the balcony and turned the snowflakes gold before winking out. Cat listened to his soft steps against the bedroom's thick carpet.

"Don't jump," Lucius said as he stepped onto the balcony behind her. "We're werewolves, not werecats."

Cat shook her head without turning around.

QUEST EXCLUSIVE: "I AM ONE OF THEM!"
— BY C. K. "CAT-GIRL" MOSELLE

"You keep saying *we*. I'm not a werewolf."

The snow crunched as he moved closer to her. She could feel the heat from his body against her back.

"Not a pure blood, no."

"Not any blood."

His hand traced the line of her shoulders. "It's nothing to be ashamed of, Cat. Sometimes these things happen."

WEREWOLF RACISM
THE HEARTBREAK OF BEING A HALF-BLOOD
— BY C. K. "NOT GOOD ENOUGH" MOSELLE

"Now, come back inside before you catch your death of cold."

Cat hadn't noticed the cold until he mentioned it, but now she was shivering and her feet were numb. *Damn him.* Holding on to the pajama bottoms and shuffling warmth back into her toes against the carpet, Cat let him lead her back to the bed but shook her head when he held the blanket up and motioned her to climb in.

"I'm not tired, and I'm *not* a werewolf."

Lucius dropped the blanket and sat down on top of it. "Suit yourself, but you've had a pretty rough night. I thought you'd be exhausted."

And, instantly, she was. Her legs barely made it to the end of the bed before giving out.

"Stop that," Cat said.

He smiled and fingered the silver-and-turquoise squash blossom peeking out from beneath the open collar of his shirt.

"Stop what?"

"You know what . . . all this Dracula mind-clouding shit."

Lucius fluffed one of the pillows higher against his spine and leaned back.

"Wrong monster," he said. "Cat, we're—"

"I like your necklace." She began playing with the satin-covered buttons on the pajama top to stop him from finishing whatever he was going to tell her. "It's very nice, but I never liked silver, myself. It makes me break out."

"Cat."

"I'm not a fucking werewolf."

This time she didn't hear or feel him move. Lucius was suddenly there, sitting on the end of the bed next to her, his arms around her as she sobbed.

"Cat, listen to me. We've always existed . . . pure blood and human-breed. At one time humankind not only knew we were real, but hunted us. Not from fear, that's part of the movie legend. MAN hunted us because we were different. We looked like man, but not enough. But our species had other problems besides being hunted. We were tottering on the verge of extinction, Cat.

"Maybe God knew he'd made a mistake by creating us and was trying to remedy that error. Only a few of our pure-blood females are born fertile, maybe one out of every hundred births, if that. The males, on the other hand, seem to be able to mate with any female, Lycanthrope or human, they came across and produced offspring."

He tightened his hold on her, moving her head to the crook of his neck. Cat burrowed against him, gasping when her chin accidentally touched the silver necklace. It made her flesh crawl . . . tingle . . . all pins and needles as if it had fallen asleep.

She yelped without realizing it.

Oh God.

"Cat, what's the matter?"

"I-I touched your necklace and it . . . I've never felt anything from silver before. I just didn't like it."

"No, you wouldn't." Leaning away from her, Lucius wrapped his hand around the heavy silver squash blossom. Cat could feel the tremor race through his body. "Until now. But you know what you are now. What you just felt was a long-buried genetic memory. I'm sorry."

Cat rubbed her chin against the back of her hand. "So am I. I don't understand. If I'm . . . if half-breeds have the same powers as—"

"But they don't," Lucius said quickly, "and that was the problem. My ancestors' attempts to bring these . . . children into the Family weren't always successful. Many were destroyed at birth." Cat felt his lips brush against her hair. "They didn't exactly look . . . *human* when they were born. It's a trait that continues to this day, I'm afraid."

Cat wiped her nose with a satin sleeve. "My mother said I was beautiful when I was born!"

It was a lie, but *he* didn't need to know that.

"You were the ugliest baby I'd ever seen, Catherine Kelly. If the nurses hadn't threatened to sue, I would have gladly left you at the hospital."

"Really. Beautiful."

He kissed the top of her head. "I'm not saying you weren't, Cat. Unless it's actively . . . pursued, the trait weakens from generation to generation."

Cat sat up and looked into his face. There was *a story* here. A *major story* that would go far beyond *QUEST* and Denver's local papers.

WEREWOLVES AMONG US

She could see the headlines now.

EXCLUSIVE:
"LIVING WITH THE HIDDEN TRUTH"
— BY C. K. MOSELLE

She licked her lips.

"I do like my meat really rare, and sometimes I even sneak some raw hamburger while I'm making dinner."

Lucius smiled and slid his hands beneath her hair, fingers cupping the back of her head.

"And I do get a little . . . *hyper* once a month. But that's probably only PMS . . . right?"

He cocked his head to one side as he lowered his face to hers.

"Who do you think invented that excuse?"

"Then I really am a . . ."

"Hush," he whispered as he kissed her.

And Cat hushed, obeying without thought of argument, without fear at the touch of his hands against her back, his chest against her breasts as he pushed her down onto the bed . . .

. . . the hardness of his cock against her belly as he slipped the satin pajamas from her body.

"You're beautiful, Cat." His breath tickled her ear, her neck, her throat and hardened her nipples. "So beautiful."

She arched her back, curling her fingers into the thickness of his hair as he kissed and licked his way from her breasts to her belly and finally to the trembling wetness between her legs.

"CATHERINE KELLY MOSELLE! What do you think you're DOING?"

Her mother's voice. Loud and clear. If what Lucius said was right . . . about her being a half-breed werewolf, then at least she knew which side of the family tree she got it from.

The bitch.

Groaning, Cat pushed Lucius up and helped him take off his shirt and pants with all the restraint of a wind-whipped forest fire. Naked, the silver necklace gleaming against his skin, Lucius pushed her higher on the bed . . . then stopped.

Naked, her own body glistening with precoital sweat, she writhed against his legs as he straddled her.

"Are you sure you want this, Cat?" His voice was low and deep, rumbling through her like thunder.

She reached down and cupped him in her hands, sat up, and slipped her lips over the first two inches of his massive shaft. His moan trembled across her tongue.

He tasted of salt and vinegar, smelled of musk and raw meat. Another inch slipped into her mouth and he began moving, slowly at first; tiny thrusts with his hips, back and forth . . . moving . . . getting faster . . . moving . . . her jaw opening to accept more of him . . . her teeth aching to close over the hard, hot flesh.

She growled, and Lucius answered in kind as he withdrew and rolled her over onto her belly.

No! Cat tried to pull away, to run, but he caught her, lifted her hips and held them tight against his own. She shook her head, whimpering suddenly as his fingers found the lips of her vagina and parted them, gently, slipping deep inside to massage the tight muscles into acceptance.

A wordless cry erupted from Cat's throat as she pushed

back against his fingers, lowering her shoulders and wiggling her ass to signal her readiness.

"Are you sure?"

She felt the silken head of his cock press against her, waiting for an answer. He was teasing her. Making her beg for it.

Making her.

Mating her.

"Yes!"

The heavy necklace hit the mattress with a dull thud as he entered her, his body curling over hers as he drove himself in again and again . . . harder and deeper . . . tearing her apart with each stroke . . .

. . . humping her doggie-style.

Werewolf-style.

Cat screamed, fingers digging into the bed as she came, her nails leaving shallow furrows across the mattress. But it was nothing compared to the damage Lucius made with his claws.

She screamed again, when she saw them . . . but it changed as it left her mouth . . . rising higher and higher until it sounded like a howl.

Which Lucius answered a moment later.

21

Lucius pressed his forehead against the window glass and exhaled. His breath fogged the glass and added a layer of frost to the multicolored lights below. It went well with the soft jazz coming from the stereo . . .

. . . and the continuous thrum of water gushing from the shower in the master bath.

Lucius drew a sad face in the condensation. Cat had been in there long enough to scrub every inch of her skin five times over.

Which was probably what she was doing—trying to scrub the feel of him off her.

And in her.

Even though she seemed to like it. Or maybe it was because she had liked it. Acceptance was always hard—finding out what you were and where you fit in the order of things.

His first time wasn't any easier than Cat's had been. So long ago. The night MOTHER had bundled him and Scooter into the back of the rusted International Harvester Jeep his "uncles" took into the high country each fall on hunting trips, and drove east to the wide, empty grasslands.

Except they weren't empty, not really. Even at six and not

yet knowing what was to happen, Lucius could sense *them* . . . the hidden people . . . and it made him giggle and jump around the backseat until MOTHER threatened to turn the car around unless he settled down.

Scooter had felt the people in the grass, too, but his reaction was the opposite of Lucius's. He curled himself into the narrow foot well behind the front seats and pulled his coat up over his head. His corduroy-covered stumps bounced each time the worn shocks failed to compensate for a rut in the road.

The trip itself was nothing exciting—just a midnight trip into Kansas farmland, where they met a weathered old man with silver hair and red skin. An Indian, just like the ones in the black-and-white Westerns their great-uncle Donovan liked to watch on Saturday mornings.

"Your FATHER," MOTHER said as she stopped the car and told him to get out.

He did, greeting the man who was his FATHER and never noticing that Scooter had stayed hidden in the backseat. Or that MOTHER had let him.

His FATHER was one of the hidden people. It would be the first, last, and only time Lucius would ever see him. And the first time, on the drive back to Denver, that MOTHER would explain why they weren't like everyone else.

Lucius wiped the sad face off the window with the side of his hand. *"We are Lycanthropes, Lucius . . . Scooter. That means we can change our shapes from man to wolf,"* MOTHER told him without emotion or hesitation. *"It is an ancient race, far superior to any on this world. Your father is Alpha Male of his Family. I am Alpha Female of ours. Lucius will be Alpha Male when he's older. Scooter, stop that sniveling right now, or I'll leave you by the side of the road for the vultures."*

End of discussion. And probably no less traumatic than the way he finally told Cat.

He shouldn't have told her.

That one thought had snapped at the back of his mind since leaving his MOTHER's house. She didn't belong to a Lycanthrope Family, her own parents had made her a virtual orphan by keeping the lineage a secret. It wouldn't help her now, not in her present life . . . so why the hell had he told her?

Good question. And only one answer—he'd told her to keep her on her guard against the OTHER. Ed.

Not the most selfless reason he could think of.

Turning from the window, Lucius reached up and looped one finger over the squash blossom. The numbing sensation coincided with the squeal of the shower taps being turned off. *Finally,* he thought, and quickly walked to the couch in front of the gas fireplace. The cheerful glow went with the music and dimmed lights, the chilled wine and light meal he'd prepared. To set a mood.

Although he wasn't sure if it was tenderness or forgiveness he was attempting to portray.

He was staring into the fire, watching the blue-tinted flames dance across the ceramic log, when she came into the room.

Cat.

His Cat.

She was wearing a pair of his old CU sweats, the shirt hanging to mid-thigh, the pant legs bunched in layers around her bare feet. She looked like a little girl who decided to play dress-up in her father's clothes.

Lucius stood up as she walked toward the couch, dabbing at the ends of her wet hair with the towel she had in her hands. She smelled of soap and shampoo—of honey and lilac and mountain pine—and that, at the moment, was ideal. His control had begun to slip the moment he heard the shower stop.

"I thought you might be hungry," he said, sitting only after she tucked herself into one corner of the couch, the one farthest from him, and pointing to the tray of cold cuts. "If you'd like something else . . ."

She looked at the tray and increased the efforts on her hair.

"No. I'm fine."

He nodded. "There's a hair dryer in the bathroom, if you'd like me to get it for you. . . ."

"No. Thanks anyway."

He nodded again. Without knowing how exactly, Lucius suddenly felt as green and tongue-tied as the Juvenile he'd been the night MOTHER had taken him to her bed for their initial mating. He hadn't known what to say then and all the years and matings in between hadn't given him any insight into handling his current situation.

His stomach, having sensed the food on its own, grumbled loudly.

Her laughter was the only thing that saved the moment. And his upper GI track.

"Sounds like you're the one who's hungry," Cat said as she draped the towel over her neck and began fluffing her hair by hand. "Why don't you eat something?"

"Because I was taught that it's impolite to eat in front of guests . . . unless there's a dominance issue at stake."

He took a sliver of raw sirloin and held it out to her. If she'd been raised in a True Family, she would have understood the honor he was showing her—Alpha Males take, they don't serve. As it was, Cat looked at his offering and inched farther back into the couch cushions.

"No. Really. I'm not. Hungry."

A ruby-colored drop of blood fell from the meat, sparkling in the firelight. Cat yelped as Lucius caught it before it reached the sand-colored carpet and licked it off the palm of his hand.

"Waste not, want not," Lucius said, suddenly embarrassed at his display. "As my MOTHER always said."

"Mine, too," Cat answered, although he doubted her punishment for leaving food on her plate had been as severe as his. One meal of putrefied squirrel had more than enforced the difference between predator and scavenger.

Lucius set the hardening strip down and selected a fresh one.

"Think of it as sushi. Besides, I hate to eat alone."

Cat reached out and took the meat, gingerly, between thumb and forefinger.

"Thanks." She licked her lips, chewed the bottom one nervously for a moment, then closed her eyes and stuffed the meat into her mouth. Lucius watched her throat work—once, twice as it struggled to get the morsel down.

"Are you all right?" he asked, leaning forward, hand hovering above hers. "Cat?"

Her eyes popped open, started. "Fine." She pressed her back against the couch, nodded. "Thanks. That was great."

Lucius returned to his original position on the couch and lifted the drying strip of meat to his mouth, ate it without tasting and watched the captive fire dance.

"Thank *you* for lying," he said. "And I'm sorry I'm pushing so hard. I"—*shouldn't have told you*—"could get you something else, if you'd rather."

"No. Thanks. I'm fine." Silence. Silence. Silence. "Nice place you've got here."

Lucius looked up as if seeing his "den" for the first time through her eyes. It was nice. Clean and large and far enough away from the congested concrete canyons and his MOTHER's house to enhance the illusion of separation. Of isolation. And independence.

Now he realized just how empty the condo looked. And how empty it would be when Cat left.

"That's beautiful," she said about something, and Lucius looked up to see her staring at the wolf head he'd carved from a cottonwood burl the year he turned fourteen.

The year he became Alpha Male.

"Thanks."

"You made that?" The disbelief in her tone made him laugh.

"What? You think a werewolf can't be artistic?" Lucius snatched another strip of meat and tossed it into his mouth. It was getting easier to be himself around her. "I'll tell you something . . . if you promise not to write about it."

Cat pouted, getting into the game, and made a cross from left to right over the top of the CU Buffalo. "Promise."

"Da Vinci, Frank Lloyd Wright, Ambrose Bierce, Freud were all Alpha Males. Although we don't like to talk about Freud too much."

Cat's pout dropped into an openmouthed stare. "You're kidding."

Lucius shook his head and handed her another piece of meat. This time she took it without question and chewed slowly before swallowing.

"Christ, how many of you . . . us are there?"

"It doesn't matter, Cat, believe me."

But he couldn't tell if she did or not when their eyes met.

"So I guess it's not such an exclusive club after all?"

"No."

Cat wiped her mouth with one edge of the towel and held it there. "Will I change? Into . . . you know."

"Not physically," he told her. "Breeds generally don't experience transformation."

She nodded. "Good." She smiled. "I'd hate to have a bad hair day all over my body."

She broke down into tears. Lucius closed the distance between them and pulled her into his arms.

"Listen to me, Cat, this has been a part of you since birth. I know it's hard to understand and accept, but there's nothing to be afraid of. Think of it as having a hidden birth defect . . . you've lived with it this long without any side effects, so why get upset now that you know what it's called?"

"But what if I have children?"

"That depends on whom you mate . . . marry," he said softly. "Think for a minute. How many stories do you read about *monsters* being born? I mean other than in *QUEST*?"

Cat lifted her head and looked at him. There were tears glistening in her eyes, but she was smiling.

"Touché. So where did we come from?"

"No one knows for sure, but my guess is that there's always been Lycanthropes. Nearly every human culture has legends about shapeshifters. My FATHER . . ." Lucius took a deep breath and looked into the fire.

"My FATHER was a pure-blood Cherokee as well as a pure-blood Lycanthrope. MOTHER chose him as a mate to strengthen our line and add a little variety to the strain. He was a werefox, not wolf. That's where the hair color comes from."

He shivered and closed his eyes as she ran her fingers through his hair, from forehead to nape.

"I like it," she whispered.

Their lips brushed gently against each other, barely touching, the scent of raw meat and estrogen on her tongue as she pushed it into his mouth.

His hand slid beneath the loose sweatshirt and found her bare breast, felt the nipple harden against his fingers.

Their bodies curled toward each other just as the telephone rang—the warbling trill slamming into Lucius's brain like a silver bullet and snapping his head back.

He couldn't tell if he was panting more or if she was. But one thing was certain, the mating scent had evaporated.

"DAMMIT!"

Lucius sat up and glared at the phone.

"D-don't you think you should get that?" Cat asked, sitting up, furiously working the towel over her damp hair.

"The machine will get it," he said, wolfing down another half dozen slices of meat without tasting any. "Besides, it's probably only my MOTHER checking up on me."

He pointed in the direction of the answering machine as his prerecorded message came on. It sounded tinny and weak and very, *very* human.

"Hello, you've reached Lucius Currer. At the sound of the tone please leave a message. Thank you."

beep

"Hey, dude . . . How're they hangin'?"

Lucius felt Cat tense. "Ed."

"Hey, Alpha? You there, man? Or are you and Kit-Cat still bumping uglies?"

The hand unit's plastic creaked under the pressure from Lucius' fingers as he grabbed it and pressed it to his ear.

"How the hell did you get this number?"

The wereman chuckled. "How the hell do you think I got it, Lukie? Your mama can be real cooperative if you give her a chance. Ain't that right, Mrs. C? Oops, forgot . . . she can't come to the phone right now. Indisposed, you know."

Someone was crying in the background, a child. Halona.

The muscles along Lucius's back and shoulders twitched beneath his skin as the beast struggled to be released. Lucius curled his fingers around the squash blossom.

"What have you done to my sister?"

The pseudo-human chuckle deepened into a wolfish growl.

"oh . . . she's your sister? huh. i didn't do anything to her . . . yet."

The chain snapped. Lucius threw the broken necklace onto the couch next to Cat. She looked up at him, silent, her eyes reflecting the fire as she watched the beast emerge.

"You touch her and you're dead."

"jesus, wolfman, chill out. you're even more hyper than that crippled brother of yours. wanna know something, luke?"

No.

"that no-rank died whimpering like a cub. i tore out his throat just so i wouldn't have to hear it anymore. really pitiful, man i mean, i was doing him a favor, something you should have done a long time ago."

The beast fell away, leaving Lucius behind. Scooter was dead. His twin was dead and he hadn't felt a thing. Cat's hand touched his arm, and he shook it off, snarled at her. *It was all her fault. If she hadn't written that damned story Scooter would still be alive and Halona . . . Halona . . .*

"Lucius?" Her eyes were wide, brimming with tears. "What's the matter? What happened?"

"Hey, Luke," Ed shouted into his ear, "you two having your first lover's quarrel, man?"

"I'm going to tear out your fucking heart, *man!*"

"Looking forward to you trying. A pack can only have one Alpha Male . . . and that's what they got." Glass shattered in the background. "Uh-oh, gotta go. The boys are getting a little bored. *Ciao*, cuz."

The line went dead. Like Scooter. And God knew who else.

Howling without transforming, Lucius picked up the phone and tore it from its jack, threw it across the room and watched it shatter.

"Lucius . . . what's *wrong?*"

Cat. His Cat.

All. Her. Fault.

She had the good sense not to scream or even struggle

when he grabbed her arm and half dragged, half carried her to the front door. He didn't trust himself to say anything. Or to open his mouth.

For fear his fangs would find her throat.

For fear that they wouldn't.

22

Ed threw the cordless handset over his shoulder and smiled as it hit the bloodstained parquet.

Lucius's Beta Bitch had put up one hell of a fight, leaving claw marks halfway across the expensive flooring before three of his middle-rankers could pry her legs open.

But from the amount of yelling and screaming that went on after, it must have been worth the effort.

Hell, *all* of them had been worth the effort.

Ed scratched a flake of dried blood off his chest and crossed his legs, settling back into what was left of the old Alpha Female's velvet throne and watching one of his younger bachelors celebrate his recent upgrade from Juvenile with a female who couldn't be more than thirteen or fourteen without her pelt. The mating probably wouldn't take, but Ed wasn't about to put a kibosh on the kid's fun . . . especially not after he himself had picked more cherries in the last couple of hours than a whole truckload of itinerant farm-workers.

Damn, life was good . . . and it just seemed to be getting better all the time.

Yawning contentedly, Ed looked down at the pack's new

Alpha Female. She was curled in a fetal position next to the disemboweled body of the Old Bitch, red hair twisted into tangles, whimpering every time a male came within sniffing distance of her. Not that any of the males would touch her now . . . at least none of *his* males. Lucius's bunch, well, that was another matter. The werewolves hadn't been taught proper Lycanthrope etiquette from the git-go. But they'd learn.

Or they'd end up like their mama and stepbrother.

"Hey, pretty thing," Ed whispered, leaning over his knees. "You okay?"

She shivered and tucked her bruised legs in tighter against her belly. Her bare little bottom was bruised, too, but that was from the floor. Ed felt bad about that, but couldn't help it if she'd literally brought the beast out in him.

"I'm talking to you, sweetie," he said. "And I expect an answer. Are you okay?"

She nodded quickly.

"Good girl. Okay, you just rest now."

He'd chosen her over the mature females because of the scent she carried. Her daddy. The Big Bad Denver Werewolf himself. Lucius.

His whelp. With the tongue-twisting moniker.

Renamed Hallie.

Just looking at her lying there, her naked little body on the verge of ripening up, dropped another quart of blood into the ol' crankshaft and stiffened it right up.

"Changed my mind," Ed told her as he sat back and patted his legs. "Come on up here, Hallie-girl and be sociable."

The whimpering stopped when she got to her feet. She'd learned that lesson quick.

"You sure are a pretty little thing," he said, taking her hand when she got close enough and helping her find room on his lap. "Even with the runny nose and teary eyes."

She wiped her nose off on the back of her hand and lifted her chin. Defiance? Maybe, considering who her parents were.

Had been.

The light from the few chandeliers that hadn't been broken

danced through the tangles in her hair as Ed brushed his hand over them, then continued down and around until he came to the smear of vaginal/virginal blood on her thigh.

"I'm sorry about this," he said, tracing the smear back to its source and tightening his hold on her when she flinched. "But it wasn't really all *that* bad, now was it, Hallie-girl?"

"Don't touch her!"

Ed glanced across the room to where a cowering group of Juveys was being held in check by Killer—their once-beloved brother/cousin—and two of his own mid-ranked males. They were all on their sides, curled into the same position Hallie'd been in . . . and for the same reason.

Cornholed into submission.

"Did one of you boys say something?" Ed asked.

Limbs shifted, eyes darted, but not one mouth opened up. *They* were quick learners, too.

"Looks like we got us a bunch of *were-pussies* here," Arthur, one of the middle-rankers, said. "I swear that cripple turd showed more guts than any of these."

"Literally." Ed chuckled and looked at the mantel over the fireplace. The stuffed wolf's head had been replaced by the cripple's, "mounted" to the wall by an andiron jammed through one eye socket. In a way, it was a tribute . . . Ed doubted the cripple's head would ever have made it up among the honored dead without his help.

"And remind me to get one of you guys to clean up those guts before we split this joint. You let one gut pile go bad and the smell stays forever . . . and I wouldn't want ol' Lucius to think we were bad houseguests. Now," he stopped the banter to turn his attention back to the sweet meat on his lap, "where was I?"

She tensed when he began bouncing her on his knees, her entire little body going rigid and hard . . . much like he was. Ed leaned in and licked the tears off her cheek.

"Ride a cock horse to Banbury Cross, to see a fine lady dressed in fine silk. So what do you say, Hallie-girl . . . you want to take another ride?"

Before she could answer, although Ed thought she'd probably already learned the lesson about only opening her mouth to take (and swallow), not give, one of Lucius's cubs got to his feet.

And was instantly knocked back to the floor.

"Shut up, Pascal," Killer snarled at him.

"B-but, Kieran . . ."

"It's okay, Killer," Ed said, waving his newest bachelor back. "Yes? Did you have something you wanted to say . . . Pascal?"

Shit . . . the names *she gave her young . . .*

The boy—lanky, lackluster, with limp brownish gold hair and heavy-lidded eyes, a standard mid-ranker with no hopes of advancement—lifted himself from the cower and met Ed's eyes.

After three tries.

"P-please. Leave her alone."

Ed stopped bouncing his little bitch and stared at the boy with open admiration. The kid almost had as much guts as his brother/cousin, Killer.

"Why?" Ed asked, wanting to see how long the kid would be able to handle a one-on-one. "I know yo' mama didn't exactly provide you guys with the rules of the *road*, Lycanthrope-speaking, but even you should know that an Alpha Male *always* takes a new Alpha Female." Ed patted Hallie-girl's plump little bottom. "And I've chosen."

"B-but she's *ours*," Pascal whimpered. It was an annoying sound, really got on his nerves.

Ed sighed and pressed his head against her matted hair. She still smelled like Ivory soap and baby shampoo despite everything.

"There is no more *yours*, kid," he said softly. "There's only mine. Now the question is . . . can you and the other happy little campers live with that? 'Cause if you can't, I can have Killer answer that question for you. And, by the way . . . if you decide to live, your name's gonna be Pac-Man. Okay?"

The boy nodded. "O-okay."

"Okay what?" Ed asked. "You wanna live or you like the name."

"B-both."

"Cool." He pulled the little girl/bitch tighter against his chest. "Killer, hobble him. I don't want any of his stuttering genes passed on. Now, my little Hallie-honey . . . how 'bout that ride?"

He entered her again, as easy and gentle as you please while her onetime sibling screamed in typical low-rank male fashion.

Man . . . this was the life! He could hardly wait for the challenge to come. Ol' Lucius wouldn't be able to back down now . . . not after all this . . . and the minute he did, he lost.

Ed dug his nails into the soft flesh along her back as the pressure built. *Oh yeah . . . once I tear ol' Lucius stem from stern all* this *is gonna be mine.*

And no one, man or beast or both, deserves it more.

23

Cat read the note a fourth time even though she already knew what it said, had already memorized it . . . because it was easier than looking at the destruction . . . the *slaughter* around her.

Dear Kit-Cat,
Sorry to have missed you two, but you know how kids are when they get new toys . . . they don't want to do anything but play. And you should see HOW they play. We may have a whole litter of new toys in the spring. Guess I spoil them, but what's a daddy to do, right? Tell Lucius I look forward to finally meeting him. Already met that sweet little girl of his . . . but don't you fret, Kit-Cat, my HEART will always belong to you! You know where to find me. Just make sure to wipe your feet on the mat before you come in. I hate messes. Catch you later, sweet-potater.
Love,
Ed

"Where is he?"
Cat looked up, the bloodied note dragging her arm down

to her side. It'd been pinned to a woman's amputated breast
. . . no . . . not amputated, ripped off, laid out on a silver serv-
ing dish, a single white candle glowing next to it.

Ed's *QUEST* business card leaning up against the base of
the candlestick. A single bloodied thumbprint at one corner.

A perfect set-up for a cover shot: THE *REAL* DENVER
WEREWOLF INVITES YOU FOR TEA.

Too bad she hadn't thought to bring a camera.

Or a new photographer.

"Cat!"

She looked up at Lucius as he pulled her into his arms,
then hid her face against his chest. It didn't help . . . she
could still see the bodies, could still smell the blood. Cat let
the note slip from her fingers.

"Where is he, Cat?"

She stepped back and looked at him. There was blood on
his face, the front of his shirt and coat. He went silent when
they got to the house and saw . . . them, the bodies, leaving
her at the door while he entered the great room to kneel and
touch and check the torn bodies.

The dismembered, and in some cases, partially devoured
wolf carcasses were bad enough to look at. It would have
been worse if the bodies had stayed in human form.

A decapitated, gutted wolf, gray-white coat covered in
blood, had been draped over the broken remains of the velvet
throne where Lucius's mother once sat. A lump of meat re-
sembling a chunk of hamburger shared the blood-stiff seat
with the carcass.

Lucius said it was a fetus, the remains of his child by his
mother.

"He killed everyone?" Cat asked. "Every . . . one?"

"All the mature males and . . . nonfertile females are dead.
And . . . my mother, of course. He wouldn't have wanted
her." Lucius's voice sounded hollow, like it was coming directly through his chest instead of his mouth. "I couldn't find
Cybil. She was pregnant, so they might let her live long
enough to whelp. They killed all the half-bloods and their
offspring. I guess your friend doesn't think as highly of your
kind as we do. Present company excluded."

My kind, Cat thought. *My blood. Half-blood. Present company excluded.*

Cat stepped back and kept stepping back, across the floor, the soles of her feet, still wrapped in Lucius's athletic socks, sticking to the coagulating pools of blood.

"I have to go now," she whispered.

Yes. Go. Now.

Home.

Go home now, Cat. Get the hell out of here.

Cat nodded. "Okay. I'll call you tomorrow and we'll talk, but I have to go now, okay? I don't like it here, Lucius. I really d—"

She should have seen the slap coming, should have noticed that he'd been keeping pace with her, the distance between them the same as she backed up. But she hadn't noticed a damned thing but the blood and bodies.

The slap was like getting hit in the face with a bucket of ice water.

His hands, however, were warm against the tops of her shoulders as he held her.

"I'm sorry, Cat, but I need your help, and I can't let you fall apart right now. Later, I promise . . . and I might even join you, but right now I need you to be as strong as I know you can be. Okay?"

Her eyes were watering but she nodded. "Okay."

"Where is Ed, Cat? I have to find him and save my children."

Children. His children. Like the little pile of hamburger meat next to its mother. *His* mother.

He lifted Cat's chin, making her look at him, when she didn't answer.

"I need you. Please. He's taken my children and will use them to breed his own. Cat, please help me. Tell me where he is."

Cat felt fire and ice crawl up from her stomach to fill in the space below her throat. "I-I don't know. His house, I guess, but I was only there once . . . and I was . . . I don't know where it is."

Pain and loss finally came to Lucius' eyes. He was helpless, there was nothing he could do to avenge his family's death. He was beaten. He'd lost and Ed had won.

Ed, the old hippy-dippy, dirty old man in wolf's clothing had won.

The hell he had! The ice in Cat's throat melted. The fire grew hotter.

"I know where we can get his address," she said. "Tanner's office. Ed's address has to be in the files. Tanner wouldn't hire somebody without an address. I have a key. . . ."

Cat looked down just as she remembered where her purse—with the *QUEST* office key—was. Back at Lucius's apartment. With her clothes. Her own unstained, unbloodied clothes.

Noticing the blood had probably not been the best idea.

"Oh God, Lucius . . ."

Grabbing her by one arm, he hauled her from the room and up the long, sweeping staircase to the second floor.

"You can borrow some of Cybil's clothes," he said as he led her toward the door at the far end of the hall, "black, if at all possible . . . I don't want either of us to be too obvious a target."

"But my key?"

"There are other ways of getting into places, Cat. You just worry about getting dressed and I'll—"

The brass doorknob was smeared with blood, the white lacquered wood around the latch splintered.

"Stay here," Lucius told her as he let go of her arm and entered the brightly lit room.

She should have listened, she really should have.

Ed didn't take Cybil with him.

At least, not *all* of her.

24

they are coming.

He sniffed the air, taking in their scent as if it was a full-course meal, and noisily swallowed the drool that filled his mouth. A hunger unlike any he'd ever known gnawed holes in his belly big enough to drive a semi through.

they are coming.
and they are close.

Dropping to all fours, he scurried into the shadows beneath the desk and tried to make himself as small as possible. Which wasn't easy, given his size.

His *power*.

But he had to. Had to wait in silence and stealth until they were close enough to take.

To kill.

To eat.

To fucking tear out their hearts and swallow them whole, yum-yum.

Drool filled his mouth again and dribbled out the sides—unnoticed—as the sound of their voices echoed up from the elevator shaft.

Toward him.

they're here.

"Suppertime," he whispered, and smacked the frayed edges of his mouth.

Cat bumped her thigh into a corner of the reception-ist's desk and cursed softly.

When she'd grabbed the black cashmere tunic/leggings outfit from the dead female werewolf's closet, along with a *real* ranch mink fur coat, as per Lucius's instructions, Cat hadn't thought the dark camouflage would work against her. But the pain helped. It made damn sure she realized she was still alive and would remain so only if her mind and body cooperated.

"Can't we turn on a couple of lights?" she whispered. Without the bustle and noise and profane tirades that occasionally drifted over the labyrinth of cubbies, the silent, murky room made Cat think of the inside of a church. Or library.

Or tomb.

"I wouldn't unless you're sure it would be normal for lights to be on this late at night. Is it?"

Cat rubbed her leg through the coat's soft fur and shrugged, knowing Lucius could see her as well as she could see him . . . even without the lights. As a child she never questioned *why* she could see so well at night, she just could and thought everyone saw the same pale phosphorescent glow that surrounded people. It was like looking at the color blue and thinking everyone saw the same shade.

She'd thought so many things as a child, believed in so many fairy tales and fantasies. Like seeing the color blue and knowing that monsters were fun to think about but not real.

Damn Lucius for telling her the truth.

Cat turned and watched him study the room.

"Let's keep it dark," he said. "All we need is for some dedicated Denver policeman to notice the light and come up to investigate."

He looked at her and smiled. The silver necklace glowed with its own ghostly luminescence, brightening his features from underneath . . . like kids holding flashlights under their chins to scare their friends. But Cat had already seen too much to be frightened of that.

"Can you access the personnel files from any of these terminals," he asked, "or is it locked into the mainframe of the systems?"

Cat stopped rubbing the bruise on her thigh. "Huh?"

Lucius brushed the hair away from her face and smiled. "Hey, I'm a modern werewolf, lady. Now, can I access it from here, or do I have to hack into your boss's terminal?"

"Oh." *Damn.* "You'll have to use Tanner's computer. I tried to get into the files to check my pay scale . . ." *Back when that sort of thing seemed important.* ". . . and couldn't." He keeps all the personnel records under a password lock in his machine's C drive. Stupid. Especially if the drive crashes, but . . ."

She stopped talking when Lucius nodded and took off in the general, but roundabout, direction of Tanner Boswell's office.

"Here," Cat grabbed his arm and began leading him through the maze, "follow me. Even with night vision—"

"Hunting vision."

"Whatever . . . if you don't know the layout you can get turned around real easy. My first week here I kept getting lost trying to find the ladies' room. Kept ending up at the lunchroom and let me tell you, the smell of espresso when your bladder's about to burst is no—"

Lucius's hand snaked across her mouth as he jerked them both to a stop. They were standing right in front Tanner's office door.

"Humph?"

"Quiet." He'd whispered the word directly into Cat's ear, but he might as well have shouted it at the top of his lungs. "We're not alone."

they know i'm here

He cowered deeper into the shadow under the desk.

they know i'm here and they're leaving!

He could feel them, smell them backing away. *so close so close and now they are going to get away.*

not fair!

He whimpered and drew his nails slowly over the foot-worn carpet. The hunger was digging its own nails into his belly, raking it open. *not fair! not fair!* The leader had given them to him—*now they're leaving*—had promised him their blood and guts and now . . .

. . . now . . .

not. fair!

He pulled himself from the desk with a guttural cry, rising from the shadows like an angry god. Like an angry, *dark* god!

Claws extended, he turned and glared at them through the glass that separated them.

Hunter and prey.

Together again.

For the last time.

The desk chair squealed as he lifted it over his head and threw it at *them*.

It was a good sound.

Lucius strong-armed Cat into one of the narrow cubi-cles as the chair crashed into the front of the flimsy press-board "wall" directly to their right and started a domino effect that toppled the makeshift offices one after another.

The man/beast followed the chair's path a moment later, the soles of his shoes crunching against the glass as he took a step toward them.

"Is it Ed?" She clung to him, pulling him deeper into the cubicle. "Lucius?"

He sniffed the air—sweat and urine, coffee and orange blossoms (?)—and shook his head.

"No. He's human. Ed turned him just enough to be dangerous. Stay here and don't come out until I tell you to, all right?"

For an answer, she reached up and unsnapped the necklace from around his throat. A sound rose from the other side of the partition—a deep, rumbling growl that made the hairs on

Lucius's back and shoulders lift without benefit of transformation.

"Kill him," she whispered.

"Will do," another voice answered.

Cat screamed and dropped the necklace, the silver chain slashing against Lucius's leg as it fell. He barely felt it as he turned and found himself staring into the raw, fleshless skull of a man.

"Oh, I guess I should ask," the man said, standing on tiptoes to look at Cat over Lucius's shoulder. "You *were* talking to me, weren't you, Kit-Cat?"

Lucius had been a moment too late in recognizing the OTHER's scent at the office door, and his timing didn't seem to be improving.

Cat's ex-employer drove a knee deep into Lucius's groin and all hell broke loose.

it is the enemy...and he's a lot harder to bring down than the leader said he'd be.

His knee was still throbbing as he lunged for the big male's throat and got nothing for his trouble except a mouthful of fire-engine red pelt.

Some of the NOT FAIRness came tumbling back at him. The leader had promised him fangs and claws as soon as he killed the ENEMY ... but promises didn't mean much when all you had were stubby fingers and a friggin' partial bridge.

But he'd show 'em ... he'd show 'em both-the leader *and* the ENEMY.

Backing up to get a good running start, he attacked again-coming in low and hard, twisting at the last moment just like when he'd been a center back at East High.

The ENEMY saw it coming and did his own little Elway Twist at the last moment, one clawed fist swiping down from out of nowhere to brush him off as easily as a glob of birdshit.

And *that* made him mad.

He growled when he picked himself up off the floor, but it didn't sound half as powerful as the ENEMY's rumbling threat. But that would come later. Maybe even as soon as he killed the big red male.

"Yeah."

Head down, arms out and forward, he lunged; kicking and biting, grunting with pleasure at the scream of pain and surprise when he got double handful of pelt and ripped it out.

"Ain't so tough now, are you, Mister Man?"

The Silverback leader had told him to be careful and not to take any chances, to kill him quick and clean and be done with it. Not to screw around with macho mind games.

But the leader wasn't here now.

And he was.

And the ENEMY was nothing but a puny li'l . . .

. . . a puny . . . li'l . . .

doesn't matter.

nothing matters but killing the enemy.

and bringing back his heart for the leader's supper.

"Right."

He came in low and fast and found himself heading backwards over the tops of broken cubicles and shattered glass.

Incoming!

He hit, forgot to tuck or roll, and lay there panting. The leader had also promised that nothing would ever hurt him again . . . once he killed the ENEMY . . . but, damn, it sure did hurt *now*!

Wiping the blood and broken teeth off his lips—before he remembered he didn't have lips anymore—he stood up and, after swaying only in three of the four accepted directions, got ready to make another run. *Her* voice stopped him. *Her.* The leader's wanna-be-bitch.

"Lucius?"

He sniffed the air and got nothing but snot.

"Lucius . . . what's going on?"

"Stay where you are, Cat."

yeah, stay right where you are, cat, he thought. *'cause once i'm done with your hairy boyfriend, you and me are gonna have us a little party. and the leader can go fuck himself.*

"Here I come, suckah," he growled—still wimpy, but

strong enough to get the ENEMY'S attention. The big shaggy head turned, eyes glittering, fangs glistening. "I'll get you and your little bitch, Toto . . . and there ain't gonna be nothin' you can do to stop me."

He heard the bitch gasp.

"Tanner?"

she knows.

"Mr. Boswell?"

and she wants me.

Tanner Boswell, Werewolf-in-Training, tossed the shredded remains of his face from side to side as he dropped into a crouch and darted forward.

"That's my boss!" Cat screamed just as the faceless man charged.

His only mistake was to look away, to try to catch her eye and offer some sort of comfort—but it was big enough. The man/beast caught him low, sinking his teeth into Lucius's scrotum.

Wolf or man, that kind of pain laid him out.

"Lucius!"

"Lucius, get up."

"Please?"

Nothing. Times three.

Cat couldn't tell if he was dead or . . . or *what*? He was flat on his back with Tanner Boswell, her usually easygoing boss, standing over him like a vulture waiting for the dinner bell to ring. If Lucius wasn't dead yet, he soon would be unless she did something fast.

"M-Mr. Boswell?"

The thing that was her boss stumbled when he lifted his head in order to look at her. *God.* He was worse than any monster she'd ever seen. Bone gleamed, stark white, against the stripped muscles on his face and now his smile really did go from ear to ear.

"Mr. Boswell?"

The bare muscle bunched up against the bottom edge of his eye sockets. Without lids, they looked like they were constantly about to pop out of his skull. Cat hugged the coat tighter to herself as he stepped over Lucius's still body.

"Why don't you call me Ol' Tannenbutt like you used to, Kit-Cat," he said, words slurred and mumbled. "Like all of you poor upright and uptight *humans* used to. After all, we're still friends, aren't we?"

Cat nodded. "Of course. We're still friends."

"Liar!" he screamed at her, bloody spittle spraying from his mouth. "We were never friends, pussycat. You were my employee and I was your boss and that's all there was. Right?"

She nodded, and that seemed to calm him. "Right. Ed told me all about you . . . half-blood. Damn shame if you ask me. You coulda been really special if you were pure . . . or made, like me."

He lifted his hands to the front of his blood-soaked shirt and straightened his tie. The normal hot-cocoa color of his skin had faded to a pasty tan, like a Hershey Kiss that had gone far beyond its expiration date.

"Ed ain't gonna do more with you than fuck you, you know that, don't you, pussy?" Tanner said, still walking, backing her into a corner. "Too bad, too, 'cause once he's done he'll let the rest of us have a taste and after that there won't be much left. You ain't good enough to be Alpha Bitch . . . but you're good enough for me. Stick with me and I'll protect you. Whadda you say?"

Cat watched the glowing form rise slowly behind her soon-to-*really*-be ex-boss.

"Come on, sweet-thang, whadda you say?"

What do *I say?* "Good-bye."

Lucius reached through the man/beast's spine as eas-ily as a knife slipping through whipped cream.

And heard his belly rumble.

hunger

pain

Real motherfucking, pucker factor of ten PAIN!

Tanner looked down at the bloodied claw protruding from his chest and lifted his hands until they were at the same level. Turned them palm up and then palm down. Only two of them moved, the third just sat there, so to speak, holding on to his heart.

damn

Watching his heart slow down made him sleepy. Shit, the leader was really going to be pissed off. His heart shivered once, like it was cold, and was still. Shaking his head, he looked up at Cat and shrugged.

"Well . . . shit."

The floor, even in his heaviest days of suckin' down the hooch, never felt as good as that moment. When it came up to kiss him good night.

Lucius tried not to inhale the heart's inviting aroma.

It was his right, as victor, to devour the organ and then piss on the remains. His *right*.

As a lasting and unmistakable warning to any other interloper that might think to Challenge him.

It *was* his right. By the ancient law of his ancestors.

Lucius hefted it in, feeling the weight, then threw the heart as hard as he could across the room. It made a soft, snowball *splat* when it hit the far wall.

He'd probably been hanging around Cat too long . . . or maybe it was just the fact that they were standing amid the wreckage of *QUEST* headquarters, because the first question that popped into his mind as he stepped across the stiffening body of the man/beast was what kind of headline all this would make.

DENVER WEREWOLF IN LOVE TRIANGLE
TEARS OUT RIVAL'S HEART
EXCLUSIVE
—BY C. K. MOSELLE

And apparently he wasn't the only one thinking this. Cat was sitting on the floor, knees drawn up to her chin, rocking slowly back and forth.

"It's all my fault," she said. "If I hadn't written that stupid story, none of this would have happened."

As much as he wanted to comfort her, Lucius agreed with her one hundred percent.

"Cat, we can't stay here." He offered her his paw and watched her jerk back when she noticed the blood. Cursing himself under his breath, he switched paws and helped her to her feet. "We made enough noise to wake the dead. The police may already be on their way."

She didn't look too steady, but at least she was standing. More or less perpendicular.

"All right, get the address from the main computer. I'll clean up out here."

Cat's eyes moved from Lucius's muzzle to the body of her ex-employer.

"I can't go in there, Lucius. I . . ."

He snapped the air an inch from her face.

"I said get the address." Lucius let his voice lower naturally into a snarl and watched her cower. "Ed wouldn't have let him erase the files. All of this was an invitation, Cat. He's expecting us."

Expecting me.

He reached out to brush the hair out of her eyes and pretended not to notice how she recoiled at the touch of his paw.

"Go on."

She slipped past him without another word, the soles of her shoes—Cybil's shoes—grinding the glass shards into dust as she hurried to the office. She'd learn. One way or the other, she would learn.

Turning, Lucius walked back to the dead man and tore through his shirtfront, and flesh, with his claws. Although it would never be as satisfying as wolfing down the heart, the liver was still warm and juicy . . .

. . . and would give the papers much more than they needed for a front-page scoop.

Lucius was right: Ed hadn't let Tanner erase the personnel files. He'd left them up and running . . . waiting for them. The terminal's green screen added another layer of depth to Cat's already enhanced perception as she picked her way through the papers and broken bottles that littered the office floor.

A single sheet of paper lay across the keyboard, a hand-drawn black arrow pointing to the screen.

Hey there, Kit-Cat!
Knew you'd be stopping by, so I had Ol' Tannenbutt
bring up my address. Wasn't that nice of him? Didn't
think you'd remember where I lived, considering it's
nowhere near the country club, but it ain't too far. So
why don't you get that cute little rump of yours on over
here. We can't start the party until the guests of honor
show up. And it's gonna be a hell of a party. See ya
soon.
Kiss, kiss.
Love, love—
Ed
B.Y.O.W.*
(*Werewolf!)

"Oh God, Ed . . ."

"That's the name, don't wear it out."

Cat felt a stabbing pain in her lower back as she spun around. To nothing.

"Ed?"

His chuckle drifted through the murky green darkness toward her. "Something wrong, Kit-Cat? You sound a little stressed? I'm down here, sweet-cheeks. On the squawk box. But use the handset . . . you sound funny this way."

Cat stared at the phone, the only thing that hadn't been knocked off the desk, and slowly picked up the receiver.

"Hello? You still there, Kit-Cat? Hey, come on . . . pick it up already."

The phone was splattered with blood, the plastic scored with claw marks.

"I'm not joking, Cat." Ed's voice growled at her from the speaker. "Pick it up right now or you won't like what's going to happen."

Cat stared at the handset . . . took a deep breath . . .

"Listen, you half-blood cunt, you talk to me right now or—"

. . . then slammed it down, again and again and again and again, against the desk until the plastic snapped in half and the room echoed with the sound of her screams.

Sometimes hysterics weren't only a girl's best friend. Sometimes they were the *only* thing a girl could call her own.

25

Ed smiled and dropped the headset back onto its cradle. All that pounding and screaming had reminded him of the first AC/DC concert he'd ever attended. It'd been wild . . . sex and meat just waiting to be snatched . . . but even that couldn't hold a candle to the frenzy that swept the eighteenth-century Italian courts when the castrati took the stage.

What would be next?

And just how much, if any of it, would he show his sweet little Kit-Cat?

If she was *really* good, he might make her his Beta Bitch; if she wasn't he'd have her fixed and give her to the pack as a humping dummy. Either way, she was going to be with them for a long, *long* time—walking bowlegged to whatever was going to take the place of concerts in the next couple of centuries.

If she was good.

Smiling at the thought, Ed took another swig off the can of Original Coors he was holding and watched the silent street outside the front window. It was snowing again—big, wet flakes that clung to everything in sight and added a bit of class to the streets where the hookers and crackheads usually walked.

But not tonight.

Those who hadn't gotten the fifteen-below hint had been cordially invited to dinner by Carmine and the boys. Down in the rumpus room there'd been quite a rumpus . . . for about five minutes.

There were, after all, more mouths to feed now.

Besides, he didn't want Cat to think he lived in a trashy neighborhood.

Ed burped back beer and whore's liver and smacked his lips when a car, headlights cutting a golden path through the bright blue night, took the turn at the end of the block and slowly crept up the street.

His claws punched holes in the can and drained it as the car, nondescript primer and rust, shimmied across the black ice and moved on.

Not them. This time.

Ed tossed the can into the cold fireplace and stretched the anticipation out of his shoulders and arms. He'd never been any good at waiting. Never. For as long as he could remember . . . and that was a long, *long* time.

But it was going to be worth it, he promised himself, *this* time. He'd already put up with more shit from his little Kit-Cat than from any other bitch he'd ever had, and he was going to make her pay for every piece of it.

A piece for a piece.

Ed finished the stretch with a yawn, cocking his head to one side to listen to the rhythmic grunts and groans that seemed to be coming from every room of the house. He'd lied in the note he'd left her . . . the party was already going full force.

The thought of her, raven black snatch spread open and waiting, stiffened his resolve . . . among other things. He'd keep her whole, for a while, maybe breed up a couple of litters until Lucius's red-haired daughter became sexually mature. Yeah . . . then he'd make her beg for it . . . come crawling to him like the cat she was named for. Maybe even hold a little competition to see which of them wanted it worse—his Kit-Cat or Hallie-girl.

It was sad that Lucius wouldn't be around to watch, but a pack could only have one Alpha Male.

Ed sucked the beer off his fingers as he watched the snow pile up outside.

"And may the best Alpha win," he said.

And he would.

26

Cat leaned against the beaded backrest and pulled the collar of the pea coat higher against her cheeks. Lucius had "appropriated" the coat, along with the matching watch cap and gypsy cab from the driver, who had been verbally unwilling to let Cat into his only means of financial support when he saw her "dog."

Having shredded his clothes during the transformation back in the office, he thought a woman seen walking a *big* dog would cause less panic than a woman walking a naked man.

Even in Lo-Do.

The snow and icy roads had made driving the two miles to Ed's house a joy Cat didn't want to repeat any time in the near or far future. She'd slipped and fishtailed on black ice more times than a novice hockey player, but only slid across all four lanes on Speer Boulevard once.

While Lucius, hunkered down in the backseat like a *good* little doggie, barked instructions.

Cat shivered and pulled Cybil's fur coat over her legs. The snow had piled up quickly on the windshield and back window, softening the glow of Christmas lights that decorated the houses lining Ed's block and turning the interior of the car into a deep freeze. She couldn't take a chance on Ed noticing the plume of exhaust coming from a seemingly empty car a half block away from his equally seemingly empty house.

Cat was finally beginning to understand just how much illusion and subterfuge went with being a werewolf.

She pulled the fur up to her chin and decided the one thing she *wouldn't* mind learning was the werewolf ability to keep warm with nothing but the fur on your back.

Like Lucius.

He was out there, somewhere, moving like a shadow through the snow while she sat in the car and quietly froze to death.

ABOMINABLE SNOW-WOMAN FOUND
EXPLAINS THE MEANING OF LIFE
QUEST Exclusive by C. K. Moselle . . . one sick were-puppy
In training.

It would have made a good story, maybe even better than any she'd written—including the *Denver Werewolf* saga—except that *QUEST*, her career, and Tanner Boswell, didn't exist anymore.

Cat stopped short of thinking how her fellow associate editors would react when they got to the office and saw the *mess* they had left.

Her stomach twisted over on itself. *Good thing she wasn't going to* think *about that.* Instead, she would focus on her future.

Maybe she'd send her resume to the *National Enquirer* in the morning.

Cat swung her legs onto the seat and watched the snow continue to pile up while she waited for her werewolf lover to get back.

Like a good little half-blood.

Even though she'd tried to talk him out of it.

"He'll kill you."

"He'll try."

"Then let me go with you."

"No. If you came I'd have to watch out for you as well as me and I can't do that."

"Please, Lucius."

"No."

"Then let's call the police."

"And tell them what? My children are in there, Cat, and I have to go after them myself. Besides, he's expecting me."

"And if you don't come back?"

"If you see anyone besides me, get the hell out of here and don't stop until sunrise. Understand? And don't worry."

Right. Don't worry.

Almost everything Lucius had said was macho bullshit except for the part about the children.

Cat squirmed against the beads until she could see out the back side window, more or less. Nothing moved in the darkness except the snow. All was calm, all was bright . . . and she was stuck in it alone.

"Give 'em hell, hairy," she whispered.

The wind was coming from the west, carrying the scent of blue snow on the mountains and mixing it with his own. Lucius wasn't worried about it. Ed knew he was coming, there was no reason to hide that fact by trying to outflank the wind.

Besides, he wanted Ed to smell him long before he saw him.

Let him know exactly what . . . who he was up against.

It was MAN he hoped to avoid. The cold may have stopped most of the self-deluded werewolf hunters, but the neighborhood was the type that probably had more than one NRA member or gangbanger just itching to prove themselves a marksman.

And the last thing he needed at the moment were armed reinforcements come to keep the peace. If that was to happen, Ed would kill Halona and the rest of the children without hesitation.

Put in a similar situation he might do the same.

And *that* terrified him.

Lucius shook his head, scattering the flakes that settled across the top of his muzzle, and leaned forward until his front paws almost touched the higher drifts. The snow crunched underpaw as he moved and the wind hissed through the bare limbs of trees, but other than that the night was silent.

Empty.

Keeping to the deeper shadows that encircled the neighboring house, Lucius vaulted a low wire fence that separated the properties and ran on all fours to the protection of the sagging porch. What sounds there were—the wind and snow—were silenced by the brick . . . but there was something that bristled the frozen hairs along his spine.

When he pressed his nose into the crack between the porch window and its frame and inhaled, he knew exactly what the *something* was.

The smell of his children, matured beyond their years.

Lucius squeezed his thighs together to stop the erection before it started. The reek of testosterone and vaginal fluid permeated the air surrounding the house. This time he wouldn't stop at simply removing Ed's heart. This time he would honor the old ways.

And swallow it whole.

The rumbling growl followed him as he left the porch and trotted stiff-legged to the back of the house, scanning the winter-bare shrubs that lined the property on that side for the slightest movement, the smallest sound.

Their scent met him before he'd gotten halfway, and he followed it—the olfactory impulses creating their images in his mind . . . skinny, raw-boned creatures that had lived by instinct and cunning for so long they knew no other way.

They were beasts, just like MOTHER said.

But beasts with a sense of humor.

However odd or misplaced.

Three helium-filled Mylar balloons fluttered above a hand lettered sign that had been attached to the open basement door.

PARTY DOWN(stairs)

A paw, gnawed through at the wrist and wrapped with

wire so that one claw-tipped pad extended into a point, had been nailed to the door beneath the sign.

A low growl erupted from Lucius's throat as he leaned forward and sniffed the paw. But the sound died quickly.

It belonged to Pascal . . .

Lucius closed his eyes against the sting of tears. *Pascal, forgive me. I'm so sorry.*

. . . but there was a second scent that opened Lucius's eyes to a red-tinted haze. The scent of the attacker, the mutilator trapped within the frozen beads of saliva that hung like diamonds to the shredded flesh, the gnawed wristbone. Even masked by the stench of decay Lucius knew the scent as well as his own.

No. No. Nonononononononono.

Kieran. His firstborn male cub by Cybil. Pascal's half brother.

Lucius could feel the hackles rise like swords along the back of his neck. Kieran had always been the troublemaker, always picking fights with the other Juveniles to show his dominance, and MOTHER had encouraged it. The Family needed a strong line. . . .

Lucius reached out and brushed the stiff fur. *"i'm sorry, kieran i failed you, too."*

"Hey, water under the bridge, Luke," Ed said from the dark basement. "Besides, he's coming along. Ain'cha, Killer?"

Silence from below and then a slap, flesh against flesh.

"I asked you a question, boy. Now answer before big Luke thinks I can't handle my own pack."

"Y-yes."

Another slap, just as hard.

"Yes, sir. I'm coming along."

It was the pain and fear in Kieran's voice that triggered Lucius's attack instinct. Without thinking, without planning, he ripped Pascal's paw free and sprang, hitting the concrete floor eight feet below in a tight crouch.

They hadn't been expecting him to react like that.

Still in a crouch, Pascal's paw clutched in his own, Lucius

watched them scatter, claws slipping against the uneven foundation, eyes glowing amber.

There were only five that Lucius counted—too easy—and three of those were still in MANskin, standing guard on the children. . . .

Lucius stood and took a step toward them. *His children.* They were bruised and naked, their hair tangled and matted . . . their sweet, clean scents masked by the stench of the monsters that defiled them. All of them . . . the Juveniles and she-cubs, Kieran crouched in one corner, his face marked by Ed's handprint and tears, holding Pascal in his arms. The younger boy looked dazed, feverish, the bandaged stump against his belly.

His children.

All of them.

Except one.

Hair bristling, Lucius threw back his head and bellowed. *"ed!"*

"You rang?"

A paunchy, middle-aged man with long, stringy hair and mustache stepped out from behind the furnace and smiled, bowed until the purple bathrobe he wore flared open to reveal his swollen, glistening penis.

"where is she?"

Ed frowned and scratched his chin. "She, who? I thought Kit-Cat was with you, Luke. Don't tell me you *lost* her already."

"halona."

"Oh . . . her. Well, why didn't you say so, cuz. Hallie-girl, come on out here and say howdy to your old papa."

Ed snapped his fingers and a tiny figure limped slowly, painfully along the same path the wereman had taken.

Lucius felt Pascal's paw slip from his claws as he watched her cross the room. Halona, his angel. He almost didn't recognize her.

Head down, haunches tucked tight, she was the perfect image of a low-ranking female. Her normally burnished copper pelt, silken from the million bedtime brushings Cybil had lavished on it, hung matted and dusty from her trembling body.

Each step seemed an effort greater than she was able to make, but still she came ... one step after the other ... whimpering softly in the back of her throat ... until her nose nudged Ed's outstretched hand.

"Good girl," he told her, patting her on the head like any common *dog*. "Now sit."

Lucius flinched at the sound she made when her little bottom hit the floor.

Ed looked down and blew her a kiss.

"But where are my manners?" the wereman asked. Hand to his chest, he seemed shocked to find himself exposed and quickly closed the gap in the robe before returning his gaze to Lucius. "First, let me tell you what an honor it is to finally meet the *Denver Werewolf*. I'm your biggest fan, dude ... and I mean that, I really do. Wow. Up until Kit-Cat told me about that paw print of yours turning into a handprint, I thought werewolves were only in stories.

"But I tell you, when I saw that, woo, you could have knocked me over with a sledgehammer. I mean, my little pack may be as uncivilized as you get, but we never left any kind of proof of our existence behind. Jeez, you got balls, wolfman ... I can't argue with that."

He reached down and lifted Halona's muzzle. Lucius watched a tear soak into the fur beneath her eyes.

"And you'll never know what meeting you and your family has done for us," Ed continued. "We were dying out, bro ... come to the end of a long genetic strand. See, *my* kind has to mate *in* kind. Screw a human bitch and all you get's a happy human bitch. No cubs." He shrugged and opened the robe, slipped it off his shoulders and let it fall to the floor. "But you stick it into a blood relation ... Well, here, let me show you."

The wereman was reaching for Halona as Lucius lunged, full force, for his throat. A big black male with glowing eyes intercepted the attack, tearing a ragged wound in Lucius's left shoulder.

The pain threw Lucius off-balance and he almost fell,

catching himself at the last moment as the black pelt turned and came at him again. But this time Lucius was ready. Crouching until the male was almost on him, Lucius suddenly stood on his hind legs and slashed with his claws.

The tall black man began to transform almost before his body . . . and head hit the floor at opposite ends of the basement.

"Shit, I liked Myron," Ed said as he looked from one piece to the other, "I really did. Okay, Killer . . . you're up."

Kieran looked down at Pascal and then up at Lucius, eyes pleading for help.

"Please, I—I can't—"

Ed's features shifted and, for only an instant, Lucius saw the beast.

"What did you say, boy?"

Fear replaced the silent plea for help as Kieran let go of his brother and pushed his way through the group of children to Ed's side, opposite his sister.

"killer?" Lucius asked.

"A whole lot easier to pronounce than the name your mama saddled him with." Ed turned and smiled at Lucius's heir. "Personally, I think it suits him. Go on, Killer, make me proud."

Kieran didn't look up at Lucius as he walked to one of the basement support beams.

"kieran."

"I—" Kieran shook his head. His whole body shook. There were tears in his eyes when he finally looked up. "I told Pascal I was sorry but . . . I'm sorry, I—I don't have a choice."

Lucius rushed forward, his only thought to comfort his son, when Kieran reached up and knocked a metal stake out of the wood. A net, heavy and burning into Lucius's flesh, covered him like a glittering shroud.

"There you go! See, I knew you had it in you, Killer," Ed said, knuckling the boy's shoulder as he walked to where Lucius lay panting. "Pretty cool, huh? I saw this at some artsy-fartsy boutique gallery on Larimer and just couldn't pass it up. Now, to be honest with you, I don't know what *normal* people would use an eighty pound silver-wire net for, but . . . damn it looks good on you."

"take it off me."

Ed squatted next to Lucius, making sure he wasn't anywhere near the silver net, and clapped. Hanging down between his thighs, his engorged penis swung back and forth like a metronome.

"You're kidding, right? Don't think so, Luke, so you just stretch out and relax while we go get the other guest of honor. Stan . . . why don't you slip into something less comfortable and invite Ms. Moselle to the party. She's in the beat-up Lincoln, five houses down."

"No."

Ed stood up and watched the beast shiver and shrink back beneath Lucius's skin. Directly behind Ed, gleaming pale green in the dark, a lanky red-haired boy was letting his beast out. There was no way Cat could mistake the dull red pelt and blunt muzzle for his own . . . unless . . .

—If you see anyone besides me, get the hell out of here and don't stop until sunrise. Understand?—

She wouldn't be expecting him in human form. She'd expect to see a red wolf . . . and that's what she'd see, more or less.

"Leave her alone."

Ed cocked his head to one side and smiled down at him.

"You're always asking for stuff I can't do, and it's pissing me off. Make's me feel like a poor host, y'know." Walking back to the transformed Juvenile, he lifted the boy under the arms and forced him into a semistanding position. "His kind walks upright, you do the same. Now, go fetch."

The wereman nodded and staggered awkwardly up the basement stairs. *—She wouldn't notice the difference. She would only see a red werewolf . . . "We all look alike to them."—*

Lucius tried to push himself off the floor only to fall back under the net's weight.

"Hey, chill out, dude," Ed told him, "Stan ain't gonna hurt your bitch . . .

". . . I get to do that."

27

Cat buried her nose deeper into the coat's thick pelt and tried to find a spot on the worn seat that was comfortable and didn't rattle every time she moved.

The search proved to be as fruitless as it had ten minutes ago . . . and ten minutes before that. The dashboard clock clicked over another digit. It wasn't exactly her idea of how to spend an evening—slowly freezing to death in a gypsy cab (minus the gypsy), draped in fur and wool while her boyfriend . . .

Whoa.

Cat spun around in the seat, ignoring the rattling and the sharp pain of kneecaps coming into contact with bottom of steering wheel, and took a deep, ragged breath. *What the hell do I mean boyfriend?* He'd raped her.

Whoa again, Pocahontas.

Leaning forward, Cat slid her arms up over the wheel and pressed her chin against the back of her hands. It wasn't rape. They'd made love. And the strength of their combined orgasms had almost knocked her out.

She could still feel it, and him, inside her.

"Dammit."

What she wouldn't give to be back home, in bed . . . with the covers pulled up over her head. Just like when she was little—when monsters only existed under beds and didn't make a habit of walking around pretending to be like everybody else.

Cat turned her head to the right and squinted at the houses she could barely see through the condensation and frost on the passenger's side window. Televisions flickered behind front-room curtains and multicolored Christmas lights blinked on and off, or just twinkled in the chill. How many of those seemingly nice, normal people were really monsters under the skin?

With or without being Lycanthrope.

Cat lifted her head and looked at her hands, willed them to change—sprout hair, develop claws, something.

Nothing.

Except a scream that shattered the night and added another bruise to the top of her knees.

Turning, her untransformed hands grabbing the back of the seat, Cat watched two shadows suddenly appear on the frosted back window as something slammed into the rear bumper.

"Pablo! Stop it, you're going to tear my coat!"

The shadows moved past the passenger window and did their own transformation—into a Hispanic couple in their early twenties. Before they disappeared behind the snow-covered windshield, Cat watched the man throw his arm around the woman's waist and hug her to him.

Love.

"What a bitch of a thing to happen to someone," Cat whispered, while the young couple transformed back into shadows and then into nothing. "Jesus, Lucius, where the hell are—"

Lucius tapped on the driver's side window, smiling wide and toothy as only a werewolf could.

"SHIT!"

He chuckled at her through the glass, his breath steaming. "You scared me!"

He stopped chuckling and flattened his ears against the sides of his skull.

"sorry . . . ki-cat"

"What?"

A sheepish grin, if that was possible on a wolfish face.

"sorry, cat." The door latch rattled. *"open the door. cat. it's cold out here."*

His voice was different. Cat's hand stopped an inch above the button lock. A small groove ruffled the fur between his eyes. He was frowning above the toothy grin.

"what's the matter, cat?"

"Where are the children . . . Lucius?"

He cocked his head, the frown deepening. *"children?"*

Shit. Cat shook her head and slid away from the door.

"Where's Lucius? What have you done to him?"

The eyes flared bright green and all pretense faded.

"shit, you think you're so smart, don't you? but you're dumber than dirt. you're nuthin' but a stinkin' half-blood bitch and that's all you'll ever be. now open this door before i rip it off the hinges. do it!"

Cat pressed her back against the passenger-side door. He was bluffing. If he could really tear the door off, he'd already have done it by now.

"Fuck you."

"maybe later . . . after papa ed's done with you . . . if there's anything left. last chance, half-blood, open it."

The neighborhood might be old and run-down, but if there were TVs in the houses there was a chance those TVs were sometimes tuned to the reruns of *Emergency 911*. Cat pulled as much of the freezing air into her lungs as they would hold and then let it out all at once:

"FIRE!"

That was the first thing they taught her in her college self-defense course—you never yell Rape! or Murder! or Help! because no one is going to help, because no one wants to get involved.

No one, on the other hand, will miss the opportunity to watch a good inferno.

"FYE-ERR!"

Curtains rustled, parted when the werewolf shattered the window. Memories of other glass breaking—of Tanner Boswell, bloodied and insane, throwing his chair through the wall of his office and then following—made her do the exact opposite of everything she'd been taught.

She panicked.

As the werewolf was reaching for her through the missing driver's side window, Cat was going out the passenger's side door.

He caught her before she'd gone three steps and pulled her into the shadows next to the house.

If there had been anyone behind the rustling curtains they would have seen a woman being mauled by a large, shaggy dog . . . and that just wasn't the stuff to bother 9-1-1 about.

At least not on a cold, snowy night where you might be expected to go out and give your report in person. Nope, not worth bothering with.

Cat would have laughed at that thought, if she hadn't been so busy getting torn apart.

"Aw, c'mon, sweet-cakes, open those pretty little eyes of yours."

Damn. I'm not dead after all.

Cat opened her eyes to soft, gentle darkness and sat up as much as the oversize beanbag chair would permit. She was in a basement—the overhead pipes and unfinished ceiling, combined with the remembered smells of laundry soap and mildew from her parents' house, told her that much.

But she'd never been in a basement quite like this one.

And *never* one that had been hosted.

Ed looked like a New Age Potentate.

Seated in a white Brentwood rocker on cushions that matched the purple-satin robe he was wearing, he was surrounded by a dozen or more naked supplicants. Slack-bellied men, biker dudes, teenaged boys, and little girls all *(naked!)* jostled and bumped each other as they stroked Ed's body.

Cat swallowed the bile that filled her mouth when she recognized one of the naked children, Lucius's daughter, sitting at Ed's right knee, shoulders slumped forward, her loose hair all but covering her face.

Lucius lay wrapped in only a glittering web under Ed's slippered left foot.

Despite all that naked flesh, or maybe because of it, Cybil's cashmere tunic and pants suddenly seemed useless to keep out the chill that began to creep into Cat's arms and legs.

DENVER WEREWOLF, PART II

DIRTY OLD MAN REALLY DIRTY OLD DOG

Okay, girl, she said to herself, *let's see some of that talent you're so proud of . . .*

"Ed . . ." It took some doing, but Cat managed to flutter her lashes. "Oh, God, why didn't you tell me?"

He smiled and lifted his arms in benediction. "Naw, nothing so exalted. Just Ed'll do, but thanks for the thought. But why didn't I tell you what?"

Another flutter. "About being a werewolf? I mean, if I'd known, I would have written about you and not even bothered about . . ." She wrinkled her nose at the children and felt her heart skip a beat. Fewer than half of them could meet her gaze. "What did you *do* to them? I mean, I'm not up on werewolf domestic situations and I—"

Ed's laughter stopped her rambling.

"You are something else, woman. You know that? Here you are, smack dab in the middle of a den of shapeshifters and you want to take notes. I'm surprised you don't *clank* when you walk. But as for what I *did* . . ." Ed looked at the huddled group of children and shrugged. "Nothing. At least by werewolf standards. Whenever a new leader takes over the rules of dominance have to be reestablished. It's standard procedure, ain't it, Hallie-girl?"

He reached down and ran a hand slowly over her naked shoulder. Cat pressed her elbows into the pit of her stomach when the child tried to shrink away from the touch.

"Goddammit, Ed, leave her alone."

"What? And here I thought you wanted to write an article on me. I'm hurt, seriously hurt." But despite being *hurt* Ed stopped and sat back, then swept the air with his hand. "So, what do you think about *my* palatial estate, huh? Not really up to Luke's usual scale of grandeur, but pretty nice I think."

Cat didn't move her eyes off his face. "It sucks."

Ed pouted, his lower lip protruding below the bristling hair, and instantly became the image of the person Cat had first thought him to be—sweet, gentle, not to be taken seriously on any account, dirty old man who never grew up.

"Aw, and here I thought you'd love your new home."

The chill in her arms and legs got worse. "My new what?"

"Home, Kit-Cat. Digs, the place to hang your hat, you know . . . where meals get cooked and babies get born." He leaned back into the stilted touches of his kidnaped admirers. "*Our* babies, for instance. Yours and mine."

"You're fucking out of your mind if you think I'll let you . . ."

Ed lifted one hand and Cat felt her jaw snap shut. It felt as if her teeth had suddenly grown together, and each time she tried to pull them apart a stinging pain brought tears to her eyes.

She glared at him.

"And you were *trying* to say?" Ed smiled at her glare and lowered his hand to scratch his chest. "Honey, I could make you want it worse than you've ever wanted anything in your life. But that's not the way *we* play. See, me and mine are just regular Joes trying to scratch out a living the best we can. Not like a fortunate few who are literally born with silver collars around their necks."

Without moving his eyes from hers, Ed raised his foot and slammed it into the point of Lucius's chin . . . just in case Cat hadn't guessed who belonged to the fortunate few.

"Ain't that right, Luke?" He nudged Lucius again, careful to keep the slipper between him and the glittering net. "Guess Mr. Denver Werewolf doesn't feel like talking right now. Not that I blame him, but I'm sure he'll be talking up a storm once you and I get going."

Cat grunted at the pain as she tried to manually pry her jaws apart.

"My God, will you look at that, Luke? Seems like I underestimated our girl again, didn't I? The pain, I'm told, is not real cool . . . must be that ounce or so of wereblood you got in you, huh? Anyway, sorry, sweet-cakes, here, allow me."

He didn't move but suddenly Cat's mouth and tongue were back in working order and the pain was gone.

"Now, as you were saying," Ed prompted.

So Cat continued.

"You fucking bastard! If you think I'm going to let you touch me, you're out of your mind!" Cat pushed her hands down against the bulging, but constantly shifting sides of the beanbag and tried to lever herself out of it. There was no way she was going to get out of there without help. Which was probably why Ed put her there. "You shithead! I'll kill you before I let that happen."

Ed applauded. Slowly. And yawned around teeth that were suddenly too long and pointed for his mouth.

"*Brava*, but a little overdone, don't you think? I said I didn't want to make you want me . . . but that don't mean I ain't going to screw you seven ways from Sunday while Luke watches. You're *letting* me has nothing to do with it. Look, baby, I'll be honest with you. You're not exactly every wereman's idea of a dream girl, okay. I mean, you can't even transform into a more accessible shape. I just need someone to start producing offspring until my little honey Hallie here grows up enough to provide the pack with a lineage of true cross-breeds."

Ed waved the adoring touches away and stood up. On Lucius.

"So tell me, Luke," he said, looking down, "is Kit-Cat a noisy lover or is she meek and quiet like your daughter?"

"I'm going to enjoy killing you, Ed," Lucius hissed from beneath the net.

"Oh my, oh my," Ed said as he stepped down and back kicked Lucius in the side of the head. "I is so scared, Massa Luke, I surely is!"

"Leave him alone, Ed, and I'll do whatever you want," Cat yelled. Both Ed and Lucius turned to look at her. "I mean it. You leave him alone . . . and let him live and I'll . . . I'll let you do whatever you want."

Three of the naked men standing around the chair broke out laughing, and even though Ed managed to keep a straight face, his eyes were glistening.

"What an offer. Looks like the little bitch has a soft spot for you, cuz. But I'm touched, Cat, really." Ed untied his robe and flashed her. "Your boy's big, but you think you can handle The Exterminator?"

Cat balled her hands into fists, driving her nails deeper into her palms in an effort to stay calm while Ed wiggled his massive, purple-veined penis at her. *God, if only I could transform.*

"Handle what?" she asked innocently. "I don't see anything."

The boy who had impersonated Lucius feigned coughing into a fist to hide his smile, but he wasn't fast or clever enough. Ed's attack came so suddenly that Cat never saw him move. One minute the red-haired boy was standing next to the chair, pretending to cough, and the next he was watching his blood snake down his chest from the opening where his throat had been only a moment before.

The man next to him—blond, with a scarred face and biker tattoos on his arms—finished the job by snapping what remained of the boy's neck.

"Alas, poor Stanley, we knew him well," Ed misquoted as the blond man cracked the boy like a walnut and tossed him the heart. Blood splattered across the concrete floor in an arc that ended just inches from Cat's feet.

"A lad of *finite* jest, but one who never learned to keep it to himself." Ed ate the heart in four bites, then rubbed the blood that had spurted from it into his face and chest. "Aw, 1980 . . . a good year." He clapped, noticed the blood on his hands, and began licking it from his fingers. "Now, where were we, Kit-Cat? Oh yeah . . . fucking."

Cat pulled her legs up to her chest as the beanbag closed in around her.

"I should have known what you were the first time I saw you."

"Oh?" Wiping his hands off on his robe, Ed walked slowly

across the room and squatted down next to her. "And what, pray tell, is that?"

Cat smiled, gathering a good sized wad of spit on her tongue.

"Discipline, Cat" he warned, "that's just what I was demonstrating. Discipline in everything. See, Stanley forgot who was in charge, and you saw what happened. Now, let's try this one more time. Answer me, little Kit-Cat or I'll—"

The wad of spit landed, with perfect accuracy, in the center of his right eye.

"You're a monster . . . and it has nothing to do with the fact that you can shapeshift."

He chuckled and wiped the sticky froth off his face with one sleeve.

"Cute, I love a woman who's feisty." He blew her a kiss and then grabbed her knees, wrenching them open. "But not too feisty. That thing with Stanley was a demonstration of what can happen if you piss me off."

His fingers eased down over her knees toward her thighs. Cat covered her crotch with her hands, but as hard as she tried, she couldn't close her legs.

"Modest, how sweet. You do the same thing with ol' Luke? Didn't think so. But anyway, back to the demonstration. Think of it as a freebie. You get the message, great. You don't, and you'll wish you died as easy as Stan did. Understand?"

No, she didn't understand . . . wouldn't understand. No, no, NO! Wasn't that what every stupid female victim kept shouting over and over while the monster sank his fangs into her neck, or sliced her open, or rammed a pitchfork through her belly, or . . .

. . . raped her?

Ed's eyes flashed emerald green, and he leaned forward. "I asked you if you understood, Kit-Cat . . . do you?"

Her hand came up and slashed his face—from ear to lip, opening four bloody trails across the no-man's-land of wrinkles on his cheek.

The emerald light in Ed's eyes flared into a chartreuse fire. His hand was even faster than Cat's had been. He ripped the

leggings and panties off before she had a chance to scream.
Then he slapped her, hard enough to knock her out of the
beanbag's clinging grasp.

"No more freebies," he growled, kicking her onto her back
and spreading her legs in the same manner. "And, to para-
phrase Randy Newman . . . you can keep your top on. Your
tits aren't that much to look at, anyway. And you only got
the two."

He ripped the robe trying to get it off. His penis quivered
as he positioned himself over her, hands pinning her shoulders to the cold concrete floor, knees pressing outward
against knees.

"You're gonna love this, Kit-Cat," Ed whispered as he
lowered his face to her, the tip of his penis poised at the
outer lips of her vagina. "Holler, if you don't."

"LUCIUS!

"Let her go!"

Ed lifted himself just enough to glance over his shoulder
and Cat took the opportunity to tuck and roll out from under
him. He hardly noticed she was gone, all his attention—as
well as hers once she'd gotten to the far end of the basement
and turned around—was on Lucius.

He was glaring at Ed through the silver strands. His entire
body shook, but Cat couldn't tell if it was from pain or anger.

Ed didn't seem to care. He pushed himself into a sitting
position and shook his head.

"Well, well . . . my footstool is giving me orders. Now
that's something you don't see every day, especially since I
thought all that silver was supposed to keep you quiet."

"That's part of the legend we don't like to spread around."
The net tore as easily in Lucius's hands as if it was tissue,
filling the basement with an ear-piercing metallic hum. "Silver has a calming effect on the beast within us . . . but any
strong emotion can free it. My kind wears silver as a reminder, not a cure."

Ed stood up, shaking his head. "You're one sneaky bastard, Luke, I have to tell you that."

Lucius, in full pelt, tossed the ruined net aside and bowed.
"praise from the master. if i had a master."

"Jesus Christ," Cat screamed, "what the hell are you waiting for? Kill him, Lucius!"

Both of them looked at her Man-in-Beast and Beast-in-Man. Ed was the first to look away, shaking his head slowly as he did.

"That's not the way it's done, Kit-Cat," he explained, "at least not in polite Lycanthrope society. You just can't take another Male's pack without a little ritual combat. With probably a whole lot less ritual than usual."

"probably," Lucius answered.

"You see, Kit-Cat," Ed said, waving the naked men and children back toward the opposite wall, "if I was to kill ol' Luke here on the sly, his family would be less likely to accept me as the Big Kahuna Alpha Male, but this way . . . when they *see* me kill him, they'll have to accept me." He looked back over his shoulder at Cat. "They won't like it, but they won't have a choice . . . you can't have a pack without an Alpha Male."

Cat looked past Ed to Lucius.

"You fucking bastard!" Even Ed seemed shocked. "You could have stopped him before he touched me?"

She pulled the tunic down over her naked thighs and let tears form in her eyes. "I believed you . . . when you told me about being the Alpha Male, but you're nothing. You let him touch me . . . you let him touch your children and you . . . you did nothing to stop it."

Cat felt a tear slid down one cheek. "You're not worth anything. I hate you."

Ed pretended to dab one eye with the corner of his sleeve.

"Oh, Kit-Cat . . . don't be so hard on Luke. Why would he do more for a half-blood than he did for his own family? Besides, if he jumped the gun any sooner, just think of all that dramatic tension that would have been lost." He nodded to Lucius. "A wonderful bit of business. But I sure wished Killer had mentioned that thing with the silver . . . sort of surprising you forgot, isn't it . . . Killer?"

A thin whimper came from the shivering boy.

"Well, we'll talk about that when I finish up here. Tell

you what . . . you go stand by Kit-Cat and keep her company, and I'll forget what you tried to do."

Cat saw Lucius watch the boy she remembered from the brightly lit room at the Currer mansion take a step toward her.

"kieran, stay where you are."

Another whine squeezed past the boy's throat as he shifted from foot to foot. Without another sound, he transformed into a pale, shivering wolf and continued to limp in her direction. It was obvious from his posture—head down, haunches tight—that he didn't want to be there, but had no choice.

But it was just as obvious that he feared Ed more than he did his own father.

Cat could understand that feeling.

"Oh, don't take it too hard," Ed said when they were again facing each other. "Killer's already on thin ice as far as this pack's concerned. But don't worry, he won't touch Kit-Cat . . . unless I tell him to. Right, Killer?"

Cat felt the cashmere snag against the rough plaster wall as the frightened cub swung his head toward her and snapped listlessly at the air between them. He wouldn't touch her. Yet.

Ed rubbed his hands together like a man about to heft a sledgehammer at a county fair.

"Okay, Luke, looks like we're just about ready to rumble." His voice had dropped an octave, the words lengthening into growls. "Fangs and claws and may the best *man* win."

He turned and winked at Cat. "It's just like doctorin' a print, Kit-*cat. presto—*"

28

—chango!"

The transformation started from the inside—the sinewy wolf shape pushing up through Ed's doughy, "Regular Joe" body; the layers of soft, paunchy flesh stretching until they hugged the lengthening bones.

Winking at Cat as he fell to all fours, Ed arched his back and groaned through clenched jaws. The change from man to beast seemed harder on him than it had on Lucius—he'd simply changed, Cat remembered, without the violent tremors and dry heaves that rocked Ed's body.

"really something . . . ain't it, kit- . . . cat?" Bile dribbled from the corners of his mouth and collected in his beard. *"sure like to see . . . david copperfield try . . . this on . . . stage."*

With a sound like someone eating celery, Ed's rib cage began folding in on itself, the bottommost ribs curving upward as the middle and upper ribs expanded. Ed gasped for air to fill the re-formed lungs as his thin, shoulder-length hair thickened and spilled down over his spine and quivering ass to meet the coarse silver hair that sprouted on his arms and legs.

Ed sneezed and Cat watched the whole front of his face—nose, cheeks, and jaw—shoot forward into a blunt, tooth-lined muzzle. The scraggly beard boiled down over his throat, continuing until it covered his entire belly and genitals.

Cat looked away when another convulsion forced the shaft of his bloodred penis from its fur-covered sheath.

Ed lowered his nose to the concrete floor and rubbed away the thin layer of human skin. He winked at her as he lifted his head.

It was still Ed. Fur-covered and wolf-shaped, it was still Ed. Good old Ed. Ed the ex-hippie. Ed the photography wizard.

Ed the Wereman.

STORY AT ELEVEN

QUEST FIRSTHAND REPORT

Cat dug her fingers into the thick cashmere and wondered what it must feel like—to transform from the something you thought you were to the thing you really were. And thank God that she would never have to go through it.

If there was anything good about being a half-blood, it was that. Unless Lucius had lied to her.

"No," she whispered, and heard the wolf/boy who had been Kieran snarl weakly, letting her know he was still there and watching.

Just like his father.

Just watching and not *doing* anything.

Body hunched forward at the shoulders and resting on the pads of his hind legs, claws on his front paws clicking as he slowly flexed and relaxed, Lucius did just that—*watched* the metamorphosis with detached indifference. Waiting patiently for his rival to finish transforming from man to beast so their stupid, macho . . . *lupus* contest could start.

"Lucius, now's your chance!" Cat hissed at him. "For God's sake . . . Do something."

His black eyes shifted toward her for only a moment before turning away. The greenish glow that surrounded him shimmered when he shook his head. No.

Kieran whimpered low and soft at her side. *"he can't do anything yet, we have rules."*

Their eyes met, and Kieran was the first to look away.

"Your rules suck," she said.

"but they're all we have," he whispered.

If it had been possible at that moment, Cat would have felt sorry for the frightened boy. As it was, the moment was filled with much more important things.

Ed had finished transforming.

STARTLING NEW *WEREWOLF* DIET

TRANSFORM THOSE UNSIGHTLY BULGES INTO SINEWY MUSCLES!

Blood mixed with the saliva that pooled around his fangs and dripped onto the hard-packed floor. Still panting, Ed licked his muzzle, then shook his head. Gray/red spittle arced through the air and landed on both Lucius and his daughter.

Neither of them moved to brush the drops away.

The silver wolf turned his head toward Cat and smiled. Even with the muzzle and pointed ears, he still looked remarkably like Ed.

"pretty cool, don't you think, kit-cat? i mean, seriously, don't you think this would have made a better story for quest?" He shook his head and more spittle flew. *"too bad you'll never get a chance to write it. but i think you're gonna be way too busy servicing me and my boys to even think about it for a long, long time. if ever."*

He winked again and clicked his tongue up against his fangs.

Cat closed her eyes and instantly saw one last headline flash across the tabloid of her mind:

THE CONTINUING DENVER WEREWOLF SAGA
"TORN BETWEEN TWO LOVERS—
LITERALLY"—BY C. K. "ALPHA BITCH" MOSELLE

Two howls rose from the silence behind her closed lids to fill the basement. Cat opened her eyes just as Ed broke the howl and lowered his head. Lucius's voice fell silent a moment later.

"to the death, cuz?" Ed asked, although Cat had the feeling it was more of a formality than a real question.

And Lucius answered, *"to the death."*

Lucius feigned a lunge and watched the Silverback start. He still had the advantage of height over the wereman, standing upright while Ed was confined to true wolf form, and that was good. Lucius's entire body felt like one giant cramped muscle. What he'd told Ed about the silver was only half true—although strong emotion could trigger transformation even in the presence of silver, the inherited allergy his kind had to the metal still left him feeling weak.

MOTHER had taken great sadistic joy in telling him and Scooter what would happen to them if they didn't wear silver. One scratch, one bullet would end their centuries-long life span in an instant.

That's why she made them wear silver collars or chains or braided strands, to build up a tolerance. And to protect them from their lesser selves.

MOTHER said.

But looking into the OTHER's eyes, Lucius decided MOTHER hadn't known what the fuck she was talking about. Wearing silver of any kind only prevented them from being what nature, and perhaps God, had intended them to be. While his kind tried to emulate MAN, Ed and his fellow shapeshifters had been content with the pelt they'd been born into.

But even so, he was as much Lycanthrope as Ed and no amount of silver or self-doubt was ever going to change that.

"something the matter, ed?" Lucius asked as he raised his hackles and eased forward a step. Pins and needles pricked each nerve as he moved.

"not at all, luke. just wondering why you're limping."

Before Lucius could answer, Ed feigned his own attack—left then right, snapping the air just above Lucius's groin when he didn't react.

"mister cool, huh? either that or you never saw it coming." Ed let his tongue loll to one side. *"man, this is gonna*

be too easy. wonder what your little piece of tail over there's gonna think when i kill her big bad wolfie boyfriend. i'll ask her when i have her spread facedown on the fl—"

Lucius charged, grabbing Ed around the forelegs and using his shoulder to keep the savage jaws away from his throat.

"one of the benefits of being bipedal," he said as he flipped Ed over onto his back. He could have finished him then, leaned forward and torn out the Silverback's throat, like Cat was screaming for him to do, but Lucius backed away and let Ed clamber back to his feet. His claws had left grooves in the concrete by the time he'd gotten on all fours. *"what's the matter, ed? don't like an opponent that can fight back?"*

This time it was Ed's turn to attack, and he did. And that was what the beast in Lucius had been waiting for. As Ed came in, low and quick, Lucius sidestepped at the last possible moment and slashed downward with his claws. But the old Silverback was faster than Lucius thought. Four-inch-deep rents parted flesh and fur above Ed's left haunch.

But the blood he licked from his claws was satisfying nonetheless.

"first blood," Lucius said, holding up his paw.

Ed glared as he turned, favoring the dripping wounds. *"doesn't count in this match, luke. we're playing for all the cookies."*

Lucius flicked the blood from his paw. Only death counted in this challenge for dominance . . . and death came for him wrapped in a silver pelt.

MOTHER was wrong about that, too. Silver could kill him.

Or at least it would try to.

Rage foam flew from Ed's muzzle as he came at Lucius a second time, but the pain that toppled him came from behind . . . spiraling up from his right ankle until it had set its claws into his brain. He'd never felt pain before, not like this . . . not real, like this. He'd been stifled, crippled.

Cat's scream echoed above and around him like the wind pouring through a canyon. There was no place he could move to escape it.

There was no way he could move, period.

Lucius saw the big yellow wolf glance back at him before slinking back into the dull green shadow, the scent of garlic and Brut trailing after him as he licked the blood from his muzzle.

Ed's front paws pinned Lucius's shoulders to the floor; hind paws braced squarely on Lucius's forearms.

"aw, now why are you looking at me like that, luke?" Ed asked. *"like i said, this is for all the cookies . . . and i've always had me a real bad sweet tooth."*

Lucius felt a minute shift in balance and instantly jerked in that same direction as Ed lunged for his throat. Ed's fangs missed his throat entirely and sank into the thick ruff of fur at the base of Lucius's neck.

Pelt and skin tore as Lucius swung his muzzle over the top of Ed's silver skull to break the hold. The painful diversion should have worked—a mouth and nose filled with loose pelt hair should have had Ed gagging.

Instead Lucius felt a slow, but ever-increasing pressure against his windpipe.

"who do you think you're dealing with, luke?" Lucius felt Ed's voice—deep and muffled—rattle against the back of his tongue. *"i've been an alpha male before your granddaddy was a sperm."*

The pressure increased, and the air stopped.

Lucius's body relaxed, arms and legs tingling slightly as they grew numb. It was almost as if the Silverback standing over him really was made of silver . . . the feeling was the same.

MOTHER was wrong. MOTHER had always been wrong.

MOTHER . . . was dead and waiting for him . . . her arms gnawed off at the wrists but open and inviting, welcoming him to rest to sleep to . . .

Lucius snapped his eyes open. The hunting vision had shifted colors, from green to red . . . the color of blood . . . the color of death . . . to darkness and shadows.

He tried to open his eyes again only to discover that they were already open, the vision behind them failing, but open and staring unblinking at the murky shapes and halftones he could see with human sight.

Any strong emotion can trigger transformation, Lucius thought as the shadows crept closer. And death is the ultimate emotion. I'm dying, I really am dy—

"Goddammit, Lucius . . . FIGHT!"

Her voice.

Cat.

"BE A MAN!"

Ed's laugh tickled his ears. Be a man. Funny. Be. A. Man.

The shadows came, soft and peaceful . . . calm, everything was finally so—

be a man.

—calm. And he wasn't afraid. For the first time in his life he wasn't a—

MAN

Be a man.

Be a MAN.

Lucius opened his eyes through the gathering shadows. The Silverback winked, and Lucius lifted his hands—*man hands*—to pat him on the head. Good boy, nice doggie. Go to hell. His fingers felt swollen, detached . . . but they were still long enough to push through the jelly of Ed's red-rimmed eyes.

They popped like green grapes, squirting their juice across Lucius's face.

The sound the air made as it raced back into Lucius's lungs was only slightly less intense then the baying shriek that came from Ed. Jellied fluid clung to the fur around the raw sockets as Ed stumbled across the floor, shaking his head violently as if he thought he could shake sight back into his missing eyes.

If he even knew they were missing.

But Lucius wasn't going to give him the chance or time to find out. *Being a man*, he balled his right hand into a fist and swung it hard against the hollow just above Ed's ruined left eye. The temple bone shattered with an audible crack.

Digestive juice and chunks of undigested meat gushed from Ed's gaping jaws as he fell. The death scent was on him when Lucius rolled him onto his back, but he was still struggling, still trying to roll onto his feet and snap at the transforming paw that reached for his throat.

The skin beneath the thin ruff was covered with scars. Ed hadn't come by his status as Alpha Male easily.

Nose wriggling, Ed followed the scent until he was facing Lucius.

"couldn't win as a wolf, could you?" Ed chuckled even as he instinctively curled into a submission posture. *"but you can finish wearing the skin. pitiful, really, pitiful."*

Ed closed the lids over his empty sockets and tilted his head back, exposing the throbbing artery beneath the fur.

"do it. i don't want to live in a world with your kind."

"Lucius . . . No!"

He looked over at Cat, his Cat, all soft and weak and *human* now that the fighting was over and she'd have to answer to her conscience. Pitiful, as Ed would say.

"Lucius."

He was merciful, perhaps more than he should have been, but he snapped the Silverback's neck before ripping out the throat and feasting on the blood that rushed into his mouth. It was different than all the other times he'd tasted blood . . . richer and sweeter and carried with it the power of the Alpha Male he'd just killed.

The blood woke something in him that Lucius had never felt, that MOTHER had never spoken about—the true sense of what it meant to be Lycanthrope and leader.

Lucius sat back on his haunches, cradling Ed's body in his arms until it mutated back into human form and became just another carcass to be disposed of.

"Lucius."

He let the dead man slip from HIS paws as HE stood. The black-haired half-blood was staring at HIM, her eyes wide, the color of a stagnant pond. What *had* HE ever seen in her besides the obvious mating impulse?

"You . . . you killed him."

"There wasn't any choice," HE said. "A pack can only have one Alpha Male, and he wasn't the type to be satisfied with a subordinate role. Besides, he was crippled."

"Like Scooter?" she yelled at him. "Like your own son?"

Cowering on the floor, Pascal whimpered and shifted his weight, trying to hide his impairment. HE smiled and felt the hair along his muzzle bristle.

"It won't be like that, Pascal. As long as you can run with the pack you're more than welcome to stay."

"My God, Lucius."

HE turned and looked at the half-blood. She was on her feet and moving toward HIM. HE could feel the tension in the air, like static electricity growing to discharge as she closed the distance between them.

"What?" HE asked.

"Did you hear what you just said, Lucius? You said *pack*. You used to call this your *family*. What's happening to you?"

HE growled at her. She stopped moving and stared at him—fear stench filling the air between them, the fear stench filling the entire basement as HE looked from one member of the pack to the next.

And accepted their submission.

HE left the half-blood standing openmouthed and walked slowly to HIS beloved copper-haired Alpha Female. SHE'd been hurt badly by the OTHER, but with enough time SHE would heal and become MOTHER.

HE leaned forward and licked the tears from HER muzzle.

"Lucius?" HE turned back to the half-blood. "I—I really think she needs a doctor. Ed . . . you know. She might be torn up . . . inside."

HE gathered HER into HIS arms, nuzzling HER matted ruff. "I'll take care of HER. Cat. You can leave now."

Shock filled her pond-water eyes. "Leave? But I thought we—"

"There is no 'we,' Cat. I have a great many things to do before someone discovers the wolf mutilations at the Currer mansion. They'll come looking for us . . . right after they come looking for you."

The half-blood staggered back a step, her bare legs pale and thin and decidedly too human.

"Me?"

"Who else would the police think responsible for a mass

killing of wolves and the possible homicide of the *QUEST* editor than the woman who thought up the Denver Werewolf in the first place? I'd leave right now if I were you, Ms. Moselle. Maybe even head for that border I mentioned earlier tonight."

"But I haven't done anything wrong. I could tell the po-lice—"

"What?" HE bellowed. "That you were the innocent pawn in a battle for dominance between a werewolf and a were-man?" HE lowered HIS voice to a soft laugh. "You'd prob-ably get off on an insanity plea . . . but you'd spend the rest of your life cutting out paper dolls with safety scissors in a psycho ward. Leave, Cat. It's the only choice *you* have."

She stood there while HE carried the new MOTHER to the stairs leading to the outside world. The rest of the pack hurried to fall in line behind THEM, HIS three-legged son bringing up the rear. Maybe HE'd change the boy's name to Scooter . . . for old times' sake.

"Lucius?"

Her again. HE stopped halfway up the stairs and looked down at her. Her scent had changed, the fear replaced by need.

"Can I come with you?"

HE shook his head, and her scent changed again—from need back to fear.

"Lucius, please. I don't want to leave you . . . not after everything we've been through. Please, I—" She took a deep, ragged breath and tugged helplessly at the hem of the tunic. "I love you, Lucius."

One of the OTHERS chuckled softly. Lucius growled it back into submission.

"Lucius, look . . . you told me I'm half-werewolf, so I have to come with you, right?"

HE hugged the MOTHER and felt HER nuzzle HIS neck.

"No," HE said, "you can't come with us, Cat. I'm sorry."

Anger in her voice and posture, begging in her scent. "Lu-cius, I'm not looking for fairy-tale endings. I just want to come with you."

HE led the pack up the stairs and into the cold night. The

snow had stopped falling, and the clouds were drifting eastward. The moon, small and alone, hung above the bare trees almost directly overhead.

The half-blood stopped on the first step, looking at the crusted piles of snow and then at her own inadequate bare feet. She'd never survive with full-bloods; she didn't know how.

She was shivering even now with the cold. "What do I do, Lucius?"

HE handed the MOTHER to one of HIS males and walked back to her, HIS Cat. Past tense.

"Find someplace away from here and settle down. Get married. have children. Do what humans do, Cat."

"But I'm not human, Lucius."

HE touched her cheek. "You're not Lycanthrope either, Cat."

"Will I ever see you again?"

HE dipped HIS head toward hers as the moon slipped behind a cloud. Her cheeks were wet with tears that tasted surprisingly similar to those HE'd lapped from Halona's muzzle.

"Yes," HE whispered. "You *both* will."

Moonset.

Epilogue

Three months and fourteen days later.

Three cycles of the moon.

Plus.

And just *why* she'd waited this long without wondering what the hell she was going to do when reality finally showed up and bit her on the ass was *anyone's* guess. Including hers.

Three months and fourteen days and reality had finally shown up in the form of a little red *PLUS* in the indicator slot of the home pregnancy test she'd bought after missing her first period.

"Shit," Cat whispered just like she had when she saw that happy little *PLUS* earlier that morning and hugged herself through the front of the paper gown the nurse had given her in exchange for her clothes. "Shit."

Three months and fourteen days and still no clue why she *had* waited.

Liar.

Okay, so maybe she had been hoping for a fairy-tale ending, where Lucius would somehow know she'd moved back to Philadelphia and would suddenly show up at her doorstep, a genetic mis-matched Native American with fox red hair,

holding a bouquet of white roses and asking her to forgive
him.

That he'd been a fool.

And couldn't live without her.

And that he'd given up being a werewolf/bartender and
was now the CEO of a major pet food company.

You've lost it, girlfriend.

"Yeah, well," she said out loud to the nagging little voice
that still sounded like her mother, "pregnancy will do that to
a woman."

Pregnant.

Cat sighed and rubbed the goose bumps on her arms. The
air whispered through the vent above the door—neither hot
nor cold, cool to keep anxiety at a minimum, or so the sadist
who first came up with the concept of pelvic exams must
have thought.

She hoped the speculum would at least be warmer than
room temperature, and then shivered involuntarily at the very
thought of it sliding up inside her.

"Calm down, girl," Cat told herself. "Deep breath. You
don't want the doctor to think you're not serious about going
through with this."

This being the reason she'd made the appointment after
having breakfast with reality that morning.

An abortion. Nice and simple and protected—for the moment—by the law as a woman's choice. Or so the form she
filled out while waiting for her appointment stated.

Yes. I want to terminate the pregnancy.

Yes. I realize I waited too long for a simple D&C.

Yes. I understand there are other options.

No. I don't want any information on them.

Nice and simple and protected. Her choice. Hers alone.

Cat took another deep breath and tried to swallow the
lump that had formed halfway down her throat. Nice and
simple and easy . . . except when she looked at all the baby
pictures on the exam-room walls. Smiling babies. Sleeping
babies. Crying babies. Babies in every size and color.

But not one of them covered with fur.

Not one three-quarter-blood werewolf cub among 'em.

Cat slid her hands across the tiny bulge beneath her navel. Three months and fourteen days and although she knew it was impossible *(it* was, *wasn't it?)* Cat was certain she could feel a sluggish ripple under her palm. From the inside out.

She really should have asked Lucius what was the normal gestation period for a three-quarter-blood.

Except she never thought she'd have to ask that particular question. At least not after only three months and fourteen days.

Gone.

But not forgotten.

Neither by her or the Jefferson County Sheriff's Department.

Someone had heard her yell "FIRE" and called 911. Emergency vehicles and a squad car showed up fifty-eight minutes later—a record given the weather conditions . . . and the neighborhood. An EMT found her, weeping and hysterical in a corner of the basement, a moment after he'd called two uniformed officers about the "naked dead guy down here with his throat torn out."

The tears and hysterics, combined with the fact that all she'd been wearing at the time was a blood-flecked tunic, gave credence to her story about being raped by the Denver Werewolf.

A physical exam confirmed the rape, although it was obvious neither the police nor doctors bought the story about the werewolf.

Until the reports started coming in about the *other* killings that might be linked to her supposedly mythical assailant.

Cat didn't even have to lie when they questioned her. She'd simply told the truth. Mostly. About Lucius and Ed and the werewolves and weremen and how Ed had been killed by the Denver Werewolf while trying to save her from being raped.

The truth . . . sugarcoated and swallowed by the police who finally, Cat learned from the sympathetic rape counselor who visited in the hospital, attributed the double homicide to a psychopath with a moon fetish.

Case closed.

And never a mention of finding the dead wolves in the Currer home. Except in *QUEST*.

The new owner/managing editor had gone to a full-color cover and splashed the story onto it in vibrant reds.

DENVER WEREWOLF KILLS EDITOR AND PHOTOG
DISMEMBERED WOLVES FOUND IN MANSION
EXCLUSIVE
— BY RON A. BRYANT

He'd come, microcassette in hand, while she was still drifting in and out of a Demerol cloud and caught all of her blathering for posterity.

Page 1.

No photos.

But a wonderful half-page black-and-white cartoon that showed *her*, scanty outfit rendered even more scanty by the monstrous (obviously male) werewolf that loomed over her.

The cartoon was better than a photograph.

The story, for which she got the standard $25 and contributor's copy, worse than anything she could have written ... even with the drugs and hysterical exhaustion.

Before the month was out, the public's memories of the Denver Werewolf, Tanner Boswell, ed., and one C. K. Moselle were relegated to the annals of urban legend.

Where they belonged.

Cat didn't read the tabs anymore—except for the recipes—but that morning, while walking through the clinic's lobby, she'd cursed herself under her breath and succumbed to temptation.

It took a little searching, but she finally found *QUEST*—tucked behind copies of the *National Enquirer* and *The Globe*—and smiled.

BIGFOOT FINDS GOD AND ELVIS
SEEKS LIFE OF DEVOTION AND ROCK-N-ROLL
—PLUS—
ELVIS DROPS 100 LBS. ON "BIGFOOT" DIET

Well, it was nice that some things would never change.

Cat arched the stiffness out of her back and shoulders and again felt the impossible sluglike ripple beneath her navel.

"Stop that," she told it. "Besides, you're probably only gas anyway."

The impossible gas moved again, just to prove it could.

Cat sat up and folded her hands against the paper sheet on her lap when the nurse practitioner who'd showed her into the room and taken her urine sample opened the door and walked in.

The woman was short and chubby, with curly blond hair and bright green eyes that matched the green teddy bears on her lab coat. And the plush teddy face that had been stitched to the cuff of the pastel pink sphygmomanometer she had draped over the top of a clipboard. A white stethoscope hung like a medallion from the slope of her ample breasts.

"Sorry to keep you waiting," the nurse said as she opened Cat's manila folder. MOSELLE, CATHERINE K. "We've been running our legs off this morning. Seems like everyone in Philly has a bun in the oven."

The woman winked knowingly. But how many of those are werebuns?, Cat wanted to ask. She smiled instead.

"Okay, let's just go over this once more." The nurse pursed her lips as she skimmed Cat's chart. "You said you came in because you got a positive read on an HPT . . . home pregnancy test . . . and that your last period was three months ago." She looked up and smiled. "HPTs aren't always the most actuate, but your urine sample was. Congratu—Oh. You're interested in terminating."

Cat nodded, fingers throbbing under the pressure she was putting on them.

"Yes. I . . . It's for the best."

The nurse didn't lose any of her professionalism while she proceeded to warm the stethoscope's metal disk against her cheek before placing it against Cat's chest. *She's just lost a bit of her smile,* Cat thought, *but haven't we all?*

"So I guess I shouldn't ask if you bought any baby-name books yet, huh? Deep breaths . . . that's it. Good. Now the back. In, hold, out. Again. Good."

"No," Cat said, as the nurse tossed the stethoscope around her neck. "No names."

"Of course. Okay, blood pressure next." The Velcro behind the green teddy face snarled at Cat when the nurse pulled the cuff open and slipped it over Cat's upper arm. The goo-goo eyes bulged outward slightly as the pressure on Cat's arm increased. "Ninety over one-twenty . . . great."

Cat waited until the teddy was deflated and on the counter next to the exam table before asking the next question.

"Is three months and fourteen days too late to terminate?"

The nurse patted Cat's hand. Her hands were so warm.

"You already know that a D&C isn't an option, but there are a number of other procedures. I'll just run out to the reception area and get some pamphlets for you." Her hand pressed down on Cat's. "I understand."

"No," Cat whispered, "you don't."

"You're probably right. But if you're not one hundred percent sure about this . . ."

Cat was about to say she was . . . one hundred and fifty percent sure . . . but couldn't get the words out of her mouth.

"Are you sure?"

She shook her head. "No."

The nurse exhaled slowly and smiled, relief easing the tension from her face.

"I didn't think so. After so many years of this I can tell when a woman really wants her baby. I'll bring some of *those* options, too. Okay?"

"Yeah. Okay."

The nurse closed the file, happy now, and stared at the carefully typed name. "Wait a minute. Oh God, I know this is probably going to sound stupid but . . . Ah, did you use to be a writer?"

A writer. Cat smiled. "Sort of, in a way."

The nurse clasped the folder to her chest and beamed. "I *knew* it! You were C. K. Moselle, weren't you? I mean, you still are but . . . Oh, you know what I mean. I can't believe this, I read *QUEST* all the time. Oh my God, Miss Moselle, I mean when you wrote about the Denver Werewolf and . . ." She stopped and looked at Cat's paper-covered belly. "I am

so sorry, Miss Moselle, I never even thought. Will you forgive me?"

Cat nodded, still smiling but afraid to answer.

"Oh dear. It's his, isn't it?"

"Yeah." Not as bad as she'd thought it would be. Talking
about it. Without giving any details.

"I'm sorry to have brought up such a painful memory."

"No, it's okay."

"The Denver Werewolf," the nurse repeated, shaking her
head. "How awful for you. What was his name again?"

Cat couldn't help but smile. The woman was a fan . . .
probably the only one Cat, ex-writer that she was, would ever
have.

"Lucius."

"That's right . . . what a waste."

"Waste?"

"Such a beautiful name for a monster. It means 'bringer
of light' in Latin . . . did you know that?" The nurse smiled
and rolled her eyes. "Baby-name books . . . sometimes that's
all there is to read around this place. Okay, you sit tight, and
I'll go get those pamphlets . . . *all* of the pamphlets?"

Cat nodded as the impossible moved inside her. "Sure."

"Good. Be right back, and then we can do the pelvic and
talk about things like vitamins and whatever. Okay?"

Cat nodded. "Okay."

"May be another wait."

"No problem," Cat said, "I'm between jobs at the moment."

"Understand." The nurse gave her hand one more pat before walking to the door. "You just rest easy, Cat. I'll be
right back."

Cat watched the door close and slowly leaned forward
over her knees while Lucius's baby stretched lazily inside
her. She was still feeling the impossible fluttering inside her
body and thinking about baby names, when she suddenly sat
up and stared at the door.

"What did she just call me?"

———

HE flipped the cellular phone shut and let HIS eyes travel to the seventh window from the left, four stories up, and took a deep breath. Spring was still locked in winter's grasp, but HE could smell it within the cold, just like HE could smell HIS child within her.

HIS Cat.

Run all this way to keep HIM from HIS child . . . the first to be born of the new pack.

HE would have found them even without Carmine's help. The big male had proven himself a most useful tracker. From Denver to Philadelphia, to the seventh window/fourth floor of a medical arts clinic.

HIS child, verified.

LUCIUS slid the phone into the pocket of HIS coat and felt the day begin to die, the last rays of the cooling sun against HIS back, and the gentle pull of the moon against HIS upturned face.

soon, HE promised HIS child, *i'll come for you soon*.

Smiling, HE turned and slipped back into the depths of the man-made canyons of HIS new hunting ground.

Moonrise.

And the start of another night.